More Praise for

MACBETH

"Inventive and deeply satisfying . . . [Nesbø] offers a dark but ultimately hopeful *Macbeth*, one suited to our troubled times."

—*New York Times Book Review*

"The legions of readers who adore the dark Scandinavian noir of Jo Nesbø will also love *Macbeth*."

—*USA Today*

"Nesbø has adhered to his contract, delivering a book that plays off of Shakespeare's work but succeeds as his own."

—NPR.org

"*Macbeth* is a modern-day drug-war, power-struggle, double-cross, lawmen-versus-gangsters recast of Shakespeare's Scottish play."

—*Associated Press*

"Nesbø infuses the mythic elements of the tragedy with bold strokes of horrific, Don Winslow–like drug-war realism. The result displays in a strikingly original way both the timelessness of Shakespeare's art and the suppleness of noir to range well beyond the strictures of formula."

—*Booklist* (starred review)

"[Nesbø is] the writer most likely to take the ice-cold crown in the critically acclaimed—and now bestselling—category of Nordic noir."

—*Los Angeles Times*

"I am the world's greatest living crime writer. [Jo Nesbø] is a man who is snapping at my heels like a rabid pitbull poised to take over my mantle when I dramatically pre-decease him."

—James Ellroy

"The next Munch or Ibsen could be Jo Nesbø."

—CNN

ALSO BY JO NESBØ

MACBETH
JO NESBØ

VINTAGE CANADA

Published by Vintage Canada, a division of Penguin Random House Canada
Limited, in 2019. Originally published in hardcover by Knopf Canada,
a division of Penguin Random House Canada Limited, in 2018, and
simultaneously in the United States by Hogarth, an imprint of the Crown
Publishing Group, a division of Penguin Random House LLC, New York, and
in Great Britain by Hogarth UK, a division of Penguin Random House UK,
London. Published by agreement with Salomonsson Agency. Distributed in
Canada by Penguin Random House Canada Limited, Toronto.

Vintage Canada with colophon is a registered trademark.

www.penguinrandomhouse.ca

Library and Archives Canada Cataloguing in Publication

Nesbø, Jo, 1960–, author
Macbeth / Jo Nesbø. — Vintage Canada trade paperback edition.

(Hogarth Shakespeare)
Translated by Don Bartlett. First published in English.
Previously published: Toronto: Knopf Canada, 2018.
ISBN 978-0-345-80921-6
eBook ISBN 978-0-345-80922-3

1. Shakespeare, William, 1564–1616. Macbeth. I. Bartlett, Don,
translator II. Title. III. Series: Hogarth Shakespeare

PT8951.24.E83M33 2019   839.82'374   C2017-906529-7

Cover design: VINTAGE, Penguin Random House UK
Cover photographs: (background) Amble Design/Shutterstock;
(man) Tim Robinson/Arcangel

Printed and bound in the United States of America

2 4 6 8 9 7 5 3

Penguin
Random House
VINTAGE CANADA

MACBETH

PART ONE

1

THE SHINY RAINDROP FELL FROM the sky, through the darkness, toward the shivering lights of the port below. Cold gusting northwesterlies drove the raindrop over the dried-up riverbed that divided the town lengthwise and the disused railway line that divided it diagonally. The four quadrants of the town were numbered clockwise; beyond that they had no name. No name the inhabitants remembered anyway. And if you met those same inhabitants a long way from home and asked them where they came from they were likely to maintain they couldn't remember the name of the town either.

The raindrop went from shiny to gray as it penetrated the soot and poison that lay like a constant lid of mist over the town despite the fact that in recent years the factories had closed one after the other. Despite the fact that the unemployed could no longer afford to light their stoves. In spite of the capricious but stormy wind and the incessant rain that some claimed hadn't started to fall until the Second World War had been ended by two atom bombs a quarter of a century ago. In other words, around the time Kenneth was installed as police commissioner. From his office on the top floor of police HQ Chief Commissioner Kenneth had then misruled the town with an iron fist for twenty-five years, irrespective of who the mayor was and what he was or wasn't doing, or what the powers-that-be were saying or not saying over in Capitol, as the country's second-largest and once most important industrial center sank into a quagmire of corruption, bankruptcies, crime and chaos. Six months ago Chief Commissioner Kenneth had fallen from a chair in his summer house. Three weeks later he was dead. The funeral had been paid for by the town—a council decision made long ago that Kenneth himself had incidentally engineered. After a funeral worthy of a dictator the council and mayor had brought in

Duncan, a broad-browed bishop's son and the head of Organized Crime in Capitol, as the new chief commissioner. And hope had been kindled among the city's inhabitants. It had been a surprising appointment because Duncan didn't come from the old school of politically pragmatic officers, but from the new generation of well educated police administrators who supported reforms, transparency, modernization and the fight against corruption—which the majority of the town's elected get-rich-quick politicians did not.

And the inhabitants' hope that they now had an upright, honest and visionary chief commissioner who could drag the town up from the quagmire had been nourished by Duncan's replacement of the old guard at the top with his own hand-picked officers. Young, untarnished idealists who *really* wanted the town to become a better place to live.

The wind carried the raindrop over District 4 West and the town's highest point, the radio tower on top of the studio where the lone, morally indignant voice of Walt Kite expressed the hope, leaving no "r" unrolled, that they finally had a savior. While Kenneth had been alive Kite had been the sole person with the courage to openly criticize the chief commissioner and accuse him of some of the crimes he had committed. This evening Kite reported that the town council would do what it could to rescind the powers that Kenneth had forced through making the police commissioner the real authority in town. Paradoxically this would mean that his successor, Duncan the good democrat, would struggle to drive through the reforms he, rightly, wanted. Kite also added that in the imminent mayoral elections it was "Tourtell, the sitting and therefore fattest mayor in the country, versus no one. Absolutely no one. For who can compete against the turtle, Tourtell, with his shell of folksy joviality and unsullied morality, which all criticism bounces off?"

In District 4 East the raindrop passed over the Obelisk, a twenty-story glass hotel and casino that stood up like an illuminated index finger from the brownish-black four-story wretchedness that constituted the rest of the town. It was a contradiction to many that the less industry and more unemployment there was, the more popular it had become among the inhabitants to gamble away money they didn't have at the town's two casinos.

"The town that stopped giving and started taking," Kite trilled over the radio waves. "First of all we abandoned industry, then the railway so that no one could get away. Then we started selling drugs to our citizens, supplying them from where they used to buy train tickets, so that we could rob them at our convenience. I would never have believed I would say I missed the profit-sucking masters of industry, but at least they worked in respectable trades. Unlike the three other businesses where people can still get rich: casinos, drugs and politics."

In District 3 the rain-laden wind swept across police HQ, Inverness Casino and streets where the rain had driven most people indoors, although some still hurried around searching or escaping. Across the central station, where trains no longer arrived and departed but which was populated by ghosts and itinerants. The ghosts of those—and their successors—who had once built this town with self-belief, a work ethic, God and their technology. The itinerants at the twenty-four-hour dope market for brew; a ticket to heaven and certain hell. In District 2 the wind whistled in the chimneys of the town's two biggest, though recently closed, factories: Graven and Estex. They had both manufactured a metal alloy, but what it consisted of not even those who had operated the furnaces could say for sure, only that the Koreans had started making the same alloy cheaper. Perhaps it was the town's climate that made the decay visible or perhaps it was imagination; perhaps it was just the certainty of bankruptcy and ruin that made the silent, dead factories stand there like what Kite called "capitalism's plundered cathedrals in a town of drop-outs and disbelief."

The rain drifted to the southeast, across streets of smashed streetlamps where jackals on the lookout huddled against walls, sheltering from the sky's endless precipitation while their prey hurried toward light and greater safety. In a recent interview Kite had asked Chief Commissioner Duncan why the risk of being robbed was six times higher here than in Capitol, and Duncan had answered that he was glad to finally get an easy question: it was because the unemployment rate was six times higher and the number of drug users ten times greater.

At the docks stood graffiti-covered containers and run-down freighters with captains who had met the port's corrupt representatives in deserted spots and given them brown envelopes to ensure quicker entry permits and mooring slots, sums the shipping companies would log in their miscellaneous-expenses accounts swearing they would never undertake work that would lead them to this town again.

One of these ships was the MS *Leningrad*, a Soviet vessel losing so much rust from its hull in the rain it looked as if it was bleeding into the harbor.

The raindrop fell into a cone of light from a lamp on the roof of one two-story timber building with a storeroom, an office and a closed boxing club, continued down between the wall and a rusting hulk and landed on a bull's horn. It followed the horn down to the motorbike helmet it was joined to, ran off the helmet down the back of a leather jacket embroidered with NORSE RIDERS in Gothic letters. And to the seat of a red Indian Chief motorbike and finally into the hub of its slowly revolving rear wheel where, as it was hurled out again, it ceased to be a drop and became part of the polluted water of the town, of everything.

Behind the red motorbike followed eleven others. They passed under one of the lamps on the wall of an unilluminated two-story port building.

The light from the lamp fell through the window of a shipping office on the first floor, onto a hand resting on a poster: MS *GLAMIS* SEEKS GALLEY HAND. The fingers were long and slim like a concert pianist's and the nails well manicured. Even though the face was in shadow, preventing you from seeing the intense blue eyes, the resolute chin, the thin, miserly lips and nose shaped like an aggressive beak, the scar shone like a white shooting star, running diagonally from the jaw to the forehead.

"They're here," Inspector Duff said, hoping his men in the Narcotics Unit couldn't hear the involuntary vibrato in his voice. He had assumed the Norse Riders would send three to four, maximum five, men to get the dope. But he counted twelve motorbikes in the procession slowly emerging from the darkness. The two at the back each had a pillion rider. Fourteen men to his nine. And there was every reason to believe the Norse Riders were armed. Heavily armed. Nevertheless, it wasn't the sight of superior numbers that had produced the tremor in his vocal cords. It was that Duff had achieved his dearest wish. It was that *he* was leading the convoy; finally *he* was within striking distance.

The man hadn't shown himself for months, but only one person owned that helmet and the red Indian Chief motorbike. Rumor had it the bike was one of fifty the New York Police Department had manufactured in total secrecy in 1955. The steel of the curved scabbard attached to its side shone.

Sweno.

Some claimed he was dead, others that he had fled the country, that he had changed his identity, cut off his blond plaits and was sitting on a *terraza* in Argentina enjoying his old age and pencil-thin cigarillos.

But here he was. The leader of the gang and the cop-killer who, along with his sergeant, had started up the Norse Riders some time after the Second World War. They had picked rootless young men, most of them from dilapidated factory-worker houses along the sewage-fouled river, and trained them, disciplined them, brainwashed them until they were an army of fearless soldiers Sweno could use for his own purposes. To gain control of the town, to monopolize the growing dope market. And for a while it had looked as if Sweno would succeed, certainly Kenneth and police HQ hadn't stopped him; rather the opposite, Sweno had bought in all the help he needed. It was the competition. Hecate's homemade dope, brew, was much better, cheaper and always readily available on the market. But if the anonymous tip-off Duff had received was right, this consignment was big enough to solve the Norse Riders' supply problems for some time. Duff had hoped, but not quite believed, that what he read in the brief typewritten lines addressed to him was true. It was simply too much of a gift horse. The sort of gift that—if handled correctly—could send the head of the Narco Unit farther up the ladder. Chief Commissioner Duncan still hadn't filled all the important positions at police HQ with his own people. There was, for example, the Gang Unit, where Kenneth's old rogue Inspector Cawdor had managed to hang on to his seat as they still had no concrete evidence of corruption, but that could only be a question of time. And Duff was one of Duncan's men. When there were signs that Duncan might be appointed chief commissioner, Duff had rung him in Capitol and clearly, if somewhat pompously, stated that if the council didn't make Duncan the new commissioner, and chose one of Kenneth's henchmen instead, Duff would resign. It was not beyond the bounds of possibility that Duncan had suspected a personal motive behind this unconditional declaration of loyalty, but so what? Duff had a genuine desire to support Duncan's plan for an honest police force that primarily served the people, he really did. But he also wanted an office at HQ as close to heaven as possible. Who wouldn't? And he wanted to cut off the head of the man out there.

Sweno.

He was the means *and* the end.

Duff looked at his watch. The time tallied with what was in the letter, to the minute. He rested the tips of his fingers on the inside of his wrist. To feel his pulse. He was no longer hoping; he was about to become a believer.

"Are there many of them, Duff?" a voice whispered.

"More than enough for great honor, Seyton. And one of them's so big, when he falls, it'll be heard all over the country."

Duff cleaned the condensation off the window. Ten nervous, sweaty police officers in a small room. Men who didn't usually get this type of assignment. As head of the Narco Unit it was Duff alone who had taken the decision not to show the letter to other officers; he was using only men from his unit for this raid. The tradition of corruption and leaks was too long for him to risk it. At least that is what he would tell Duncan if asked. But there wouldn't be much caviling. Not if they could seize the drugs and catch thirteen Norse Riders red-handed.

Thirteen, yes. Not fourteen. One of them would be left lying on the battlefield. If the chance came along.

Duff clenched his teeth.

"You said there'd only be four or five," said Seyton, who had joined him at the window.

"Worried, Seyton?"

"No, but you should be, Duff. You've got nine men in this room and I'm the only one with experience of a stakeout." He said this without raising his voice. He was a lean, sinewy, bald man. Duff wasn't sure how long he had been in the police, only that he had been in the force when Kenneth was chief commissioner. Duff had tried to get rid of Seyton. Not because he had anything concrete on him; there was just something about him, something Duff couldn't put his finger on, that made him feel a strong antipathy.

"Why didn't you bring in the SWAT team, Duff?"

"The fewer involved the better."

"The fewer you have to share the honors with. Because unless I'm very much mistaken that's either the ghost of Sweno or the man himself." Seyton nodded toward the Indian Chief motorbike, which had stopped by the gangway of MS *Leningrad*.

"Did you say Sweno?" said a nervous voice from the darkness behind them.

"Yes, and there's at least a dozen of them," Seyton said loudly without taking his eyes off Duff. "Minimum."

"Oh shit," mumbled a second voice.

"Shouldn't we ring Macbeth?" asked a third.

"Do you hear?" Seyton said. "Even your own men want SWAT to take over."

"Shut up!" Duff hissed. He turned and pointed a finger at the poster on the wall. "It says here MS *Glamis* is sailing to Capitol on Friday at oh-six-hundred hours and is looking for galley staff. You said you wanted to take part in this assignment, but you hereby have my blessing to apply for employment there instead. The money and the food are supposed to be better. A show of hands?"

Duff peered into the darkness, at the faceless, unmoving figures. Tried to interpret the silence. Already regretting that he had challenged them. What if some of them actually did put up their hands? Usually he avoided putting himself in situations where he was dependent on others, but now he needed every single one of the men in front of him. His wife said he preferred to operate solo because he didn't like people. There could have been something in that, but the truth was probably the reverse. People didn't like him. Not that everyone actively disliked him, although some did; there was something about his personality that put people off. He just didn't know what. He knew his appearance and confidence attracted a certain kind of woman, and he was polite, knowledgeable and more intelligent than most people he knew.

"No one? Really? Good, so let's do what we planned, but with a few minor adjustments. Seyton goes to the right with his three men when we come out and covers the rear half of them. I go to the left with my three men. While you, Sivart, sprint off to the left, out of the light, and run in an arc in the darkness until you're behind the Norse Riders. Position yourself on the gangway so that no one can escape into the boat. All understood?"

Seyton cleared his throat. "Sivart's the youngest and—"

"—fastest," Duff interrupted. "I didn't ask for objections, I asked if my instructions were *understood*." He scanned the blank faces in front of him. "I'll take that as a yes." He turned back to the window.

A short bowlegged man with a white captain's hat waddled down the gangway in the pouring rain. Stopped by the man on the red motorbike. The rider hadn't removed his helmet—he had just flipped up the visor—nor had he switched off his engine. He sat with his legs splayed obscenely astride the saddle and listened to the captain. From under the helmet protruded two blond plaits, which hung down over the Norse Rider logo.

Duff took a deep breath. Checked his gun.

The worst was that Macbeth *had* rung. He had been given the same tip-off via an anonymous phone call and offered Duff the SWAT team. But Duff had turned down his offer, saying all they had to do was pick up a lorry, and had asked Macbeth to keep the tip-off quiet.

At a signal from the man in the Viking helmet one of the other bikers moved forward, and Duff saw the sergeant's stripes on the upper arm of his leather jacket when the rider opened a briefcase in front of the ship's captain. The captain nodded, raised his hand, and a second later iron screamed against iron, and light appeared in the crane swinging over its arm from the quayside.

"We're almost there," Duff said. His voice was firmer now. "We'll wait until the dope and the money have changed hands, then we'll go in."

Silent nods in the semidarkness. They had gone through the plans in painstaking detail, but they had imagined a maximum of five couriers. Could Sweno have been tipped off about a possible intervention by the police? Was that why they had turned up in such strength? No. If so, they would have called it all off.

"Can you smell it?" Seyton whispered beside him.

"Smell what?"

"Their fear." Seyton had closed his eyes and his nostrils were quivering. Duff stared into the rainy night. Would he have accepted Macbeth's offer of the SWAT team now? Duff stroked his face with his long fingers, down the diagonal scar. There was nothing to think about now; he had to do this, he'd always had to do this. Sweno was here now, and Macbeth and SWAT were in their beds asleep.

Macbeth yawned as he lay on his back. He listened to the rain drumming down. Felt stiff and turned onto his side.

A white-haired man lifted up the tarpaulin and crept inside. Sat shivering and cursing in the darkness.

"Wet, Banquo?" Macbeth asked, placing the palms of his hands on the rough roofing felt beneath him.

"It's a bugger for a gout-ridden old man like me to have to live in this piss-hole of a town. I should grab my pension and move into the country. Get myself a little house in Fife or thereabouts, sit on a veranda where the sun shines, bees hum and birds sing."

"Instead of being on a roof in a container port in the middle of the night? You've got to be joking."

They chuckled.

Banquo switched on a penlight. "This is what I wanted to show you."

Macbeth held the light and shone it on the drawing Banquo passed him.

"There's your Gatling gun. Beautiful job, isn't she?"

"It's not the appearance that's the problem, Banquo."

"Show it to Duncan then. Explain that SWAT needs it. Now."

Macbeth sighed. "He doesn't want it."

"Tell him we'll lose as long as Hecate and the Norse Riders have heavier weaponry than us. Explain to him what a Gatling can do. Explain what *two* can do!"

"Duncan won't agree to any escalation of arms, Banquo. And I think he's right. Since he's been the commissioner there *have* been fewer shooting incidents."

"This town is still being depopulated by crime."

"It's a start. Duncan has a plan. And he wants to do what's right."

"Yes, yes, I don't disagree. Duncan's a good man." Banquo groaned. "Naive though. And with this weapon we could clear up and—"

They were interrupted by a tap on the tarpaulin. "They've started unloading, sir." Slight lisp. It was SWAT's young new sharpshooter, Olafson. Along with the other equally young officer Angus, there were only four of them present, but Macbeth knew that all twenty-five SWAT officers would have said yes to sitting here and freezing with them without a moment's hesitation.

Macbeth switched off the light, handed it back to Banquo and slid the drawing inside his black SWAT leather jacket. Then he pulled away the tarpaulin and wriggled on his stomach to the edge of the roof.

Banquo crawled up beside him.

In front of them in the floodlights, over the deck of MS *Leningrad*, hovered a prehistoric-looking military-green lorry.

"A ZIS-5," Banquo whispered.

"From the war?"

"Yep. The S stands for Stalin. What do you reckon?"

"I reckon the Norse Riders have more men than Duff counted on. Sweno's obviously worried."

"Do you think he suspects the police have been tipped off?"

"He wouldn't have come if he did. He's afraid of Hecate. He knows Hecate has bigger ears and eyes than us."

"So what do we do?"

"We wait and watch. Duff might be able to pull this off on his own. In which case, we don't go in."

"Do you mean to say you've dragged these kids out here in the middle of the night to sit and *watch*?"

Macbeth chortled. "It was voluntary, and I did say it might be boring."

Banquo shook his head. "You've got too much free time, Macbeth. You should get yourself a family."

Macbeth raised his hands. His smile lit up the beard on his broad dark face. "You and the boys are my family, Banquo. What else do I need?"

Olafson and Angus chuckled happily behind them.

"When's the boy going to grow up?" Banquo mumbled in desperation and wiped water off the sights of his Remington 700 rifle.

Bonus had the town at his feet. The glass pane in front of him went from floor to ceiling, and without the low cloud cover he would have had a view of absolutely the whole town. He held out his champagne glass, and one of the two young boys in riding jodhpurs and white gloves rushed over and recharged it. He should drink less, he knew that. The champagne was expensive, but it wasn't him paying. The doctor had said a man of his age should begin to think about his lifestyle. But it was so good. Yes, it was as simple as that. It was so good. Just like oysters and crawfish tails. The soft, deep chair. And the young boys. Not that he had access to them. On the other hand, he hadn't asked.

He had been picked up from reception at the Obelisk and taken to the penthouse suite on the top floor with a view of the harbor on one side and the central station, Workers' Square and Inverness Casino on the other. Bonus had been received by the great man with the soft cheeks, the friendly smile, the dark wavy hair and the cold eyes. The man who was called Hecate. Or the Invisible Hand. Invisible, as very few people had ever seen him.

The Hand, as most people in the town over the last ten years had been affected in some way or other by his activities. That is, his product. A synthetic drug he manufactured himself called brew. Which, according to Bonus's rough estimate, had made Hecate one of the town's four richest men.

Hecate turned away from the telescope on the stand by the window. "It's difficult to see clearly in this rain," he said, pulling at the braces of his own jodhpurs, and took a pipe from the tweed jacket hanging over the back of the chair. If he'd known that they would turn out dressed as an English hunting party he would have chosen something other than a boring everyday suit, Bonus thought.

"But the crane's working, so that means they're unloading. Are they feeding you properly, Bonus?"

"Excellent food," Bonus said, sipping his champagne. "But I have to confess I'm a little unsure what it is we're celebrating. And why I'm entitled to be here."

Hecate laughed and raised his walking stick, pointing to the window. "We're celebrating the view, my dear flounder. As a seabed fish you've only seen the belly of the world."

Bonus smiled. It would never have occurred to him to object to the way Hecate addressed him. The great man had too much power to do good things for him. And less good.

"The world is more beautiful from up here," Hecate continued. "Not more real but more beautiful. And then we're celebrating this, of course." The stick pointed to the harbor.

"And this is?"

"The biggest single stash ever smuggled in, dear Bonus. Four and a half tons of pure amphetamine. Sweno has invested everything the club owns plus a little more. What you see below is a man who has put all his eggs in one basket."

"Why would he do that?"

"Because he's desperate, of course. He can see that the Riders' mediocre Turkish product is outclassed by my brew. But with such a large quantity of quality speed from the Soviets, bulk discount and reduced transport costs will makes it competitive in price and quality per kilo." Hecate rested the stick on the thick wall-to-wall carpet and caressed its gilt handle. "Well calculated by Sweno, and if he succeeds it's enough to upset the balance of power in this town. So here's to our worthy competitor."

He raised his glass, and Bonus obediently followed suit. But as Hecate was about to put it to his lips he studied the glass with a raised eyebrow, pointed to something and handed the glass back to one of the boys, who immediately cleaned it with his glove.

"Unfortunately for Sweno," Hecate continued, "it's difficult to obtain such a large order from a completely new source without someone in the same line of business catching wind of it. And unfortunately it seems this 'someone' may have passed on to the police an anonymous, though reliable, tip-off about where and when."

"Such as you?"

Hecate smirked. Took the glass, turned his broad bottom toward Bonus and leaned down to the telescope. "They're lowering the lorry now."

Bonus got up and went over to the window. "Tell me, why didn't you launch an attack on Sweno instead of watching from the sidelines? You would have got rid of your sole competitor and acquired four and a half tons of quality amphetamine at a stroke. And you could have sold it on the street for how many millions?"

Hecate sipped from his glass without raising his eye from the telescope. "Krug," he said. "They say it's the best champagne. So it's the only one I drink. But who knows? If I'd been served something else I might have acquired a taste for it and switched brands."

"You don't want the market to try anything else but your brew?"

"My religion is capitalism and the free market my creed. But it's everyone's right to follow their nature and fight for a monopoly and world domination. And society's duty to oppose us. We're just playing our roles, Bonus."

"Amen to that."

"Shh! Now they're handing over the money." Hecate rubbed his hands. "Showtime . . ."

Duff stood by the front door with his fingers around the handle listening to his breathing while trying to get eye contact with his men. They were standing in a line on the narrow staircase right behind him. Busy with their thoughts. Releasing the safety catch. A last word of advice to the man next to them. A last prayer.

"The suitcase has been handed over," Seyton called down from the first floor.

"Now!" Duff shouted, wrenching open the door and hugging the wall.

The men pushed past him into the darkness. Duff followed. Felt the rain on his head. Saw figures moving. Saw a couple of motorbikes left unmanned. Raised the megaphone to his mouth.

"Police! Stay where you are with your hands in the air! I repeat, this is the police. Stay where—"

The first shot smashed the glass in the door behind him, the second caught the inside leg of his trousers. Then came a sound like when his kids made popcorn on a Saturday night. Automatic weapons. Fuck.

"Fire!" Duff screamed, throwing down the megaphone. He dived onto his stomach, tried to raise his gun in front of him and realized he had landed in a puddle.

"Don't," whispered a voice beside him. Duff looked up. It was Seyton. He stood stationary with his rifle hanging down by his side. Was he sabotaging the action? Was he . . . ?

"They've got Sivart," Seyton whispered.

Duff blinked filthy water from his eyes and kept looking, a Norse Rider in his sights. But the man was sitting calmly on his motorbike with his gun pointed at them, not shooting. What the hell was going on?

"Nobody move a fuckin' finger now and this'll be fine."

The deep voice came from outside the circle of light and needed no megaphone. Duff saw first the abandoned Indian Chief. Then saw the two figures in the darkness merge into one. The horns sticking up from the helmet of the taller of the two. The figure he held in front of him was a head shorter. With every prospect of being another head shorter. The blade of the saber glinted as Sweno held it to young Sivart's throat.

"What will happen now—" Sweno's bass voice rumbled from out of the visor opening "—is that we'll take our stuff with us and go. Nice and quietly. Two of my men will stay and make sure none of you does anything stupid. Like trying to come after us. Got that?"

Duff hunched up and was about to stand.

"If I were you I'd stay in the puddle, Duff," Seyton whispered. "You've screwed this up enough as it is."

Duff took a deep breath. Let it out. Drew another. Shit, shit, shit.

"Well?" said Banquo, training the binoculars on the protagonists on the quayside.

"Looks like we'll have to activate the young ones after all," Macbeth said. "But not quite yet. We'll let Sweno and his men leave the scene first."

"What? We're going to let them get away with the lorry and all the stash?"

"I didn't say that, dear Banquo. But if we start anything now we'll have a bloodbath down there. Angus?"

"Sir?" came the quick response from the lad with the deep blue eyes and the long blond hair unlikely to have been allowed by any other team leader but Macbeth. His emotions were written all over his open face. Angus and Olafson had the training; now they just needed some more experience. Angus especially needed to toughen up. During his job interview Angus had explained that he had dropped out of training to become a priest when he saw there was no god; people could only save themselves and one another, so he wanted to become a policeman instead. That had been good enough for Macbeth; he liked the fearless attitude, the boy dealing with the consequences of his beliefs. But Angus also needed to learn how to master his feelings and realize that in SWAT they became practical men of action, the long, and rough, arm of the law. Others could take care of reflection.

"Go down the back, fetch the car and be ready by the door."

"Right," Angus said, got up and was gone.

"Olafson?"

"Yes?"

Macbeth glanced at him. The constant slack jaw, the lisping, the semi-closed eyes and his grades at police college meant that when Olafson had come to Macbeth, begging to be moved to SWAT, he had had his doubts. But the lad had *wanted* the move, and Macbeth decided to give him a chance, as he himself had been given a chance. Macbeth needed a sharpshooter, and even if Olafson was not spectacularly talented in theoretical subjects, he was a highly gifted marksman.

"At the last shooting test you beat the twenty-year-old record held by him over there." Macbeth nodded to Banquo. "Congratulations, that's a damn fine achievement. You know what it means right here and now?"

"Er . . . no, sir."

"Good, because it means absolutely nothing. What you have to do here is watch and listen to Inspector Banquo and learn. You won't save the day today. That's for later. Understand?"

Olafson's slack jaw and lower lip were working but were clearly unable to produce a sound, so he just nodded.

Macbeth laid a hand on the young man's shoulder. "Bit nervous?"

"Bit, sir."

"That's normal. Try to relax. And one more thing, Olafson."

"Yes?"

"Don't mess up."

"What's happening?" Bonus asked.

"I know what's going to happen," Hecate said, straightening his back and swinging his telescope away from the quay. "So I don't need this." He sat down beside Bonus. Bonus had noticed that he often did that. Sat down beside you instead of opposite. As though he didn't like you looking straight at him.

"They've got Sweno and the amphetamine?"

"On the contrary. Sweno's seized one of Duff's men."

"What? Aren't you worried?"

"I never bet on one horse, Bonus. And I'm more worried about the bigger picture. What do you think of Chief Commissioner Duncan?"

"His promise that you'll be arrested?"

"That doesn't concern me at all, but he's removed many of my former associates in the police and that's already created problems in the markets. Come on, you're a good judge of character. You've seen him, heard him. Is he as incorruptible as they say?"

Bonus shrugged. "Everyone has a price."

"You're right there, but the price is not always money. Not everyone is as simple as you."

Bonus ignored the insult by not perceiving it as such. "To know how Duncan can be bribed you have to know what he wants."

"Duncan wants to serve the herd," Hecate said. "Earn the town's love. Have a statue erected he didn't order himself."

"Tricky. It's easier to bribe greedy vermin like us than pillars of society like Duncan."

"You're right as far as bribery is concerned," Hecate said. "And wrong with respect to pillars of society and vermin."

"Oh?"

"The foundation of capitalism, dear Bonus. The individual's attempt to get rich enriches the herd. It's mechanics pure and simple and happens without us seeing or thinking about it. You and I are pillars of society, not deluded idealists like Duncan."

"Do you think so?"

"The moral philosopher Adam Hand thought so."

"Producing and selling drugs serves society?"

"Anyone who supplies a demand helps to build society. People like Duncan who want to regulate and limit are unnatural and in the long run harmful to us all. So how can Duncan, for the good of the town, be rendered harmless? What's his weakness? What can we use? Sex, dope, family secrets?"

"Thank you for your confidence, Hecate, but I really don't know."

"That's a shame," said Hecate, gently tapping his stick on the carpet as he observed one of the boys remove the wire from the cork of a new bottle of champagne. "You see, I've begun to suspect Duncan has only one weak point."

"And that is?"

"The length of his life."

Bonus recoiled in his chair. "I really hope you haven't invited me here to ask me to . . ."

"Not at all, my dear flounder. You'll be allowed to lie still in the mud."

Bonus heaved a sigh of relief as he watched the boy struggle with the cork.

"But," Hecate said, "you have the gifts of ruthlessness, disloyalty and influence that give you power over the people I need to have power over. I hope I can rely on you when help is needed. I hope you can be my invisible hand."

There was a loud bang.

"There we are!" Bonus laughed, patting the boy on the back as he tried to get as much of the unrestrained champagne into the glasses as he could.

Duff lay still on the tarmac. Beside him his men stood equally still watching the Norse Riders, less than ten meters away, preparing to leave. Sivart and Sweno stood in the darkness outside the cone of light, but Duff could see the young officer's body shaking and Sweno's saber blade, which rested against Sivart's throat. Duff could see that the least pressure or movement would pierce the skin and the artery and drain the man's blood in seconds.

And Duff could feel his own panic when he considered the consequences. Not only the consequences of having one of his men's blood on his hands and record, but the consequences of his privately orchestrated actions failing miserably just as the chief commissioner was about to appoint a head of Organized Crime. Sweno nodded to one of the Norse Riders, who dismounted from his motorbike, stood behind Sivart and pointed a gun at his head. Sweno pulled down his visor, stepped into the light, spoke to the man with the sergeant's stripes on his leather jacket, straddled his bike, saluted with two fingers to his helmet and rode off down the quayside. Duff had to control himself not to loose off a shot at him. The sergeant gave some orders and a second later the motorbikes growled off into the night. Only two unmanned motorbikes were left after the others had followed Sweno and the sergeant.

Duff told himself not to give way to panic, told himself to think. Breathe, think. Four men in Norse Rider regalia were left on the quay. One stood behind Sivart in the shadows. One stood in the light keeping the police covered with an assault rifle, an AK-47. Two men, presumably the pillion riders, got into the lorry. Duff heard the continuous strained whine as the ignition key was turned and for a second he hoped that the old iron monster wouldn't start. Cursed as the first low growl rose to a loud rumbling rattle. The lorry moved off.

"We'll give them ten minutes," shouted the man with the AK-47. "Think of something pleasant in the meantime."

Duff stared at the lorry's rear lights slowly fading into the darkness. Something pleasant? A mere four and a half tons of drugs heading away from him, along with what would have been the biggest mass arrest this side of the war. It didn't help that they *knew* Sweno and his people had been there right in front of them if they couldn't tell the judge and jury they had *seen* their faces and not just fourteen sodding helmets. Something *pleasant*? Duff closed his eyes.

Sweno.

He'd had him here in the palm of his hand. Shit, shit, shit!

Duff listened. Listened for something, *anything*. But all that could be heard was the meaningless whisper of the rain.

"Banquo's got the guy holding the lad in his sights," Macbeth said. "Have you got the other one, Olafson?"

"Yes, sir."

"You have to shoot at the same time, OK? Fire on the count of three. Banquo?"

"I need more light on the target. Or younger eyes. I might hit the boy as it is."

"My target has lots of light," Olafson whispered. "We can swap."

"If we miss and our lad is killed, we'd prefer it if it was Banquo who missed. Banquo, what's the maximum speed of a fully loaded Stalin lorry, do you reckon?"

"Hm. Sixty maybe."

"Good, but time's getting short to achieve all our objectives. So we'd better do a bit of improvising."

"Are you going to try your daggers?" Banquo asked Macbeth.

"From this distance? Thanks for your confidence. No, you'll soon see, old man. As in *see*."

Banquo looked up from his binoculars and discovered that Macbeth had stood up and grabbed the pole on to which the light on the roof was bolted. The veins in Macbeth's powerful neck stood out and his teeth shone in either a grimace or a grin, Banquo couldn't decide which. The pole was screwed down to withstand the feisty northwesterlies that blew for eight of the year's twelve months, but Banquo had seen Macbeth lift cars out of snowdrifts before now.

"Three," Macbeth groaned.

The first screws popped out of their sockets.

"Two."

The pole came loose and with a jerk tore the cable away from the wall below.

"One."

Macbeth pointed the light at the gangway.

"Now."

It sounded like two whiplashes. Duff opened his eyes in time to see the man with the automatic weapon topple forward and hit the ground helmet first. Where Sivart stood there was now light, and Duff could see him clearly and also the man behind him. He was no longer holding a gun to Sivart's head but resting his chin on Sivart's shoulder. And in the light Duff also saw the hole in the visor. Then, like a jellyfish, he slid down Sivart's back to the ground.

Duff turned.

"Up here, Duff!"

He shaded his eyes. A peal of laughter rang out behind the dazzling light and the shadow of a gigantic man fell over the quay.

But the laughter was enough.

It was Macbeth. Of course it was Macbeth.

2

A SEAGULL SWEPT IN OVER Fife through the silence and moonlight under a cloud-free night sky. Below, the river shone like silver. On the west of the river—like an immense fortress wall—a steep black mountain rose to the sky. Just short of the top a monastic order had once erected a large cross, but as it had been put up on the Fife side the silhouette appeared to be upside down to the residents of the town. From the side of the mountain—like a drawbridge over the fortress moat—jutted an impressive iron bridge. Three hundred and sixty meters long and ninety meters high at its tallest point. Kenneth Bridge, or the new bridge, as most people called it. The old bridge was by comparison a modest but more aesthetically pleasing construction farther down the river, and it meant a detour. In the middle of the new bridge towered an unlovely marble monument in the shape of a man, meant to represent former Chief Commissioner Kenneth, erected at his own orders. The statue stood inside the town boundary by a centimeter as no other county would give the rogue's posthumous reputation a centimeter of land for free. Even though the sculptor had complied with Kenneth's order to emphasize his visionary status by creating a characteristic horizon-searching pose, not even the most benevolent of artists could have refrained from drawing attention to the chief commissioner's unusually voluminous neck and chin area.

The seagull flapped its wings to gain height, hoping for better fishing on the coast across the mountain, even though that meant crossing the weather divide. From good to bad. For those wishing to travel the same way there was a two-kilometer-long narrow black hole from the new bridge through the mountain. A mountain and a partition many appeared to appreciate—neighboring counties referred to the tunnel as a rectum with an anal orifice at each end. And indeed as the seagull passed over the mountain peak it was like flying from a world of quiet harmony into a freezing-cold filthy shower falling onto the foul-smelling town beneath. And as if to show its contempt the seagull shat, then continued to swerve between the gusts of wind.

The seagull shit hit the roof of a shelter, below which an emaciated trembling boy crept onto a bench. Although the sign beside the shelter indicated it was a bus stop the boy wasn't sure. So many bus routes had been stopped over the last couple of years. Because of the decreasing population, the mayor said, the fathead. But the boy had to get to the central station for brew; the speed he had bought from some bikers was just crap, icing sugar and potato flour rather than amphetamine.

The oily wet tarmac glinted beneath the few streetlamps that still worked, and the rain lay in puddles on the potholed road leading out of town. It had been quiet, not a car to be seen, only rain. But now he heard a sound like a low gurgle.

He raised his head. Pulled on the string of his eyepatch, which had slipped over from his empty eye cavity and now covered the remaining eye. Perhaps he could hitch a lift to the center?

But no, the sound came from the wrong direction.

He drew up his knees again.

The gurgle rose to a roar. He couldn't be bothered to move, besides he was already drenched, so he just covered his head with his arms. The lorry passed, sending a cascade of filthy water into the bus shelter.

He lay there thinking about life until he realized it was wiser not to.

The sound of another vehicle. This time?

He struggled upright and looked out. But no, it was coming from the town too. Also at great speed. He stared into the lights as they approached. And the thought came into his head: one step into the road and all his problems were solved.

The van passed him without going into any of the potholes. Black Ford Transit. Cops, three of them. Great. You don't want a lift with them.

"There it is, ahead of us," Banquo said. "Step on it, Angus!"

"How do you know it's them?" Olafson asked, leaning forward between the front seats of the SWAT Transit.

"Diesel smoke," Banquo said. "My God, no wonder there's an oil crisis in Russia. Get right behind them so that they can see us in their rearview mirror, Angus."

Angus maintained his speed until they reached the black exhaust. Banquo rolled down his window and steadied his rifle on the wing mirror. Coughed. "And now alongside, Angus!"

Angus pulled out and accelerated. The Transit drew alongside the snorting, groaning lorry.

A puff of smoke came from the lorry window. The mirror under Banquo's rifle barrel broke with a crack.

"Yes, they've seen us," Banquo said. "Get behind them again."

The rain stopped suddenly and everything around them became even darker. They had driven into the tunnel. The tarmac and the hewn black walls seemed to swallow the lights of the headlamps; all they could see was the lorry's rear lights.

"What shall we do?" Angus asked. "The bridge at the other end, and if they pass the middle . . ."

"I know," Banquo said, lifting his rifle. The town stopped by the statue, their area of jurisdiction stopped, the chase stopped. In theory of course they could carry on, it had happened before: enthusiastic officers, rarely in the Narco Unit though, had arrested smugglers on the wrong side of the boundary. And every time they'd had a nice fat juicy case thrown out of court and had to face censure for gross misjudgment in the course of duty. Banquo's Remington 700 recoiled.

"Bull's-eye," he said.

The lorry began to swerve in the tunnel; bits of rubber flew off the rear wheel.

"Now you'll feel what a heavy steering wheel is *really* like," Banquo said and took aim at the other rear tire. "Bit more distance, Angus, in case they go straight into the tunnel wall."

"Banquo!" came a voice from the back seat.

"Olafson?" Banquo said, slowly pressing the trigger.

"Car coming."

"Whoops."

Banquo lifted his cheek off the rifle as Angus braked.

In front of them the ZIS-5 veered from side to side, alternately showing and cutting off the headlights of the oncoming car. Banquo heard the horn, the desperate hooting of a saloon car that saw a lorry bearing down on it and knew it was too late to do anything.

"Jesus . . ." Olafson said in a lisped whisper.

The sound of the horn rose in volume and frequency.

Then a flash of light.

Banquo automatically glanced to the side.

Caught a glimpse of the back seat in the car, the cheek of a sleeping child, resting against the window.

Then it was gone, and the dying tone of the horn sounded like the disappointed groan of cheated spectators.

"Faster," Banquo said. "We'll be on the bridge in no time."

Angus jammed his foot down, and they were back in the cloud of exhaust.

"Steady," Banquo said while aiming. "Steady . . ."

At that moment the tarpaulin on the back of the lorry was pulled aside, and the Transit's headlamps lit up a flatbed piled with plastic bags containing a white substance. The window at the back of the driver's cab had been smashed. And from the top of a gap between the kilo bags pointed a rifle.

"Angus . . ."

A brief explosion. Banquo caught sight of a muzzle flash, then the windscreen whitened and fell in on them.

"Angus!"

Angus had taken the point and swung the wheel sharply to the right. And then to the left. The tires screamed and the bullets whined as the fire-spitting muzzle tried to track their maneuvers.

"Jesus Christ!" Banquo shrieked and fired at the other tire, but the bullet just drew sparks from the wing.

And suddenly the rain was back. They were on the bridge.

"Get him with the shotgun, Olafson," Banquo yelled. "Now!"

The rain pelted through the hole where the windscreen had been, and Banquo moved so that Olafson could lay the double-barreled gun on the back of his seat. The barrel protruded above Banquo's shoulder, but disappeared again at the sound of a thud like a hammer on meat. Banquo turned to where Olafson sat slumped with his head tipped forward and a hole in his jacket at chest height. Gray upholstery filling fluffed up when the next bullet went right through Banquo's seat and into the seat beside

Olafson. The guy on the lorry had got his eye in now. Banquo took the shotgun from Olafson's hands and in one swift movement swung it forward and fired. There was a white explosion on the back of the lorry. Banquo let go of the shotgun and raised his rifle. It was impossible for the guy on the lorry to see through the thick white cloud of powder, but from the darkness rose the floodlit white marble statue of Kenneth, like an unwelcome apparition. Banquo aimed at the rear wheel and pulled the trigger. Bull's-eye.

The lorry careered from side to side, one front wheel mounted the pavement, a rear wheel hit the curb, and the side of the ZIS-5 struck the steel-reinforced fence. The scream of metal forced along metal drowned the vehicles' engines. But, incredibly, the driver in front managed to get the heavy lorry back on the road.

"Don't cross the bloody boundary, please!" Banquo yelled.

The last remnant of rubber had been stripped from the lorry's rear wheel rims and a fountain of sparks stood out against the night sky. The ZIS-5 went into a skid, the driver tried desperately to counter it, but this time he had no chance. The lorry veered across the road and skidded along the tarmac. It was practically at the boundary when the wheels gained purchase again and steered the lorry off the road. Twelve tons of Soviet military engineering hit Chief Commissioner Kenneth right under the belt, tore him off the plinth and dragged the statue plus ten meters or so of steel fencing along before tipping over the edge. Angus had managed to stop the Transit, and in the sudden silence Banquo observed Kenneth falling through the moonlight and slowly rotating around his own chin. Behind him came the ZIS-5, bonnet first, with a tail of white powder like some damned amphetamine comet.

"My God . . ." the policeman whispered.

It felt like an eternity before everything hit the water and colored it white for an instant, and the sound reached Banquo with a slight time delay.

Then the silence returned.

Sean stamped his feet on the ground outside the clubhouse, staring out through the gate. Scratched the NORSE RIDER TILL I DIE tattoo on his forehead. He hadn't been so nervous since he was in the hospital delivery room. Wasn't it just typical that he and Colin had drawn the short straw and had to stand guard on the night when excitement was at fever pitch? They hadn't been allowed to string along and collect the dope or go to the party either.

"Missus wants to call the kid after me," said Sean, mostly to himself.

"Congrats," said Colin in a monotone, pulling at his walrus mustache. The rain ran down his shiny pate.

"Ta," said Sean. Actually he hadn't wanted either. A tattoo that would stamp him for life or a kid he knew would do the same. Freedom. That was the idea of a motorbike, wasn't it? But the club and then Betty had changed his notion of freedom. You can only truly be free when you belong, when you feel real solidarity.

"There they are," Sean said. "Looks like everything's gone well, eh?"

"Two guys missing," Colin said, spitting out his cigarette and opening the high gate with barbed wire on top.

The first bike stopped by them. The bass rumbled from behind the horn helmet. "We were ambushed by the cops, so the twins will come a bit later."

"Right, boss," Colin said.

The bikes roared through the gate one after the other. One of the guys gave a thumbs-up. Good, the dope was safe, the club saved. Sean breathed out with relief. The bikes rolled across the yard past the shed-like single-story timber house with the Norse Rider logo painted on the wall and disappeared into the big garage. The table was laid in the shed; Sweno had decided that the deal should be celebrated with a piss-up. And after a few minutes Sean heard the music turned up inside and the first shouts of celebration.

"We're rich." Sean laughed. "Do you know where they're taking the dope?"

Colin said nothing, just rolled his eyes.

He didn't know. Nobody did. Only Sweno. And those in the lorry, of course. It was best like that.

"Here come the twins," Sean said, opening the gate again.

The motorbikes came slowly, almost hesitantly, up the hill toward them.

"Hi, João, what happ—?" Sean began, but the bikes continued through the gate.

He watched them as they stopped in the middle of the yard as though considering leaving their bikes there. Then they nudged one another, nodded to the open garage door and drove in.

"Did you see João's visor?" Sean said. "It had a hole in it."

Colin sighed heavily.

"I'm not kidding!" Sean said. "Right in the middle. I'll go and see what really happened down on the quay."

"Hey, Sean . . ."

But Sean was off, ran across the yard and entered the garage. The twins had dismounted. Both stood with their backs to him, still wearing their helmets. One twin by the door leading straight from the garage into the club's function room held the door ajar, as though not wanting to show himself but seeing what the party was like first. João, Sean's best mate, stood by his bike. He had removed the magazine from his ugly-looking AK-47 and seemed to be counting how many bullets he had left. Sean patted him on the back. That must have been quite a shock because he spun round with a vengeance.

"What happened to your visor, João? Stone chip, was it?"

João didn't answer, just appeared to be busy inserting the magazine back into his AK-47. He was strangely clumsy. The other strange thing was that he seemed . . . taller. As though it wasn't João standing there, but . . .

"Fuck!" Sean shouted, took a step back and reached for his belt. He had realized what the hole in the visor was and that he wasn't going to see his best pal again. Sean pulled out his gun, released the safety catch and was about to point it at the man still struggling with the AK-47 when something struck him in the shoulder. He automatically swung the gun in the direction from which the blow had come. But there was no one there. Only the guy in the Norse Rider jacket standing over by the door. At that moment his hand seemed to wither and Sean dropped his gun to the floor.

"Not a peep," a voice said behind him.

Sean turned again.

The AK was pointing at him, and in the reflection of the holed visor he saw a dagger sticking out of his shoulder.

Duff put the barrel of the AK to the tattoo on the guy's forehead. Looked into his gawping, ugly features. His finger squeezed the trigger, just a fraction . . . He heard the hiss of his own breathing inside the helmet and his heart pounding beneath the somewhat too tight leather jacket.

"Duff," Macbeth said from the clubroom doorway. "Easy now."

Duff squeezed the trigger a fraction more.

"Stop that," Macbeth said. "It's our turn to use a hostage."

Duff let go of the trigger.

The man's face was as white as a sheet. From fear or loss of blood. Both probably. His voice shook. "We don't save—"

Duff hit him across the tattoo with the gun barrel. Leaving a stripe that for a moment shone white like a copy of Duff's own trademark. Then it filled with blood.

"You shut up, son, and everything'll be fine," said Macbeth, who had joined them. He grabbed the young man's long hair, pulled his head back and put the blade of his second dagger to his throat. Pushed him forward to the clubroom door. "Ready?"

"Remember Sweno's mine," Duff said, making sure the curved magazine sat properly in the weapon, and strode after Macbeth and the Norse Rider.

Macbeth kicked open the door and went in with the hostage in front and Duff hard on his heels. Grinning and loud-mouthed, the Norse Riders were sitting at a long table in the large, open but already smoke-filled clubroom. All of them with their backs to the wall facing the three doors that led from the room. Probably a club rule. Duff estimated there were twenty of them. The music was on loud. The Stones. "Jumpin' Jack Flash."

"Police!" Duff shouted. "No one move or my colleague will cut the throat of this fine young man."

Time seemed to come to an abrupt halt, and Duff saw the man at the end of the table raise his head as if in slow motion. A ruddy porcine face with visible nostrils and plaits so tight they pulled the eyes into two narrow hate-filled straight lines. From the corner of his mouth hung a long thin cigarillo. Sweno.

"We don't save hostages," he said.

The young man lost consciousness and fell.

In the next two seconds everything in the room froze and all you could hear was the Rolling Stones.

Until Sweno took a drag of his cigarillo. "Take them," he said.

Duff registered at least three of the Norse Riders reacting at the same time and pulled the trigger of his AK-47. Held it there. Spraying chunks of lead with a diameter of 7.62 millimeters, which smashed bottles, raked the table, lashed the wall, carved flesh and stopped Mick Jagger between two *gas*ses. Beside him Macbeth had reached for the two Glocks he had removed from the Norse Rider bodies on the quay. Along with their jackets, helmets and bikes. In Duff's hands, his gun felt warm and soft like a woman. Darkness fell gradually as lamps were shot to pieces. And when Duff finally let go of the trigger, dust and feathers hovered in the air, and one lamp swung to and fro from the ceiling sending shadows scurrying up the walls like fleeing ghosts.

3

"**I LOOKED AROUND, AND IN** the semidarkness Norse Rider guys were strewn across the floor facedown," Macbeth said. "Blood, broken glass and empty shell cases."

"Jesus!" Angus shouted with a slur over the lively babble at the Bricklayers Arms, the SWAT's local behind the central station. The glazed blue eyes looked at Macbeth with what seemed to be adoration. "You just swept them off the face of the earth! Holy Jesus! Cheers!"

"Now, now, careful with your language, you priest-in-waiting," Macbeth said, but when many of the eighteen SWAT officers in attendance raised their beer mugs to him, he eventually smiled, shaking his head, and then raised his glass too. Took a long draft and looked at Olafson, who was holding a heavy Bricklayers Arms pint mug in his left hand.

"Does it hurt, Olafson?"

"It's all the better for knowing that one of them has a sore shoulder as well," Olafson lisped and shyly straightened the sling when the others burst into loud laughter.

"The ones who actually got things rolling were Banquo and Olafson here," Macbeth said. "I was just holding the light like some bloody photographer's assistant for these two artists."

"Keep going," Angus said. "You and Duff had all the Norse Riders on the floor. What happened then?" He flicked his blond hair behind his ears.

Macbeth gazed at the expectant faces around the table and exchanged glances with Banquo before continuing. "Some of them screamed they were surrendering. The dust settled and the music system was shot to pieces, so it was finally quiet but still dark, and the situation was rather unclear. Duff and I started checking them out from our end of the room.

There were no fatalities, but a number of them required medical attention, you might say. Duff shouted that he couldn't find Sweno." Macbeth ran a finger through the condensation on the outside of his glass. "I spotted a door behind the end of the table where Sweno had been sitting. At that moment we heard motorbikes starting up. So we left the others and charged out into the yard. And there we saw three motorbikes on their way out of the gate, one of them was red, Sweno's. And the guard, a bald guy with a mustache, jumped on his bike and followed. Duff was furious, wanted to give chase, but I said there were a few badly injured guys inside . . ."

"Did you think that would stop Duff?" a voice whispered. "Bastards lying around bleeding when he could catch Sweno?"

Macbeth turned. The voice in question was sitting alone in the next booth, his face hidden in the shadow beneath the dart club's trophy cupboard.

"Did you think Duff would consider a few ordinary people's lives when a heroic exploit was within reach?" A beer mug was raised in the shadows. "After all there are careers to consider."

Macbeth's table had gone quiet.

Banquo coughed. "To hell with careers. We in SWAT don't let defenseless people just die, Seyton. We don't know what you in Narco do."

Seyton leaned forward and the light fell on his face. "None of us in Narco quite know what we're doing either, that's the problem with a boss like Duff. But don't let me interrupt your story, Macbeth. Did you go back in and tend their wounds?"

"Sweno's a murderer who would kill again if he had the chance," Macbeth said without letting go of Seyton's eyes. "And Duff was worried they would escape across the bridge."

"I was afraid they'd get across the bridge, as the lorry had tried to do," Duff said. "So we jumped back on our bikes. We rode them as hard as we could. Plus a bit more. One miscalculated bend on the wet tarmac . . ." Duff pushed the golden half-eaten crème brûlée across Lyon's damask cloth, took the bottle of champagne from the cooler and refilled the other three's glasses. "After the first hairpin bend at the bottom of the valley I saw the rear lights of four bikes and pressed on. In my mirror I saw Macbeth was still following."

Duff cast a furtive glance at Chief Commissioner Duncan to see if his account was being well received. His gentle, friendly smile was hard to interpret. Duncan still hadn't directly commented on the night's stakeout, but wasn't the fact that he had come to this little celebration an acknowledgment in itself? Perhaps, but the chief commissioner's silence unsettled Duff. He felt more secure with the pale redhead leader of the Anti-Corruption Unit, Inspector Lennox, who with his customary enthusiasm leaned across the table swallowing every word. And the head of the Forensic Unit, Caithness, whose big green eyes told him she believed every scrap and crumb.

Duff put down the bottle. "On the stretch leading to the tunnel we were side by side and the lights ahead were growing. As though they had slowed down. I could see the horns on Sweno's helmet. Then something unexpected happened."

Duncan moved his champagne next to his red-wine glass, which Duff didn't know whether to interpret as tension or just impatience. "Two of the bikes turned off straight after the bus shelter, by the exit road to Forres, while the other two continued toward the tunnel. We were seconds away from the junction and I had to make a decision . . ."

Duff emphasized the word *decision*. Of course he could have said *make a choice*. But *choosing* was just something any idiot might be forced to do while *making a decision* is pro-active, it requires a mental process and character, it is taken by a leader. The kind of leader the chief commissioner needed when he appointed the head of the newly established Organized Crime Unit. The OCU was a grand merging of the Narco Unit and the Gang Unit, and a logical fusion as all the drug dealing in town was now split between Hecate and the Norse Riders, who had swallowed the other gangs. The question was who would lead the unit, Duff or Cawdor, the experienced leader of the Gang Unit, who had a suspiciously large fully paid-off house on the west side of town. The problem was that Cawdor had a supporting cast on the town council and among Kenneth's old conspirators at police HQ, and even though everyone knew Duncan was prepared to stick his neck out to get rid of the various Cawdors he also had to show some political nous so as not to lose control at HQ. What was clear was that one of Cawdor or Duff would emerge as the winner and the other would be left without a unit.

"I signaled to Macbeth that we should follow the Forres pair."

"Really?" said Lennox. "Then the other two would cross the county boundary."

"Yes, and that was the dilemma. Sweno's a sly fox. Was he sending two men to Forres as decoys while he drove to the boundary as he's the only Norse Rider we've got anything on? Or was he counting on us thinking that was what he was thinking and he would therefore do the opposite?"

"Have we?" Lennox asked.

"Have we what?" Duff asked, trying to conceal his irritation at being interrupted.

"Got anything on Sweno? The Stoke Massacre is time-barred, as far as I know."

"The two post office robberies in District 1 five years ago," Duff said impatiently. "We've got Sweno's fingerprints and everything."

"And the other Norse Riders?"

"Zilch. And we didn't get anything tonight either because they were all wearing helmets. Anyway, when we turned off for Forres we saw the helmet—"

"What's the Stoke Massacre?" Caithness asked.

Duff groaned.

"You probably weren't born then," Duncan said in a friendly voice. "It happened in Capitol straight after the war. Sweno's brother was about to be arrested for desertion and was stupid enough to draw a weapon. The two arresting policemen, who had both spent the war in the trenches, shot holes in him. Sweno avenged his brother several months later in Stoke. He went into the local police station and shot down four officers, among them one very pregnant woman. Sweno disappeared off our radar, and when he reappeared the case was time-barred. Please, Duff, continue."

"Thank you. I thought they weren't aware we were so close on their tails that we could see Sweno's helmet when he turned off for Forres and the old bridge. We caught them up only a couple of kilometers or so later. That is, Macbeth fired two shots in the air when they were still a good way in front, and they stopped. So we stopped too. We had left the valley behind us, so it wasn't raining. Good visibility, moonlight, fifty to sixty meters between us. I had my AK-47 and ordered them to get off their bikes, walk five steps toward us and kneel down on the tarmac with their hands behind their heads. They did as we said, we got off our bikes and walked toward them."

Duff closed his eyes.

He could see them now.

They were kneeling.

Duff's leather gear creaked as he walked toward them, and a drop of water hung in his peripheral vision from the edge of his open visor. Soon it would fall. Soon.

"There was probably a distance of ten to fifteen strides between us when Sweno pulled out a gun," Macbeth said. "Duff reacted at once. He fired. Hitting Sweno three times in the chest. He was dead before his helmet hit the ground. But in the meantime the second man had drawn his gun and aimed at Duff. Fortunately though he never managed to pull the trigger."

"Holy shit!" Angus shouted. "You shot him, did you?"

Macbeth leaned back. "I got him with a dagger."

Banquo studied his superior officer.

"Impressive," whispered Seyton from the shadows. "On the other hand, Duff reacted quicker than you when Sweno went for his gun? I'd have bet you'd be quicker, Macbeth."

"But there you're wrong," Macbeth said. *What was Seyton doing, what was he after?* "Just like Duff," Macbeth said, lifting his beer mug to his mouth.

"I made a mistake," Duff said, signaling to the head waiter for another bottle of champagne. "Not about shooting, of course. But choosing which bikes to follow."

The head waiter came to the table and quietly informed them that unfortunately they would have to close, and it was illegal to sell alcohol after midnight. Unless the chief commissioner . . .

"Thank you, but no," said Duncan, who was a master of the art of smiling roguishly while raising his eyebrows in reproof. "We'll keep to the law."

The waiter took his leave.

"Making the wrong choice can happen to the best of us," Duncan said. "When did you realize? When you removed his helmet?"

Duff shook his head. "Immediately before, when I knelt down beside the body and happened to glance at his bike. It wasn't Sweno's bike, the saber wasn't there. And the Riders don't swap bikes."

"But they swap helmets?"

Duff shrugged. "I should have known. After all, Macbeth and I had just employed the same trick ourselves. Sweno swapped his helmet, and they slowed down enough for us to see his helmet was on one of the Riders going to Forres. He himself went through the tunnel, over the bridge and escaped."

"Smart thinking, no doubt about it," Duncan said. "Shame his people weren't as smart."

"What do you mean?" Duff asked, looking down at the leather folder with the bill the waiter had placed before him.

"Why pull guns on the police when they know—as you yourself said—we have no evidence against anyone except Sweno? They could have just allowed themselves to be arrested and left the police station as free men a few hours later."

Duff shrugged. "Perhaps they didn't believe we were policemen. Perhaps they thought we were Hecate's men and we were going to kill them."

"Or as the chief commissioner says," Lennox said, "they're stupid."

Duncan scratched his chin. "How many Norse Riders did we lock up?"

"Six," Duff said. "When we returned to the clubhouse it was mainly the seriously injured who were still there."

"I didn't think gangs like the Norse Riders left their injured for the enemy."

"They knew they would get medical aid faster. They're being treated now, but we're expecting to get more in custody tomorrow. And then they'll be questioned about Sweno. However much pain they're in. We'll find him, sir."

"Fine. Four and a half tons of amphetamine. That's a lot," said Duncan.

"It is indeed." Duff smiled.

"So much that you almost have to ask yourself why you didn't inform me about the stakeout beforehand."

"Time," Duff replied quickly. He had weighed up the pros and cons of how to answer the inevitable question. "There wasn't enough time between receiving the tip-off and going into action. As head of the unit I had to assess procedural regulations against the risk of not preventing four and a half tons of amphetamines from reaching the youths in this town."

Duff met Duncan's eyes, which were contemplating him. The chief commissioner's index finger stroked the point of his chin to and fro. Then he moistened his lips.

"There's a lot of blood too. A lot of damage to the bridge. The fish in the river are probably already junkies. And Sweno's still on the loose."

Duff cursed inwardly. The hypocritical, arrogant fool must be capable of seeing the bigger picture.

"But," said the chief commissioner, "six Norse Riders are in custody. And even if we do feel a little more invigorated than usual when eating fish over the next few weeks, better that than the dope ending up in our young people. Or—" Duncan grabbed his champagne glass "—in Seized Goods."

Lennox and Caithness laughed. It was well known that the HQ warehouse was still unaccountably losing goods.

"So," Duncan said, raising his glass, "good police work, Duff."

Duff blinked twice. His heart beat quickly and lightly. "Thank you," he said, draining his glass.

Duncan snatched the leather folder. "This is on me." He took the bill, held it at arm's length and squinted. "Although I can't see if I've been given the right bill."

"Who has!" Lennox said with a stiff smile when no one laughed.

"Let me," Caithness said, taking the bill and putting on her horn-rimmed granny glasses, which Duff knew she didn't need but wore because she thought they added a couple of years to her age and detracted from her appearance. Duncan had been brave to give Caithness the Forensic Unit. Not because anyone doubted her professional competence—she had been the best cadet at her police college and had also studied chemistry and physics—but she was younger than any of the other unit heads, single and simply too good-looking for suspicion of ulterior motives not to creep in. The candle flames made the water in her laughing eyes behind the glasses, the moisture of her full red lips and the wetness of her shining white teeth sparkle. Duff closed his eyes. The gleaming shine of the tarmac, the sound of tires on the wet road. The spattering sound. The blood that had splashed to the floor when the man had pulled the dagger from his neck. It was a like a hand squeezing Duff's chest, and he opened his eyes with a gasp.

"Everything OK?" Lennox held a carafe of water over Duff's glass, and the dregs splashed in. "Drink, Duff, so that you can dilute the champagne. You have to drive now."

"No question of that," Duncan said. "I don't want my heroes arrested for drunk driving or killed on the road. My driver wouldn't object to a little detour."

"Thank you," Duff said. "But Fife's—"

"—more or less on my way home," Duncan said. "And it's Mrs. Duff and your two wonderful children who should thank me."

"Excuse me," Duff said, pushing his chair back and standing up.

"A stupendous police officer," Lennox said as he watched Duff stagger toward the toilet door at the back of the room.

"Duff?" Duncan queried.

"Him too, but I was thinking about Macbeth. His results are impressive, his men love him, and even though he worked under Kenneth, we in the Anti-Corruption Unit know he's rock solid. It's a pity he doesn't have the formal qualifications necessary for a higher management post."

"There's no requirement to have anything higher than police college. Look at Kenneth."

"Yes, but Macbeth still isn't one of us."

"Us?"

"Well," Lennox lifted his champagne glass with a wry smile, "you've chosen heads who—whether we like it or not—are seen as belonging to the elite. We all come from the western side of town or Capitol, have an education or a respectable family name. Macbeth is seen more as someone from the broader ranks of the populace, if you know what I mean."

"I do. Listen, I'm a bit worried about Duff's unsteadiness on his feet. Could you . . . ?"

Fortunately the toilet was empty.

Duff did up his flies, stood by one of the sinks, turned on a tap and splashed water over his face. He heard the door go behind him.

"Duncan asked me to check how you were," Lennox said.

"Mm. What do you think he thought?"

"Thought about what?"

Duff grabbed a paper and dried his face. "About . . . how things went."

"He probably thinks what we all think: you did a good job."

Duff nodded.

Lennox chuckled. "You really do want the Organized Crime job, don't you."

Duff turned off the tap and soaped his hands while looking at the head of Anti-Corruption in the mirror.

"You mean I'm a climber?"

"Nothing wrong with climbing the ladder." Lennox smirked. "It's just amusing to see how you position yourself."

"I'm qualified, Lennox. So isn't it simply my duty to this town and my and your children's future to do what I can for Organized Crime? Or should I leave the biggest unit to Cawdor? A person we both know must have both dirty and bloody hands to have survived under Kenneth for as long as he did."

"Aha," Lennox said. "It's duty that drives you? Not personal ambition at all. Well, St. Duff, let me hold the door open for you." Lennox performed a deep bow. "I presume you will refuse the salary increase and other concomitant privileges."

"The salary, honor and fame are irrelevant to me," Duff said. "But society rewards those who contribute. Showing contempt for the salary would be like showing contempt for society." He studied his face in the mirror. *How can you see when a person is lying?* Is it possible when the person in question has succeeded in convincing himself that what he says is the truth? How long would it take him to convince himself that it was the truth, the version he and Macbeth had arranged to give of how they had killed the two men on the road?

"Have you finished washing your hands now, Duff? I think Duncan wants to go home."

The SWAT men took their leave of one another outside the Bricklayers Arms. "Loyalty, fraternity," Macbeth said in a loud voice.

The others answered him in slurred, to varying degrees, unison: "Baptized in fire, united in blood."

Then they walked away in every direction of the compass. Macbeth and Banquo to the west, past a street musician who was howling rather than singing "Meet Me on the Corner" and through the deserted rundown concourses and corridors of the central station. A strangely warm wind picked up through the passages and swept litter between the once beautiful Doric pillars crumbling after years of pollution and lack of maintenance.

"Now," Banquo said. "Are you going to tell me what *really* happened?"

"You tell me about the lorry and Kenneth," Macbeth said. "Ninety-meter free fall!" His laughter resounded beneath the brick ceiling.

Banquo smiled. "Come on, Macbeth. What happened out there on the country road?"

"Did they say anything about how long they would have to close the bridge for repairs?"

"You might be able to lie to them, but not to me."

"We got them, Banquo. Do you need to know anymore?"

"Do I?" Banquo waved away the stench from the stairs down to the toilets, where a woman of indeterminate age was standing bent over with her hair hanging down in front of her face as she clung to the handrail.

"No."

"All right," Banquo said.

Macbeth stopped and crouched down by a young boy sitting by the wall with a begging cup in front of him. The boy raised his head. He had a black patch over one eye and the other stared out from a doped-up state, a dream. Macbeth put a banknote in his cup and a hand on his shoulder. "How's it going?" he asked softly.

"Macbeth," the boy said. "As you can see."

"You can do it," Macbeth said. "Always remember that. You can stop."

The boy's voice slurred and slid from vowel to vowel. "And how do you know that?"

"Believe me, it's been done before." Macbeth stood up, and the boy called a tremulous "God bless you, Macbeth" after them.

They went into the concourse in the eastern part of the station, where there was a conspicuous silence, like in a church. The druggies who weren't sitting, lying or standing by the walls or on the benches were staggering around in a kind of slow dance, like astronauts in an alien atmosphere, a different gravitational field. Some stared suspiciously at the two police officers, but most just ignored them. As though they had X-ray eyes that had long ago established that these two had nothing to sell. Most were so emaciated and ravaged it was hard to know exactly how long they had been alive. Or how long they had left.

"You're never tempted to start again?" Banquo asked.

"No."

"Most ex-junkies dream of a last shot."

"Not me. Let's get out of here."

They walked to the steps in front of the west exit, stopped before they came to where the roof no longer sheltered them from the rain. Beside them, on black rails on a low plinth, stood what appeared in the darkness to be a prehistoric monster. Bertha, a hundred and ten years old, the first locomotive in the country, the very symbol of the optimism about the future that had once held sway. The broad, majestic, gently graded steps led down to the dark, deserted Workers' Square, where once there had been hustle and bustle, market stalls and travelers hurrying to and fro, but which was now ghostly, a square where the wind whistled and whined. At one end lights glittered in a venerable brick building which had at one time housed the offices of the National Railway Network but had fallen into disuse after the railway was abandoned, until it had been bought and renovated to become the most glamorous and elegant building the town had to offer: Inverness Casino. Banquo had been inside only once and immediately knew it was not his kind of place. Or, to be more precise, he wasn't their kind of customer. He was probably the Obelisk type, where customers were not so well dressed, the drinks were not so expensive and the prostitutes not so beautiful nor so discreet.

"Good night, Banquo."

"Good night, Macbeth. Sleep well."

Banquo saw a light shiver go through his friend's body, then Macbeth's white teeth shone in the darkness. "Say hello to Fleance from me and tell him his father has done a great job tonight. What I wouldn't have given to see Kenneth in free fall from his own bridge . . ."

Banquo heard his friend's low chuckle as he disappeared into the darkness and rain on Workers' Square, but when his own laughter had faded too an unease spread through him. Macbeth wasn't only a friend and a colleague, he was like a son, a Moses in a basket whom Banquo loved almost as much as Fleance. So that was why Banquo waited until he saw Macbeth reappear on the other side of the square and walk into the light by the entrance to the casino, from which a tall woman with flowing flame-red hair in a long red dress emerged and hugged him, as though a phantom had warned her that her beloved was on his way.

Lady.

Perhaps she had caught wind of this evening's events. A woman like Lady wouldn't have got to where she was without informants who told her what she needed to know about everything that moved beneath the surface of this town.

They still had their arms around each other. She was a beautiful woman and might well have been even more beautiful once. No one seemed to know Lady's age, but it was definitely a good deal more than Macbeth's thirty-three years. But maybe it was true what they said: true love conquers all.

Or maybe not.

The older policeman turned and set off north.

In Fife the chief commissioner's chauffeur turned off onto the gravel lane as instructed. The gravel crunched under the car tires.

"You can stop here. I'll walk the rest of the way," Duff said.

The chauffeur braked. In the ensuing silence they could hear the grasshoppers and the sough of the deciduous trees.

"You don't want to wake them," Duncan said, looking down the lane, where a small white farmhouse lay bathed in moonlight. "And I agree. Let our dear ones sleep in ignorance and safe assurance. A lovely little place you've got here."

"Thank you. And sorry about the detour."

"We all have to take detours in life, Duff. The next time you get a tip-off, as with the Norse Riders, you make a detour toward me. OK?"

"OK."

Duncan's index finger moved to and fro across his chin. "Our aim is to make this town a better place for everyone, Duff. But that means all the positive powers have to work together and think of the community's best interests, not only their own."

"Of course. And I'd just like to say I'm willing to do any job so long as it serves the force and the town, sir."

Duncan smiled. "In which case it's me who should thank you, Duff. Ah, one last thing . . ."

"Yes?"

"You say fourteen Norse Riders including Sweno himself were more than you'd anticipated and it would have been more discreet of them to have just sent a couple of men to drive the lorry away?"

"Yes."

"Has it struck you that Sweno might also have been tipped off? He might have suspected you'd be there. So your fear of a leak was perhaps not unfounded. Good night, Duff."

"Good night."

Duff walked down to his house breathing in the smell of the earth and grass where the dew had already fallen. He had considered this possibility and now Duncan had articulated it. A leak. An informant. And he, Duff, would find the leak. He would find him the very next day.

Macbeth lay on his side with his eyes closed. Behind him he heard her regular breathing and from down in the casino the bass line of the music, like muffled heartbeats. The Inverness stayed open all night, but it was now late even for crazed gamblers and thirsty drinkers. In the corridor overnight guests walked past and unlocked their rooms. Some alone, some with a spouse. Some with other company. This wasn't something Lady paid too much attention to as long as the women who frequented the casino complied with her unwritten rules of always being discreet, always well-groomed, always sober, always infection-free and always, but always, attractive. Lady had once, not long after they had got together, asked why he didn't look at them. And laughed when he had answered it was because he only had eyes for her. It was only later she understood he meant that quite literally. He didn't need to turn round to see her, her features were seared into his retinas; all he had to do—wherever he was—was close his eyes and she was there. There hadn't been anyone before Lady. Well, there had been women who made his pulse race and there were definitely women's hearts that had beaten faster because of him. But he had never been intimate with them. And of course there was one who had scarred his heart. When Lady had realized and had, laughing, asked him if she had been sent a genuine virgin, he told her his story. The story that hitherto only two people in the world had known. And then she had told him hers.

The suite's silk sheet felt heavy and expensive on his naked body. Like a fever, hot and cold at the same time. He could hear from her breathing that she was awake.

"What is it?" she whispered sleepily.

"Nothing," he said. "I just can't sleep."

She snuggled up to him, and her hand stroked his chest and shoulders.

Occasionally, like now, they breathed in rhythm. As though they were one and the same organism, like Siamese twins sharing lungs—that was exactly how it felt the time they had exchanged their stories, and he knew he was no longer alone.

Her hand slid down his upper arm, over the tattoos, down to his lower arm, where she caressed his scars. He had told her about them too. And about Lorreal. They quite simply kept no secrets from each other. They weren't secrets, but there were grim details he had begged her to spare him. She loved him, that was all that was important, that was all he *had* to know about her. He turned onto his back. Her hand stroked his stomach, stopped and waited. She was the queen. And her vassal obediently stood up under the silk material.

When Duff crept into bed beside his wife, listened to her regular breathing and felt the heat from her back, it was as though the memories of the night's events had already begun to recede. This place had that effect on him, it always had. They had met while he was a student. She came from an affluent family on the western side of town, and even though her parents had been initially skeptical, after a while they accepted the hardworking ambitious young man. And Duff came from a respectable family, in his father-in-law's opinion. The rest followed almost automatically. Marriage, children, a house in Fife, where the children could grow up without inhaling the town's toxic air, career, everyday grind. A lot of everyday grind with long days and promotion beckoning. And time flies by. That's the way it is. She was a good woman and wife, it wasn't that. Clever, caring and loyal. And what about him—wasn't he a good husband? Didn't he provide for them, save money for the children's education, build a cabin by the lake? Yes, neither she nor her father had much to complain about. He was the way he was, he couldn't help that. Anyway, there was a lot to say for having a home, having a family: it gave you peace. It had its own pace of life, its own agenda, and it didn't care much about what was on the outside. Not really. And he needed that perception of reality—or the lack of it—he *had* to have it. Now and then.

"You came home then—" she mumbled.

"To you and the kids," he said.

"—in the night," she added.

He lay listening to the silence between them. Trying to decide whether it was good or bad. Then she laid a tender hand on his shoulder. Pressed her fingertips carefully against his tired muscles where he knew they would soothe.

Closed his eyes.

And he saw it again.

The raindrop hanging from the edge of his visor. The man kneeling in front of him. Not moving. The helmet with the horns. Duff wanted to say something to him, but he couldn't. Instead he lifted the gun to his shoulder. Couldn't the man at least move? The raindrop would soon fall.

"Duff," Macbeth said behind him. "Duff, don't . . ."

The drop fell.

Duff fired. Fired again. Fired again.

Three shots.

The man kneeling in front of him fell sideways.

The silence afterward was deafening. He squatted down beside the dead man and removed his helmet. It was like having a bucket of ice-cold water thrown over him when he saw it wasn't Sweno. The young man's eyes were closed; he looked like he was sleeping peacefully where he lay.

Duff turned, glanced at Macbeth. Felt the tears filling his eyes, still unable to speak, just shook his head. Macbeth nodded in response and removed the other's helmet. Also a young man. Duff felt something pushing up into his throat and wrapped his hands around his face. Over his sobs he heard the man's pleas reverberate like gulls' cries across the uninhabited plains. "No, don't! I haven't seen anything! I won't tell anyone! Please, no jury will believe me anyway. I under—"

The voice was cut off. Duff heard a body smack against the tarmac, a low gurgle, then everything went quiet.

He turned. Only now did he notice the other man was wearing white clothes. They were soaking up the blood running from the hole in his neck.

Macbeth stood behind the man, a dagger in his hand. His chest was heaving. "Now," he said gruffly. Cleared his throat. "Now I've paid my debt to you, Duff."

Duff pressed his fingertips against the place where he knew they didn't soothe. He held his other hand over the man's mouth to muffle his screams and forced him down onto the hospital bed. The man pulled desperately

at the handcuffs shackling him to the bedhead. From the daylight flood-
ing in through the window Duff could clearly see the network of fine
blood vessels around the big pupils, black with shock, in his wide-open
eyes under the NORSE RIDER TILL I DIE tattoo on his forehead. Duff's forefinger and index finger went red where they pressed under the bandage
into the shoulder wound, making squelching noises.

Any job, Duff thought, *as long as it serves the force and the town.*

And repeated the question: "Who's your police informant?"

He took his hand away from the wound. The man stopped screaming.
Duff took his hand off his mouth. The man didn't answer.

Duff ripped off the bandage and pressed all his fingers into the wound.

He knew he would get an answer, it was just a question of time. There
is only so much a man can take before he gives in, before he breaks every
tattooed oath and does everything—absolutely everything—he thought
he would never do. For eternal loyalty is inhuman and betrayal is human.

4

IT TOOK TWENTY MINUTES.

Twenty minutes after Duff had walked into the hospital and poked his fingers into the shoulder wound of the man with the tattoo on his forehead, until he left, amazed, with enough information about whom, where and when for the relevant person to find it impossible to deny unless he was innocent. Amazed because—now things had got so bad that they had a mole in their midst—it was almost too good to be true.

It took thirty minutes.

Thirty minutes after Duff had got in his car, driven through the trickle of rain falling onto the town like an old man piddling, parked outside the main police station, received a gracious nod from the chief commissioner's anteroom lady to let him know he could pass, until he was sitting in front of Duncan and articulated the one word. Cawdor. And the chief commissioner leaned across his desk, asked Duff if he was sure, after all this was the head of the Gang Unit they were talking about—sat back, drew a hand over his face and for the first time Duff heard Duncan swear.

It took forty minutes.

Forty minutes from when Duncan had announced that Cawdor had a day off, lifted the phone and ordered Macbeth to arrest him, until eight SWAT men surrounded Cawdor's house, which lay on a big plot of land overlooking the sea so far to the west that refuse was still collected and the homeless removed, and Mayor Tourtell was his closest neighbor. The SWAT team parked some distance away and crept up to the house, two men from each direction.

Macbeth and Banquo sat on the pavement with their backs against the high wall to the south of the house, beside the gates. Cawdor—like most of his neighbors—had cemented glass shards into the top of the wall, but

SWAT had mats to overcome hindrances of that kind. The raid followed the usual procedure, the teams reporting via walkie-talkies when they were in their pre-arranged positions. Macbeth glanced across the street to where a boy of six or seven had been throwing a ball against a garage wall when they arrived. Now he stopped and stared at them with his mouth open. Macbeth put a finger to his lips, and the boy nodded back somnambulantly. The same expression as the white-clad young man kneeling on the tarmac the previous night, Macbeth reflected.

"Wake up." It was Banquo whispering in his ear.

"What?"

"All the teams are in position."

Macbeth breathed in and out a couple of times. Had to shut out other things from his mind now, had to get in the zone. He pressed the talk button: "Fifty seconds to going in. North? Over."

Angus's voice with that unctuous priest-like chanting tone: "All OK. Can't see any movement inside. Over."

"West? Over."

"All OK." That was the replacement's voice, Seyton. Monotone, calm. "Hang on, the sitting-room curtain twitched. Over."

"OK," Macbeth said. He didn't even need to think; this was part of the what-if procedure they drilled day in, day out. "We may have been seen, folks. Let's cut the countdown and go in. Three, two, one . . . go!"

And there it was, the zone. The zone was like a room where you closed the door behind you and nothing else but the mission, you and your men existed.

They got to their feet, and as Banquo threw the mat over the glass on the wall Macbeth noticed the boy with the ball wave slowly, robotically, with his free hand.

Within seconds they were over the wall and sprinting through the garden, and Macbeth had this feeling he could sense everything around him. He could hear a branch creak in the wind, could see a crow take off from the ridge of the neighbor's roof, could smell a rotting apple in the grass. They ran up the steps, and Banquo used the butt of his gun to smash the window beside the front door, slipped his hand through and unlocked the door from the inside. As they entered they heard glass breaking elsewhere in the house. Eight against one. When Macbeth asked Duncan if there was any reason to think Cawdor would put up resistance Duncan had answered that wasn't why he wanted a full-scale arrest.

"It's to send a signal, Macbeth. We don't treat our own more leniently. Quite the contrary. Smash glass, kick in doors, make a lot of noise and lead Cawdor out in handcuffs through the front entrance so that everyone can see and tell others."

Macbeth went in first. Pressing an assault rifle to his shoulder as his gaze swept the hall. Stood with his back to the wall beside the sitting-room door. His eyes gradually adapted to the darkness after the sharp sunlight outside. All the curtains in the house appeared to be drawn. Banquo came up to his side and carried on into the sitting room.

As Macbeth pushed off from the wall to follow him, it happened.

The attacker came swiftly and silently from the darkness shrouding one of the two staircases, hit Macbeth in the chest and sent him flying backward.

Macbeth felt hot air on his throat, but managed to get his gun barrel between him and the dog and knock its snout to the side so that the big teeth sank into his shoulder instead. He screamed with pain as an immense snarling head tore at skin and flesh. Macbeth tried to hit out, but his free hand was caught in his rifle strap. "Banquo!" Cawdor wasn't supposed to have a dog. They always checked before operations of this kind. But this was definitely a dog, and it was strong. The dog shoved the gun barrel to the side. It was going for his throat. He would soon have his carotid artery severed.

"Banq—"

The dog went stiff. Macbeth turned his head and stared into dulled canine eyes. Then its body went limp and slumped on top of him. Macbeth pushed it off and looked up.

Seyton was standing over him holding out a hand.

"Thank you," Macbeth said, getting to his feet without help. "Where's Banquo?"

"He and Cawdor are inside," Seyton answered, motioning toward the sitting room.

Macbeth went to the sitting-room door. They had opened the curtains, and in the bright light from behind he saw only Banquo's back as he stared up at the ceiling. Above him hovered an angel with a halo of sunshine and his head bowed as if in a plea for forgiveness.

It took an hour.

An hour from the moment Macbeth had said, "Go!" until Duncan had gathered all the departmental and unit leaders together in the large conference room at HQ.

Duncan stood up on the podium and looked down at some papers; Duff knew he had written some words there the way he wanted them to be said but that he would ad-lib according to the moment and the situation. Not because the chief commissioner was a loose cannon, far from it. Duff knew he had the words under control, he was as much a man of heart as he was of mind, a man who spoke how he felt and vice versa. A man who understood himself and therefore others too, Duff thought. A leader. Someone people would follow. Someone Duff wished he was, or could be.

"You all know what happened," Duncan said in a low, solemn voice, yet it carried as though he had shouted. "I just wanted to brief you fully before the press conference this afternoon. One of our most trusted officers, Inspector Cawdor, had a serious charge of corruption leveled against him. And at the present moment it appears this suspicion was justified. In the light of his close connection with the Norse Riders—against whom we launched a successful operation yesterday—there was clearly a risk that he, given the situation, might try to destroy evidence or flee. For that reason, at ten o'clock this morning I gave the order for SWAT to arrest Inspector Cawdor with immediate effect."

Duff had hoped his name would be mentioned, but he was also aware that Duncan wouldn't divulge any details. For if there is one thing you learn in the police it is that rules are rules, even when unwritten. So he was surprised when Duncan looked up and said, "Inspector Macbeth, would you be so kind as to come up here and briefly summarize the arrest?"

Duff turned and watched his colleague stride up between the lines of chairs to the podium. Obviously he had been caught by surprise as well. The chief commissioner didn't normally delegate in these contexts; he would usually say his piece, make it short and to the point and conclude the meeting so that everyone could get back to their job of making the town a better place to live.

Macbeth looked ill at ease. He was still wearing his black SWAT uniform, but the zip at the neck was undone far enough for them to see the bright white bandage on his right shoulder.

"Well," he began.

Not exactly an elegant start, but then no one expected the head of SWAT to be a wordsmith. Macbeth checked his watch as though he had an appointment. Everyone in the room knew why: it is the instinctive re-action of police officers who have been ordered to report back and feel unsure of themselves. They check their watches as though the obligatory time references for past events are written there or the watch face will jog their memory.

"At ten fifty-three," Macbeth said and coughed twice, "SWAT raided Inspector Cawdor's home. A terrace door was open, but there was no sign of a break-in or violence, or that anyone had been there before us. Apart from a dog. Nor any signs that anyone other than Cawdor himself had done it . . ." Now Macbeth stopped looking at his watch and addressed the gathering. "A chair was knocked over by the terrace door. I'm not going to anticipate the SOCOs' conclusions, but it looked as if Cawdor didn't just step off the chair when he hanged himself, he jumped, and when he swung back kicked the chair across the room. That tallies with the way the deceased's excrement was scattered across the floor. The body was cold. Suicide seems the obvious cause of death, and one of the guys asked if we could skip the procedures and cut the man down as Cawdor had been a police officer all his life. I said no . . ."

Duff noticed Macbeth's dramatic pause. As if to allow the audience to listen to his silence. It was a trick Duff might use himself, a method he had definitely seen Duncan use, but he hadn't imagined that the pragmatic Macbeth would have it in his repertoire. And perhaps he didn't, because he was studying his watch again.

"Ten fifty-nine."

Macbeth looked up and pulled his sleeve over the watch in a gesture to suggest he had finished.

"So Cawdor's still hanging there. Not for any investigative purpose, but because he was a *corrupt* policeman."

It was so quiet in the room that Duff could hear the rain lashing against the window high up the wall. Macbeth turned to Duncan and gave a cursory nod. Then he left the podium and went back to his seat.

Duncan waited until Macbeth had sat down before saying, "Thank you, Macbeth. That won't form part of the press conference, but I think it's a suitable conclusion to this internal briefing. Remember that a condemnation of all that is weak and bad in us can also be seen as an optimistic tribute to all that is strong and good. So back to your good work, folks."

The young nurse stood by the door and watched the patient take off his top. He had pulled his long black hair behind his head as the doctor unwound the bloodstained bandage from his left shoulder. All she knew about the patient was that he was a police officer. And muscular.

"Oh my goodness," the doctor said. "We'll have to give you a few stitches. And you'll need a tetanus injection, we always do that with dog bites. But first a little anaesthetic. Maria, can you . . . ?"

"No," said the patient, staring stiffly at the wall.

"Sorry?"

"No anaesthetic."

A silence ensued.

"No anaesthetic?"

"No anaesthetic."

The doctor was about to say something about pain when she caught sight of the scars on his forearms. Old scars. But the type of scar she had seen all too often after she moved to this town.

"Right," she said. "No anaesthetic."

Duff leaned back in his office chair and pressed the receiver to his ear.

"It's me, love. What are you all doing?"

"Emily's gone swimming with friends. Ewan has got a toothache. I'll take him to the dentist."

"OK. Love, I'm working late today."

"Why's that?"

"I may have to stay over here."

"Why's that?" she repeated. Her voice didn't reveal any annoyance or frustration. It just sounded as if this was information she would like, perhaps to explain his absence to the children. Not because she needed him. Not because . . .

"It'll soon be on the news," he said. "Cawdor has committed suicide."

"Oh dear. Who's Cawdor?"

"Don't you know?"

"No."

"The head of the Gang Unit. He was a strong candidate for the Organized Crime post."

Silence.

She had never taken much interest in his work. Her world was Fife, the children and—at least when he was at home—her husband. Which was great for him. In the sense that he didn't have to involve them in the grimness of his work. On the other hand, her lack of interest in his ambition meant she didn't always show much understanding for what the job demanded of his time. For his sacrifice. For . . . what he needed, for goodness' sake.

"The head of Organized Crime, who will be number three in the chain of command at HQ, after Duncan and Deputy Commissioner Malcolm. So, yes, this is a big deal, and it means I have to be here. Probably for the next few days, too."

"Just tell me you'll be here for the pre-birthday."

The pre-birthday. Oh, hell! It was a tradition they had, the day before the child's real birthday it was just the four of them, meat broth and Mum and Dad's presents. Had he really forgotten Ewan's birthday? Perhaps the date had slipped his mind with all the events of the last few days, but he had gone out to buy what Ewan said he wanted after Duff told him how the undercover officers worked in the Narco Unit—sometimes they donned a disguise so that they wouldn't be recognized. In the drawer in front of Duff there was a nicely wrapped gift box containing a false beard and glue, fake glasses and a green woolly hat, all adult sizes so that he could assure Ewan it was *exactly* what Daddy and the others in the Narco Unit wore.

A light flashed on his telephone. An internal call. He had an inkling who it might be.

"Just a mo, love."

He pressed the button below the light. "Yes?"

"Duff? Duncan here. It's about the press conference this afternoon."

"Oh yes?"

"I'd like to show we haven't been rendered impotent by what's happened and we're thinking about the future, so I'm going to announce the name of the acting head of Organized Crime."

"Organized Crime? Er . . . already?"

"I'd have done it at the end of the month anyway, but as the Gang Unit no longer has a leader it's expedient to appoint an acting head straightaway. Can you come up to my office?"

"Of course."

Duncan rang off. Duff sat staring at the extinguished light. It was unusual for the chief commissioner to ring personally; it was always his secretary or one of his assistants who called meetings. Acting head. Who would probably take over the post when the formalities—application phase, appointment board's deliberations and so on—were at an end. His gaze picked up another light. He had completely forgotten his wife was on hold.

"Love, something's happened. I've got to run."

"Oh? Nothing awful, I hope."

"No." Duff laughed. "Nothing awful. Not at all. I think you should switch on the radio news this afternoon and listen to what they say about the new appointment for Organized Crime."

"Oh?"

"Kiss on the neck." They hadn't used this term of endearment for years. Duff rang off and ran—he couldn't stop himself—out of his office and up the stairs to the top floor. Up, up, up, higher and higher.

The secretary told Duff to go straight in. "They're waiting for you." She smiled. Smiled? She never smiled.

Around the circular oak table in the chief commissioner's large, airy but soberly furnished office sat four people, not counting Duncan. Deputy Chief Commissioner Malcolm, prematurely gray and bespectacled. He had studied philosophy and economics at the university in Capitol, spoke accordingly and was seen by many as a strange bird in HQ. He was an old friend of Duncan's, who claimed he had brought him in because they needed his broad range of management skills. Others said it was because Duncan needed Malcolm's unqualified "Yes" vote at management meetings. Beside Malcolm, Lennox leaned forward, as keen as ever, albino-pale. His section, the Anti-Corruption Unit, had been established during Duncan's reorganization. There had been a brief discussion as to whether *anti* should be in the title, some arguing that they didn't say the Anti-Narcotics Unit or the Anti-Homicide Unit. Yet under Kenneth the Narcotics Unit had been known as the corruption unit in local parlance. On the other side of Duncan sat an assistant taking minutes of the meeting, and beside her, Inspector Caithness.

As Duncan didn't allow smoking in his office there were no ashtrays on the table with cigarette ends to tell Duff roughly how long they had been sitting there, but he registered that some of the notepads on the table had coffee stains and some of the cups were nearly empty. And the open, gentle, almost relaxed atmosphere suggested they had reached a conclusion.

"Thank you for coming so quickly, Duff," Duncan said, showing him to the last vacant chair with an open palm. "Let me get straight to the point. We're pushing forward the merging of your Narcotics Unit with the Gang Unit to become the Organized Crime Unit. This is our first crisis since I took over the chair of—" Duff looked in the direction Duncan was nodding, to the desk. The chief commissioner's chair was high-backed and large, but didn't exactly look comfortable. Bit too straight. No soft upholstery. It was a chair to Duff's taste "—so I feel it's important we show some vim."

"Sounds sensible," Duff said. And regretted it at once. The remark made it seem as if he had been brought in to assess top management's reasoning. "I mean, I'm sure you're right."

There was a moment's silence around the table. Had he gone too far the other way, suggesting that he didn't have opinions of his own?

"We have to be absolutely one hundred percent certain that the person is not corrupt," Duncan said.

"Of course," Duff said.

"Not only because we can't afford any similar scandals such as this one with Cawdor, but because we need someone who can help us to catch the really big fish. And I'm not talking Sweno but Hecate."

Hecate. The silence in the room after articulating the name spoke volumes.

Duff straightened up in his chair. This was indeed a big mission. But it was clear this was what the job demanded: slaying the dragon. And it was magnificent. For it started here. Life as a different, better man.

"You led this successful attack on the Norse Riders," Duncan said.

"I didn't do it on my own, sir," Duff said. It paid dividends to show a bit of humility, and especially in situations where it wasn't required; it was precisely then you could afford to be humble.

"Indeed," Duncan said. "Macbeth helped you. Quite a lot, I understand. What's your general impression of him?"

"Impression, sir?"

"Yes, you were in the same year at police college. He's undoubtedly done a good job with SWAT, and everyone there is enthusiastic about his leadership qualities. But of course SWAT is a very specialized unit. You know him, and that's why we'd like to hear whether you believe Macbeth could be the man for the job."

Duff had to swallow twice before he could get his vocal cords to produce a sound. "If Macbeth could be the man to lead the Organized Crime Unit, you mean?"

"Yes."

Duff needed a couple of seconds. He placed a hand over his mouth, lowered his eyebrows and forehead and hoped this made him look like a deep thinker—not a deeply disappointed man.

"Well, Duff?"

"It's one thing leading men in a raid on a house, shooting criminals and saving hostages," Duff said. "And Macbeth's good at that without any doubt. Leading an organized crime unit requires slightly different qualifications."

"We agree," Duncan said. "It requires *slightly* different and not *completely* different qualifications. Leading is leading. What about the man's character? Is he trustworthy?"

Duff squeezed his top lip between thumb and first finger. Macbeth. Bloody Macbeth! What should he say? This promotion belonged to him, Duff, and not some guy who could equally well have ended up as a juggler or knife thrower in a traveling circus! He focused his gaze on the painting on the wall behind the desk. Marching, loyalty, leadership and solidarity. He could see them in his mind's eye on the country road: Macbeth, himself, the two dead men. The rain washing the blood away.

"Yes," Duff said. "Macbeth is trustworthy. But above all he's a craftsman. That was perhaps clear from his performance on the podium today."

"Agreed," Duncan said. "That was why I got him up there, to see how he would tackle it. Around the table we agreed unanimously that what he demonstrated today was an excellent example of a practitioner's respect for established reporting routines, but also a true leader's ability to enthuse and inspire. *Cawdor's still hanging there because he was a corrupt policeman.*"

Muted laughter around the table at Duncan's imitation of Macbeth's rough working-class dialect.

"If he really has these qualities," Duff said, hearing an inner voice whispering that he shouldn't say this, "you have to ask yourself why he hasn't got further since his police college years."

"True enough," Lennox said. "But this is one of the strongest arguments in *favor* of Macbeth." He laughed—an ill-timed, high-pitched trill. "None of us sitting round this table had high posts under the last chief commissioner. Because we, like Macbeth, weren't in on the game, we refused to take bribes. I have sources who can say with *total* certainty that this stalled Macbeth's career."

"Then you have answered the question already," Duff said stiffly. "And of course you've taken into consideration his relationship with the casino owner."

Malcolm glanced at Duncan. Received a nod from him in return and spoke up. "The Fraud Unit's now looking into businesses that were allowed to prosper under the previous administration and, with respect to that, they've just carried out a thorough investigation of Inverness Casino. Their conclusion is unambiguous: the Inverness is run in exemplary fashion with regard to accounts, tax and employment conditions. Which is not a matter you can take for granted in gambling joints. At this moment they're taking a closer look at the Obelisk's—" he smiled wryly "—cards. And let me say quite openly that this is a different kettle of fish. To be continued, as they say. So, in other words, we have no objections to Lady and her establishment."

"Macbeth's from the east end of town and an outsider," Duncan said, "while all of us around this table are considered to belong to an inner circle. We're known to have stood up to Kenneth, we represent a change of culture in the force, but we've also had private educations and come from privileged homes. I think it's a good signal to send. In the police, in *our* police force, everyone can get to the top, whatever background, whatever connections they have, as long as they work hard and are honest, with emphasis on the *honest*."

"Good thinking, sir," Lennox said.

"Fine." Duncan brought his hands together. "Duff, anything you'd like to add?"

Haven't you seen the scars on his arms?

"Duff?"

Haven't you seen the scars on his arms?

"Anything wrong, Duff?"

"No, sir. I have nothing to add. I'm sure Macbeth is a good choice."

"Good. Then let me thank all of you for attending this meeting."

Macbeth stared at the red traffic lights as the wipers went to and fro across the windscreen of Banquo's Volvo PV544. The car was as small as Banquo, a good deal older than the others around them, but fully functional and reliable. There was something about the design of the car, especially the set-back bonnet and protruding lower front, that made it look a bit like a throwback to before the war. But internally and under the bonnet, according to its owner, it had everything a man could demand of a modern car. The wipers struggled to dispose of the rain, and the running water reminded Macbeth of melting glass. A boy in a wet coat ran across the road in front of them, and Macbeth saw that the light for pedestrians had changed from a green man to red. A human body covered with blood from head to toe. Macbeth shuddered.

"What is it?" Banquo asked.

"I think I'm getting a temperature," Macbeth said. "I keep seeing things."

"Visions and signs," Banquo said. "It's flu then. No wonder. Soaked all day yesterday and bitten by a dog today."

"Talking about the dog, have we found out where it came from?"

"Only that it wasn't Cawdor's. It must have come in through the open veranda door. I was wondering how it died."

"Didn't I tell you? Seyton killed it."

"I know that, but I couldn't see any marks on it. Did he *strangle* it?"

"I don't know. Ask him."

"I did, but he didn't give me a proper answer, just—"

"It's green, Dad." The boy on the back seat leaned forward between the two men. Macbeth glanced at the lanky nineteen-year-old. Fleance had inherited more of his mother's modesty than his father's good-natured joviality.

"Who's driving, you or your dad, son?" Banquo said with a warm smile and accelerated. Macbeth looked at the people on the pavement, the housewives shopping, the unemployed men outside the bars. In the last ten years the town had become busier and busier in the mornings. It should have lent the town an atmosphere of hustle and bustle, but the opposite was true, the apathetic, resigned faces were more reminiscent of the living dead. He had searched for signs of change over recent months. To see whether Duncan's leadership had made any difference. The most glaring and brutal street crimes were perhaps rarer, probably because there were more patrols out. Or maybe they had simply shifted to the back streets, into the twilight areas.

"Afternoon lectures at police college," Macbeth said. "We didn't have them in my day."

"It's not a lecture," the boy said. "Me and a couple of others have a colloquium."

"A colloquium? What's that?"

"Fleance and some of the keener ones swot together before exams," Banquo said. "It's a good idea."

"Dad says I have to study law. Police college isn't enough. What do you think, Uncle Mac?"

"I think you should listen to your dad."

"But you didn't do law either," the boy objected.

"And look where it got him." Banquo laughed. "Come on, Fleance. You have to aim higher than your wretched father and this slob."

"You say I don't have leadership qualities," Fleance said.

Macbeth arched an eyebrow and glanced at Banquo.

"Really? I thought it was a father's job to make his children believe they can do anything if they try hard enough."

"It is," Banquo said. "And I didn't say he hasn't got leadership qualities, only skills. And that means he has to work on it. He's smart; he just has to learn to trust his own judgment, which means taking the initiative and not always following others."

Macbeth turned to the back seat. "You've got a hard nut of a father."

Fleance shrugged. "Some people always want to give orders and take charge while others aren't like that—is that so weird?"

"Not weird," Banquo said. "But if you want to get anywhere you have to try to change."

"Have *you* changed?" asked Fleance with a touch of annoyance in his voice.

"No, I was like you," Banquo said. "Happy to let others take charge.

But I wish I'd had someone to tell me my opinion was as good as anyone else's. And sometimes better. And if you've got better judgment you *should* lead, it's your damned duty to the community."

"What do you think, Uncle? Can you just change and *become* a leader?"

"I don't know," Macbeth said. "I think some people are born leaders and become them as a matter of course. Like Chief Commissioner Duncan. People whose sense of conviction rubs off on you, who can make you die for something. While others I know have neither conviction nor leadership skills, they're just driven by the desire to climb and climb until they get the boss's chair. They might be intelligent, have charm and the gift of the gab, but they don't really understand people. Because they don't *see* them. Because they understand and see only one thing: themselves."

"Are you talking about Duff?" Banquo smiled.

"Who's Duff?" Fleance pleaded.

"It doesn't matter," Macbeth said.

"Yes, it does. Come on, Uncle. I'm here to learn, aren't I?"

Macbeth sighed. "Duff and I were friends at an orphanage and at police college, and now he's head of the Narco Unit. Hopefully he'll learn the odd thing on the way and that will change him."

"Not him." Banquo laughed.

"The Narco Unit," Fleance said. "Is he the one with the diagonal scar across his mug?"

"Yes," his father said.

"Where did he get it?"

"He was born with it," Macbeth said. "But here's the school. Be good."

"Yeah, yeah, Uncle Mac."

The "Uncle" came from when Fleance was small; now he mostly used it ironically. But as Macbeth watched the boy sprinting through the rain to the gates of the police college it gave him a feeling of warmth anyway.

"He's a good lad," he said.

"You should have children," Banquo said, pulling away from the curb. "They're a gift for life."

"I know, but it's a bit late for Lady now."

"Then with someone younger. What about someone of your own age?"

Macbeth didn't answer, staring out the window rapt in thought. "When I saw the red man at the lights I thought about death," he said.

"You were thinking about Cawdor," Banquo said. "By the way, I spoke to Angus while he was staring at Cawdor dangling there."

"Religious musings?"

"No. He just said he didn't understand rich, privileged people who took their own lives. Even if Cawdor had lost his job and maybe had to do a short stretch, he was still well set up for a long, carefree life. I had to explain to the boy that it's the fall that does it. And the disappointment when you see that your future won't live up to your expectations. That's why it's important not to have such high expectations, to start slowly, not to have success too young. A planned rise, don't you think?"

"You're promising your son a better life than yours if he studies law."

"It's different with sons. They're an extension of your life. It's their job to ensure a steady rise."

"It wasn't Cawdor."

"Eh?"

"It wasn't Cawdor I was thinking of."

"Oh?"

"It was one of the young men on the country road. He was—" Macbeth looked out of the window "—red. Soaked in blood."

"Don't think about it."

"Cold blood."

"Cold . . . what do you mean?"

Macbeth took a deep breath. "The two men by Forres, they'd surrendered. But Duff shot the guy wearing Sweno's helmet anyway."

Banquo shook his head. "I knew it was something like that. And the other one?"

"He was a witness." Macbeth grimaced. "They'd run out of the party and he'd only been wearing a white shirt and white trousers. I took out my daggers. He started to plead; he knew what was coming."

"I don't need to hear anymore."

"I stood behind him. But I couldn't do it. I stood there with a dagger in the air, paralyzed. But then I saw Duff. He was sitting with his face in his hands sobbing like a child. Then I struck."

A siren was heard in the distance. A fire engine. What the hell could be burning in this rain? Banquo thought.

"I don't know if it was because his clothes were drenched," Macbeth said, "but the blood covered *all* of him. All his shirt and trousers. And lying there on the tarmac with his arms down and slightly to the side, he reminded me of the traffic light. Stop now. Don't walk."

They went on in silence, past the entrance to the garage under police HQ. Only unit leaders and higher-ranking officers had parking spots there. Banquo turned into the car park at the rear of the building. He stopped and switched off the engine. The rain beat down on the car roof.

"I understand," Banquo said.

"What do you understand?"

"Duff knew that if you arrested Sweno, hauled him before a greedy judge in the country's most corrupt town, how long would he have got? Two years? Maximum three? Full acquittal? And I understand you."

"Do you?"

"Yes. What would Duff have got if Sweno's lackey had taken the stand against him? Twenty years? Twenty-five? In the force we take care of our own. No one else does. And even more importantly, another police scandal would do so much harm just as we have a chief commissioner who's beginning to give the public back some faith in law and order. You have to see the bigger picture. And sometimes cruelty is on the side of the good, Macbeth."

"Maybe."

"Don't give it another thought, my friend."

The water streaming down the windscreen had distorted the police headquarters building in front of them. They didn't move, as though what had been said had to be digested before they could get out.

"Duff should be grateful to you," Banquo said. "If you hadn't done that he would've had to do it himself, both of you knew that. But now you've both got something on each other. A balance of terror. That's what allows people to sleep at night."

"Duff and I are not the U.S. and the Soviet Union."

"No? What are you actually? You were inseparable at police college, but now you barely talk. What happened?"

Macbeth shrugged. "Nothing much. We were probably an odd couple anyway. He's a Duff. His family had property once, and that kind of thing lingers. Language, upper-class manners. At the orphanage it isolated and exposed him, then he seemed to gravitate toward me. We became a duo you didn't mess with, but at college you could see he was drawn to his own sort. He was released into the jungle like a tame lion. Duff studied at university, found himself an upper-class girl and got married. Children. We drifted apart."

"Or did you just get sick of him behaving like the selfish, arrogant bastard he is?"

"People often get the wrong idea about Duff. At police college he and I swore we would get the big bad boys. Duff really *wants* to change this town, Banquo."

"Was that why you saved his skin?"

"Duff's competent and hardworking. He has a good chance of getting Organized Crime, everyone knows that. So why should one mistake in the heat of battle stop the career of a man who can do something good for us all?"

"Because it's not like you to kill a defenseless man in that way."

Macbeth shrugged. "Maybe I've changed."

"People don't change. But I see now you saw it simply as your soldier's duty. You, Duff and I are fighting on the same side in this war. You've cut short the lives of two Norse Riders so that they can't continue to cut short the lives of our children with their poison. But you don't perform your duty by choice. I know what it costs you when you start seeing your dead enemies in traffic lights. You're a better man than me, Macbeth."

Macbeth smirked. "You see more clearly than me in the mists of battle, old man, so it's some solace to me that I have your forgiveness."

Banquo shook his head. "I don't see better than anyone else. I'm just a chatterbox with doubt as my sole guide."

"Doubt, yes. Does it eat you up sometimes?"

"No," Banquo answered, staring through the windscreen. "Not sometimes. All the time."

Macbeth and Banquo walked from the car park up to the staff entrance at the rear of HQ, a two-hundred-year-old stone building in the center of District 3 East. In its time the building had been a prison, and there was talk of executions and mumblings of torture. Many of those who worked late also claimed they felt an inexplicably cold draft running through the offices and heard distant screams. Banquo had said to Macbeth it was only the somewhat eccentric caretaker, who turned down the heating at five on the dot every day, and his screams when he saw someone leaving their desk without turning off the lamp.

Macbeth noticed two Asiatic-looking women shivering on the pavement among the unemployed men, looking around as if they were waiting for someone. The town's prostitutes used to gather in Thrift Street behind the National Railway Network offices until the council chased them out a few years ago, and now the market had split into two: those attractive enough to work the casinos, and those forced to endure the hard conditions of the streets, who felt safer wall to wall with the law. Moreover, when the police, after periodic pressure from politicians or the press, "cleaned" the "sex filth" off the streets with mass arrests, it was convenient for all sides if the clear-up was brief and quick. Soon everything would be back to normal, and you couldn't rule out the possibility that some of the girls' punters came from police HQ anyway. But Macbeth had politely declined the girls' offers for so long that they left him in peace. So when he saw the two women moving toward him and Banquo he assumed they were new to the area. And he would have remembered them. Even by the relatively low standard of these streets their appearance did not make a favorable impression. Now it was Macbeth's experience that it was difficult to put a precise age on Asiatic women, but whatever theirs was, they must have been through hard times. It was in their eyes. They were the cold, inscrutable kind that don't let you see in, that only reflect their surroundings and themselves. They were stooped and dressed in cheap coats, but there was something else that caught his attention, something which didn't add up, the disfiguration of their faces. One opened her mouth and revealed a line of dirty, brown, neglected teeth.

"Sorry, ladies," Macbeth said cheerfully before she managed to speak. "We'd have liked to say yes, but I've got a frighteningly jealous wife and him there, he's got a terrible VD rash."

Banquo mumbled something and shook his head.

"Macbeth," said one of them in a staccato accent and squeaky doll-like voice at variance with her hard eyes.

"Banquo," said the other woman—identical accent, identical voice.

Macbeth stopped. Both women had combed their long raven-black hair over their faces, probably to conceal them, but they couldn't hide the big un-Asiatic fiery-red noses hanging over their mouths like glass glowing beneath the glassblower's pipe.

"You know our names," he said. "So how can we help you, ladies?"

They didn't answer. Just nodded toward a house on the other side of the street. And there, from the shadows of an archway, a third person stepped into the daylight. The contrast to the two others couldn't have been greater. This woman—if it was a woman—was as tall and broad-shouldered as a bouncer and dressed in a tight leopardskin-print outfit that emphasized her female curves the way a swindler emphasizes the false benefits of his product. But Macbeth knew what she was selling, at least what she used to sell. And the false benefits. Everything about her was extreme: her height, width, bulging breasts, the claw-like red nails that bent around her strong fingers, the wide-open eyes, the theatrical makeup, boots up to her thighs with stiletto heels. To him the only shock was that she hadn't changed. All the years had passed without apparently leaving a mark on her.

She crossed the street in what seemed to be two gigantic steps.

"Gentlemen," she said in a voice so deep Macbeth thought he could hear the glass panes behind him quiver.

"Strega," Macbeth said. "Long time, no see."

"Likewise. You were a mere boy then."

"So you remember me?"

"I remember all my clients, Inspector Macbeth."

"And who are these two?"

"My sisters." Strega smiled. "We bring Hecate's congratulations."

Macbeth saw Banquo automatically reach inside his jacket at the sound of Hecate's name, and he placed a guarded hand on his arm. "What for?"

"Your appointment as head of Organized Crime," Strega said. "All hail Macbeth."

"All hail Macbeth," the sisters echoed.

"What are you talking about?" Macbeth said, scanning the unemployed men across the street. He had spotted a movement when Banquo went for his gun.

"One man's loss, another man's gain," Strega said. "Those are the laws of the jungle. More dead, more bread. And who will get the bread, I wonder, if Chief Commissioner Duncan dies?"

"Hey!" Banquo took a step toward her. "If that's Hecate threatening us, then . . ."

Macbeth held him back. He had seen it now. Three of the men across the road had looked up, braced themselves. They were standing apart but among the others, and there was a similarity: they all wore gray lightweight coats. "Just let her talk," Macbeth whispered.

Strega smiled. "There's no threat. Hecate won't do anything; he's just stating an interesting fact. He thinks you'll be the next chief commissioner."

"Me?" Macbeth laughed. "Duncan's deputy would take over of course, and his name's Malcolm. Be off with you."

"Hecate's prophecies never err," said the man-woman. "And you know that." She stood opposite Macbeth without moving, and Macbeth realized she was still taller than him.

"Well?" she said. "Is your casino lady keeping you clean?"

Banquo saw Macbeth stiffen. And thought this Strega should be happy to be considered a woman. Macbeth snorted, looked as if he was going to say something but changed his mind. Shifted his weight from one foot to the other. Opened his mouth again. Nothing came out this time either. Then he turned and strode toward the entrance of police HQ.

The tall woman watched him. "And as for you, Banquo, aren't you curious to know what's in store for you?"

"No," he said and followed Macbeth.

"Or your son, Fleance?"

Banquo stopped in his tracks.

"A good, hardworking boy," Strega said. "And Hecate promises that if he and his father behave and follow the rules of the game, in the fullness of time he'll also become chief commissioner."

Banquo turned to her.

"A planned rise," she said. Gave a slight bow and smiled, turned and grabbed the other two under her arms. "Come on, sisters."

Banquo stared after this bizarre trio until they had rounded the corner of HQ. So out of place had they seemed that when they were gone he had to ask himself if they had really been there.

"Lots of fruitcakes on the streets nowadays," Banquo said as he caught up with Macbeth in the foyer before the reception desk.

"Nowadays?" Macbeth said, pressing the lift button impatiently again. "Fruitcakes have always prospered in this town. Did you notice the ladies had minders?"

"Hecate's invisible army?"

The lift doors glided open.

"Duff," Macbeth said, stepping to the side. "Now how . . . ?"

"Macbeth and Banquo," said the blond man, striding past them toward the door to the street.

"Goodness me," Banquo said. "A stressed man."

"That's what it's like when you've got the top job." Macbeth smiled, walked in and pressed the button for the basement floor. The SWAT floor.

"Have you noticed how Duff's shoes always creak?"

"It's because he always buys shoes too big for him," Macbeth said.

"Why?"

"No idea," Macbeth replied and managed to stop the doors closing in front of the officer running over from reception.

"Just had a call from the chief commissioner's office," he said, out of breath. "Telling us to ask you to go up the minute you arrive."

"Right," Macbeth said and let go of the doors.

"Trouble?" Banquo asked after they had closed.

"Probably," Macbeth said, pressing the button for the fourth floor. Feeling the stitches in his shoulder begin to itch.

5

LADY WALKED THROUGH THE GAMING ROOM. The light from the immense chandeliers fell softly on the dark mahogany where they were playing blackjack and poker, on the green felt where the dice would dance later in the evening, on the spear-shaped gold spire that stood up like a minaret in the middle of the spinning roulette wheel. She'd had the chandeliers made as smaller copies of the four-and-a-half-ton chandelier in Dolmabahçe Palace in Istanbul, while the spire pointing from the middle of the ceiling down to the roulette table was a copy of the spire in the roulette wheel. The chandeliers were anchored with cords tied to the banisters of the mezzanine in such a way that they could be lowered every Monday and the glass cleaned. This was the kind of detail that passed straight over most customers' heads. Like the small, discreet lilies she'd had sewn into the thick, sound-muffling burgundy carpets she had bought in Italy for a tiny fortune. But they didn't go over *her* head, she saw the matching spires and only she knew what the lilies commemorated. That was enough. For this was hers.

The croupiers automatically stood up straight whenever she passed. They knew their jobs, they were efficient and careful, they treated the customers with courtesy but were firm, they had manicured hands, groomed hair and were immaculately dressed in Inverness Casino's elegant red-and-black croupier uniform, which was changed every year and tailor-made for every single member of staff. And, most important of all, they were honest. This wasn't something she assumed, it was something she *saw* and *heard*. *Saw* it in people's eyes, involuntary tics, muscular twitches or theatrically relaxed states. *Heard* it in the tiny distinctions of quivering vocal cords. It was an innate sensitivity she had, inherited from her mother and grandmother. But while this sensitivity had led them as they aged into the dark shadows of insanity, Lady had used her skills to flush out dishonesty. Away from childhood's vale of woe, up to where she was today. The rounds of inspection had two functions. One was to keep her employees on their toes that little bit more so that every day, every night, they would show themselves to be at least one class higher than those at the Obelisk. The second was to uncover any dishonesty. Even though they had been honest and honorable yesterday, people were like wet clay: they were shaped by opportunity, motive and what you told them today, and they could blithely do what had been inconceivable the day before. Yes, that was the only thing that was fixed, the only thing you could count on: the heart was greedy. Lady knew that. She had that kind of heart herself. A heart she alternately cursed and counted herself lucky to have, which had brought her affluence but had also deprived her of everything. But it was the heart that beat in her chest. You can't change anything, you can't stop it, all you can do is follow it.

She nodded to the familiar faces gathered around the roulette table. Regular customers. They all had their reasons for coming here and playing. There were those who needed to switch off after a challenging working day and those who, after a boring working day, needed a challenge. And those who had neither work nor a challenge, but money. Those who had none of the above ended up at the Obelisk, where you were given a tasteless but free lunch if you gambled more than five hundred. You had idiots who thought they had a system which promised long-term gains, a breed that kept dying but curiously never died out. And then you had those who—and no casino-owner would admit this aloud—formed the bedrock of their business. Those who had to. Those who felt compelled to come here because they couldn't stop themselves risking everything, night after night, fascinated by the roulette ball whizzing around the shiny wheel like a little globe caught in the sun's gravitational field, the sun that gave them daily life but which in the end, with the inevitability of physics, would also burn them up. The addicted. Lady's bread and butter.

Talking about addiction. She looked at her watch. Nine. It was still a bit early in the evening, but she wished the tables were fuller. Reports from the Obelisk suggested they were continuing to take business away from her despite the heavy investment she had made in interior design, the kitchen and the upgrade of the hotel rooms. Some thought she was in the process of pricing herself out of the market and, because the three-year-old

Obelisk was well established in people's minds as the more reasonable alternative, she could and should cut down on the standards and expenses. After all, she wouldn't lose her status as the town's exclusive option. But they didn't know Lady. They didn't know that for her it wasn't primarily about the bottom line but being the exclusive option. Not only more elegant than the Obelisk but better, whatever the comparison. Lady's Inverness Casino should be the place you wanted to be seen, the place you wanted to be associated with. And she, Lady, should be the person you wanted to be seen and associated with. The moneyed came here and the top politicians, actors and sports personalities from the celebrity firmament, writers, beauties, hipsters and intellectuals—everyone came to Lady's table, bowed respectfully, kissed her hand, met her discreet rejection of their equally discreet inquiry about gambling credit with a smile and gratefully accepted a Bloody Mary on the house. Profit or no profit, she hadn't come all this way to run a bloody bordello, as they were doing at the Obelisk, so they could have the dregs, those she would rather not see beneath Inverness Casino's chandeliers. *Genuine* chandeliers. But of course the tide had turned. The creditors *had* started asking questions. And they hadn't liked her answer: what the Inverness needed was not cheaper drinks but more and bigger chandeliers.

Business wasn't on her mind now though. Addiction was. And the fact that Macbeth hadn't got here yet. He always said if he was going to be late. And what had happened during the Sweno raid had affected him. He didn't say so, but she could sense it. Sometimes he was strangely softhearted, it seemed to her—a man she had seen kill with her own eyes. She had seen the calculated determination before the killing, the cold efficiency during it and the remorseless smile afterward.

But this had been different, she knew. The man had been defenseless. And even if on occasion she had problems understanding the code of honor men like Macbeth upheld, she knew this sort of issue could cause him to lose his bearings. She crossed the floor, caught the stares of two men at the bar. Both younger than her. But they didn't interest her. Although she had always done everything to feel desired she despised men who desired her. Apart from one man. It had surprised her at first that someone could fill her thoughts and heart so fully and completely. And often she had asked herself why she, who had never loved any man, loved this particular man. She had concluded it was because he loved that part of her which frightened other men. Her strength. Willpower. An intelligence that was superior to theirs and she couldn't be bothered to hide under a bushel. It took a man to love that in a woman. She stood by the large window facing Workers' Square, looked over toward Bertha, the black locomotive guarding the entrance to the disused station. To the swamp where, over the years, she had seen so many get stuck and sink. Could he—?

"Darling."

How many times had she heard this voice whisper this word in her ear? And yet every time was like the first. He lifted her long red hair to the side, and she felt currents run through her body as his lips touched her neck. It was unprofessional—she knew the two men at the bar were watching—but she let it go. He was here.

"Where've you been?"

"In my new office," he said, wrapping an arm around her midriff.

"New office?" She caressed his forearm. Felt the scar tissue under her fingertips. He had told her the reason the scars were there was because he'd had to inject in the dark and couldn't see his veins, so he would feel his way to the wound from the previous injection and shoot up in the same spot. If you did that enough times, for several years, plus the unavoidable infection now and then, you ended up with forearms that looked like his, as though they had been dragged through barbed wire. But she couldn't feel any fresh wounds. It was some years ago now. So long that sometimes—in fits of childlike optimism—she considered him cured.

"I didn't think you called those coal bins in the cellar 'offices.'"

"On the third floor," Macbeth said.

Lady turned to him. "What?"

His white teeth shone in his dark beard. "You see before you the new head of Organized Crime in this town."

"Is that true?"

"Yes." He laughed. "And now you look as shocked as I imagine I did in Duncan's office."

"I'm not shocked, my love. I'm . . . I'm just happy. It's so deserved! Haven't I kept telling you? Haven't I said you're worth more than that office in the basement?"

"Yes, you have. Again and again, darling. But you were the only one." Macbeth leaned back and laughed again.

"And now we're going up, my love. Out of your cellar obscurity! I hope you demanded a good salary."

"Salary? No, I forgot to ask. My sole demand was that I had Banquo as my deputy, and they both agreed. It's quite mad—"

"Mad? Not at all. It's a wise appointment."

"Not the appointment. On the way to HQ we met three sisters sent by Hecate, who prophesied I would get the job."

"Prophesied?"

"Yes!"

"They must have known."

"No. When I got to Duncan's office he said the decision had been made just five minutes before."

"Hm. Witchcraft, nothing less."

"They were probably high on their own dope and talking nonsense. They said I'd be the chief commissioner, too. And do you know what? Duncan suggested we celebrate my appointment here, at the Inverness!"

"Hang on a moment. What did they say?"

"He wanted to celebrate it here. Wouldn't the chief commissioner choosing to organize a party in your casino be good for your reputation?"

"No, I mean the sisters. Did they *say* you'd be chief commissioner?"

"Yes, but forget it, darling. I suggested to Duncan that we make an evening of it, and he and all the people who live out of town can stay overnight in the hotel. You've got quite a lot of unoccupied rooms at the moment, so . . ."

"Of course we'll do that." She stroked his cheek. "I can hear you're happy, but you still look pale, my love."

He shrugged. "I don't know. I think I'm sickening for something. I see dead men in traffic lights."

She put a hand under his arm. "Come on. I've got what you need, my boy."

He smiled. "Yes, you do."

They sailed through the casino. She knew it was her high heels that made her half a head taller than him. Knew her young figure, elegant evening gown and stately, lissom walk made the men at the bar still stare after her. Knew this was something they didn't have at the Obelisk.

Duff lay on the large double bed staring at the ceiling, at the crack in the paint he knew so well.

"Afterward, as I was leaving the meeting, Duncan took me aside and asked if I was disappointed," he explained. "He said we both knew I'd have been the natural candidate for the post."

The crack had offshoots spreading in an apparently random way, but when he scrunched up his eyes, thereby losing focus, the crack seemed to follow a pattern, form an image. He just couldn't work out what it was.

"And what did you answer?" came the voice over the running water in the bathroom. Even now, after having seen as much of each other as any two people can, she disliked him seeing her until she was ready. And that was fine by him.

"I answered that, yes, I was disappointed. When he said they wanted Macbeth *because* he didn't belong to the inner circle, my being one of those who had supported Duncan's project right from the start was used *against* me."

"Well, that's true. What did—?"

"Duncan said there was another reason, but he didn't want to mention it with the others present. The Sweno raid had only been partly successful as Sweno had got away. And it turned out I had received the tip-off so early that there would have been enough time to inform him. I had almost undone a year's undercover work by what looked a lot like an ego trip. And Macbeth and SWAT had saved the whole operation. Therefore it would seem suspicious to choose me ahead of him. But at least he did give me a consolation prize."

"He gave you the Homicide Unit, and that's not bad, is it?"

"It's smaller than Narco, but at least I escaped the humiliation of being a subordinate officer in Organized Crime."

"Who persuaded Duncan anyway?"

"What do you mean?"

"Who argued Macbeth's case? Duncan's a listener; he likes consensus and goes for group decisions."

"Believe me, my dearest, no one lobbies for Macbeth. I doubt he knows what the word means. All he wants in life is to catch baddies and make sure his casino queen is happy."

"Speaking of which." She posed by the bathroom door. The gauzy negligee revealed more than it hid of course. Duff liked a lot about this woman, some things he wasn't even able to articulate, but what he idolized was plain enough: her youth. The glow from the candles on the floor made the moisture in her eyes, on her red lips, on her shining teeth, sparkle. And yet tonight he needed something more. He wasn't in the mood. After what had happened he didn't feel like the buck he had been when he had started the day. But that could perhaps be changed.

"Take it off," he said.

She laughed. "I've just put it on."

"It's an order. Stay where you are and take it off. Slowly."

"Hm. Maybe. If I'm given a clearer order . . ."

"Caithness, you are hereby ordered by a superior officer to turn your back, pull what you're wearing over your head, lean forward and take a good hold of the door frame."

Duff heard her little girlie gasp of shock. Perhaps it was put on for his sake, perhaps not. It was fine by him. He was getting in the mood.

Hecate strode across the damp floor of the central station, between the peeling walls and mumbling drug addicts. He noticed the gaze of two guys stooped over a spoon and syringe they were obviously sharing. They didn't know him. No one knew him. Perhaps they were thinking the big man with the mustard-yellow cashmere coat, the carefully groomed, almost unnaturally black hair and the resplendent heavy Rolex looked like perfect prey which had just walked into the lion's den. Or they may have had suspicions; perhaps there was something about the self-assured, determined gait, something about the gold-capped walking stick, which made a rhythmic *tick-tock* in time with the stiletto heels of the tall broad-shouldered woman who walked two steps behind him. If she was a woman. There might also have been something about the three men, all wearing gray lightweight coats, who had entered the station immediately before him and taken up a position by the wall. Perhaps that was why they sensed that they were in his den. *He* was the lion.

Hecate stopped, and let Strega go first down the narrow stairs reeking of urine to the toilet. Saw the two druggies lower their heads and concentrate on the task in hand—heating and injecting. Addicts. For Hecate this was a statement of fact without contempt or irritation. After all, they were his bread and butter.

Strega opened the door at the bottom of the stairs, lifted a sleeping man to his feet, bared her teeth to show him her mood and a thumb to point him in the right direction. Hecate followed her in between the cubicles and the running sinks. The stench was so intense that Hecate could still get tears in his eyes. But it also had a function: it kept away curious eyes and made even the hardened addicts keep their visits as brief as possible. Strega and Hecate went into the farthest cubicle with the sign DO NOT USE on the door and a bowl filled to the brim with excrement. Furthermore, the neon tube in the ceiling above had been removed, so it was impossible to see or hit veins in there. Strega removed one of the tiles above the disconnected loo, turned a handle and pushed. The wall swung open, and they stepped inside.

"Close it quickly," Hecate said and coughed. He looked around the room. It had been a railway storeroom, and the other door led to the tunnel for the southern lines. He had moved his production here two years after the train traffic had ceased. He'd had to chase out some tramps and junkies, and although no one ever came here and Chief Commissioner Kenneth had been their highest-ranking protector he had installed camouflaged CCTV in the tunnel and over the stairs down to the toilet. There were twelve people in total on the evening shift, all wearing masks and white coats. On this side of the glass partition dividing the room into two, brew was chopped up, weighed and packed into plastic bags by seven people. By the tunnel door sat two armed guards keeping an eye on the workers and the CCTV monitors. Inside the glass partition was what they called the inner sanctum or simply the kitchen. The tank was there, and only the sisters had access. The kitchen was hermetically sealed for many reasons. First, so that nothing outside could contaminate the processes inside and because some idiot might inadvertently flick a lighter or throw down a lit cigarette end, blowing them all to pieces. But mostly because everyone in the room would soon be hooked if they inhaled the molecules floating in the air on a daily basis.

Hecate had found the sisters in a Chinatown opium den in Bangkok, where the two had set up a homemade laboratory to make heroin from the opium in Chang Rai. He didn't know much about them, only that they had fled China with Chiang Kai-shek's people, the disease that had ravaged their faces had reportedly spread through the village they came from, and as long as he paid them punctually they would deliver whatever he asked. The ingredients were well known, the proportions the same, and others could follow the procedures through the glass window. Yet there was a mystery about the way they mixed and heated the ingredients. And Hecate saw no reason to deny the rumors that they used toads' glands, bumblebee wings, juice from rats' tails and even blew their noses into the tank. It created a sense of black magic, and if there was something that people would pay for in their all-too-real working lives, it was precisely that: black magic. And brew was going down a bomb. Hecate had never seen so many become so desperately addicted in such a short time. But it was equally obvious that the day the sisters produced a slightly less potent product he would have to get rid of them. That was how it was. Everything had its day, its cycle. Like the two decades under Kenneth. The good times. And now with Duncan, who if he was allowed to go his merry way would mean bad times for the magic industry. It is obvious that if the gods bring good and bad times, short human lives and death, you have to make sure you become a god yourself. It is easier than you might think. The obstacle to most people achieving god-like status is that they are afraid and superstitious, and in their anxiety-ridden submission they believe there is a morality, a set of heaven-sent rules that apply to all people. But these rules are made by precisely those that tell you they are gods, and in some strange way the rules serve these gods. Well, OK, not everyone can be a god, and every god needs followers, a client base. A market. A town. Many towns.

Hecate took up a position at the end of the room, placed both hands on the top of his stick and just stood there. This was his factory. Here he was the factory owner. In a growing industry. He would soon have to expand. If he didn't meet the demand others would, those were the simple rules of capitalism. He'd long had plans to take over one of the town's disused factories, set up some fictitious business as a cover while he concocted his brew in the back rooms. Guards, barbed-wire fences, his own lorries going in and out. He could increase production tenfold and export to the rest of the country. But it would be more visible and would require police protection. It would require a chief commissioner who was in his pocket. It would require a Kenneth. So what do you do if Kenneth is dead? You make a new one and clear a path for him.

He received stiff smiles and brief nods from his choppers and packers before they launched themselves at their tasks with renewed energy. They were frightened. That was the principal purpose of these inspections. Not to stop the cycle—it was inevitable—but to delay it. Everyone in this cellar room would at some point try to cheat him, take a few grams home and sell it themselves. They would be found out, and the sentence would be carried out speedily. By Strega. She seemed to enjoy her varied assignments. Like being a messenger together with the sisters.

"Well, Strega," he said. "Do you think the seed we sowed in Macbeth will grow?"

"Human ambition will always stretch toward the sun like a thistle and overshadow and kill everything around it."

"Let's hope so."

"They're thistles. They can't help themselves. They're evil and foolish. If people see the soothsayer's first prophecy fulfilled they'll believe the next one blindly. And now Macbeth has found out he's the new head of Organized Crime. The only question is whether Macbeth has enough of the thistle's ambition in him. And the necessary cruelty to go the whole way."

"Macbeth doesn't," Hecate said. "But she does."

"She?"

"Lady, his beloved dominatrix. I've never met her, yet I know her innermost secrets and understand her better than I understand you, Strega. All Lady needs is time to reach the inescapable conclusion. Believe me."

"Which is?"

"That Duncan has to be got rid of."

"And then?"

"Then," Hecate said, tapping his stick on the ground, *tap-tap.* "The good times will roll again."

"Are you sure we can control Macbeth? Now he's clean he's probably . . . moralistic, isn't he?"

"My dear Strega, the only person more predictable than a junkie or a moralist is a love-smitten junkie and moralist."

Banquo lay in the bedroom on the first floor listening to the rain, to the silence in the room, to the train that never came. The railway track ran past outside, and he visualized the wet, glistening gravel where some of the rails and the sleepers had been removed. Well, stolen. They had been happy here, he and Vera. They'd had good times. He had met Vera while she was working for the goldsmith Jacobs & Sons, where the finer folk

went to buy wedding rings and gifts for each other. One evening the burglar alarm went off, and Banquo—who was on patrol—arrived on the
spot, sirens howling, within a minute. Inside, a terrified young woman
was desperately shouting over the ear-piercing bell that she was only closing up, she was new and must have done something wrong when she was
putting the alarm on. He had only caught the odd word here and there
and had had all the more time to observe her. And when eventually she
burst into tears he had put a gentle, consoling arm around her. She felt like
a warm, tremulous, fledgling bird. During the next few weeks they went
to the cinema, walked on the sunny side of the tunnel and he had kissed
her at the gate. She came from a working-class family and lived at home.
Right from a young girl she'd had to make a contribution and had worked
at the Estex factory like her parents. Until she got a bad cough, unofficial
advice from a doctor to work elsewhere and a job at Jacobs via recommen-
dations.

"The pay's worse," she said, "but you live longer."

"You still cough?"

"Only on rainy days."

"We'd better make sure you get more sunshine. Another walk on
Sunday?"

After six months Banquo went to the jeweler's shop and asked her if
she had an engagement ring she could recommend. She looked so bewildered he had to laugh.

After getting married they moved into a poky two-bed flat, with
neighbors beneath them on the ground floor. They had saved up for,
bought and made love in the bed where he was lying now. Out of consideration for their neighbors, Vera—who was a passionate but shy woman—
would wait for a train until she came. When a train thundered past,
shaking the walls and ceiling lamps, she let herself go, screamed and dug
her nails into his back. She did the same when she gave birth to Fleance in
that very bed—waited until the train came and then screamed, dug her
nails into his hand and squeezed out a son.

They bought the ground floor the following year to have more room.
There were three of them and could soon be many more. But five years
later there were only two of them: a boy and a man. It was her lungs. The
doctors blamed the polluted air, all the toxins from the factories forced
down by low-pressure weather systems hovering over the town like a lid.

And with lungs that were already damaged . . . Banquo blamed himself. He hadn't been able to scrape enough money together to move the family to the other side of the tunnel, to Fife, to somewhere with a bit of sunshine and fresh air you could breathe.

Now they had too much room. He could hear the radio on downstairs and knew Fleance was doing his schoolwork. Fleance was conscientious, he wanted so much to do well. It was some consolation that those who found school easy and got off to a good start often lost their enthusiasm when life became tougher. And then students like Fleance, who was forced to employ strict working routines and knew that learning required effort, got their turn. Yes, it would all be fine. And, who knows, perhaps the boy would meet a girl and start a family. Here in this house, for example. Perhaps new and better times were coming. Perhaps they would be able to help Duncan even more, now that Macbeth was in charge of fighting organized crime in this town. The news had come as a huge surprise to Banquo and most at HQ. Down in the SWAT cellar Ricardo had put it bluntly: he couldn't imagine Macbeth and Banquo sitting behind their desks in suits and ties. Drawing diagrams and presenting budgets. Or making polite conversation at cocktail parties with chief commissioners, council members and other fine folk. But they would see. There wouldn't be any lack of will. And perhaps it was now the turn of people like Macbeth, who were used to having to put in a shift, to achieve their aims.

There was no one else at HQ apart from Duff who knew how addicted to speed Macbeth had been when he was a teenager, how crazy it had made him, how hopelessly lost he had been. Banquo had been on the beat, tramping round the rain-lashed streets, when he came across the boy curled up on a bench in a bus shelter, out of his head on dope. He woke him, wanting to move him on, but there was something about his pleading brown eyes. Something in his alert movements when he stood up, something about his fit, compact body that told Banquo he was going to waste. Something that might have been developing. Something that could still be saved. Banquo took the fifteen-year-old home that night, got him some dry clothes. Vera fed him and they put him to bed. The next day, a Sunday, Vera, Banquo and the boy drove through the tunnel, came out into sunshine on the other side and went for a long walk in the green hills. Macbeth talked with a stammer at first, then less so. He had grown up in an orphanage and dreamed about working in a circus. He showed them how he could juggle and then took five paces from a tall oak and threw Banquo's penknife into the tree, where it quivered. The boy found it more difficult to show them the scars on his forearm and talk about them. That didn't happen until later, when he knew Banquo and Vera were people he could trust. Even then he only said it had started after he fled the home, not how or what triggered it. After that there were more Sundays, more conversations and walks. But Banquo remembered the first especially well because Vera had whispered to him on the way home, "Let's make a son like him." And when, four years later, a proud Banquo had accompanied Macbeth to police college, Fleance had been three and Macbeth clean for just as long.

Banquo turned and looked at the photograph on the bedside table. It was of him and Fleance; they were standing under the dead apple tree in the garden. Fleance's first day at police college. He was wearing his uniform, it was early morning, the sun was out, and the shadow of the photographer fell across them.

He heard a chair scrape and Fleance stomping around. Angry, frustrated. It wasn't always easy to grasp everything straight off. It took time to acquire understanding. Like it took time and willpower to renounce drugs, the escape you had become so addicted to. Like it took time to change a town, to redress injustice, to purge the saboteurs, the corrupt politicians and the big-time criminals, to give the town's citizens air they could breathe.

It had all gone quiet downstairs. Fleance was back at his desk.

It was possible if you took one day at a time and did the work that was required. Then one day the trains might run again.

He listened. All he heard was silence. And rain. But if he closed his eyes, wasn't that Vera's breathing beside him in bed?

Caithness's panting slowly subsided.

"I have to call home," Duff said, kissing her sweaty forehead and swinging his legs out of bed.

"Now?" she exclaimed. He could see from the way she bit her lower lip that it had come out more angrily than she had intended. Who said he didn't understand people?

"Ewan had a toothache yesterday. I have to see how he is."

She didn't answer. Duff walked naked through the flat. He usually did as it was an attic flat and no one could see in. Besides, being seen naked didn't bother him. He was proud of his body. Perhaps he was especially fond of his body because he had grown up feeling ashamed of the scar that divided his face. The flat was large, larger than you would have imagined a young woman working in the state sector would have. He had offered to help her with the rent as he spent so many nights there, but she said her father took care of that side of things.

Duff went into the study, closed the door after him and dialed the Fife number.

He listened to the rain drumming on the attic window right above his head. She answered after the third ring. Always after the third ring. Regardless of where she was in the house.

"It's me," he said. "How did it go with the dentist?"

"He's better now," she said. "I'm not sure if it was a toothache."

"Oh? What was it then?"

"There are other things that can hurt. He was crying, and when I asked him why, he wouldn't tell me and said the first thing that came into his head. He's in bed now."

"Hm. I'll be home tomorrow and then I'll have a chat with him. What's the weather like?"

"Clear sky. Moonlight. Why?"

"We could go to the lake tomorrow, all of us. For a swim."

"Where are you, Duff?"

He stiffened, there was something about her intonation. "Where? At the Grand, of course." And added in an exaggeratedly cheery voice, "Beddy-byes for tired men, you know."

"I rang the Grand earlier this evening. They said you hadn't booked in."

He stood up straight with the phone in his hand.

"I rang you because Emily needed help with some maths. And, as you know, I'm not that good at putting two and two together. So where are you?"

"In my office," Duff said, breathing through his mouth. "I'm sleeping on the sofa in the office. I'm up to my ears in work. I'm sorry I said I was at the Grand, but I thought you and the children didn't need to know how hard things were at the moment."

"Hard?"

Duff gulped. "All the work. And I still didn't get the Organized Crime post." He curled his toes. He could hear how pathetic he sounded, as though he were asking her to let him off the hook out of sympathy.

"Well, you got the Homicide Unit anyway. And a new office, I hear."

"What?"

"On the top floor. I can hear the rain drumming on a window. I'll ring off then."

There was a click and she was gone.

Duff shivered. The room was chilly. He should have put on some clothes. Shouldn't have been so naked.

Lady listened to Macbeth's breathing and shivered.

It was as though a chill had passed through the room. A ghost. The ghost of a child. She had to get out of the darkness that weighed down on her, force her way out of the mental prison that had imposed itself on her mother and grandmother, up into the light. Fight for her liberation, sacrifice whatever had to be sacrificed to be the sun. To be a star. A shining mother who was consumed in the process and gave life to others. The center of the universe as she burned up. Yes. Burned. As her breath and skin burned now, forcing the cold from the room. She ran a hand down her body, feeling her skin tingle. It was the same thought, the same decision as then. It had to be done, there was no way round it. The only way was onward, straight on at whatever lay in their path, like a bullet from a gun.

She laid a hand on Macbeth's shoulder. He was sleeping like a child. It would be the last time. She shook him.

He turned to her, mumbling, put out his hands. Always ready to serve. She held his hands firmly in hers.

"Darling," she whispered, "you have to kill him."

He opened his eyes; they shone at her in the darkness.

She let go of his hands.

Stroked his cheek. The same decision as then.

"You have to kill Duncan."

6

LADY AND MACBETH HAD FIRST met one late summer's evening four years
ago. It had been one of those rare days when the sun shone from a cloud-
less sky, and Lady was sure she had heard a bird singing in the morning.
But when the sun had set and the night shift came on an evil moon had
risen above Inverness Casino. She had been standing outside the main
entrance to the casino, in the moonlight, when he rolled up in a SWAT
armored vehicle.

"Lady?" he said, looking straight into her eyes. What did she see?
Strength and determination? Maybe. Or perhaps it was because that was
what she wanted to see at that moment.

She nodded. Thinking he seemed a little too young. Thinking the man
behind him, an elderly man with white hair and calm eyes, looked more
suited for the job.

"I'm Inspector Macbeth. Any changes in the situation, ma'am?"

She shook her head.

"OK, is there anywhere we can see them from?"

"The mezzanine."

"Banquo, assemble the men and I'll recce."

Before they went up the stairs to the mezzanine the young officer whispered that she should take off her high heels to make less noise. That
meant she was no longer taller than him. On the mezzanine they first kept
to the back, by the windows looking out over Workers' Square, so that
they couldn't be seen from the gaming room below. Halfway along they
moved toward the balustrade. They were partially hidden by the rope to
the central chandelier and the genuine suit of Maximilian armor from the
sixteenth century which she had bought at an auction in Augsburg. The
idea was that when gamblers saw it up there it would give them an

unconscious sense of being either protected or watched. Their own conscience would determine which. Lady and the officer crouched and peered
down into the room, where twenty minutes earlier customers and staff had
fled in panic. Lady had been standing on the roof looking up at the full
moon and instinctively felt the evil when she heard the crash and screams
from down below. She went down, grabbed one of the fleeing waiters, who
said that some guy had fired a gun into the chandelier and was holding
Jack.

She had already calculated the cost of a new chandelier, but it was
obvious that would be nothing compared to the cost of the gun—which
was at present pointing at the head of Jack, her best croupier—being fired
one more time. After all, part of what her casino offered was safe excitement and relaxation; for a while you didn't need to think about the crime
in the streets outside. If the impression was created that Inverness Casino
couldn't offer that, the gaming room would be as empty as it was now. The
only two people left were sitting at the blackjack table below the mezzanine on the other side. Poor Jack was ramrod-stiff and as white as a sheet.

Right behind him, holding a gun, sat the customer.

"It would be hard to get a shot in from such a distance as long as he's
hiding behind your croupier," Macbeth whispered, taking out a little telescope from his black uniform. "We have to get closer. Who is he and what
does he want?"

"Ernest Collum. He says he'll kill my croupier unless he's given back
everything he's lost at the casino."

"And is that a lot?"

"More than we have in cash here. Collum's one of the addicts. An engineer and a number-crunching genius, so he knows the odds. They're the
worst. I've told him we'll try and get the money, but the banks are closed,
so it could take a while."

"We don't have much time. I'm going in."

"How do you know?"

Macbeth moved back from the balustrade and tucked the telescope
inside his uniform. "His pupils. He's high and he's going to shoot." He
pressed a button on his walkie-talkie. "Code Four Six. Now. Take command, Banquo. Over."

"Banquo in command. Over."

"I'll go with you," Lady said, following Macbeth.

"I don't think—"

"This is my casino. *My* Jack."

"Listen, ma'am—"

"Collum knows me, and women calm him down."

"This is a police matter," Macbeth said and ran down the stairs.

"I'm coming," Lady said and ran after him.

Macbeth came to a halt and stood in front of her.

"Look at me," he said.

"No, you look at me," she said. "Do I look as if I'm *not* going with you? He's expecting me to bring the money."

He looked at her. He had a good look. Looked at her in a way other men had looked at her. But also in a way no men or women had looked at her. They looked at her with fear or admiration, respect or desire, hatred, love or subservience, measured her with their eyes, judged her, misjudged her. But this young man looked at her as though he had finally found something. Which he recognized. Which he had been looking for.

"Come on then," he said. "But keep your mouth shut, ma'am."

The thick carpet muffled the sound of their feet as they entered the room.

The table where the two men were sitting was less illuminated than usual because of the smashed chandelier. Jack's face, stiffened into a mask of transfixed shock, didn't change when he saw Lady and Macbeth coming toward him. Lady noticed the hammer of the gun rise.

"Who are you?" Collum's voice was thick.

"I'm Inspector Macbeth from SWAT," said the policeman, pulling out a chair and taking a seat. Laying both palms on the table so that they were visible. "My job is to negotiate with you."

"There's nothing to negotiate, Inspector. I've been cheated by this bloody casino for years. It has ruined me. They fix the cards. *She* fixes the cards."

"And you've arrived at that conclusion after taking brew?" Macbeth asked, tapping his fingers soundlessly on the felt. "It distorts reality, you know."

"The reality, Inspector, is that I have a gun and I see better than ever, and if you don't give me the money I'll first shoot Jack here, then you, as you'll try to draw a gun, and then Lady, so-called, who will at that point either try to flee or overpower me, but it will be too late for both. Then possibly myself, but we'll have to see whether I'm in a better mood after dispatching you three to hell and blowing this place sky-high." He chuckled. "I don't see any money, and these negotiations are thereby called off. So let's get started . . ."

The hammer rose higher. Lady automatically grimaced and waited for the bang.

"Double or quits," Macbeth said.

"I beg your pardon?" Collum said. Immaculate pronunciation. Immaculate shave and immaculate dinner suit with a pressed white shirt. Lady guessed his underclothes were clean too. He had known this was unlikely to finish with him leaving the casino holding a suitcase full of money. He would be carried out as bankrupt as when he came in. But, well, immaculate.

"You and I play a round of blackjack. If you win, you get all the money you've lost here, times two. If I win, I get your gun with all the bullets and you drop all your demands."

Collum laughed. "You're bluffing!"

"The suitcase with the money you asked for has arrived and is in the police vehicle outside. The owner has said she's willing to double up if we agree. Because we *know* there's been some jiggery-pokery with the cards, and fair's fair. What do you say, Ernest?"

Lady looked at Collum, at his left eye, which was all that was visible behind Jack's head. Ernest Collum was not a stupid man; quite the opposite. He didn't believe the story about the suitcase. And yet. Sometimes it seemed as if it was the most intelligent customers who refused to see the inevitability of chance. Given enough time everyone was doomed to lose against the casino.

"Why would you do this?" Collum said.

"Well?" Macbeth said.

Collum blinked twice. "I'm the dealer and you're a player," he said. "She deals."

Lady looked at Macbeth, who nodded. She took the pack, shuffled and laid two cards in front of Macbeth face up.

A six. And the king of hearts.

"Sweet sixteen." Collum grinned.

Lady laid two cards in front of Collum, one face up. Ace of clubs.

"One more," Macbeth said, stretching out a hand.

Lady gave him the top card from the pack. Macbeth held it to his chest, sneaked a look. Glanced up at Collum.

"Looks like you've bust, sweet sixteen," Collum said. "Let's see."

"Oh, I'm pretty happy with my hand," Macbeth said. Smiling at Collum. Then he threw the card to the right, where the table was in part-shadow. Collum automatically leaned across a fraction to see the card better.

The rest happened so fast Lady remembered it as a flash. A flash of a hand in motion, a flash of steel that caught the light as it flew across the table, a flash of Collum's one eye staring at her, wide open in aggrieved protest, light glistening in a cascade of blood streaming out both sides of the blade that sliced his carotid artery. Then the sounds. The muffled sound of the gun hitting the thick, much-too-expensive carpet. The splash of blood landing on the table. Collum's deep gurgle as his left eye extinguished. Jack's one quavering sob.

And she remembered the cards. Not the ace, not the six. But the king of hearts. And, half in shadow, the queen of spades. Both sprayed with Ernest Collum's blood.

They came in wearing their black uniforms, quick, soundless, obeying his every sign. They didn't touch Collum; they led out a sobbing Jack. She pushed away an offer of help. Sat looking at the young head of SWAT, who leaned back in his chair looking content. Like someone thinking he had taken the last trick.

"Collum will take the last trick," she said.

"What?"

"Unless we find it."

"Find what?"

"Didn't you hear what he said? *After dispatching you three to hell and blowing this place sky-high.*"

He stared at her for a couple of seconds, first with surprise, then with something else. Acknowledgment. Respect. Then shouted, "Ricardo! There's a bomb!"

Ricardo was a SWAT guy with calm self-assurance in his gaze, his movements and the softly spoken orders he gave. His skin was so black Lady thought she could see her reflection. It took Ricardo and his men four minutes to find what they were searching for, inside a locked toilet cubicle. A zebra-striped suitcase Collum had brought in after the doorman had checked the contents. Collum had explained it was four gold bars. He intended to use them as a stake at the exclusive poker table where, until the Gambling and Casino Board had forbidden it, they had accepted cash, watches, wedding rings, mortgage deeds, car keys and anything else, provided that the players agreed. Behind the gold-painted iron bars engineer and numbers genius Collum had placed a homemade time bomb, which the SWAT bomb expert later praised for its craftsmanship. Exactly how many minutes were left on the timer Lady couldn't remember. But she remembered the cards.

The king of hearts and the queen of spades. That evening they met under an evil moon.

Lady invited him over for dinner at the casino the next evening. He accepted the invitation but refused the aperitif. No to wine, but yes to water. She had the table on the mezzanine laid with a view of Workers' Square, where the rain was trickling down and running quietly over the cobblestones from the railway station to the Inverness. The architects had built the station a few meters higher up because they thought the weight of all the marble and trains like Bertha would over time cause the floor to sink in the town's constantly waterlogged, marshy terrain.

They talked about this and that. Avoided anything too personal. Avoided what had happened the evening before. In short, they had a nice time. And he was—if not polite—so charming and witty. And unusually attractive in a gray a-little-too-tight suit that he said he had been given by his older colleague, Banquo. She listened to stories about the orphanage, a pal called Duff and a traveling circus which he had joined one summer as a boy. About the nervous lion tamer who always had a cold, about the skinny sisters who were trapeze artists and only ate oblong food, about the magician who invited members of the audience into the ring and made their possessions—a wedding ring, a key or a watch—float in the air in front of their very eyes. And he listened with interest to Lady talking about the casino she had built from scratch. And finally, when she felt she had told him everything that could be told, she raised her glass of wine and asked, "Why do you think he did it?"

Macbeth shrugged. "Hecate's brew drives people crazy."

"We ruined him, that's true, but there's no duplicity with the cards."

"I didn't think there was."

"But two years ago we had two croupiers who worked a number with players on the poker table and stole from others. I kicked them out of course, but I hear they've got together with some financiers and have applied to the council to have a new casino built."

"The Obelisk? Yes, I've seen the drawings."

"Perhaps you also know a couple of the players they worked with were politicians and Kenneth's men?"

"I've heard that, yes."

"So the casino will be built. And I promise you people like Ernest Collum will have every reason to feel they're being cheated."

"I'm afraid you're right."

"This town needs new leaders. A new start."

"Bertha," Macbeth said, nodding toward the window facing the central station, where the old black locomotive stood glistening in the rain on the plinth by the main entrance, its wheels on eight meters of the original rails that ran to Capitol. "Banquo says she needs to be started up again. We need to have a new, healthy activity. And there's good energy in this town too."

"Let's hope so. But back to last night . . ." She twiddled her wineglass. Knew he was looking at her cleavage. She was used to men doing that and it didn't make her feel anything either way; she only knew that her female attributes could be used now and then, sometimes should not be used, like any other business tool. But his eyes were different. *He* was different. He wasn't anyone she needed, merely a sweet policeman on a low rung of the ladder. So why was she spending time with him? Of course she could have shown him a sign of her appreciation other than her presence. She observed his hand as he took the glass of water. The thick veins on the suntanned hand. Obviously he made sure to get out of town when he could.

"What would you have done if Collum hadn't agreed to play blackjack?"

"I don't know," he said, looking at her. Brown eyes. People in this town had blue eyes, but of course she had known men with brown eyes before. Not like these though. Not so . . . strong. And yet vulnerable. My God, was she falling for him? So late in life?

"You don't know?" she asked.

"You said he was an addict. I was counting on him not being able to resist the temptation to gamble one more time. With everything."

"You've been to a lot of casinos, I can see."

"No." He laughed. A boy's laughter. "I didn't even know whether my cards were any good."

"Sixteen versus an ace? I would say they weren't. So how could you be so sure he would play? The story you told him wasn't exactly convincing."

He shrugged. She looked into her glass of wine. And saw what she knew. He knew what addiction was.

"Did you at any point have any doubt you'd be able to stop him before he shot Jack?"

"Yes."

"Yes?"

The young policeman sipped from his glass. He didn't seem to be relishing this topic of conversation. Should she let him off the hook? She leaned across the table. "Tell me more, Macbeth."

He put down his glass. "For a man to lose consciousness before he has time to pull the trigger in such a situation, you have to either shoot him in the head or cut his carotid artery. As you saw, cutting his artery produced a brief but thick jet of blood, then the rest trickled out. Well, the oxygen the brain needed was in the first jet, so that meant he was unconscious before the blood even hit the table. There were two problems. Firstly, the ideal distance for throwing a knife is five paces. I was sitting much closer, but fortunately the daggers I use are balanced. That makes them harder to throw for someone without sufficient experience, but for an experienced thrower it's easier to adjust the rotation. The second problem was that Collum was sitting in such a way that I could only get at the artery on the left-hand side of his face. And I would have to throw with my right hand. I am, as you can see, left-handed. I was dependent on a bit of luck. And usually I'm not lucky. What was the card by the way?"

"Queen of spades. You lost."

"See."

"You're not lucky?"

"Definitely not at cards."

"And?"

He considered. Then he shook his head. "Nope. Not lucky in love either."

They laughed. Toasted each other and laughed again. Listened to the falling rain. And she closed her eyes for a moment. She thought she had heard ice clinking in glasses at the bar. The click of the ball on wood spinning round the roulette wheel. Her own heartbeats.

"What?" He blinked in the dark bedroom.

She repeated the words: "You have to kill Duncan."

Lady heard the sound of her own words, felt them grow in her mouth and drown her beating heart.

Macbeth sat up in bed, looking at her carefully. "Are you awake or talking in your sleep, darling?"

"No. I'm here. And you know it has to be done."

"You were having a bad dream. And now—"

"No! Think about it. It's logical. It's him or us."

"Do you think he wishes us any harm? He's only just promoted me."

"In name you may be the head of Organized Crime, but in practice you're at the mercy of his whims. If you want to close the Obelisk, if you want to chase the drug dealers out of the area around the Inverness and increase police presence on the streets so that people feel safe, you have to be chief commissioner. And that's just the small things. Think of all the big things we could achieve with you in the top job, darling."

Macbeth laughed. "But Duncan wants to do big things."

"I don't doubt that he honestly and genuinely wants to, but to achieve big things a chief commissioner must have broad support from the people. And for this town's inhabitants Duncan is just a snob who landed the top post, as Kenneth did too, as Tourtell did in the town hall. It isn't beautiful words that win over the populace, it's who you are. And you and I are part of them, Macbeth. We know what they know. We want what they want. Listen. *Of the people. For the people. With the people.* Do you understand? We are the only ones who can say that."

"I understand, but . . ."

"But what?" She stroked his stomach. "Don't you want to be in charge? Aren't you a man who wants to be at the top? Are you happy to lick the boots of others?"

"Of course not. But if we just wait we'll get there anyway. As head of Organized Crime I'm still number three."

"But the chief commissioner's office is not for the likes of you, my love! Think about it. You've been given this job so that it *looks* as if we're as good as them. They'll *never* give you the top job. Not willingly. We have to *take* it."

He rolled over onto his other side, with his back to her. "Let's forget this, darling. The way you've forgotten that Malcolm will be chief if anything happens to Duncan."

She grabbed his shoulder, pulled him back over so that he lay facing her again.

"I haven't forgotten anything. I haven't forgotten that Hecate said you'll be the chief commissioner, and that means he has a plan. We take care of Duncan and he'll take care of Malcolm. And I haven't forgotten the evening you took care of Ernest Collum. Duncan is Collum, my sweet. He's holding a pistol to the head of our dream. And you have to find the courage you displayed that evening. You have to be the man you were that night, Macbeth. For me. For us." She placed a hand on his cheek and softened her voice. "Life doesn't give the likes of us that many opportunities, darling. We have to grasp the few that offer themselves."

He lay there. Silent. She waited. Listened, but no words drowned out the beating of her heart now. He had ambition, dreams and the will, she knew that, they were what had raised him from the mess he had found himself in—they had turned a youth addicted to drugs into a police cadet and later the head of SWAT. That was the affinity they had: they had both made good, paid the price. Should he stop now, halfway there, before they could enjoy the rewards? Before they could enjoy the respect and admire the view? He was courageous and a ruthless man of action, but he had failings that could prove costly. A lack of evil. The evil that you needed, if only for one decisive second. The second when you have to cope with not having restrictive morality on your side, when you mustn't lose sight of the bigger picture, mustn't torment yourself by asking if you're doing the right thing in this, the smaller one. Macbeth loved what he called justice, and his loyalty to the rules of others was a weakness she could love him for. In times of peace. And despise him for now, when the bells of war were ringing. She ran her hand from his cheek to his neck, slowly over his chest and stomach. And back up. Listened. His breathing was regular, calm. He was asleep.

Macbeth breathed deeply, as though he were sleeping. She took away her hand. Moved to lie down along his back. She was breathing calmly too now. He tried to breathe in time with her. *Kill Duncan?* Impossible. Of course it was impossible.

So why couldn't he sleep? Why did her words persist, why did his thoughts whirl around in his head like bats?

Life doesn't give the likes of us that many opportunities, darling. We have to grasp the few that offer themselves. He thought of the opportunities life had given him. The one that night in the orphanage, which he hadn't grasped. And the one Banquo had given him, which he *had.* How the first one had almost killed him and the second had saved him. But isn't it that you don't take some opportunities that are offered because they will condemn you to unhappiness anyway, opportunities that will cause regret for the rest of your life whether you take them or not? Oh, the insidious dissatisfaction that will always poison the most perfect happiness. And yet. Had fate opened a door that would soon shut? Was his courage letting him down again, the way it had let him down that night in the orphanage? He visualized the man in the bed that time, asleep, unsuspecting. Defenseless. A man who stood between him and the freedom every human being deserved. Between him and the dignity every human being should crave. Between Macbeth and the power he would gain. And the respect. And the love.

Day had started to break when he woke Lady.

"If I did this . . ." he said, "I would be beholden to Hecate."

She opened her eyes as though she had been awake the whole time. "Why do you think like that, darling? Hecate has only prophesied that something will happen, so there is no debt to be paid."

"So what has he to gain by my becoming chief commissioner?"

"You'd better ask him, but it's obvious—he must have heard that Duncan has sworn he won't rest until he has arrested Hecate. And he probably knows it's not inconceivable that you would prioritize action against the drugs gangs who use violence and shoot each other in the streets."

"The Norse Riders, whose back has already been broken?"

"Or against establishments that cheat good people out of their savings."

"The Obelisk?"

"For example."

"Hm. You said something about the big things we could do. Were you thinking of something good for the town?"

"Of course. Remember, the chief commissioner decides which politicians need to be investigated and which do not. And anyone who has any knowledge of the town council knows that everyone in a position of power during the last ten years has paid for services in ways that would not bear close scrutiny. And that they in turn have demanded payment. Under Kenneth they didn't need to bother to camouflage their corruption, the evidence was there for all to see. We know that, they know that, and it means we can control them as we wish, my love."

She stroked his lips with her forefinger. She had told him the first night they spent together that she loved his lips. They were so soft and thin-skinned she could taste his blood with no more than a little nibble.

"Make them finally keep their promises to implement initiatives that would save this town," he whispered.

"Exactly."

"Get Bertha running again."

"Yes." She nibbled his lower lip, and he could feel the trembling, hers and his, their hearts racing.

He held her.

"I love you," he whispered.

Macbeth and Lady. Lady and Macbeth. They were breathing in rhythm with each other now.

7

LADY LOOKED AT MACBETH. He was so handsome in a dinner jacket. She turned, checked that the waiter had put on white gloves as she had asked. And that the champagne flutes on the silver tray were the ones with the narrow bowls. She had, mostly for fun, put a small but elegant silver whisk on the tray, even though very few customers had seen one before and even fewer knew what it was for. Macbeth rocked back on his shoes as they sank into the deep carpet in the Inverness, and stared stiffly at the front door. He had seemed nervous all day. Only when they went through the practical details of the plan did he regain concentration and become the professional policeman of a rapid-response unit and forget the target had a name. Duncan.

The guards outside opened the door, and a gust of rain swept in.

The first guests. Lady switched on her happiest, most excited smile and placed her hand under Macbeth's arm. She felt him instinctively straighten up.

"Banquo, old friend!" she exclaimed. "And you've brought Fleance. He's become such a good-looking young man—I'm jolly glad I don't have any daughters!" Hugs and clinking glasses. "Lennox! You and I should have a little chat, but first some champagne. And there's Caithness! You look ravishing, my dear! Why can't I find dresses like that? Deputy Chief Commissioner Malcolm! But your title's simply too long. Is it all right if I just call you Chief? Don't tell anyone, but sometimes I tell Macbeth to call me Director General just to hear how it sounds."

She had barely said a word to most of them before, yet she still managed to make them feel they had known each other for years. Because she could see inside them, see how they wanted to be seen—it was the blessing of super-sensitivity among all its curses. It meant she could skip the preliminary skirmishes and get straight to the point. Perhaps it was her unpretentious manner that made them trust her. She broke the ice by telling them apparently intimate details of her life, which made them daring, and when they noticed their little secrets were rewarded with an "Ah" and conspiratorial laughter, they ventured on to slightly bigger secrets. It was unlikely any other person in the town knew more about its inhabitants than this evening's hostess.

"Chief Commissioner Duncan!"

"Lady. Apologies for my late arrival."

"Not at all. It is indeed your privilege. We don't want a chief commissioner who arrives first. I always ensure I arrive last, in case anyone should be in any doubt as to who is considered the queen."

Duncan laughed quietly, and she laid a hand on his arm. "You're laughing, so in my eyes the evening is already a success, but you should try our exquisite champagne, dear Chief Commissioner. I assume your bodyguards won't . . ."

"No, they'll probably be working all night."

"All night?"

"When you publicly threaten Hecate you have to sleep with at least one eye open. I sleep with two pairs open."

"Apropos sleeping. Your bodyguards have the adjacent room to your suite with an intervening door, as they requested. The keys are at reception. But I insist your guards at least taste my homemade lemonade, which I promise was not made using the town's drinking water." She signaled to the waiter holding a tray bearing two glasses.

"We—" one bodyguard said, clearing his throat.

"Refusals will be taken personally and as an insult," Lady interrupted.

The bodyguards exchanged glances with Duncan, then they each took a glass, drained the contents and put it back on the tray.

"It's very magnanimous of you to host this party, ma'am," Duncan said.

"It's the least I can do after you made my husband head of the Organized Crime Unit."

"Husband? I didn't know you were married."

She tilted her head. "Are you a man to stand on formality, Chief Commissioner?"

"If by formality you mean rules, I probably am. It's in the nature of my work. As it is in yours, I assume."

"A casino stands or falls on everyone knowing that the rules apply in all cases, no exceptions."

"I have to confess I've never set foot in a casino before, ma'am. I know you have your hostess duties, but might I ask for a tiny guided tour when it suits you?"

"With pleasure." Lady smiled and linked her arm with his. "Come on."

She led Duncan up the stairs to the mezzanine. If his eyes and secret thoughts were drawn to the high split in her dress as she strode ahead, he concealed them well. They stood at the balustrade. It was a quiet evening. Four customers at the roulette table; the blackjack tables were empty; four poker players at the table underneath them. The others at the party had gathered by the bar, which they had almost to themselves. Lady watched Macbeth nervously fidgeting with his glass of water as he stood with Malcolm and Lennox, trying to look as though he was listening.

"Twelve years ago this was a water-damaged vandalized ruin after the railway administration moved out. As you know we're the only county in the land to allow casinos."

"Thanks to Chief Commissioner Kenneth."

"Bless his blackened soul. Our roulette table was built according to the Monte Carlo principle. You can put your bets on identical slots on both sides of the wheel, which is made of mostly mahogany, a little rosewood and ivory."

"It is, frankly, very impressive what you've created here, Lady."

"Thank you, Chief Commissioner, but it has come at a cost."

"I understand. Sometimes you wonder what drives us humans."

"So tell me what drives you."

"Me?" He deliberated for a second or two. "The hope that this town may one day be a good place to live."

"Behind that. Behind the fine principles we can so easily articulate. What are your selfish, emotional motives? What is your dark motive, the one that whispers to you at night and haunts you after all the celebratory speeches have been made?"

"That's a searching question, Lady."

"It's the *only* question, my dear Chief Commissioner."

"Maybe." He rolled his shoulders inside his dinner jacket. "And maybe I didn't need such a strong motivation. I was dealt good cards when I was born into a relatively affluent family where education, ambition and career were a matter of course. My father was unambiguous and plainspoken about corruption in the public sector. That was probably why he didn't get very far. I think I just carried on where he left off and learned from the strategic mistakes he made. Politics is the art of the possible, and sometimes you have to use evil to fight evil. I do whatever I have to do. I'm not the saint the press likes to portray me as, ma'am."

"Saints achieve little apart from being canonized. I'm more for your school of tactics, Chief Commissioner. That's always been my way."

"I can understand that. And although I don't know any details of your life, I do know you've had a longer and steeper path to tread than me."

Lady laughed. "You'll find me in the faded files of your archives. I supported myself on the oldest profession in the world for a few years— that's not exactly a secret. But we all have a past and have—as you put it—done what we had to do. Does the Chief Commissioner gamble? If so, I'd like you to do so on the house tonight."

"Thank you for your generosity, Lady, but it would break my rules to accept."

"Even as a private individual?"

"When you become chief commissioner your private life ceases to exist. Besides, I don't gamble, ma'am. I prefer not to rely on the gods of fate but to merit any winnings I might make."

"Nevertheless you got where you are—as you yourself said—because the gods of fate dealt you good cards at birth."

He smiled. "I said *prefer*. Life's a game where you either play with the cards you have or throw in your hand."

"May I say something, Chief Commissioner? Why are you smiling?"

"At your question, ma'am. I think you'll ask anyway."

"I just wanted to say that I think you, my dear Duncan, are a thoroughly decent person. You're a man with spine, and I respect who you are and what you stand for. Not least because you have dared to give an unknown quantity like Macbeth such a prominent position in your management team."

"Thank you, ma'am. Macbeth has only himself to thank."

"Does the appointment form part of your anti-corruption campaign?"

"Corruption is like a bedbug. Sometimes you have to demolish the whole house to get rid of the plague. And start building again with non-infected materials. Like Macbeth. He wasn't part of the establishment, so he isn't infected."

"Like Cawdor."

"Like Cawdor, ma'am."

"I know what it costs to pare away the infected flesh. I had two disloyal servants in my employ." She leaned over the balustrade and nodded toward the roulette table. "I still cried when I sacked them. Being tempted by money and wealth is a very common human weakness. And I was too softhearted, so instead of crushing the bedbugs under my heel I let them go. And what was my thanks? They used *my* ideas, the expertise *I* had given them and probably money they had stolen from here to start a dubious establishment that is not only destroying the reputation of the industry but taking bread from the mouths of the people who created this market, from us. If you chase away bedbugs they come back. No, I'd have done the same as you, Chief Commissioner."

"As me, ma'am?"

"With Cawdor."

"I couldn't let him get away with working with Sweno."

"I mean, you did the job properly. All you had on him was the testimony of a Norse Rider who even the most stupid judge and jury know would have been willing to tell the police whatever he needed to keep himself out of prison. Cawdor could have got away."

"We had a bit more on him than that, ma'am."

"But not enough for a watertight conviction. Cawdor the bedbug *could* have come back. And then the scandal would have dragged on interminably. A court case with one hell of a shit-storm that could easily have left stains here and there. Not exactly what the police need when they're trying to win back the town's trust. You have my full support, Chief Commissioner. You have to crush them. One turn of your heel and it's over."

Duncan smiled. "That's quite a detailed analysis, but I hope you're not suggesting I had anything to do with Cawdor's premature demise, ma'am."

"No, God forbid." She placed a hand on the chief commissioner's arm. "I'm only saying what Banquo usually says: there are several ways to skin a cat."

"Such as?"

"Hm. Such as ringing a man and telling him that Judgment Day has come. The evidence is so overwhelming he'll have SWAT at his door in minutes; he'll be publicly humiliated, stripped of all his honors, his name will be dragged through the gutters to the stocks. He has only a few minutes."

Duncan studied the poker table beneath. "If I had some binoculars," he said. "I'd be able to see their cards."

"You would."

"Where did you get your binoculars, ma'am? A gift from birth?"

She laughed. "No, I had to buy them. With experience. Dearly bought."

"Of course I haven't said anything, but Cawdor served in the force for many years. Like most of us he was neither a-hundred-percent good nor a-hundred-percent bad. Perhaps he deserved, perhaps his family deserved, to have had a choice as to which way out he took."

"You're a nobler person than me, Chief Commissioner. I'd have done the same, but exclusively for selfish reasons. *Santé.*"

They raised glasses and clinked.

"Talking about binoculars," Lady said, nodding toward the others in the bar. "I see Inspector Duff and young Caithness have their antennae tuned in."

"Oh?" Duncan arched an eyebrow. "They're standing at opposite ends of the bar, from what I can see."

"Exactly. They're keeping the maximum distance between them. And still checking every fifteen seconds where the other is."

"Not much escapes your eye, does it?"

"I saw something when I asked you what your dark, selfish motive was."

Duncan laughed. "Can you see in the dark too?"

"My sensitivity to the darkness is inherited, Chief Commissioner. I sleepwalk in the darkest night without hurting myself."

"I suppose the motive for the best charitable work can be called selfish, but my simple view is that the end justifies the motive."

"So you'd like a statue like the one Kenneth got? Or the love of the people, which he didn't get?"

Duncan held her gaze, checked the bodyguards behind them were still outside hearing range, then emptied his glass and coughed. "For myself I wish to be at peace in my soul, ma'am. The satisfaction of having done my duty. Of having maintained and improved my forefathers' house, so to speak. I know it's perverse, so please don't tell anyone."

Lady took a deep breath, pushed off from the balustrade and lit up in a big happy smile. "But what is your hostess doing? Interrogating her guests when there's supposed to be a party! Shall we go and meet the others? And then I'll go down to the cellar and get a bottle that has been waiting for an occasion just like this."

After enduring Malcolm's lengthy analysis of the loopholes in the new tax law Duff made an excuse and went to sit at the bar to reward himself with a whiskey.

"Well?" said a voice behind him. "How was your day off with the family?"

"Fine, thanks," he said without turning. Pointed to a bottle for the waiter and showed with two fingers that he wanted a double.

"And tonight?" Caithness asked. "You still want to stay over at . . . the hotel?"

The code word for her bed. But he could hear that the question was not only about tonight but the nights to come. She wanted him to repeat the old refrain: the assurance that he wanted her, he *didn't* want to return to his family in Fife. But this all took time; there were many aspects to consider. It was incomprehensible to him that Caithness didn't know him any better, that she doubted this could be what he really wanted. Perhaps that was why he answered with a certain defiance that he had been offered a bed at the casino.

"And do you want that? To stay here?"

Duff sighed. What did women want? Were they all going to tie him up, tether him to the bedhead and feed him in the kitchen so that they could milk his wallet and testicles to overwhelm him with more offspring and a guilty conscience?

"No," he said, looking at Macbeth. Considering he was the focus of the party, he seemed strangely burdened and ill at ease. Had the responsibility and gravity of his new post already intimidated the happy, carefree boy in him? Well, now it was too late, both for Macbeth and for himself. "If you go first I'll wait a suitable length of time and follow you."

He noticed her hesitate behind him. He met her eyes in the mirror behind the shelves of bottles. Saw she was about to touch him. Sent her an admonitory glance. She desisted. And left. *Jesus.*

Duff knocked back his drink. Got up to go over to Macbeth, who was leaning on the end of the bar. Time to congratulate him properly. But right at that moment Duncan came between them; people flocked around him, and Macbeth was lost in the melee. And when Duff saw him again, Macbeth was on his way out, rushing after Lady's skirt tails, which he saw leaving the room.

Macbeth caught Lady up as she was unlocking the wine cellar.

"I can't do it," he said.

"What?"

"I can't kill my own chief commissioner."

She looked at him.

She grabbed the lapels of his jacket, pulled him inside and closed the door. "Don't fail me now, Macbeth. Duncan and his guards are set up in their rooms. Everything's ready. You've got the master key, haven't you?"

Macbeth took the key from his pocket and held it up for her. "Take it. I can't do this."

"Can't or won't?"

"Both. I *won't* do it because I *can't* find the will for such villainy. It's wrong. Duncan's a good chief commissioner, and I can't do anything better than him. So what's the point, apart from feeding my ambition?"

"*Our* ambition! Because after hunger, cold, fear and lust there is nothing more than ambition, Macbeth. Because honor is the key to respect. And that is the master key. Use it!" She was still holding his lapels, and her mouth was so close to his he could taste the fury in her breath.

"Darling—" he began.

"No! If you think Duncan is such an honorable man listen to how he killed Cawdor to spare himself the embarrassing revelations that might have leaked out if Cawdor had lived."

"That's not true!"

"Ask him yourself."

"You're only saying that to . . . to . . ."

"To steel your will," she said. She let go and instead pressed her palms against the lapels as if to feel his heartbeat. "Just think that you're going to kill a murderer, the way you killed the Norse Rider; then it'll be easy."

"I don't *want* it to be easy."

"If it's your morals that are getting the better of you, then just remember you're bound by the promise you made to me last night, Macbeth. Or are you telling me that what I saw and interpreted as courage when you killed Ernest Collum was just a young man's recklessness because it wasn't your life at stake but my croupier's? While now, when you have to risk something yourself, you flee like a cowardly hyena."

Her words were unreasonable but still hit home. "You know that's not how it is," he said in desperation.

"So how *can't* you keep the promise you made to me, Macbeth?"

He gulped. Searched feverishly for words. "I . . . Can you say you keep *all* your promises?"

"Me? *Me?*" She emitted a piercing laugh of astonishment. "To keep a promise to myself I wrenched my suckling child from my breast and smashed its head against a wall. So how could I break a promise to you, my only beloved?"

Macbeth stood looking at her. He was inhaling her breath now, her poisonous breath. He felt it weakening him second by second. "But you do realize, don't you, that if this fails Duncan will cut your head off too?"

"It won't fail. Listen. I'm going to give Duncan a glass of this burgundy, and I'll insist that his bodyguards at least *taste* it. They won't notice anything, but they might become a little muddled later in the evening. And sleep like logs when they go to bed . . ."

"Yes, but—"

"Shh! You'll be using your daggers so there's no chance of them waking. Afterward smear the blood on the blades all over the guards and leave the daggers in their beds. And later when you wake them—"

"I remember our plan. But it has weaknesses, and—"

"It's *your* plan, my love." She grasped his chin with one hand and bit the lobe of his ear hard. "And it's perfect. Everyone will realize the guards have been bought by Hecate; they were just too drunk to hide the traces of their crime."

Macbeth closed his eyes. "You can only give birth to boys, can't you?"

Lady gave a low chuckle. Kissed him on the neck.

Macbeth held her shoulders and pushed her away. "You'll be the death of me, Lady, do you know that?"

She smiled. "And you know everywhere you go, I go."

8

THE DINNER WAS HELD IN the casino restaurant. Duff was placed next to the hostess, who had Duncan on her other side. Macbeth sat opposite them with Caithness as his neighbor. Duff noticed that neither Caithness nor Macbeth spoke or ate much, but the atmosphere was still good and the table so wide it was hard to have a conversation across it. Lady chatted and seemed to be enjoying herself with Duncan, while Duff listened to Malcolm and concentrated on not yawning.

"Caithness looks beautiful tonight, doesn't she?"

Duff turned. It was Lady. She smiled at him, her large blue eyes innocent beneath fiery red hair.

"Yes, nearly as beautiful as you, ma'am," Duff said but could hear his words lacked the spark that could have brought them to life.

"She's not only beautiful," Lady said. "I suppose, as a woman in the police, she must have sacrificed a lot to get where she is. Having a family, for example. I can see she's sacrificed having a family. Can't you too, Duff?"

Gray eyes. They were gray, not blue.

"All women who want to get on have to sacrifice something, I suppose," Duff said, lifting his wineglass and discovering it was empty again. "Family isn't the be-all and end-all for everyone. Don't you agree, ma'am?"

Lady shrugged. "We humans are practical. If decisions we made once can't be changed, we do our best to defend them so that our errors won't haunt and torment us too much. I think that's the recipe for a happy life."

"So you're afraid you'd be haunted if you saw your decisions in a true light?"

"If a woman is to get what she wants, she has to think and act like a man and not consider the family. Her own or others'."

Duff recoiled. He tried to catch her eye, but she had leaned forward to fill the glasses of the guests around her. And the next moment Duncan tapped his glass, stood up and coughed.

Duff watched Macbeth during the inspired thank-you speech, which paid homage not only to the hostess's dinner and the host's promotion but to the mission they had all signed up to: to make the town a place where it was possible to live. And he rounded off by saying that after a long week they deserved the rest the merciful Lord had granted them and they would be wise to use it because there was a good chance the chief commissioner wasn't going to be such a merciful god in the weeks to come.

He wished them a good night, stifled a yawn and proposed a toast to their hosts. During the ensuing applause Duff glanced across at Macbeth, wondering if he would return the toast—after all, Duncan was the chief commissioner. But Macbeth just sat there, pale-faced and as stiff as a board, apparently caught off guard by the new situation, his new status and the new demands that he would have to face.

Duff pulled out Lady's chair for her. "Thank you for everything this evening, ma'am."

"Likewise, Duff. Have you got the key for your room?"

"Mm, I'll be staying . . . elsewhere."

"Back home in Fife?"

"No, with a cousin. But I'll be here early tomorrow morning to pick up Duncan. We live in Fife, not far apart."

"Oh, what time?"

"At seven. Duncan and I both have children and . . . Well, it's the weekend. All go, you know how it is."

"Actually I don't," Lady said with a smile. "Sleep well and my regards to your cousin, Duff."

One by one the guests left the bar and the gaming tables and went to their rooms or homes. Macbeth stood in reception shaking hands and mumbling hollow goodbyes, but at least there he didn't have to make conversation with the stragglers in the bar.

"You really don't look well," Banquo said with a slight slur. He had just come out of the toilet and placed a heavy paw on Macbeth's shoulder. "Get to bed now, so you don't infect other folk."

"Thanks, Banquo. But Lady's still in the bar entertaining."

"It's almost an hour now since the chief went to bed, so you're allowed to go too. I'll just drink up in the bar, then Fleance and I will go too. And I don't want to see you standing here like a doorman. OK?"

"OK. Good night, Banquo."

Macbeth watched his friend walk somewhat unsteadily back to the bar. Looked at his watch. Seven minutes to midnight. It would happen in seven minutes. He waited for three. Then he straightened up, looked through the double doors to the bar, where Lady was standing and listening to Malcolm and Lennox. At that moment, as though she had felt his presence, she turned and their eyes met. She gave an imperceptible nod and he nodded back. Then she laughed at something Malcolm said, countering with something that made both of the men laugh. She was good.

Macbeth went up the stairs, let himself into his and Lady's suite. Put his ear to the door of the bodyguards' room. The snoring from inside was even, safe. Almost artless. He sat on the bed. Ran his hand over the smooth bedcover. The silk whispered beneath his rough fingertips. Yes, she was good. Better than he would ever be. And perhaps they could pull this off—perhaps the two of them, Macbeth and Lady, could make a difference, shape the town in their image, carry on what Duncan had started and take it further than he would ever have managed. They had the will, they had the strength and they could win people over. Of the people. For the people. With the people.

His fingers stroked the two daggers he had laid out on the bed. But for the fact that power corrupts and poisons, they wouldn't have needed to do this. If Duncan's heart had been pure and idealistic they could have discussed it, and Duncan would have seen that Macbeth was the best man to realize his dream of leading the town out of the darkness. For whatever dreams Duncan had, the common people of the town wouldn't follow an upper-class stranger from Capitol, would they? No, they needed one of their own. Duncan could have been the navigator, but Macbeth would have to be the captain—as long as he could get the crew to obey, to guide the boat to where they both wanted, into a safe harbor. But even if he accepted that a transfer of power was in the best interests of the town, Duncan would never surrender his post to Macbeth. Duncan, for all his virtue, was no better than any other person in power: he put his personal ambitions above everything else. See how he killed those who could damage his reputation or threaten his authority. Cawdor's body had still been warm when they got there.

Wasn't that so? Yes, it was. It was, it was.

Twelve o'clock.

Macbeth closed his eyes. He had to get into the zone. He counted down from ten. Opened his eyes. Swore, closed them again and counted down from ten again. Looked at his watch. Grabbed the daggers, stuffed them in the especially made shoulder holster with sheaths for two knives, one on each side. Then he went into the corridor. Passed the bodyguards' door and stopped outside Duncan's. Listened. Nothing. He drew a deep breath. Evaluations of a variety of scenarios had been done beforehand; the only thing left was the act itself. He inserted the master key into the lock, saw his reflection in the shiny doorknob of polished brass, then gripped it and turned. Observed what he could in the corridor light, then he was inside and had closed the door behind him.

He held his breath in the darkness and listened to Duncan's breathing. Calm, even.

Like Lorreal's. The director of the orphanage.

No, don't let that thought out now.

Duncan's breathing told him he was in bed and asleep. Macbeth went to the bathroom door, switched on the light inside and left the door slightly ajar. Enough light for what he was going to do.

What he was going to do.

He stood beside the bed and looked down at the unsuspecting sleeping man. Then he straightened up. What an irony. He raised a dagger. Killing a defenseless man—could anything be easier? The decision had been taken, now all he had to do was carry it out. And hadn't he already killed his first defenseless victim on the road to Forres, wasn't his virginity already gone, hadn't he paid his debt to Duff there and then, paid him back in the same currency Duff had run it up: cold blood. Seen Lorreal's hot blood streaming onto the white sheet, the blood that had looked black in the darkness. So what was stopping him now? How was this conspiracy different from when he and Duff had changed the crime scene so that all the evidence found in Forres would tally with the story they agreed they would tell? And the story at the orphanage they agreed they would tell. *And sometimes cruelty is on the side of the good, Macbeth.* He looked up from the blade glinting in the light from the bathroom.

He lowered the dagger.

He didn't have it in him.

But he had to do it. He *had to*. He had to have it in him. But what could he do if he wasn't up to it even in the zone?

He had to become the other Macbeth, the one he had buried so deep, the crazy flesh-eating corpse he had sworn he would never be again.

Banquo stared at the big, lifeless locomotive as he unbuttoned his flies. He swayed in the wind. He was a bit drunk, he knew that.

"Come on, Dad," came Fleance's voice from behind him.

"What's the time, son?"

"I don't know, but the moon's up."

"Then it's past twelve. There's a storm forecast tonight." The gun holster hanging between the first and second loops on his belt was in his way. He unhooked it and passed it to Fleance.

His son took it with a resigned groan. "Dad, this is a public place. You can't—"

"It's a public urinal, that's what it is," Banquo slurred and at that moment registered a black-clad figure coming round the steam engine. "Give me the gun, Fleance!"

The light fell on the man's face.

"Oh, it's just you."

"Ah, it's you, is it?" Macbeth said. "I was out for some air."

"And I just had to air the old fella," Banquo slurred. "No, I *wasn't* about to piss on Bertha. After all, that would be—now they've closed St. Joseph's Church—desecrating the last holy thing in this town."

"Yes, maybe."

"Is there anything up?" Banquo said, trying to relax. He always found it difficult to get going with strangers nearby, but Macbeth and his son?

"No," Macbeth said in a strangely neutral tone.

"I dreamed about the three sisters last night," Banquo said. "We haven't talked about it, but they got their prophecies spot on, didn't they. Or what do you reckon?"

"Oh, I'd forgotten them. Let's talk about it another time."

"Whenever," Banquo said, sensing the flow coming.

"Well," Macbeth said. "Actually I was going to ask you—now you're my deputy in Organized Crime—but suppose something like that did happen, just as the sisters said it would?"

"Yes?" Banquo groaned. He had lost patience, started forcing it, and with that the flow stopped.

"I'd appreciate it if you joined me then too."

"Become your deputy CC? Ha ha, yes, pull the other one." Banquo suddenly realized that Macbeth wasn't joking. "Of course, my boy, of course. You know I'm always willing to follow anyone who'll fight the good fight."

They looked at each other. And then, as if a magic wand had been waved, it came. Banquo looked down, and there was a majestic golden jet splashing intrepidly over the locomotive's large rear wheel and running down onto the rail beneath.

"Good night, Banquo. Good night, Fleance."

"Good night, Macbeth," answered father and son in unison.

"Was Uncle Mac drunk?" Fleance asked when Macbeth had gone.

"Drunk? You know he doesn't drink."

"Yes, I know, but he was so strange."

"Strange?" Banquo grinned grimly as he watched the continuous stream with satisfaction. "Believe me, that boy isn't *strange* when he gets high."

"What is he, then?"

"He goes crazy."

The jet was suddenly swept to the side by a strong gust of wind.

"The storm," Banquo said, buttoning up.

Macbeth went for a walk around the central station. When he came back Banquo and Fleance had gone, and he went into the large waiting room.

He scanned the room and instantly sorted the individuals there into the four relevant categories: those who sold, those who used, those who did both and those who needed somewhere to sleep, shelter from the rain, and would soon be joining one of the first three. That was the path he himself had followed. From orphanage escapee receiving food and drink from officers of the Salvation Army to user who financed dope and food by selling.

Macbeth went over to an older, plump man in a wheelchair.

"A quarter of brew," he said, and just the sound of the words made something that had been hibernating in his body wake up.

The man in the wheelchair looked up. "Macbeth," he said, spitting the name out in a shower of saliva. "I remember you and you remember me. You're a policeman, and I don't sell dope, OK? So get the hell away from me."

Macbeth walked on to the next dealer, a man in a checked shirt who was so hyped up he couldn't stand still.

"Do you think I'm an idiot?" he shouted. "I am, by the way. Otherwise I wouldn't be here, would I. But selling to a cop and ending up in clink for twenty-four hours when you know you can't go four hours without a fix?" He leaned back, and his laughter echoed beneath the ceiling. Macbeth went farther in, along the corridor to the departures hall, and heard the dealer's cry resound behind him: "Undercover cop coming, folks!"

"Hi, Macbeth," came a thin, weak voice.

Macbeth turned. It was the young boy with the eye patch. Macbeth went over to him and crouched down by the wall. The black patch had ridden up, allowing Macbeth to see inside the cavity's mysterious darkness.

"I need a quarter of brew," Macbeth said. "Can you help me?"

"No," said the boy. "I can't help anyone. Can you help me?"

Macbeth recognized something in his expression. It was like looking into a mirror. What the hell was he actually doing? He had, with the help of good people, managed to get away, and now he was back to this? To perform an act of villainy even the most desperate drug addict would shy away from? He could still refuse. He could take this boy with him to the Inverness. Give him food, a shower and a bed. Tonight could be very different from the way he had planned it, there was still that possibility. The possibility of saving himself. The boy. Duncan. Lady.

"Come on. Let's—" Macbeth started.

"Macbeth." The voice coming from behind him rumbled like thunder through the corridor. "Your prayers have been heard. I have what you need."

Macbeth turned. Lifted his eyes higher. And higher. "How did you know I was here, Strega?"

"We have our eyes and ears everywhere. Here you are, a present from Hecate."

Macbeth gazed down at the little bag that had dropped into his hand. "I want to pay. How much?"

"Pay for a present? I think Hecate would take that as an insult. Have a good night." Strega turned and left.

"Then I won't take it," Macbeth called out and threw the bag after her, but she had already been swallowed up by the darkness.

"If you don't . . ." said the one-eyed reedy voice. "Is it OK if I . . . ?"

"Stay where you are," Macbeth snarled without moving.

"What do you want to do?" the boy asked.

"Want?" Macbeth echoed. "It's never what you *want* to do, but what you have to do."

He walked toward the bag and picked it up. Walked back. Passing the boy's outstretched hand.

"Hey, aren't you going . . . ?"

"Go to hell," Macbeth growled. "I'll see you there."

Macbeth went down the stairs to the stinking toilet, chased out a woman sitting on the floor, tore open the bag, sprinkled the powder onto the sink below the mirrors, crushed the lumps with the blunt side of a dagger and used the blade to chop it up into finer particles. Then he rolled up a banknote and sniffed the yellowy-white powder first up one nostril, then the other. It took the chemicals a surprisingly short time to pass through the mucous membranes into his blood. And his last thought before the dope-infected blood entered his brain was that it was like renewing an acquaintance with a lover. A much too beautiful, much too dangerous lover who hadn't aged a day in all these years.

"What did I tell you?" Hecate banged his stick on the floor by the CCTV monitors.

"You said there was nothing more predictable than a love-smitten junkie and moralist."

"Thank you, Strega."

Macbeth stopped at the top of the steps in front of the central station.

Workers' Square swayed like a sea ahead of him; the breakers crashed beneath the cobblestones, sounding like the chattering of teeth as they rose and fell. And down below the Inverness there was a paddle steamer filled with the noise of music and laughter, and the light made it sparkle in the water running from its slowly rotating, roaring wheel.

Then he set off. Through the black night, back to the Inverness. He seemed to be gliding through the air, his feet off the ground. He floated through the door and into the reception area. The receptionist looked at him and gave him a friendly nod. Macbeth turned to the gaming room and saw that Lady, Malcolm and Duff were still talking in the bar. Then he went up the stairs as though he were flying, along the corridor until he stopped outside Duncan's door.

Macbeth inserted the master key in the lock, turned the knob and went in.

He was back. Nothing had changed. The bathroom door was still ajar, and the light inside was on. He walked over to the bed. Looked down at the sleeping police officer, put his left hand inside his jacket and found the handle of the dagger.

He raised his hand. It was so much easier now. Aimed for the heart. The way he had aimed at the heart carved into the oak tree. And the knife bored a hole between the names there. Meredith and Macbeth.

"Sleep no more! Macbeth is murdering sleep."

Macbeth stiffened. Was it the chief commissioner, the dope or he himself who had spoken?

He looked down at Duncan's face. No, the eyes were still closed and his breathing calm and even. But as he watched, Duncan's eyes opened. Looked at him quietly. "Macbeth?" The chief commissioner's eyes went to the dagger.

"I thought I heard s-s-sounds coming from here," Macbeth said. "I'll check."

"My bodyguards . . ."

"I h-h-heard them snoring."

Duncan listened for a few moments. Then he yawned. "Good. Let them sleep. I'm safe here, I know. Thanks, Macbeth."

"Not at all, sir."

Macbeth walked toward the door. He wasn't floating any longer. A sense of relief, *happiness* even, spread through his body. He was saved. The chief commissioner had liberated him. Lady could do and say what she liked, but this stopped here. Five paces. He grabbed the doorknob with his free hand.

Then a movement in the reflection on the polished brass.

As if in a fairground mirror and in the light from the bathroom door he saw—like in some absurd, distorted film—the chief commissioner pull something from under his pillow and point it at his back. A gun. Five paces. Throwing distance. Macbeth reacted instinctively. Whirled round. He was off-balance, and the dagger left his hand while he was still moving.

9

OF COURSE IT HAD BEEN Duff who had approached the two girls and asked to join them at their table. Macbeth went to the bar and bought them all beers, came back and heard Duff sounding off about Macbeth and him being the best two cadets in the final year at police college. Their future prospects looked more than rosy, and the girls should make a move if they knew what was good for them, he said. The two girls laughed, and the eyes of the girl called Meredith glinted, but she looked down when Macbeth tried to hold her gaze. When the bar closed, Macbeth accompanied Meredith to the gate and was rewarded with a friendly handshake and a telephone number. While, next morning, Duff went into great detail about how he had serviced the friend, Rita, in a narrow bed at the nurses' hall of residence, Macbeth rang Meredith the same evening and in a trembling voice invited her out for dinner.

He had ordered a table at Lyon's and knew it was a mistake the moment he saw the head waiter's knowing gaze. The elegant suit Duff had lent him was much too big, so he'd had to go for Banquo's, which was two sizes too small and twenty years out of date. Fortunately Meredith's dress, beauty and calm polite nature compensated. The only part of the French menu he understood was the prices. But Meredith explained and said that was how the French were: they refused to accept that they spoke a language that was no longer international, and they were so bad at English they couldn't bear the double ignominy of appearing idiots in their rivals' tongue.

"Arrogance and insecurity often go together," she said.

"I'm insecure," Macbeth said.

"I was thinking of your friend Duff," she said. "Why are you so insecure?"

Macbeth told her about his background. The orphanage. Banquo and Vera. Police college. She was so easy to talk to he was almost tempted to tell her everything, for one crazy moment even about Lorreal. But of course he didn't. Meredith said she had grown up in the western part of town, with parents who made sure their children lacked for nothing but who also made demands on them and were ambitious on their behalf, especially for her brothers.

"Protected, privileged and boring," she said. "Do you know I've never been to District Two East?" She laughed when Macbeth refused to accept that could be true. "Yes, it is! I never have!"

So after dinner he took her down to the riverbed. Walking along the potholed road alongside the run-down houses as far as Penny Bridge. And when he said good night outside the gate she leaned forward and kissed him on the cheek.

When he returned to his room Duff was still up. "Spill the beans," he ordered. "Slowly and in detail."

Two days later. Cinema. *Lord of the Flies.* They walked home under the same umbrella, Meredith's hand under his arm. "How can children be so cruel and bloodthirsty?" she said.

"Why should children be any less cruel than adults?"

"They're born innocent!"

"Innocent and without any sense of morality. Isn't peaceful passivity just something that adults force children to learn so that we recognize our place in society and let them do what they like with us?"

They kissed at the gate. And on Sunday he took her for a walk in the woods on the other side of the tunnel. He had packed a picnic basket.

"You can cook!" she exclaimed excitedly.

"Banquo and Vera taught me. We used to come to this very spot."

Then they kissed, she panted and he put his hand up her cotton dress. "Wait . . ." she said.

And he waited. Instead he carved a heart in the big oak and used the point of his knife to write their names. Meredith and Macbeth.

"She's ready to be plucked," Duff told Macbeth when he came home and told him the details. "I'm going to Rita's on Wednesday. Invite her here."

Macbeth had opened a bottle of wine and lit candles when Meredith rang at the door. He was prepared. But not for what happened—for her loosening his belt as soon as they were inside the door and stuffing her hand down his trousers.

"D-d-don't," he said.

She looked at him in surprise.

"S-s-stop."

"Why are you stammering?"

"I d-d-don't want you to."

She withdrew her hand, her cheeks burning with shame.

Afterward they drank a glass of red wine in silence.

"I have to get up early tomorrow," she said. "Exams soon and . . ."

"Of course."

Three weeks passed. Macbeth tried ringing several times, but the few times he got an answer Rita said that Meredith wasn't at home.

"You and Meredith are no longer dating, I take it," Duff said.

"No."

"Rita and I aren't either. Do you mind if I meet Meredith?"

"You'd better ask her."

"I have."

Macbeth gulped. It was as if he had a claw around his heart. "Oh yes? And what did she say?"

"She said yes."

"Did she? And when are you . . . ?"

"Yesterday. Just for a bite to eat, but . . . it was nice."

The day after, Macbeth woke up and was sick. And it was only later he realized what this sickness was and that there was no remedy for a broken heart. You had to suffer your way through it and he did. Suffered in silence without mentioning her name to anyone but an old oak tree on the healthy side of the tunnel. And after a while the symptoms passed. Almost completely. And he discovered that it wasn't true what people said, that we can only fall in love once. But unlike Meredith, Lady was the sickness and remedy in one. Thirst and water. Desire and satisfaction. And now her voice reached him from across the sea, from across the night.

"Darling . . ."

Macbeth drifted through water and air, light and darkness.

"Wake up!"

He opened his eyes. He was lying in bed. It had to be night still, for the room was dark. But there was a grainy element, a kind of imperceptible grayness that presaged dawn.

"At last!" she hissed in his ear. "Where have you been?"

"Been?" Macbeth said, trying to hold on to a scrap of the dream. "Haven't I been here?"

"Your body has, yes, but I've been trying to wake you for hours. It's as if you've been unconscious. What have you done?"

Macbeth was still holding on to the dream, but suddenly he didn't know whether it was a good dream or a nightmare. Duncan . . . He let go, and images whirled in the darkness.

"Your pupils," she said, holding his face between her hands. "You've taken dope, that's why."

He squirmed away, from her, from the light. "I needed it."

"But you've done it?"

"It?"

She shook him hard. "Macbeth, darling, answer me! Have you done the deed you promised you would?"

"Yes!" He groaned and ran a hand across his face. "No, I don't know."

"You don't *know*?"

"I can see him in front of me with a dagger in him, but I don't know if it really happened or I just dreamed it."

"There's a clean dagger here on the bedside table. You were supposed to have put both daggers in with the bodyguards after killing Duncan, one with each of them."

"Yes, yes, I remember."

"Is the other dagger with them? Pull yourself together!"

"Sleep no more! Macbeth is murdering sleep."

"What?"

"He said that. Or I dreamed it."

"We'd better go in and check."

Macbeth closed his eyes, reached out for the dream—perhaps it could tell him. Rather that than go back in. But the dream had already slipped through his fingers. When he reopened his eyes Lady was standing with an ear to the wall.

"They're still snoring. Come on." She grabbed the dagger from the bedside table.

Macbeth breathed in deeply. The day and its revealing light would soon be here. He swung his legs out of bed and discovered he was still fully dressed.

They went into the corridor. Not a sound to be heard. Those who stayed at the Inverness didn't usually get up early.

Lady unlocked the guards' room, and she and Macbeth went in. Each was lying asleep in an armchair. But there were no daggers anywhere, and there was no blood smeared over their suits and shirts, as per their plan.

"I only dreamed it," Macbeth whispered. "Come on, let's drop this."

"No!" Lady snarled and strode off to the door connecting to Duncan's room. Shifted the dagger to her right hand. Then, without any sign of hesitation, she tore open the door and went in.

Macbeth waited and listened.

Nothing.

He walked over to the door opening.

Gray light seeped in through the window.

She was standing on the opposite side of the bed with the dagger raised by her mouth. Squeezing the handle with both hands, her eyes wide with horror.

Duncan was in the bed. His eyes were open and seemed to be staring at something by the other door. Everything was sprayed with blood. The duvet, the gun lying on the duvet, the hand on the gun. And the handle of the dagger sticking out of Duncan's neck like a hook.

"Oh darling," Lady whispered. "My man, my hero, my savior, Macbeth."

Macbeth opened his mouth to say something, but at that moment the total Sunday silence was broken by a barely audible but continuous ringing sound from below.

Lady looked at her watch. "That's Duff. He's early! Darling, go downstairs and keep him busy while I sort this out."

"You've got three minutes," Macbeth said. "Don't touch the blood. It's semi-coagulated and will leave prints. OK?"

She angled back her head and smiled at him. "Hi," she said. "There you are."

And he knew what she meant. At last he was there. The zone.

———

Standing in front of the door to the Inverness, Duff shivered and longed to be back in Caithness's warm bed. He was about to press the bell a second time when the door opened.

"Sir, the entrance to the casino is down there."

"No, I'm here to collect Chief Commissioner Duncan."

"Oh, right. Come in. I'll ring and say you're here. Inspector Duff, isn't it?"

Duff nodded. They had really first-class staff at the Inverness. He sank down into one of the deep armchairs.

"No answer, sir," said the receptionist. "Neither there nor in his bodyguards' room."

Duff looked at his watch. "What's the chief commissioner's room number?"

"Two thirteen, sir."

"Would you mind if I went up to wake him?"

"Not at all."

Duff was on his way up the stairs when a familiar figure came bounding down toward him.

"Morning, Duff," Macbeth called cheerily. "Jack, could you go to the kitchen and get us both a cup of strong coffee?"

The receptionist went off.

"Thanks, Macbeth, but I've been told to collect Duncan."

"Is it that urgent? And aren't you a bit early?"

"We've arranged a time to be home, and I remembered that Kenneth Bridge was still out of action, so we'll have to take the detour over the old bridge."

"Relax." Macbeth laughed, grabbing Duff under the arm. "She won't be setting a stopwatch, will she? And you look exhausted, so if you're driving you'll need some strong coffee. Come on, let's sit down."

Duff hesitated. "Thanks, my friend, but that'll have to wait."

"A cup of coffee and she won't notice the smell of whiskey quite as easily."

"I'm considering becoming a teetotaler like you."

"Are you?"

"Booze leads to three things: a colorful nose, sleep and pissing. In Duncan's case, obviously sleep. I'll go up and—"

Macbeth held on to his arm. "And booze is lust's dupe, I've heard. Increases your lust but reduces performance. How was your night? Tell me. Slowly and in detail."

Duff arched an eyebrow. Slowly and in detail. Was he using the interrogation term from their police college days as a jokey parody or did he know something? No, Macbeth didn't talk in riddles. He didn't have the patience or the ability. "There's not much to tell. I stayed with a cousin."

"Eh? You never told me you had any family. I thought your grandfather was the last relation you had. Look, here's the coffee. Just put it on the table, Jack. And try ringing Duncan again."

Reassured that the receptionist was on the case, Duff went down the steps and greedily reached for the coffee. But stayed standing.

"The family, yes," Macbeth said. "It's a source of a constant guilty conscience, isn't it?"

"Yes, maybe," said Duff, who had burned his tongue with his first sip and was now blowing on the coffee.

"How are they? Are they enjoying Fife?"

"Everyone enjoys Fife."

"Duncan still isn't answering his phone, sir."

"Thanks, Jack. Keep trying. Lots of people will have heavy heads this morning."

Duff put down his cup. "Macbeth, I think I'll wake him first and drink coffee afterward, so we can get going."

"I'll go up with you. He's next to us," Macbeth said, taking a sip of his coffee. He spilled it on his hand and jacket sleeve. "Whoops. Have you got a paper towel, Jack?"

"I'll just—"

"Hang about, Duff. That's it, yes. Thanks, Jack. Come on, let's go."

They walked up the stairs.

"Have you hurt yourself?" Duff asked.

"No. Why?"

"I've never seen you climb stairs so slowly."

"I might have pulled a muscle during the Norse Rider chase."

"Hm."

"Otherwise. Sleep well?"

"No," Duff said. "It was a terrible night. Thunder, lightning and rain."

"Yes, it was a bad night."

"So you didn't sleep either?"

"Well, I did—"

Duff turned and looked at him.

"—after the worst of the storm had died down," Macbeth finished. "Here we are."

Duff knocked. Waited and knocked again. Grabbed the doorknob. The door was locked. And he had a sense, a sense something was not as it should be.

"Is there a master key?"

"I'll go and ask Jack," Macbeth said.

"Jack!" Duff shouted. And then again, from the bottom of his lungs: "Jack!"

After a few seconds the receptionist's head appeared over the edge of the stairs. "Yes, sir?"

"Have you got a master key?"

"Yes, sir."

"Come here and open the door at once."

The receptionist ran up to them, taking short steps, rummaged in his jacket pocket and pulled out a key, put it in the lock and twisted.

Duff opened the door.

They stood staring. The first person to speak was the receptionist.

"Holy shit."

Macbeth examined the scene, conscious of the door threshold pressing against the sole of his foot, and heard Duff smash the glass of the fire alarm, which immediately began to howl. The dagger had been removed from the right-hand side of Duncan's neck and Lady had added a stab on the left. The gun on the duvet had also been removed. Otherwise everything appeared to be how it had been.

"Jack!" Duff called over the howl. "Get everyone out of their rooms and assemble them in reception now. Not a word about what you've seen, all right?"

"All r-right, sir."

Doors down the corridor opened. Out of the closest came Lady, barefoot and in her dressing gown.

"What's up, darling? Is there a fire?"

She was good. They were back following the plan, he was still in the zone, and Macbeth felt at this second, at this moment, with everything apparently in chaos, that everything was actually on track. Right now he and the woman he loved were unbeatable, right now they were in total control—of the town, fate, the orbit of the stars. And he felt it now, it was like a high, as strong as anything Hecate could offer.

"Where on earth are his bodyguards?" Duff shouted, furious.

They hadn't imagined it would be Duff in the role of witness to what was about to happen, but one of the more perplexed and frightened over-night guests they had placed in neighboring rooms, such as Malcolm. But now Duff was here he was impossible to ignore.

"In here, darling," Macbeth said. "You too, Duff."

He pushed them into Duncan's room and closed the door. Took his service pistol from the holster on his trouser belt. "Listen carefully now. The door was locked and there was no sign of a break-in. The only person who has a master key to this room is Jack . . ."

"And me," said Lady. "I think so, anyway . . ."

"Apart from that, there's only one possibility." Macbeth pointed to the door to the adjacent room.

"His own bodyguards?" Lady said in horror and put a hand to her mouth.

Macbeth cocked his gun. "I'm going in to check."

"I'll go with you," Duff said.

"*No*, you won't," Macbeth said. "This is my business, not yours."

"And I choose to ma—"

"You'll choose to do what I tell you, Inspector Duff."

Macbeth initially saw surprise in Duff's face. Afterward it slowly sank in: the head of Organized Crime outranked the head of Homicide.

"Take care of Lady, will you, Duff?"

Without waiting for an answer Macbeth opened the door to the guards' room, stepped inside and closed the door behind him. The body-guards were still in their chairs. One of them grunted; perhaps the fire alarm was penetrating the heavy veil of drugs.

Macbeth struck him with the back of his hand.

One eye half-opened, its gaze floated around the room and landed on Macbeth. It remained there before gradually taking in his body.

Andrianov registered that his black suit jacket and white shirt were covered with blood, then he felt that something was missing. The weight of his gun in its holster. He put a hand inside his jacket and down into the holster, where his fingers found instead of his service pistol cold sharp steel and something sticky . . . The bodyguard removed his hand and looked at it. Blood? Was he still dreaming? He groaned, a section of his brain received what it interpreted as signals of danger, and he desperately tried to collect himself, automatically looked around, and there, on the floor beside his chair he saw his gun. And his colleague's gun, beside the chair where he lay, apparently asleep.

"What . . ." Andrianov mumbled, looking into the muzzle of the gun held by the man in front of him.

"Police!" the man shouted. It was Macbeth. The new head of . . . of . . . "Hold the guns where I can see them or I'll shoot."

Andrianov blinked in his confusion. Why did it feel as if he was lying in a bog? What had he taken?

"Don't point that gun at me!" Macbeth shouted. "Don't . . ."

Something told Andrianov that he shouldn't reach for the gun on the floor. The man in front of him wouldn't shoot him if he sat still. But it didn't help. Perhaps all the hours, days, years as a bodyguard had created an instinct, a reaction which was no longer steered by will, *to protect without a thought for your own life.* Or perhaps that was just how he was and why he had applied to work in this branch of service.

Andrianov reached out for the gun, and his life and reasoning were interrupted by a bullet that bored through his forehead, his brain and the back of the chair and didn't stop until it met the wall with the golden-thread wallpaper that Lady had bought for a minor fortune in Paris. The explosion sent a convulsion through his colleague's body, but he never managed to regain consciousness before he too got a bullet through the forehead.

Duff made for the door as the first shot went off.

But Lady held him back. "He said you—"

A second shot rang out, and Duff freed himself from her grasp. Ripped open the door and charged in. And stood in the middle of the floor looking around. Two men, each in a chair with a third eye in his forehead.

"Norse Riders," Macbeth said, putting the smoking gun back in its holster. "Sweno's behind this."

There was shouting and banging on the corridor door.

"Let them in," Macbeth said.

Duff did as he was told.

"What's going on?" Malcolm gasped, out of breath. "Heavens above, are they . . . ? Who . . . ?"

"Me," said Macbeth.

"They pulled their guns," Duff said.

Malcolm's eyes jumped in bewilderment from Duff back to Macbeth. "On you? Why?"

"Because I was going to arrest them," Macbeth said.

"What for?" Lennox asked.

"Murder."

"Sir," Duff said, looking at Malcolm, "I'm afraid we have bad news."

He could see Malcolm's eyes narrowing behind the square glasses as he leaned forward like a boxer bracing himself for the punch he wouldn't see yet sensed was on its way. Everyone turned to the figure that had appeared in the doorway to the next room.

"Chief Commissioner Duncan is dead," Lady said. "Stabbed with a knife while he was sleeping."

The last sentence made Duff automatically turn toward Macbeth. Not because it said anything he didn't already know, but because it was an echo of the same sentence uttered early one morning in an orphanage so many years ago.

Their eyes met for a brief instant before both of them looked away.

PART TWO

10

THE MORNING CHIEF COMMISSIONER DUNCAN was found dead in bed at Inverness Casino was the second time in its history that Lady had immediately ordered the building to be cleared of customers and a CLOSED sign to be hung up outside.

Caithness arrived with everyone she could muster from Forensics and they closed the whole of the first floor.

The other officers who had stayed the night gathered around the roulette table in the empty gaming room.

Duff looked at Deputy Chief Commissioner Malcolm sitting at the end of the makeshift conference table. He had taken off his glasses, perhaps to clean them, at least that was what he was doing as he stared fixedly at the green felt, as though answers to all the questions lay there. Malcolm was the highest-ranking officer present, and Duff had occasionally wondered whether the reason he walked with such a stoop was that Malcolm, a bureaucrat surrounded by people with practical police experience, felt he was on such thin ice that he automatically leaned forward to catch any advice, any whispered hints. And perhaps Malcolm's wan complexion was not down to the previous night's drinking but the fact that he had suddenly become acting chief commissioner.

Malcolm breathed on his glasses and kept cleaning them. He didn't look up. As though he didn't dare meet the gazes directed at him, colleagues waiting for him to speak.

Duff was perhaps too harsh. Everyone knew that in chiseling out Duncan's program Malcolm had been both the chisel and the hammer. But could he lead them? The others had years of experience leading their respective units, while Malcolm had spent days running two stooped paces behind Duncan like a kind of overpaid assistant.

"Gentlemen," Malcolm said, staring at the green felt. "A great man has left us. And at this juncture that's all I intend to say about Duncan." He put on his glasses, raised his head and studied those around the table. "As chief commissioner he would not have allowed us to sink into sentimentality and despair at such a pass, he would have demanded that we did what we're employed to do: find the guilty party, or parties, and put them under lock and key. Tears and commemorative words will have to come afterward. At this meeting let's plan and coordinate what to do first. The next meeting will be at HQ at six this evening. I suggest the first thing you do after this meeting is to ring your wives and so on—"

Malcolm's gaze landed on Duff, but Duff couldn't work out if there was any intentional subtext.

"—and say you're unlikely to be home for a while." He paused for a moment. "Because first of all you're going to arrest the person who took Chief Commissioner Duncan from us." Long pause. "Duff, you've got the Homicide Unit. I want an interim report for the meeting in an hour, including whatever Caithness and her team have or haven't found at the crime scene."

"Right."

"Lennox, I want a full background check on the bodyguards and details of their movements before the murder. Where they were, who they spoke to, what they bought, any changes in their bank accounts, some tough questioning of family and friends. Requisition any resources you need."

"Thank you, sir."

"Macbeth, you've already contributed a lot to this case, but I need more. See if Organized Crime can link this with the big players, those who would profit most from getting rid of Duncan."

"Isn't it pretty obvious?" Macbeth said. "We've dumped Sweno's dope in the river, killed two and arrested half the Norse Riders. This is Sweno's revenge, and—"

"It's not obvious," Malcolm said.

The others stared at the deputy chief commissioner in surprise.

"Sweno has everything to gain by Duncan continuing his project." Malcolm tapped on some gambling chips that had been left on the cloth after the hasty evacuation. "What was Duncan's first promise to this town? He was going to arrest Hecate. And now, with the Norse Riders down for the count, Duncan would have focused all the police resources on precisely that. And if Duncan had succeeded what would he have done?"

"He would have cleaned up the market for Sweno so that he could make a comeback," Lennox said.

"Quite honestly," Macbeth said, "do you really think a vindictive Sweno would think that rationally?" Malcolm raised an eyebrow a fraction. "A man from the working classes, with no education or any other help, who has run one of the most profitable businesses in this town for more than thirty years. Could he be financially rational? Is he capable of putting aside a thirst for revenge when he can see what's good for business?"

"OK," Duff said. "Hecate's the one with the most to gain from Duncan's removal, so you assume he's behind this." He was looking at Malcolm.

"I'm not assuming anything, but Duncan's extreme prioritization of the hunt for Hecate has been, as we know, much debated, and from Hecate's point of view anyone who succeeds Duncan would be preferable."

"Especially if his successor were someone Hecate had tabs on," Duff said. Realizing at once what he had insinuated, he closed his eyes. "Sorry. I didn't mean to . . ."

"That's fine," Malcolm said. "We can speak and think freely here, and what you said follows from my reasoning. Hecate might think he would have an easier time than under Duncan. So let's show him how wrong he is." Malcolm pushed all the chips onto black. "So our provisional hypothesis is Hecate, but let's hope we know more by six o'clock. To work."

Banquo could feel sleep letting go. Felt the dream letting go. Felt Vera letting go. He blinked. Was it the church bells that had woken him? No. There was someone in the room. A person sitting by the window and looking down at the framed photograph, who, without looking up, asked, "Hangover?"

"Macbeth? How . . . ?"

"Fleance let me in. He's taken over my room, I see. Even the winkle-pickers you bought me."

"What's the time?"

"And there was me thinking pointed shoes were way out of fashion."

"That was why you left them here. But Fleance will wear anything if he knows it was once yours."

"Books and school stuff everywhere. He's hardworking, he's got the right attitude to get to the top."

"Yes, he's getting there."

"But, as we know, that's not always enough to get to the top. You're one of many, so it's a question of opportunity. Having the skill and the courage to strike when the opportunity presents itself. Do you remember who took this picture?"

Macbeth held it up. Fleance and Banquo under the dead apple tree. The shadow of the photographer falling across them.

"You did. What do you want?" Banquo rubbed his face. Macbeth was right: he did have a hangover.

"Duncan's dead."

Banquo's hands dropped to the duvet. "What was that you said?"

"His bodyguards stabbed him in the neck while he was asleep at the Inverness last night."

Banquo felt nausea on the march and had to breathe in several times to stop himself throwing up.

"This is the opportunity," Macbeth said. "That is, it's a parting of the ways. From here one way goes to hell and the other to heaven. I'm here to ask which you'll choose."

"What do you mean?"

"I want to know if you'll follow me."

"I've already answered that. And the answer's yes."

Macbeth turned to him. Smiled. "And you can say that without asking whether it'll lead to heaven or hell?" His face was pale, his pupils abnormally small. Had to be the sharp morning light because if Banquo hadn't known Macbeth better he would have said he was back on dope. But the moment he was about to push that thought away the certainty broke over him like a sudden freezing-cold deluge.

"Was it you?" Banquo said. "Was it you who killed him?"

Macbeth tilted his head and studied Banquo. Studied him the way you study a parachute before you jump, a woman before you try to kiss her for the first time.

"Yes," he said. "I killed Duncan."

Banquo had difficulty breathing. Squeezed his eyes shut. Hoping that

Macbeth, that *this* would be gone when he opened them again. "And what now?"

"Now I have to kill Malcolm," he heard Macbeth say. "That is, *you* have to kill Malcolm."

Banquo opened his eyes.

"For me," Macbeth said. "And for my crown prince, Fleance."

11

BANQUO SAT IN THE FRUGAL light of the cellar listening to Fleance stamping to and fro upstairs. The boy wanted to go out. Meet friends. Maybe a girl. It would be good for him.

Banquo let the chain slide through his fingers.

He had said yes to Macbeth. Why? Why had he crossed this boundary so easily? Was it because of Macbeth's promise that he was of the people, with the people and for the people, in a way that an upper-class man like Malcolm could never be? No. It was because you simply couldn't say no when it was about a son. And even less when it was about two.

Macbeth had described it as following fate's call, clearing a path to the chief commissioner's office. He hadn't said anything about Lady being the brains behind it. He hadn't needed to. Macbeth preferred simple plans. Plans that didn't require too much thinking in critical situations. Banquo closed his eyes. Tried to imagine it. Macbeth taking over as chief commissioner and running the town with absolute power, the way Kenneth had done but with the honest aim of making the town a better place for all its inhabitants. If you want to make all the drastic changes that are needed, the slowness of democracy and the free rein it gives simplemindedness are no good. A strong, just hand. And so, by the time Macbeth is too old, he will let Fleance take over at the helm. By then Banquo will have died of old age, happy. Perhaps that was why he couldn't imagine it.

Banquo heard the front door slam.

But it's obvious, even if visions of this nature take time to become completely clear.

He put on his gloves.

It was half past five and the rain was hammering down on the cobblestones and on the windscreen of Malcolm's Chevelle 454 SS as he wound his way through the streets. He was aware it was stupid to buy a petrol guzzler in the middle of an oil crisis, and even if he had bought it secondhand for what he considered a reasonable price, he had fallen short in the responsibility argument. First of all, with his ecology-conscious daughter, then with Duncan, who had underscored the significance of leaders showing moderation. In the end Malcolm had said what he felt: he had loved these American exaggerations of cars ever since he was a boy, and Duncan had said that at least it showed economists were humans too.

He had quickly popped home to have a shower and change his clothes, which fortunately didn't take long because it was a Sunday and there was very little traffic. A large press gathering awaited him at the entrance to HQ, probably hoping for a comment or a better picture than they would get at the press conference at half past seven. The mayor, Tourtell, had already been on TV to make a statement. "Incomprehensible," "tragedy," "our thoughts go out to the family" and "the town must stand united against this evil" was what he had said, only accompanied by a great many more words. Malcolm's, by contrast, minimal comment had been to ask the press for their understanding; his focus was now on the investigation, and he referred them to the press conference.

Malcolm drove down the ramp to the basement garage, nodded to the guard, who opened the barrier, and swung in. The distance from your parking slot to the lift was in direct proportion to your place in the hierarchy. And when Malcolm backed into his slot it struck him that, from a formal point of view, he *could* have actually parked in the one that was closest.

He was about to take out the ignition key when the door on the passenger side opened and someone slipped into the back, sliding over behind the driver's seat. And for the first time since Duncan's murder Malcolm confronted the thought. With the chief commissioner's job came not only a parking slot closer to the lift but also a death threat, whenever, wherever; security was a privilege accorded to those who parked farther away.

"Start up the car," the person in the back seat said.

Malcolm looked in the rearview mirror. The person had moved so quickly and so soundlessly that he could only conclude SWAT training was effective. "Anything wrong, Banquo?"

"Yes, sir. We've uncovered plans for an attack on your life."

"Inside police HQ?"

"Yes. Drive slowly, please. We have to get away. We don't know who is involved in the force yet, but we think they're the same people who killed Duncan."

Malcolm knew he should be frightened. And he *was*. But not as frightened as he could have been. Often it was trivial situations—like standing on a ladder or being surrounded by angry wasps—that could trigger pathetic panic-like reactions. But now, just like this morning, it was as though the situation didn't permit that type of fear; on the contrary, it sharpened your ability to think fast and rationally, strengthened your resolve and, paradoxically, calmed him down.

"If that's the case, how do I know you're not one of them, Banquo?"

"If I'd wanted to kill you, you would already be dead, sir."

Malcolm nodded. Something about Banquo's tone told him that the physically smaller and much older man would probably have been able to do so with his bare hands if he so wished.

"So where are we going?"

"To the container harbor, sir."

"Why not home to—"

"You don't want your family caught up in this mess, sir. I'll explain when we're there. Drive. I'll slump down in the seat. Best no one sees me and realizes you've been informed."

Malcolm drove out, received a nod from the guard, the barrier was lifted and he was back out in the rain.

"I have a meeting in—"

"That'll be taken care of."

"And the press conference?"

"That too. What you should think about now is you. And your daughter."

"Julia?" Malcolm could feel it now. The panic.

"She'll be taken care of, sir. Just drive now. We'll soon be there."

"What are we going to do?"

"Whatever has to be done."

Five minutes later they drove through the gates of the container harbor, which in recent years had been left open, as all attempts to keep the homeless and thieves out had achieved had been smashed fences and locks. It was Sunday and the quay was deserted.

"Park behind the shed there," Banquo said.

Malcolm did as instructed, parking beside a Volvo saloon.

"Sign this," Banquo said, holding a sheet of paper and a pen between the front seats.

"What is it?" Malcolm said.

"A few lines written on your typewriter," Banquo said. "Read it aloud."

"*The Norse Riders threatened they would kill my daughter—*" Malcolm stopped.

"Carry on," Banquo said.

Malcolm cleared his throat. "*—Julia, if I didn't help them to kill the chief commissioner,*" he read. "*But now they have a hold on me and they've told me to perform other services for them, too. I know that for as long as I'm alive the threat to my daughter will always be there. That is why—and because of the shame I feel for what I've done—I've decided to drown myself.*"

"That is in fact true," Banquo said. "Only the signature on that letter can save your daughter."

Malcolm turned to Banquo on the back seat. Stared into the muzzle of the gun he was holding in his gloved hand.

"There isn't any attempt on my life. You lied."

"Yes and no," Banquo said.

"You tricked me into coming here so that you could kill me and dump me in this canal."

"You'll drown yourself, as it says in the letter."

"Why should I?"

"Because the alternative is that I shoot you in the head now, drive to your house and then the suicide letter looks like this." Banquo passed him another sheet of paper. "Just the ending has been changed."

"*For as long as my daughter and I are alive, the threat will always be there. That's why I've chosen to take our lives and spare her the shame of what I've done and a life of endless fear.*" Malcolm blinked. He understood the words, they made sense, yet still he had to reread the letter.

"Sign now, Malcolm." Banquo's voice sounded almost comforting.

Malcolm closed his eyes. It was so quiet in the car that he could hear the creak of the trigger springs in Banquo's gun. Then he opened his eyes, grabbed the pen and signed his name on the first letter. Metal rattled on the back seat. "Here," said Banquo. "Put them around your waist under your coat."

Malcolm appraised the tire chains Banquo held out. A weight.

He took them and wrapped them around his waist while his brain tried to find a way out.

"Let me see," Banquo said, tightening the chains. Then he threaded through a padlock and clicked it shut. Placed the signed letter on the passenger seat and on top a key Malcolm assumed was for the padlock.

"Come on." They got out into the rain. With his gun Banquo prodded Malcolm along the edge of the quay following a narrow canal that cut in from the main docks. Containers stood like walls on both sides of the canal. Even if people were out walking on the quay they wouldn't see Malcolm and Banquo where they were.

"Stop," Banquo said.

Malcolm stared across the black sea, which lay flat, beaten down and tamed by the lashing rain. Lowered his gaze and looked down into the oil-covered greenish-black water, then turned his back to the sea and fixed his eyes on Banquo.

Banquo raised his gun. "Jump, sir."

"You don't look like someone intending to kill, Banquo."

"With all due respect, sir, I don't think you know what such people look like."

"True enough. But I'm a fairly good judge of character."

"Have been up to now."

Malcolm stretched his arms out to the side. "Push me then."

Banquo moistened his lips. Changed his grip on the gun.

"Well, Banquo? Show me the killer in you."

"You're cool for a suit, sir."

Malcolm lowered his arms. "That's because I know something about loss, Banquo. Just like you. I've learned that we can afford to lose most things. But then there are some we cannot, that will stop us existing even more than if we lose our own lives. I know that you lost your wife to the illness which this town has given to its inhabitants."

"Oh yes? How do you know that?"

"Because Duncan told me. And he did so because I lost my first wife to the same illness. And we talked about how we could help to create a town where this wouldn't happen, where even the town's most powerful industrial magnates would face trial for breaking the law, where a murder is a murder, whether it's with a weapon or by gassing the town's inhabitants until their eyes go yellow and they smell like a corpse."

"So you've already lost the unlosable."

"No. You can lose your wife and your life still has meaning. Because you have a child. A daughter. A son. It's our children who are unlosable, Banquo. If I save Julia by dying now, that's the way it has to be, it's worth it. And there will be others after me and Duncan. You might not believe me, but this world is full of people who want what is good, Banquo."

"And who decides what is good? You and the other big bosses?"

"Ask your heart, Banquo. Your brain will deceive you. Ask your heart."

Malcolm saw Banquo shift his weight from one foot to the other. Malcolm's mouth and throat were dry, he was already hoarse. "You can hang as many chains on us as you like, Banquo, it won't make any difference because we'll float to the surface. What is good rises. I swear I'm going to float to the surface somewhere and reveal your misdeeds."

"They aren't mine, Malcolm."

"Hecate. Yours. You're in the same boat. And we both know which river that boat will cross and where you'll soon end up."

Banquo nodded slowly. "Hecate," he said. "Exactly."

"What?"

Banquo seemed to be staring at a point on Malcolm's forehead. "You're right, sir. I work for Hecate." Malcolm tried to decipher Banquo's faint smile. Water was running down his face as though he were crying, Malcolm thought. Was he hesitating? Malcolm knew he would have to continue talking, to make Banquo talk, because every word, every second prolonged his life. Increased the fading tiny chance that Banquo might change his mind or someone might appear.

"Why drowning, Banquo?"

"Eh?"

"Shooting me in the car and making it look like suicide would be easier."

Banquo shrugged. "There are many ways to skin a cat. The crime scene is underwater. No traces if they suspect murder. And drowning is nicer. Like going to sleep."

"What makes you think that?"

"I know. I almost drowned twice in my youth."

The barrel of Banquo's gun had sunk a fraction. Malcolm estimated the distance between them.

Malcolm swallowed. "Why did you almost drown, Banquo?"

"Because I grew up on the east side of town and never learned to swim. Isn't it funny that here in a town on the edge of the sea there are people who die if they fall in? So I tried to teach my boy to swim. The odd thing is he didn't learn either. Perhaps because it was a non-swimmer trying to teach him. If we sink, they sink, that's how our fates are passed on. But people like you can swim, Malcolm."

"Hence the chains, I assume."

"Yes." The gun barrel was raised again. The hesitation was gone and the determination back in Banquo's eyes. Malcolm took a deep breath. The chance had been there and now it wasn't.

"Good people or not," Banquo said, "you have the buoyancy we lack. And I have to be sure you will stay under the water. And never rise to the surface again. If you don't I won't have done my job. Do you understand?"

"Understand?"

"Give me your police badge."

Malcolm took the brass badge from his jacket pocket and gave it to Banquo, who immediately threw it. It flew over the edge of the quay, hit the water and sank. "It's brass. It's shiny but will sink right to the bottom. That's gravity, sir, it drags everything with it into the mud. You have to disappear, Malcolm. Disappear forever."

In the meeting room Macbeth looked at his watch. Twenty-nine minutes past six. The door opened again, and a person Macbeth recognized as Lennox's assistant stuck her head in, said it still wasn't possible to get in contact with Malcolm; all they knew was he arrived at HQ, turned round in the garage and left, and no one, not even his daughter, Julia, knew where he was.

"Thanks, Priscilla," Lennox said and turned to the others. "Then I think we should start this meeting by—"

Macbeth knew this was the moment. The moment Lady had spoken about, the moment of the leadership void, when everyone would unconsciously regard the person who took the initiative as the new leader. For that reason his interruption came over loud and clear.

"Excuse me, Lennox." Macbeth turned to the door. "Priscilla, could you organize a search for Malcolm and his car? For the time being, radio only patrol cars. And phrase it as low-key as possible. HQ wishes to contact him ASAP. That kind of thing, thank you." He turned to the others. "Sorry to requisition your assistant, Lennox, but I think most of us here share my unease. OK, let's start the meeting. Anyone object if I chair it until Malcolm arrives?"

He scanned the table. Caithness. Lennox. Duff. Saw how they had to think before they concluded what Lennox said stiffly after a clearing of the throat: "You're the next in command, Macbeth. Away you go."

"Thank you, Lennox. Would you mind, by the way, closing the window behind you? Let's start with the bodyguards. Has Anti-Corruption got anything there?"

"Not yet," Lennox said, trying to close the latches. "There's nothing to suggest irregularities or anything one might deem suspicious. In fact, the lack of irregularities is the only suspicious thing."

"Nothing suspicious, new connections, no sudden purchasing of luxury goods or bank account movements?"

Lennox shook his head. "They seem as clean as shining armor."

"My guess is they *were* clean," Duff said. "But even the cleanest knights can be poisoned and corrupted if you can find the chink in their armor. And Hecate found that gap."

"Then we can, too," Macbeth said. "Keep searching, Lennox."

"I will." His tone suggested a space for *sir* at the end. It wasn't spoken, but everyone had heard it.

"You mentioned you spoke to the undercover guys in your old section, Duff?"

"They say the murder came as a shock to everyone working on the street. No one knew anything. But everyone takes it as a foregone conclusion that Hecate's behind it. A young guy down at the central station mentioned something about a police officer asking for dope—I don't know if it was one of our undercover drugs men, but it definitely wasn't either of the bodyguards. We'll continue to look for clues that could lead us to where Hecate is. But it's—as we know—at least as hard as finding Sweno."

"Thanks, Duff. Crime scene investigation, Caithness?"

"Predicted finds," she said, looking at the notes in front of her. "We've identified various fingerprints in the deceased's room and they match those of the three maids, the bodyguards and those who were in the room—Lady, Macbeth and Duff. As well as a set of prints we couldn't identify for a while, but now we have a match with the prints of the previous occupants of the room. So when I say 'predicted finds' that's not exactly true; usually hotel rooms are full of unidentified fingerprints."

"The owner of the Inverness takes cleaning *very* seriously," Macbeth said drily.

"Pathology confirms that the direct cause of death was two stab wounds. The wounds match the daggers that were found. And although the daggers were cleaned on the sheet and the bodyguards' own clothing there was still more than enough blood on the blades and handles to establish it came from the deceased."

"Can we say Duncan?" Macbeth asked. "Instead of deceased."

"As you wish. One dagger is bloodier than the other as it was the one that cut the dece— erm Duncan's carotid artery, hence the splash of blood over the duvet, as you can see on this photograph." Caithness pushed a black-and-white photo into the middle of the table, which the others dutifully examined. "Full autopsy report will be ready tomorrow morning. We can say more then."

"*More* about what?" Duff asked. "What he had for dinner? As we all know, we had the same. Or what illnesses he had that he *didn't* die of? If we're going to keep up the pace it's essential now that we focus on information that's important."

"An autopsy," Caithness said, and Macbeth noticed the quiver in her voice, "can confirm or deny the assumed sequence of events. And I'd assume that was pretty important."

"It is, Caithness," Macbeth said. "Anything else?"

She showed some more photos, talked about other medical and technical evidence, but none of it pointed in a direction that was different from the general consensus around the table: that the two bodyguards had killed Duncan. There was also agreement that the guards didn't seem to have a motive, therefore other forces must have been behind the murder, but the consequent discussion about whether anyone else apart from Hecate could have been responsible was brief and unproductive.

Macbeth suggested postponing the press conference until ten o'clock pending the location and briefing of Malcolm. Lennox pointed out that nine was a better time for the press as they had early deadlines on a Sunday.

"Thank you, Lennox," Macbeth said. "But our agenda is what counts and not sales figures early tomorrow."

"I think that's stupid," Lennox said. "We're the new management team, and it's unwise to make ourselves unpopular with the press at the very first opportunity."

"Your view has been noted," Macbeth said. "Unless Malcolm appears and says anything to the contrary, we meet here at nine and go through what has to be said at the press conference."

"And who will give the press conference?" Duff asked.

Before Macbeth had the chance to answer, the door opened. It was Priscilla, Lennox's assistant.

"Sorry to interrupt," she said. "A patrol car has reported that Malcolm's car is parked at the container harbor. It's empty and there's no sign of Malcolm."

Macbeth felt the silence in the room. Savored the knowledge that they didn't share. And the control it gave him.

"Where in the container harbor?" Macbeth asked.

"On the quay by one of the canals."

Macbeth nodded slowly. "Send divers."

"Divers?" Lennox said. "Isn't that a bit premature?"

"I think Macbeth's right," Priscilla interrupted, and the others turned to her in astonishment. She gulped. "They found a letter on the car seat."

12

THE PRESS CONFERENCE STARTED AT ten precisely. When Macbeth entered Scone Hall and walked to the podium, flashes fired off from all angles and cast grotesque fleeting shadows of him on the wall behind. He placed his papers on the lectern in front of him, looked down at them for a few seconds, then coughed and scanned the full rows of seats. He had never enjoyed speaking in front of audiences. Once, long ago, the very thought of it had been worse than the most hazardous mission. But it had got better. And now, this evening, he felt happy. He would enjoy it. Because he was in control and knew something they didn't. And because he had just inhaled a line of brew. That was all he needed.

"Good evening, I'm Inspector Macbeth, head of the Organized Crime Unit. As you know, Chief Commissioner Duncan was found murdered at Inverness Casino this morning at 6:42. Immediately afterward the two provisional suspects in the case, Duncan's bodyguards Police Officer Andrianov and Police Officer Hennessy, were shot and killed by the police in the adjacent room when they resisted arrest. An hour ago you were given a detailed account of the course of events, our current findings and assumptions about the case, so this can be dealt with quickly. But I would like to add a couple of things of a more technical nature."

Macbeth held his breath and one journalist was unable to restrain himself:

"What do you know about Malcolm?" the question resounded.

"Is he dead?" another journalist lobbed in.

Macbeth looked down at his notes. Put them to the side.

"If these questions mean the press considers we've covered our responsibility to report on the murder of Chief Commissioner Duncan, we can now talk about the disappearance of the deputy chief commissioner."

"No, but first things first," shouted one of the older journalists. "We have deadlines looming."

"OK," Macbeth said. "Deputy Chief Commissioner Malcolm didn't show up—as you appear to know—at our meeting in police HQ at six. On a day when the chief commissioner has been found dead that is of course disturbing. So we instigated a search, and Malcolm's car was located this afternoon in the container harbor. Subsequently the area was searched, also by divers. And they found—"

"The body?"

"—this." Macbeth held up a round piece of metal that glinted in the glare of the TV lamps. "This is Malcolm's police badge, and was found on the seabed by the quay."

"Do you think someone has killed him?"

"Possibly," Macbeth said, without batting an eyelid, in the deafening silence that followed. "If by *someone* we include Malcolm himself." He ran his eye over the audience and continued: "A letter was found on the front seat of his car."

Macbeth addressed the letter. Cleared his throat.

"The Norse Riders threatened they would kill my daughter, Julia, if I didn't help them to kill the chief commissioner. But now they have a hold on me and they've told me to perform other services for them, too. I know that for as long as I'm alive the threat to my daughter will always be there. That is why—and because of the shame I feel for what I've done—I've decided to drown myself. It is signed by the deputy chief commissioner."

Macbeth looked up at the assembled journalists. "The first question we—and I presume you, too—are asking is of course whether the letter is genuine. Our Forensic Unit has confirmed that the letter was written on Malcolm's typewriter at HQ. The paper bears Malcolm's fingerprints and the signature is Malcolm's."

It was as though the room needed a few seconds to digest the information. Then came shrill voices.

"Do you know if there's anything else to confirm Malcolm was behind Duncan's murder?"

"How could Malcolm have helped the Norse Riders to murder Duncan?"

"What's the connection between Malcolm and the bodyguards?"

"Do you think there are any other police officers involved?"

Macbeth held up his palms. "I won't answer any questions about Duncan's murder now, as it is all speculation. Only questions about Malcolm's disappearance. One at a time, please."

Silence. Then the only female journalist in the room said, "Are we to understand that you've found Malcolm's police badge, but *not* Malcolm?"

"We have a muddy seabed to contend with, and the water in our harbor is not the cleanest. A light brass badge doesn't necessarily sink into the mud the way a body does, and brass reflects light. It will take the divers time to find Malcolm."

Macbeth watched the journalists as they threw themselves over their pads and made notes.

"Isn't the most obvious reason for that the current carrying away the body?" said a voice with rolled "r"s.

"Yes," Macbeth replied, and he spotted the face behind the voice. One of the few who wasn't taking notes. Walt Kite. He didn't need to; the radio station microphone was placed in front of Macbeth.

"If Malcolm killed Duncan and regretted it, why—"

"Stop." Macbeth raised a palm. "As I said, I won't answer any questions about Duncan's murder until we know more. And now please understand that we have to return to work. The number one priority for us is to investigate this case as quickly and efficiently as we can with the resources at our disposal. We also have to appoint a chief commissioner as soon as possible so that we have continuity in the rest of the work the police are doing for this town."

"Is it correct that you're the acting chief at this moment, Macbeth?"

"In formal terms, yes."

"And in practice?"

"In practice . . ." Macbeth paused. Looked down quickly at his sheet. Moistened his lips. "We're a group of experienced unit heads who have already taken the helm, and I'm not afraid to say we are in control. Nor, however, am I afraid to say that filling Duncan's shoes will take some doing. Duncan was a visionary man, a hero who died in the fight against the powers of evil, who think today they have won a victory." He gripped the lectern and leaned forward. "But all they have achieved is to make us even more determined that this lost battle will be the start of progress toward the final victory for the power of good. For justice. For security. And through that for rebuilding, re-establishing and regaining prosperity. But we can't do that alone; to do that we need your trust and the town's trust. If we have that we will continue the work that Chief Commissioner Duncan started. And I would—" he stopped to raise his hand as if swearing an oath "—like to guarantee personally that we will not stop until we have achieved the goals that Duncan set for this town and all—*all*—its inhabitants."

Macbeth let go of the lectern and straightened up. Looked at the faces, which blurred into a sea of eyes and open mouths before him. No, he wasn't afraid. He saw the effect and was still savoring the sound of his own words. Lady's words. He had leaned forward exactly when he was supposed to. She had instructed him in front of a mirror and explained how aggressive body language gave the impression of spontaneous passion and hunger for a fight, and that body language was more important than the words he used because it bypasses the brain and speaks directly to the heart.

"The next press conference is tomorrow morning at eleven here in Scone Hall. Thank you."

Macbeth collected his papers, and there was a groan of disappointment before a hail of protests and questions. Macbeth peered across the room. He wanted to stay there a couple more seconds. He managed—with some difficulty—to stop the incipient smile at the last moment.

He looks like the bloody captain of a boat, thought Duff, sitting in the front row. A captain fearlessly looking across the stormy sea. Someone has taught him that. It's not the Macbeth I know. Knew.

Macbeth nodded briefly, marched across the podium and disappeared through the door held open by Priscilla.

"Well, what do you reckon, Lennox?" Duff asked while the journalists were still shouting for an encore behind them.

"I'm moved," said the redhead inspector. "And inspired."

"Exactly. That was more like an election speech than a press conference."

"You can interpret it like that or you can interpret it as a clever and responsible tactical move."

"Responsible?" Duff snorted.

"A town, a country, rests on notions. Notions that banknotes can be exchanged for gold, notions that our leaders think about you and me and not their own good, that crimes will be punished. If we didn't believe in those notions civilized society would disintegrate in a frighteningly short time. And in a situation where anarchy is knocking on the door Macbeth has just reassured us that the town's public institutions are fully intact. It was a speech worthy of a statesman."

"Or stateswoman."

"You think those were Lady's words, not Macbeth's?"

"Women understand hearts and how to speak to them. Because the heart is the woman in us. Even if the brain is bigger, talks more and believes that the husband rules the house, it's the heart that silently makes the decisions. The speech touched your heart and the brain gladly follows. Believe me, Macbeth doesn't have it in him; the speech is her work."

"So what? We all need a better half. As long as the result is what we want it doesn't matter if the devil himself is behind it. You're not jealous of Macbeth, are you, Duff?"

"Jealous?" Duff snorted. "Why would I be? He looks and speaks like a real leader, and if he acts like one as well, it's obviously best for all of us that he leads and no one else."

Chairs scraped back behind them. Macbeth hadn't returned and their deadline was approaching.

It was an hour to midnight. The wind had dropped, but litter and wreckage from last night's storm were still being blown through the streets. The damp northwesterly was compressed and accelerated through the corridors of the station concourse, past a bundle lying beside the wall and—a few meters farther down—a man with a scarf wrapped over his nose and mouth.

Strega went over to him.

"Afraid you'll be recognized, Macbeth?"

"Shh, don't say my name. I gave a speech this evening and I'm afraid I lost my anonymity."

"I saw the evening news, yes. You looked good up there. I believed almost everything you said. But then a handsome face has always had that effect on me."

"How come you appear as soon as I show up here, Strega?"

She smiled. "Brew?"

"Have you got anything else? Speed? Cocaine? I'm seeing things and get such terrible dreams from brew."

"It was the storm, not brew, that gave you such bad dreams, Macbeth.

I don't touch the stuff, yet I dreamed that all the dogs went mad from the thunder. I saw them going for one another with foam coming from their jaws. And while they were still alive they were eating one another. I was covered in sweat and relieved when I woke up."

Macbeth pointed at the bundle farther up the corridor. "There you have your dream."

"What is it?"

"It's the corpse of a half-eaten dog, can't you see?"

"I think you're seeing things again. Here." She put a little bag in his hand. "Brew. Don't go crazy now, Macbeth. Remember the path is simple, it runs straight ahead."

As Macbeth passed Bertha and hurried down across the deserted Workers' Square where it sloped down toward Inverness Casino's illuminated facade he saw a figure standing in the darkness and rain. And on getting closer he saw to his surprise that it was Banquo.

"What are you doing here?" Macbeth said.

"Waiting for you," Banquo said.

"Midway between Bertha and the Inverness, where neither can give you shelter?"

"I couldn't make up my mind," Banquo said.

"Which way to go?"

"What to do with Malcolm."

"You didn't put the chains around him, is that it?"

"What?"

"The divers haven't found the body yet. Without some weight the current will have taken him."

"It's not that."

"No? Let's go to the Inverness then instead of standing here and getting cold and wet."

"For me it's too late. I'm chilled to the very bottom of my heart. I was waiting for you here because there are journalists outside the casino. They're waiting for you, the new chief commissioner."

"Then we'd better do this quickly. What happened?"

"I skinned the cat in a different way. You have nothing to fear. Malcolm's gone forever and will never come back. And even if he did he has no idea you've played a part in this. He thinks Hecate's behind everything."

"What are you talking about? Is Malcolm *alive*?"

Banquo shivered. "Malcolm thinks I'm in Hecate's pocket and it was me who influenced Duncan's bodyguards. I know this wasn't what we agreed. But I solved our problem and I saved the life of a good man."

"Where's Malcolm now?"

"Gone."

"Where?" Macbeth said and saw from Banquo's face that he had raised his voice.

"I drove him to the airport and put him on a plane to Capitol. From there he'll go abroad. He knows that if he tries to contact anyone or gives the smallest sign of being alive, his daughter, Julia, will be liquidated at once. Malcolm is a father, Macbeth. And I know what that means. He will never risk his daughter's life, *never*. He'd rather let a town go to the dogs. Believe me, even in the draftiest attic a flea-bitten Malcolm will wake up every morning hungry, cold and lonely and thank his maker that his daughter can live another day."

Macbeth raised his hand and then saw something in Banquo's eyes he had only ever seen once before. Not in all the operations they had carried out together against desperadoes or lunatics who had taken children as hostages. Not the times Banquo had faced an adversary who was bigger, stronger and he knew would—and did—give him a beating. Macbeth had only seen this expression on Banquo's face once, and it was the time he came home after visiting Vera in hospital and the doctor had told him the result of the latest tests. Fear. Sheer, unadulterated fear. And for that reason Macbeth suspected it wasn't for himself that Banquo was afraid.

"Thank you," Macbeth said. He laid his hand heavily on Banquo's shoulder. "Thank you, my dear friend, for being kind where I was not. I thought one man was a small sacrifice for such an immense objective as ours. But you're right: a town can't be saved from going to the dogs by letting good men die without need. This one could be spared and so he should be spared. And perhaps you've saved us both from ending up in hell for such a gross act of cruelty."

"I'm so glad you see it that way," Banquo exclaimed, and Macbeth could feel the trembling muscles in Banquo's shoulder relax under his hand.

"Get off home and sleep now, Banquo. And say hello to Fleance from me."

"I will. Good night."

Macbeth crossed the square, pensive. Sometimes good men did die for no need, he thought. And sometimes there was a need. He entered the light from the Inverness, ignored the journalists' barked questions about Malcolm, about Duncan's bodyguards, about whether it really was he who had shot them both.

Inside, Lady received him.

"They broadcast the whole of the press conference live on TV, and you were fantastic," she said and hugged him. He wouldn't let her go again. He held her until he could feel heat returning to his body. Felt the wonderful electric currents down his back as her lips touched his ear and she whispered, "Chief Commissioner."

Home. With her. The two of them. This, this was all he wanted. But to have this you had to merit it. That is how it is in this world. And, he thought, also in the next.

"Are you home?"

Duff turned in the doorway to the children's room, to the surprised voice behind him. Meredith had put on a dressing gown and stood with her arms crossed, shivering.

"Just popped by," he whispered. "I didn't want to wake you. Doesn't Ewan want to sleep in his own room?" He nodded toward his son, who lay curled up in the bed beside his big sister.

Meredith sighed. "He's started going to Emily when he can't sleep. I thought you would be staying in town while you're working on these dreadful things?"

"Yes. Yes, but I had to escape for a while. Get some clean clothes. See if you all still existed. I thought I'd sleep a couple of hours in the guest room and then be on my way."

"All right, I'll make up the bed. Have you eaten?"

"I'm not hungry. I'll have a sandwich when I wake up."

"I can make you some breakfast. I can't sleep anyway."

"You go and sleep, Meredith. I'll be up for a bit, then I'll make up the bed."

"As you like." She stood there with her arms crossed looking at him, but in the darkness he couldn't see her eyes. She turned and went.

13

"BUT I WANT TO KNOW *why*," Duff said, placing his elbows on the table and his chin in his hands. "Why didn't Andrianov and Hennessy run off? Why would two treacherous bodyguards first kill their boss and then lie down for a sleep in the adjacent room, covered in blood and evidence from here to hell? Come on, you're detectives, you must have some bloody *suggestions* at least!"

He looked around. Several of the Homicide Unit's twelve detectives sat in the room in front of him, but the only one who opened his mouth did so to yawn. It was Monday morning—perhaps that was why they were so uncommunicative, looked so ill at ease and switched-off? No, these faces would look just as tired tomorrow unless someone got a grip on things. There was a reason the Homicide Unit had been without a formal leader for the two months that had passed since Duncan had given the previous head an ultimatum: resign or an internal inquiry will be set up to investigate suspected corruption. There were no qualified applicants. Under Kenneth, the Homicide Unit had had the lowest clear-up rate in the country, and corruption was not the only reason. While the Homicide Unit in Capitol got the best in the field, the Homicide Unit at police HQ had only the dregs: the apathetic and the dysfunctional.

"This has to be turned round," Duncan had said. "The success or failure of the Homicide Unit determines to a large extent people's confidence in the police. That's why I'm putting one of our finest officers on the case. You, Duff."

Duncan had known how to serve up bad news to his staff in an inspiring way. Duff groaned. He had a pile of reports beside him worth less than the paper they were written on—meaninglessly detailed interviews with guests at Inverness Casino all telling the same story: they hadn't seen or heard anything apart from the hellish weather. Duff knew the silence around the table might be because they were simply afraid of his fury, but he didn't give a damn. This wasn't a popularity contest, and if they had to be frightened into doing something, fine by him.

"So we think the guilty bodyguards just slept the sleep of the innocent, do we? As it had been a long day at work. Which of you idiots votes for that?"

No reaction.

"And who *doesn't* believe that?"

"Not of the innocent," said Caithness, who had just breezed in through the door. "Of the medicated. Apologies for my late arrival, but I had to pick up this." She waved something horribly resembling a report. Which it was, Duff established, as it landed in front of the pile on the table with a thud. More precisely, a forensic report. "Blood samples taken from Andrianov and Hennessy show they had enough benzodiazepines in their bodies to sleep for twelve hours." Caithness sat down on one of the unoccupied chairs.

"Bodyguards who take sleeping tablets?" Duff said in disbelief.

"They calm you down," said one guy rocking on a chair at the back of the room. "If you're going to assassinate your boss, you're probably a bit shaky. Lots of bank robbers take benzos."

"And that's why they fuck it up," said a detective with nervous twitches around his nose wearing a shoulder holster over a white polo-neck.

Laughter. Short-lived.

"What do you reckon, Caithness?" Duff said.

She shrugged. "Detection is not my field of expertise, but to me it seems pretty obvious that they needed to take something to calm their nerves, but they don't know a lot about drugs, so they messed up the dosage. During the murder the drugs worked as intended. Their reflexes were still fast, but the nervousness was gone, and the clean cuts show a steady hand. But after the murder, when the chemical really kicked in, they lost control of the situation. They wandered around getting blood all over themselves and in the end both simply fell asleep in chairs."

"Typical," said the polo-neck. "Once we nabbed two doped-up bank robbers who had fallen asleep in their getaway car at the lights. I'm not kidding. Criminals are so bloody stupid you can—"

"Thank you," Duff interrupted. "How do you know their reflexes were still fast?"

Caithness shrugged. "Whoever made the first stab managed to remove their hand from the knife before the blood spurted out. Our blood-spatter analyst says the blood on the handle is from the spurt. It didn't run, drip or get smeared on."

"In which case I agree with all your other conclusions," Duff said. "Who disagrees?"

No reaction.

"Anyone agree?"

Mute nods.

"Good, let's say that answers that then. Now let's go to the other loose thread. Malcolm's suicide." Duff stood up. "His letter says that the Norse Riders threatened to kill his daughter if he didn't help them kill Duncan. My question is: instead of doing as Sweno and the Norse Riders want and taking his own life, why not go to Duncan and have his daughter moved to a safe house? Threats aren't exactly something new for the police. What do you think?"

The others looked at the floor, one another and out the window.

"No opinions? Really? A whole Homicide Unit of detectives and no—"

"Malcolm knows Sweno has contacts in the police," said the chair rocker. "He knows Sweno would have found his daughter anyway."

"Good, we're up and running," Duff said, bent over and pacing to and fro in front of them. "Let's assume Malcolm thinks his daughter can be saved by doing as Sweno says. Or by dying so that Sweno no longer has any reason to kill his daughter. OK?" He saw that none of those present had a clue where he was going.

"So if Malcolm—as the letter suggests—cannot live if either he loses his daughter or he becomes an accessory to Duncan's murder, why didn't he commit suicide *before* Duncan was murdered and save them both?"

The faces gaped at him.

"If I might . . ." Caithness began.

"Please, Inspector."

"Your question might be logical, but the human psyche doesn't work like that."

"Doesn't it?" Duff replied. "I think it does. There's something about Malcolm's apparent suicide that doesn't tally. Our brains will always—with great accuracy and based on available information—weigh up the pros and cons and then make an irrefutably logical decision."

"If the logic's irrefutable, why, despite having no new information, do we sometimes feel remorse?"

"Remorse?"

"Remorse, Inspector Duff." Caithness looked him straight in the eye. "It's a feeling in people with human qualities that tells us we wish something that we've done, undone. We can't exclude the possibility that Malcolm was like that."

Duff shook his head. "Remorse is a sign of illness. Einstein said proof of insanity is when someone goes through the same thought process again hoping to get a different answer."

"Then Einstein's contention can be refuted if, over time, we draw different conclusions. Not because the information has changed in any way, but because people can do that."

"People don't change!"

Duff noticed that the officers in the room had woken up and were following attentively now. They perhaps suspected that this exchange with Caithness was no longer only about Malcolm's death.

"Perhaps Malcolm changed," Caithness said. "Perhaps Duncan's death changed him. That can't be ruled out."

"Nor can we rule out the possibility that he left a suicide letter, threw his police badge in the sea and did a runner," Duff said. "As regards human qualities and all that."

The door opened. It was an officer from the Narcotics Unit. "Phone call for you, Inspector Duff. He says it's about Malcolm and it's urgent. And he *only* wants to speak to you."

Lady stood in the middle of the bedroom looking at the man sleeping in her bed. In *their* bed. It was gone nine o'clock, she'd had her breakfast a long time ago, but there was still no life in the body under the silk sheets.

She sat down on the side of the bed, stroked his cheek, tugged at his thick black curls and shook him. A narrow strip of white appeared under his eyelids.

"Chief Commissioner! Wake up! The town's on fire!"

She laughed as Macbeth groaned and rolled onto his side, his back to her. "What's the time?"

"Late."

"I dreamed it was Sunday."

"You dreamed a lot, I think."

"Yes, that bloody . . ."

"What?"

"Nothing. I heard storm bells. But then I realized they were church bells. Summoning churchgoers to confession and a christening."

"I told you not to say that word."

"Christening?"

"Macbeth!"

"Sorry."

"The press conference is in less than two hours. And they'll be wondering what's happened to their chief commissioner."

He swung his legs out of bed. Lady stopped him, held his face between her hands and inspected him carefully. The pupils were small. Again.

She pulled a stray hair from his eyebrow.

"Also we've got a dinner this evening," she said, searching for more. "You haven't forgotten, have you?"

"Is it really right to have it so close after Duncan's passing-away?"

"It's a dinner to cultivate connections, not a banquet. And we still have to eat, darling."

"Who's coming?"

"Everyone I've asked. The mayor. Some of your colleagues." She found a gray hair, but it slipped between her long red nails. "We're going to discuss how to enforce the regulations for the casinos. It's in today's leader column that the Obelisk is apparently running a prostitution racket under cover of the casino and that therefore it should be closed."

"It doesn't help that your editor chum writes what you want him to if no one reads his newspapers."

"No. But now I've got a chief commissioner as my husband."

"Ow!"

"You should get a few more gray hairs. They look good on bosses. I'll talk to my hairdresser today. Perhaps he can discreetly dye your temples."

"My temples aren't visible."

"Exactly. That's why we'll get your hair cut—so they are."

"Never!"

"Mayor Tourtell might think his town should have a chief commissioner who looks like a grown man, not a boy."

"Oh? Are you worried?"

Lady shrugged. "Normally the mayor wouldn't interfere with the police hierarchy, but he's the one who appoints the new chief commissioner. We just have to be sure he doesn't get any funny ideas."

"And how can we do that?"

"Well, we might have to ensure we have some hold over Tourtell in the unlikely event that he cuts up rough. But don't you worry about that, darling."

"All right. Apropos cutting up rough . . ."

She stopped searching for unruly hairs. She recognized the tone. "Is there something you haven't told me, dearest?"

"Banquo . . ."

"What about him?"

"I've begun to wonder whether I can trust him. Whether he hasn't made some cunning plan for himself and Fleance." He took a deep breath, and she knew he was about to tell her something important. "Banquo didn't kill Malcolm yesterday, he sent him off to Capitol. He made some excuse about this not being a life we risked anything by sparing."

She knew he was waiting for her reaction. When none was forthcoming he remarked she didn't seem so dumbfounded.

She smiled.

"This is not the time to be dumbfounded. What do you think he's planning?"

"He claims he's frightened Malcolm into silence, but I'm guessing the two of them have concocted something that will give Banquo a better and surer payoff than he's getting with me."

"Darling, surely you don't think that nice old Banquo has any ambition to become chief commissioner?"

"No, no, Banquo has always been someone who wants to be led, not to lead. This is about his son, Fleance. I'm only fifteen years older than Fleance, and by the time I retire Fleance will be old and gray himself. So it's better for him to be the crown prince to an older man like Malcolm."

"You're just tired, my love. Banquo's much too loyal to want to do anything like that. You said yourself he would burn in hell for you."

"Yes, he has been loyal. And so have I to him." Macbeth got up and stood in front of the big gold-framed mirror on the wall. "But if you take a closer look, hasn't this mutual loyalty been more advantageous for Banquo? Hasn't he been the hyena who follows the lion's footprints and eats prey he hasn't killed himself? I made him second-in-command in SWAT and my deputy in Organized Crime. I would say he's been well paid for the small services he's performed for me."

"All the more reason why you can count on his loyalty, darling."

"Yes, that's what I thought too. But now I see . . ." Macbeth frowned and went closer to the mirror. Placed a hand on its surface to check if there was something there. "He loved me like a father loves a son, but that love turned to hatred when he drank the poison of envy. I passed him on the way up, and instead of him being my boss I became his. And as well as obeying my orders he has had to tolerate the unspoken contempt of his own blood, Fleance, who has seen his father bow his head to the cuckoo in the nest, Macbeth. Have you ever looked into a dog's faithful brown eyes as it looks up at you, wagging its tail and hoping for food? It sits there, still, waiting, because that's what it's been trained to do. And you smile at it, pat its head, and you can't see the hatred behind the obedience. You can't see that if it got the opportunity, if it saw its chance to escape punishment, it would attack you, it would tear at your throat; your death would be its breath of freedom and it would leave you half-eaten in some filthy corridor."

"Darling, what *is* the matter with you?"

"That's what I dreamed."

"You're paranoid. Banquo really is your friend! If he was planning to betray you he could have just gone to Malcolm and told him about your schemes."

"No, he knows he'll be stronger if he plays his ace at the end. First kill me, a dangerous murderer, and then bring back Malcolm as chief commissioner. What a heroic deed! How can you reward a man like that and his family?"

"Do you really believe this?"

"No," said Macbeth. He was standing close to the mirror now, his nose touching the glass, which had misted up. "I don't believe it, I *know* it. I can *see*. I can see the two of them. Banquo and Fleance. I have to forestall them, but how?" Suddenly he turned to her. "How? You, my only one, you have to help me. You have to help *us*."

Lady crossed her arms. However warped Macbeth's reasoning sounded, there was some sense in it. He *might* be right. And if he wasn't, Banquo was still a fellow conspirator and a potential witness and blabber. The fewer there were of them, the better. And what real *use* did they have for Banquo and Fleance? None. She sighed. As Jack would say, *If you've got less than twelve in blackjack you ask for another card. Because you can't lose.*

"Invite them here one evening," she said. "Then we know where they are."

"And we do it here?"

"No, no, there have been enough murders at the Inverness; one more would cast suspicion on us and also frighten away the clientele. We'll do it on the road."

Macbeth nodded. "I'll ask Banquo and Fleance to come by car. I'll tell them we've promised someone a lift home with them. I know exactly the route he'll take, so if I tell them to be punctual we'll know to the minute where on the route they'll be. Do you know what, woman of my dreams?"

Yes, she thought, as he embraced her, but let him say it anyway.

"I love you above everything on this earth and in the sky above."

Duff found the young boy sitting on a bollard at the edge of the quay. There was a break in the rain, and more light than usual penetrated the layer of white cloud above them. But out in the river new troops of bluish-gray clouds stood lined up ready to ride in on the northwesterly wind against them—all you could rely on in this town.

"I'm Duff. Are you the person who rang about Malcolm?"

"Cool scar," the boy said, straightening his eyepatch. "They said you weren't the head of Narco anymore?"

"You said it was urgent."

"It's always urgent, Mr. Narco Boss."

"Suits me fine. Spit it out."

"*Fork* it out, I think we say."

"Oh, so that's why it's urgent. When do you have to have your next shot?"

"A couple of hours ago. And as this is important enough for the boss himself to show up, I think we'll say you pay for not only the next one, but the next ten."

"Or I wait half an hour and you'll happily spit it out for half the price. Another half an hour and it'll cost half again . . ."

"I cannot deny this, Mr. Narco Boss, but the question is: which of us is in a greater hurry? I read about Malcolm in the papers this morning and recognized him in the photo. Drowned, kind of. Deputy chief commissioner and shit. Heavy stuff."

"Come on, lad, and I'll pay you what it's worth."

The one-eyed boy chuckled. "Sorry, Mr. Narco Boss, but I've stopped trusting the fuzz. Here's your first bite. I wake up after nodding off, sitting between the lines of containers you can see over there, where you can shoot up and have a trip without being robbed, know what I mean? No one sees me, but I can see him, Malcolm, on the other side of the canal. Well, Narco Boss? First shot's for free, the next one will cost you big time. Heard that one before?" The boy laughed.

"Not sure I'm hooked there," Duff said. "We know Malcolm was here, we found his car."

"But you didn't know he wasn't alone here. Or who was here with him."

From bitter experience Duff knew a junkie told more lies than the truth, especially if that way they could finance their next shot. But, as a rule, a junkie preferred easier and quicker ways of tricking you than ringing HQ and insisting on talking to one of the unit heads, then waiting an hour in the rain, and all of that without a guaranteed payment.

"And you know that, do you?" Duff asked. "Who this person is?"

"I've seen him before, yes."

Duff took out his wallet. Produced a wad, counted, passed the banknotes to the boy.

"I was thinking of calling Macbeth himself," the boy said as he recounted. "But then I realized he would probably refuse to believe me when I told him who it was."

"Personal?"

"That Malcolm was talking to Macbeth's sidekick," the boy said. "Old guy, white hair."

Duff gasped involuntarily. "Banquo?"

"I dunno what his name is, but I've seen him with Macbeth at the station."

"And what were Banquo and Malcolm talking about?"

"They were too far away for me to hear."

"What erm . . . did it seem as if they were talking about? Were they laughing? Or were there loud, angry voices?"

"Impossible to say. The rain was hammering down on the containers and mostly they had their backs to me. They might have been arguing.

The old boy was waving his shooter for a while. But then things quietened down, they got into a Volvo and drove off. The old boy was driving."

Duff scratched his head. Banquo and Malcolm in cahoots?

"This is too much," the boy said, holding up a note.

Duff looked down at him. A junkie giving him change? He took the note. "You didn't tell me this just for the money for another shot, did you?"

"Eh?"

"You said you'd read the papers and knew this was heavy stuff. And it is. So heavy that if you'd rung a journalist with this story you'd have got ten times more than from a policeman. So either it's Hecate who sent you to spread false info or you've got another agenda."

"Go to hell, Mr. Narco Boss."

Duff grabbed the junkie's collar and pulled him off the bollard. The boy weighed almost nothing.

"Listen to me," Duff said, trying to avoid inhaling the boy's stinking breath. "I can put you behind bars, and let's see then what you think when you hit cold turkey and you know you've got two days in the wilderness in front of you. Or you tell me now why you came to me. You've got five seconds. Four . . ."

The boy glared back at Duff.

"Three . . ."

"You piece of cop shit, you're fuckin' . . ."

"Two . . ."

"My eye."

"One . . ."

"My eye, I said!"

"What about it?"

"I only wanted to help you catch the man that took my eye."

"Who was it?"

The boy snorted. "The same guy that's busting your arse. Don't you know who's behind all this shit? There's only one person in this town who can kill a chief commissioner and get away with it, and that's the Invisible Hand."

Hecate?

14

MACBETH DROVE ALONG THE DIRTY road between the old factories. The cloud hung so low and Monday-gray over the chimneys that it was difficult to see which were smoking, but some of the gates had CLOSED signs or chains secured across them like ironic bow ties.

The press conference had passed painlessly. Painlessly because he had been too high to feel anything. He had concentrated on sitting back in a relaxed manner with his arms crossed and leaving the questions to Lennox and Caithness. Apart from those directed at him personally, which he had answered with, "We cannot comment on that at the present time," delivered with an expression that said they had much too much information and were in full control. Calm and assured. That was the impression he hoped he had given. An acting chief commissioner who did not allow himself to be affected by the hysteria around him, who answered journalists' shrill questions—"Doesn't the public have the right to know?"—with a somewhat resigned, tolerant smile.

Although then Kite, the reporter with the rolled "r"s, had said in his radio program right after the press conference that the acting chief commissioner had yawned a lot, seemed uninvolved and looked at his watch a lot. But to hell with Kite. In the Patrols Section they definitely thought the new chief commissioner was involved enough as he had personally dropped in and redirected the patrols from District 2 West to District 1 East. He explained it was time the neighborhoods of normal people were also patrolled. It was an important signal to send: the police didn't prioritize districts with money and influence. And if Kite had been annoyed, Banquo had at least been happy to receive a dinner invitation with instructions to bring along Fleance.

"Good for the lad to get used to mixing with the big boys," Macbeth had said. "And then I think you should decide what you'd like to do. Take over SWAT, Organized Crime or become the deputy chief commissioner."

"Me?"

"Don't get stressed now, Banquo. Just give it some thought, OK?"

And Banquo had chortled and shaken his head. Gentle, as always. As though he didn't have an evil thought in his mind. Or at least he didn't have a conscience about having one. Well, tonight the traitor would meet his maker and destroyer.

No one was on the gate of the Norse Riders' clubhouse. They probably didn't have anyone left to stand guard.

Macbeth got out of his car and went into the clubroom. Stopped in the doorway and looked around. It felt like a strangely long time ago since he had stood there beside Duff and scanned the same room. Now the long table had gone, and at the bar stood three men with low-slung paunches in the club's leather jackets and two women with high-slung breasts. One was holding a baby, who was wriggling around under a muscular maternal arm tattooed with the name SEAN.

"Colin, isn't that the . . . ?" she whispered.

"Yes," said the completely bald man with the walrus mustache in a low voice. "That's the one who got Sean."

Macbeth remembered the name from the report. It was strange how he kept forgetting the names of people he met, but never those that appeared in reports. Sean. He was the one who had been on guard at the gate, the one Macbeth had knifed in the shoulder and whom they had used as a hostage, one of those who was still in custody.

The man glared at the police officer in slack-jawed fury. Macbeth took a deep breath. It was so quiet he could hear the floorboards creak under his heels as he walked over to the bar. He addressed the leather jacket behind the counter and caught himself thinking as he opened his mouth that he shouldn't have sniffed that last line before leaving HQ. Brew had a tendency to make him cocky. And his concern was confirmed by what came out: "Hello, not many people here, where is everybody? Oh, yes, that's right. In the slammer. Or the morgue. A Glendoran, please."

Macbeth saw the barman's eyes flit across, knew an attack was imminent from his left and he still had oceans of time. Macbeth had always had good reflexes, but with brew he was like a fly—he could yawn, scratch his back and study his watch with its incredibly slow second hand while a fist was on its way. But then, as Colin with the walrus mustache thought he was about to connect, Macbeth swayed back, and the fist that was heading for his newly trimmed temple met air. Macbeth lifted and swung his elbow to the side, barely felt the impact, only heard a groan, the crunch of cartilage, staggering footsteps and bar stools toppling over.

"On the rocks," Macbeth said.

Then he turned to the man beside him, in time to see he had clenched his right hand and drawn his shoulder back to deliver a punch. As it arrived, Macbeth lifted his hand and met Colin's halfway. But instead of the expected crunch of bone on bone, there came the smooth sound of steel in flesh followed by a dull thud when Colin's knuckles hit the hilt. Then his long drawn-out scream when he saw the dagger running up through his clenched hand into his forearm. Macbeth pulled out the dagger with a jerk.

". . . and some soda."

The man with the walrus mustache fell to his knees.

"What the hell is going on?" said a voice.

This came from the door to the garage. The man had a big beard and a leather jacket with three chevrons on each shoulder. Plus a sawn-off shotgun in his hands.

"I'm ordering," Macbeth said, turning to the barman, who still hadn't moved.

"Ordering what?" said the man, coming closer.

"Whiskey. Among other things."

"And what else?"

"You're the sergeant. You run the shop when Sweno's not here, don't you? By the way, where's he hiding this time?"

"Say what you came to say and get outta here, cop scum."

"I won't hear a bad word about the place, but the service could be friendlier and quicker. What about you and me doing this in peace and quiet, in a back room, Sarge?"

The man looked at Macbeth for some moments. Then he lowered the gun barrel. "There's not much more damage you can do here anyway."

"I know. And Sweno's going to like my commission, I can guarantee you that."

The sergeant's little office—for that's what it was—had posters of motorbikes on the walls and a very small selection of engine parts on the shelves. With a desk, telephone and in and out trays. And a chair for visitors.

"Don't make yourself too comfortable, cop."

"My order is for a hit job."

If the sergeant was shocked he didn't show it. "Wrong address. We don't do that stuff for cops anymore."

"So the rumor's true? You used to do hit jobs for Kenneth's men?"

"If there was nothing else . . ."

"Only this time it isn't a competitor you would have to dispatch into the beyond," Macbeth said, leaning forward in his chair. "It's two cops. And the payment is your Norse Riders being set free immediately afterward and all charges dropped."

The sergeant raised an eyebrow. "And how would you do that?"

"Procedural error. Spoiled evidence. This shit happens all the time. And if the chief commissioner says we haven't got a case, we haven't got a case."

The sergeant crossed his arms. "Carry on."

"The person who has to be dispatched is the guy who ensured the dope you were going to live off ended up in the river. Inspector Banquo." Macbeth watched the sergeant nod slowly. "The other is a cop sprog who will be in the same car."

"And why are they to be expedited?"

"Is that important?"

"Usually I wouldn't ask, but this is police officers we're talking about, and that means there's going to be loads of trouble."

"Not with these ones. We know Inspector Banquo is working with Hecate, we just can't prove it, so we have to get rid of him another way. This is the best option from our point of view."

The sergeant nodded again. Macbeth had counted on him understanding this logic.

"How do we know you'll keep your part of a potential deal?"

"Well," Macbeth said, squinting at the calendar girl above the sergeant's head. "We have five witnesses in the bar who can vouch for Acting Chief Commissioner Macbeth being here in person and giving you a commission. You don't think I'd want to give you any reason to make that public, do you?"

The sergeant leaned back in his chair so far it touched the wall, studying Macbeth while making growling noises and pulling at his beard. "And when and where would this job potentially take place?"

"Tonight. You know Gallows Hill in District Two West?"

"That's where they hanged my great-great-grandfather."

"On the main road above the lanes where the West Enders go shopping there's a big junction."

"I know the one you mean."

"They'll be in a black Volvo at the lights sometime between half past six and ten to seven. Probably at exactly a quarter to. He's a punctual man."

"Hm. There are always a lot of patrol cars there."

Macbeth smiled. "Not tonight there won't be."

"Oh, really? I'll think about it and give you an answer at four."

Macbeth laughed. "*Sweno* will think about it, you mean. Great. Pick up a pen, and I'll give you my phone number and the registration number of the Volvo. And one more thing."

"Uh-huh?"

"I want their heads."

"Whose?"

"The two cops. I want their heads. Delivered to the door."

The sergeant stared at Macbeth as if he considered him insane.

"The customer requires a receipt," Macbeth said. "Last time I ordered a hit job I didn't ask for a receipt and that was an error. I didn't get what I ordered."

Late in the afternoon Duff made a decision.

His thoughts had been churning for hours in a brain where the traffic felt as slow-moving as that on the road in front of him and the way ahead as full of choices. They still hadn't replaced the railings on Kenneth Bridge, so the traffic eastbound was being redirected to the old bridge and the queue backed up to District 2, where Duff's car moved forward at a snail's pace from junction to junction, which all threw up the question: left, right, straight ahead, what's the fastest?

Duff's own particular junction was this.

Should he go to Macbeth and the others with what he had found out on the quayside? Should he keep it to himself? But suppose the one-eyed boy wasn't telling the truth or Banquo was able to deny the accusations? What would the consequences be for Duff if in this chaotic situation he made false accusations against Banquo, who, with Macbeth, had suddenly become a powerful figure?

Duff could of course simply present the information the way he had been given it and let Lennox and Macbeth evaluate it themselves, but then he would lose the chance to register a badly needed personal triumph by single-handedly arresting and unmasking Banquo.

On the other hand, he couldn't afford another blunder after his raid on the container harbor. It had cost him the Organized Crime appointment; another blunder could easily cost him his job.

Another junction: Organized Crime would be up for grabs again if Macbeth became chief commissioner, and if Duff seized the opportunity now, dared and won, the unit could be his.

He had weighed up asking Caithness for her opinion, but then the cat would be out of the bag, he couldn't play innocent and would be forced to do *something*. Take a risk.

The way he had chosen in the end was one where he didn't risk much, but where he would still get the credit if it all went as he hoped.

Duff turned off the little railway bridge and into the yard in front of the modest brick building on the other side. It had taken him more than three quarters of an hour to cover the short distance from HQ to Banquo's address.

"Duff," said Banquo, who opened the door seconds after Duff had rung the bell. "What gives?"

"A party by the looks of it," Duff said.

"Yes, and that's why I can't decide whether to take this or not." Banquo held up the holster with his service gun.

"Leave it behind. It'll only make a bulge in your suit. But that tie knot is no good."

"Isn't it?" Banquo said, pressing his chin down against his white shirt collar in a futile attempt to see the knot. "It's been good enough for fifty years, ever since I was confirmed."

"That's a poor man's knot, Banquo. Come on, let me show you . . ."

Banquo warded off Duff's helping hand by covering the knot. "I *am* a poor man, Duff. And I assume you came here to get help, not offer it."

"That's true enough, Banquo. Can I come in?"

"I'd have liked to offer you help and coffee, but I'm afraid we're on our way out." Banquo put his gun holster on the hat shelf behind him and called up the stairs: "Fleance!"

"Coming!" was the response.

"We can go outside in the meantime," Banquo said, buttoning up his coat.

They stood on the covered white steps. Rain gurgled cheerily down from the gutters while Banquo offered Duff a cigarette and lit his own when the inspector declined.

"I was back in the container harbor today," Duff said. "I met a boy, one of our young drug addicts, who wanted to talk to me. He's got only one eye. He told me how he lost the other one."

"Mmhm."

"He'd been driven crazy with his craving for dope but was broke. Down at central station he met an old man and begged him for some money. The old man had a walking stick with a gold tip."

"Hecate?"

"The old man stopped, took out a bag which he dangled in front of the boy and said it was top-quality brew straight from the pot. The boy could have it if he would do two things for him. The first was to answer the question: which sense would you be most afraid to lose? When the boy replied it would be his eyesight, the old man said he wanted one of his eyes."

"That *was* Hecate."

"When the boy asked the old man why he wanted his eye, Hecate answered that he had everything, so all that was left for him was what was most valuable to the buyer, not to himself. And after all it was only half his eyesight, well, not even that. And think how much more valuable his second eye would be afterward. Indeed loss and gain would almost be equal."

"I don't understand that."

"Maybe not, but that's the way some people are. They desire power itself more than what it can give them. They'd rather own a worthless tree than the edible fruit that grows on it. Just so that they can point to it and say, 'That's mine.' And then cut it down."

Banquo blew out a cloud of smoke. "What did the boy decide to do?"

"He was helped by a man-woman, who was with the old man, to take out the eye. And when he got his shot afterward all the pain he had ever known was gone—it smoothed all the scars, removed all the bad memories. The boy said it was so wonderful that even today he can't say he has any regrets. He's still chasing after it, the perfect shot."

"And what was he after today when you met him?"

"The same. Plus the person who had taken his eye just because he could."

"He'll have to take his place in the queue of Hecate-chasers."

"He was thinking instead that he would help us catch Hecate."

"And how would a poor brew slave do that?"

"Malcolm's so-called suicide letter tries to finger the Norse Riders. But the boy thinks Hecate's behind everything. Both the letter and the murder of Duncan. And Hecate's in league with Malcolm. And perhaps others in the force."

"A popular theory nowadays." Banquo flicked the ash off the cigarette and looked at his watch. "Was he paid for that?"

"No," Duff said. "He wasn't paid for anything until he told me he'd seen Malcolm down on the quay before he went missing. And he'd been with you."

The cigarette on its way to Banquo's mouth stopped. He laughed. "Me? I don't believe it."

"He described you and your car."

"Neither I nor my car was there. And I find it difficult to believe you could have paid public money for such a claim. So which of you is bluffing? This junkie then or you now?"

A gust of cold wind blew, and Duff shivered. "The boy says he saw Malcolm and an older man he'd seen with Macbeth. A Volvo saloon. And a gun. Wouldn't you have paid for that information, Banquo?"

"Only if I was desperate." Banquo stubbed his cigarette out on the iron railing which flanked the steps. "And not even then if it concerned a police colleague."

"Because you always rate loyalty very high, don't you?"

"A police force cannot function without the loyalty of individuals. It's a prerequisite."

"So how far does your loyalty to the force stretch?"

"I'm a simple man, Duff, and I don't understand what you mean."

"If you mean what you say about loyalty then you have to give us Malcolm. For the sake of the force."

Duff pointed out into the gray soup of rain and mist in front of them. "For this town's sake. Where is Duncan's murderer hiding in Capitol?"

Banquo blew the ash from the cigarette end and put it in his coat pocket. "I know nothing about Malcolm. Fleance! Sorry, Inspector, but we're going out to dinner."

Duff ran after Banquo, who had walked down the three steps into the rain. "Speak to me, Banquo! I can see you're weighed down by guilt and a bad conscience. You're not an evil, cunning person. You've just been led into temptation by someone higher in rank than you by trusting their judgment. And so you've been betrayed. He *has* to be arrested, Banquo!"

"Fleance!" Banquo screamed in the direction of the house as he unlocked the car in the yard.

"Do you want us to continue in this downward spiral into chaos and anarchy, Banquo? Our forefathers built railways and schools. We build brothels and casinos."

Banquo got into the car and hooted the horn twice. The house door opened, and a suited Fleance emerged onto the steps struggling to open an umbrella.

Banquo cracked open the window, presumably because the car was misting up inside, and Duff put his hands on the window and tried to press it down farther while talking through the narrow opening. "Listen, Banquo. If you do this, if you confess, there's not a lot I can do for you, you know that. But I promise you no one will be allowed to hurt Fleance. His prospects won't be those of a traitor's son but those of the son of a man who sacrificed himself for the town. You have my word."

"Hi. Inspector Duff, isn't it?"

Duff straightened up. "Hi, Fleance. That's right. Have a nice dinner."

"Thanks."

Duff waited until Fleance had got into the passenger's seat and Banquo had started the engine. Then he set off for his car.

"Duff!"

He turned.

Banquo had opened his door. "It's not as you think," he shouted.

"Isn't it?"

"No. Meet me by Bertha at midnight."

Duff nodded.

The Volvo was put into gear, and father and son went through the gate into the mist.

15

LADY WENT UP THE LAST metal rungs of the ladder to the door leading to the flat roof of Inverness Casino. She opened it and stared into the darkness. All that could be heard was the mumbled whisper of the rain. It seemed that everything and everyone had secrets. She was about to turn and go back in when a crackle of lightning lit up the roof, and she saw him. He was standing by the edge of the roof and looking down into Thrift Street, at the back of the casino. Before she had persuaded the town council to clean it up, the prostitutes had stood there in the barely lit street and not only offered themselves but often performed their services right there, in the archways, in cars, on cars or up against walls. When the National Railway Network had been here it was said that the boss had had all the windows facing Thrift Street bricked up so that his subordinates could concentrate on work and not the filth outside.

She opened her umbrella and went over to Macbeth.

"Out here getting wet, darling? I've been looking for you. The guests for dinner will be here soon." She looked down the smooth black windowless walls like a fortress that led down to Thrift Street. She knew every yard of the street. And that was reason enough to keep the windows bricked up.

"What can you see down there?"

"An abyss," he said. "Fear."

"My dearest, don't be so gloomy."

"No?"

"What would the point of all our victories be if they didn't bring a smile to our lips?"

"We've won only a couple of battles. The war has barely begun. And already I'm being consumed by this fear. God knows where it comes from.

Give me an armed biker gang coming toward me rather than this serpent we've slashed at but haven't killed."

"Stop it, my love. No one can catch us now."

"Duncan. I can see him down there. And I envy him. He's dead—I've granted him peace—while all he gives me is anxiety and these nightmares."

"It's brew, right? It's brew that gives you nightmares."

"Darling . . ."

"Do you remember what you said about Collum? You said brew drove people crazy. You have to stop taking it or you'll lose everything we've won! Do you hear me? Not another grain of brew!"

"But the nightmares aren't a product of my imagination. The sergeant called me. The deal is done. Or have you forgotten the grave deed we have planned for this evening? Have you repressed the thought that my only father and best friend are going to be slaughtered?"

"I don't know what you're talking about and nor do you. When what's done is done, there'll be nothing to brood over. And brew won't give you consolation or courage. Now your soul will receive its reward. So no more brew! Put a tie on now, my love. And a smile." She took his hand. "Come on, let's charm them to pieces."

Caithness sat in an armchair with a glass of red wine in her hand listening to the rain on the attic window and Kite on the radio. He was talking about the problem of an acting chief commissioner in practice having more power than a democratically elected mayor, all because of Kenneth's tampering with the town's laws and statutes. She liked the way he rolled his "r"s and his calm voice. Liked the way he wasn't afraid to shine with his knowledge and intelligence. But most of all she liked the way he was always *against* something. Against Kenneth, against Tourtell, yes, even against Duncan, who himself had been against so much. It had to be a lonely furrow. And who would want to be lonely if they had a choice?

She had occasionally wondered whether to send an anonymous letter to his radio station, saying how reassuring it was that there were still principled people like him, someone who took on the job of a lone, fearless watchdog. Speaking of which. Wasn't that the second time she had heard that sound from the front door? She turned down the radio. Listened.

There it was again. She crept over to the door and put her ear against it. A familiar creaking sound. She opened the door.

"Duff. What are you doing?"

"I . . . erm . . . am standing here. And thinking." He had his hands stuck deep down in his coat pockets and was rocking on his much-too-large shoes with the creaking soles.

"Why didn't you ring the bell?"

"I have," Duff said. "I . . . The bell obviously doesn't work."

She opened the door wide, but he still seemed to be caught in two minds.

"Why so glum, Duff?"

"Am I glum?"

"Sorry, I know there's not much to be cheery about right now, but are you coming or going?"

His eyes flitted around. "Can I stay until midnight?"

"Of course, but come in, will you? I'm cold."

The sergeant rested his hands on the handlebars of his Honda CB450 "Black Bomber." It was less than five years since he had bought it, and on good days he could squeeze a ton out of it. Nevertheless it felt a bit old now that the Honda CB750 superbike was on the market. He looked at his watch. Sixteen minutes to seven. The rush hour had subsided now, and darkness had fallen early. Waiting beside the road, he could see every single car that came toward the Gallows Hill junction. Sweno had sent them reinforcements from the club down south: three members, cousins they called them, had jumped on their bikes and arrived in town in less than three hours. They were sitting on their bikes, ready, by the pumps at the petrol station on the road along which the car was supposed to be coming. Appraising the models and number plates. Down the road, on the other side of the junction, he could see Colin standing on climbing irons up one of the posts by the junction box. The only entertainment they'd had so far was when they had done a trial run, and Colin had stuck a screwdriver in and turned. Brakes squealed on the road when the lights, without any warning, had changed from green to red. And seconds later, when they had changed back to green, engine revs had risen hesitantly and carefully, and cars crept across the junction while the sergeant flashed his headlights to signal to Colin that things were working as they should.

The sergeant looked at his watch again. A quarter to seven.

Sweno had needed a little time to make the decision, but the sergeant had the feeling that was more for reasons of caution than doubt. And that was confirmed when the three cousins from the south had drawn up in front of the club gate, a Harley Davidson chopper with high handlebars, a Harley FL 1200 Electra Glide and a Russian Ural with a sidecar and mounted machine gun. The guy on the Electra Glide had a sword with him, not curved like Sweno's saber, but it would do the job.

Fourteen minutes to seven.

"Fleance . . ."

Something in his father's voice made Fleance glance across. His father was always calm, but when something was wrong he had this voice that was even calmer. Like the time Fleance was seven and his father came home from the hospital after visiting Mum and said his name in that same eerily calm way.

"Change of plans for this evening." His father shifted lanes, tucked in behind a Ford Galaxie. "And the next few days."

"Really?"

"You're going to Capitol. Tonight."

"Capitol?"

"Something's happened. You'll have lots of questions, my lad, but you won't get any answers just yet. Drop me off at the Inverness, then you drive on at once. Pop home, take only what you need with you and go to Capitol. Drive steadily, not too fast, and you'll get there late tomorrow. Got that?"

"Yes, but what—"

"No questions. You should stay there a few days, maybe weeks. As you know, your mother inherited a little flat. Take the notepad from the glove compartment."

"The one-room flat she called the rat hole?"

"Yes. No wonder we never managed to sell it. Fortunately, I have to say now. The address is Sixty-six Tannery Street, District Six. Right next to the Dolphin Nightclub. Second floor on the right. You're safe there. Have you written that down?"

"Yes." Fleance tore out the page and put the notepad back in the glove compartment. "But I'll need a key, won't I? I mean, who'll let me in if it's empty?"

"It's not empty."

"Tenants?"

"Not exactly; I've let poor old cousin Alfie stay there. He's so old and deaf he might not open up when you ring the bell, so you'll have to improvise."

"Dad?"

"Yes?"

"Has this got anything to do with what Duff was after? He seemed very . . . intense."

"Yes, but no more questions, Fleance. You'll just have to stay there, study some school books you take with you, get bored, but no phone calls, no letters, don't say a peep to anyone about where you are. Just do as I say, and I'll send for you when it's safe to return."

"Are *you* safe then?"

"You heard what I said."

Fleance nodded.

They drove in silence, the worn rubbers of the windscreen wipers squeaking and sounding as if they wanted to tell them something.

"Yes," Banquo said, "I'm safe. But take no notice of the news from now on, probably just lies. There's someone else staying there as well at the moment. I think he's got a mattress on the floor, so you take the sofa. If the rats haven't eaten it."

"Funny guy. Do you promise me you're safe?"

"Don't you worry . . ."

"The lights are red!"

Banquo jumped on the brakes and almost ended up on the rear bumper of the Galaxie, which obviously hadn't seen the lights change either.

"Here," Banquo said, passing his son a thick worn wallet. "Take the money, then you've got enough to make ends meet for a while."

Fleance took out the notes

"Bloody long time on red . . ." he heard his father mutter.

Fleance glanced in the side mirror. There was already a long queue behind them. On the outside of the queue a line of motorbikes was coming toward them.

"Strange," his father said. Again his much-too-calm voice. "Looks like the road ahead is on red too. And has been for a while."

"Dad, there are some motorbikes coming."

Fleance saw his father glance in the rearview mirror for a second. Then he put his foot down on the accelerator, wrenched the steering wheel to the right and let go of the clutch. The old car spun on the wet, oily tarmac, but squeezed out to the right of the queue. The hubcaps hit the high curb, and both cars screamed as if hurt when the Volvo scraped alongside the Galaxie and knocked off its side mirror as they passed.

A huge roar came from the street ahead. The lights had changed to green.

"Dad! Stop!"

But his father didn't stop; on the contrary, he slammed his foot down. They raced into the junction on a collision course with a lorry from the left and a bus from the right. And heard two horns blaring, one from either side, roaring a jarring chord as they emerged from between them. Fleance stared in the mirror as they shot down from Gallows Hill toward the center, and the painful music sank in pitch behind them. He saw the traffic lights had changed back to green and the motorbikes were already across the junction.

Macbeth stood with both feet firmly planted on the solid tiles at the entrance to Inverness Casino yet still felt he was at sea. In front of him an overweight man in a black suit struggled to get out of the rear seat of a limousine. The Inverness's red-clad doorman held the car door open and an umbrella in his hand as he hesitated between offering to pull him up or letting him retain his dignity. After the man had finally managed to complete the job without help but with some panting, Lady rushed forward.

"Our very own . . . my very own mayor!" She laughed and embraced him. Which was no mean feat, Macbeth thought, hearing himself let slip a silly snigger as he watched Lady's slender hands grasp Tourtell's well padded turtle shell.

"You become more handsome and more virile every time we meet," she twittered.

"And you, Lady, more beautiful and more mendacious. Macbeth . . ."

Macbeth shook hands, fascinated by how the flesh on the mayor's hand oozed away from under his thumb.

"And who's this young man?" Lady asked.

A brown-eyed, smooth-skinned boy with girlish good looks, so young he must have been in his teens, scurried around the limousine from the rear door on the opposite side. He smiled tentatively at Tourtell as if for help.

"This, Lady, is my son," Tourtell said.

"Silly billy, you don't have any children," Lady said, smacking the mayor on the lapel of his jacket.

"My *extra-marital* son," Tourtell amended, stroking the base of the boy's spine and winking at Macbeth with a chuckle. "I've only just found out about him, you know. You can see the likeness though, can't you, Lady?"

"You are and always will be a sly fox, dear Tourtell. Shall we give him a name?"

"What about Kasi Tourtell Junior?" said the mayor, stroking his Salvador Dalí mustache and emitting a booming laugh when Lady rolled her eyes.

"Get yourselves some refreshment in the warm," Lady said.

The two of them went through the door as she came to stand next to Macbeth.

"How dare he, the perverted pig," Macbeth said. "I thought Tourtell was one of the respectable guys."

"He's one of the respected guys, and that's all that counts, dear. Power gives you the freedom to do what you want without people losing their respect for you. At least now you're smiling."

"Am I?"

"Like an unhinged clown." Lady was already beaming at the taxi drawing up to the entrance. "Don't overdo the grin, darling. This is Janovic, a property investor from Capitol."

"Another scavenger buying up our factory sites for a song?"

"He looks at the casinos. Be nice and say hello, and at some point let drop a comment assuring him that street crime is already on its way down."

Fleance screamed instinctively and ducked when the rear window exploded.

"How many?" his father asked calmly and swerved hard to the right, down a cobbled side street. Fleance turned. The roar of the bikes behind them rose in volume like an enraged dragon.

"Five or six," Fleance shouted. "Give me your gun!"

"It wanted to stay at home tonight," Banquo said. "Hold tight." He twisted the steering wheel; the wheels hit the curb, and the Volvo jumped and cut the corner in front of a posh clothes shop as they turned left down an even narrower street. Fleance understood the strategy: in these one-way alleys at least the bikers couldn't come alongside and finish them off. But they were getting unremittingly close. Another bang behind them. Fleance hadn't as yet learned to differentiate between all types of firearms, which he knew his father could, but even he knew that was a shotgun. Which after all was better than—

A hail of bullets hammered against the car body.

—an automatic weapon.

His father executed another sudden turn with authority, as though he knew where he was going. They were well into the shopping area now, but the shops were closed and the streets almost deserted in the rain. Did his father know a way out of this labyrinth? In response Banquo suddenly steered the car to the right, past a sign bearing bad news.

"Dad, this is a cul-de-sac!"

Banquo didn't react.

"Dad!"

Still no reaction, only his eyes staring ahead in deep concentration, his hands clutching the wheel. Fleance only discovered now that blood was running down his father's face and inside the neck of his shirt, where its white collar, like blotting paper, had assumed a pink color from the welling blood. And there was something missing from where the blood was seeping out of his father's head. Fleance shifted his gaze to the steering wheel. That was why he wasn't answering. His ear. It lay stuck to the dashboard, a small, pale scrap of skin, shreds of flesh and blood.

Fleance raised his eyes to the windscreen. And there he saw, quite literally, the end. The blind alley culminated in a solid-looking timber house. The ground floor was a large partially illuminated shop window. It was approaching fast, and they showed no signs of stopping.

"Belt on, Fleance."

"Dad!"

"Now."

Fleance grabbed his seat belt, pulled it across his chest and just managed to buckle it before the front wheels hit the curb and they reared up. The bonnet hit the shop window in the middle, and Fleance had the feeling it had opened and they were flying through a curtain of white glass into whatever was inside. Then, as he looked around in amazement, knowing something was dislocated, there was a break in the course of events and he knew he must have passed out. There was an infernal ringing in his ears. His father lay motionless with his head on the wheel.

"Dad!"

Fleance shook him.

"Dad!"

No reaction. The windscreen was gone, and something on the bonnet was shining. Fleance had to blink before he realized it was what it looked like. Rings. Necklaces. Bracelets. And in front of him on the wall was written in gold letters: JACOBS & SONS. JEWELERS. They had driven into a bloody jewelry shop. And the ringing he could hear wasn't coming from his head, it was the burglar alarm. Now it dawned on him. The burglar alarm. All the town's banks, the casinos and larger jewelry shops were connected to the central switchboard at police HQ. Who immediately contacted patrol cars in the district. Dad had known where he was going after all.

Fleance tried to undo his seat belt, but couldn't. He yanked and tugged, but the buckle refused to move.

The sergeant sat on his bike, counted the seconds and looked at the car protruding from the shop in front of them. The alarm drowned most sounds, but he could see from the smoke coming out of the exhaust pipe that the engine was running.

"Whad are we waidin' for, eh?" asked the guy on the Electra Glide. There was something irritating about the way he spoke. "Led's go ged 'em."

"We'll wait awhile longer," the sergeant said and counted. "Twenty-one, twenty-two."

"How long, eh?"

"Until we know the guy who ordered this job has kept his promise," said the sergeant. Twenty-five, twenty-six.

"Doh. I wanna finish this head-choppin' stuff and leave this shide down."

"Wait." The sergeant quietly observed him. The guy looked like a grown man. Two grown men. The guy was as broad as a barn door and had muscles everywhere, even in his face. Yet he wore a brace on his teeth, like a boy. The sergeant had seen it before, in prison, where the inmates who pumped iron and took anabolic steroids grew such powerful jaw-bones that their teeth curled. Twenty-nine, thirty. Thirty seconds and no sirens. "Away you go," the sergeant said.

"Thanks." The barn door pulled a long-barreled Colt from his waist-band and the sword from its sheath, dismounted his bike and set off to-ward the car. He nonchalantly ran the sword blade along the wall and over the post of the NO PARKING sign. The sergeant studied the back of his leather jacket. A pirate flag with the skull over a swastika. No style. He sighed. "Cover him with the shotgun, Colin."

Colin smoothed his walrus mustache with a bandaged hand, then broke open a short-barreled shotgun and inserted two shells.

The sergeant saw a couple of faces appear in windows across the road, but still heard no sirens, only the monotonous, unceasing burglar alarm as the guy entered the shop and approached the car. He put the sword under his arm, pulled open the passenger door with his free hand and pointed the revolver at the person sitting there. The sergeant automatically clenched his teeth as he waited for the bang.

Fleance tore at the belt, but the infuriating buckle was stuck. He tried to wriggle out. Fleance raised his knees to his chin, swung himself round in the seat and placed his feet against the passenger door to push himself over toward his father and the driver's seat. At that moment he caught sight of the man stepping into the shop with a sword and a revolver in his hands. It was too late to get away now, and Fleance didn't even have time to think how frightened he was.

The passenger door was wrenched open. Fleance saw the gleam of a dental brace and a revolver being raised and realized the man was out of reach for the kick he had planned. So instead he reached out with one foot for the opened door in sheer desperation. A normal shoe wouldn't have fitted behind the internal door handle, but the long thin toe of Macbeth's old winklepickers slipped in easily. He glimpsed the blackness of eternity in the revolver muzzle, then pulled the door to as hard as he could. There was a smack as the door hit the man's wrist and jammed it in the opening. And a muffled thud as the revolver hit the floor.

Fleance heard swearing, slammed the door shut with one hand while searching for the revolver with the other.

The door was torn open again, and there stood the dental-brace man with a sword raised over his head. Fleance patted the floor everywhere—under the seat—where the hell had the gun gone? Dental Brace then obviously realized that the door opening was too narrow for him to swing the sword and he would have to stab with it. He brought his elbow back, aimed the point at Fleance and leaped at him. Fleance lashed out and met him halfway with two outstretched legs, which sent the guy staggering backward through the room to finally topple back and smash a glass counter in his fall.

"Colin," sighed the sergeant. "Please go in and bring this vaudeville to an end."

"Right, boss." Before dismounting Colin checked he would still be able to pull the trigger with the hand Macbeth had impaled with a dagger.

Fleance had given up his struggle, realizing that he was trapped, he wouldn't be able to free himself from the seat belt before it was too late. So he lay sideways on the seat, watched the guy with the sword stand up from behind the smashed counter, fragments of glass falling from his broad shoulders. He was more careful this time. Took up a position beyond Fleance's reach. Checked he had a good grip on the sword. Fleance knew he was aiming for where he could do most instant damage and remain out of Fleance's reach. His groin.

"Bloody shide down," the man snarled, spat on the sword, brought back his arm, took the necessary step closer and bared a row of clenched teeth. The soft, warm shop lighting made his brace sparkle, which for one instant looked like it belonged to the shop's inventory. Fleance raised the gun and fired. Glimpsed a surprised expression and a small black hole in the middle of the brace before the man fell.

The pianoforte's soft, discreet tones tickled Macbeth's ears.

"Dear guests, acquaintances, colleagues and friends of the casino," he said, looking at the faces surrounding him, "even if not everyone has arrived yet, I'd like on behalf of the woman you all know and fear—" muted polite laughter and nods to a laughing Lady "—to wish you a warm welcome and propose a toast before we take our seats at the table."

Colin stopped when he saw his cousin from the south fall to the floor. The noise of the shot had drowned the alarm, and he saw a hand holding a revolver sticking out of the car-door opening. He reacted quickly. Fired one barrel. Saw the shell hit, saw the light-colored inside of the door turn red, the window in the door explode and the revolver fall to the shop floor.

Colin walked quickly toward the motionless car. Adrenaline had made his senses so receptive that he took everything in. The faint vibration of the exhaust pipe, the absence of any heads in the smashed rear window and a sound he just recognized through the drone of the alarm. The belching sound of revving. *Shit!*

Colin ran the last steps to the door opening. On the passenger seat sat a suit-clad boy in a strangely distorted position. With his seat belt on, a blood-covered hand and his left foot stretched over to where the driver lay lifeless slumped over the wheel. Colin raised the shotgun as the engine raced, caught traction and the car rushed backward. The open door hit Colin in the chest, but he managed to stick out his left hand and cling to the top of the door. They raced out of the shop, but Colin didn't let go. He still had the shotgun in his aching right hand, but to get a shot into the car he would have to move it to under his left arm . . .

Fleance had managed to get his foot over to the pedals, push his father's foot away and press the clutch so that he could move the gear lever out of neutral and into reverse. Then he gradually raised his heel off the clutch while pressing the accelerator with the tip of his shoe. The open passenger door had hit some guy who was still hanging on, but now they were out of the shop, on their way back. Fleance couldn't see a damn thing, but he gave it full throttle and hoped they wouldn't crash into anything.

The guy on the door was struggling to do something, and in a flash he saw what. The muzzle of a shotgun was protruding from under his arm. The next moment it went off.

Fleance blinked.

The guy with the gun was gone. Also the passenger door. He looked over the dashboard and saw the door and the guy wrapped around the post of the NO PARKING sign.

And he saw a side street.

He stamped on the brake and pressed the clutch before the engine died. Checked his mirror. Saw four men dismounting from their motor-bikes and coming toward him. Their bikes were parked side by side barri-cading the narrow street; the Volvo wouldn't be able to reverse over them. Fleance grabbed the gear lever, noticed now that his hand was bleeding, tried to find first gear but couldn't, probably because from the position he was in he couldn't press the clutch right down. *Fuck, fuck, fuck.* The en-gine coughed and spluttered, about to breathe its last. He saw in his mirror they had drawn guns. No, machine guns. This was it. This was where it ended. And a strange thought struck him. How bitter it was that he wouldn't be taking his final exam in law now that he had finally cracked the code and understood the thinking: the difference between wrong and illegal, moral and regulation. Between power and crime.

He felt a warm hand on his, on top of the gear stick.

"Who's driving, son? You or your dad?"

Banquo's eyes were a little dimmed, but he sat upright in the seat with both hands on the wheel. And the next second the engine's old voice rose to a hoarse roar, and they skidded away on the cobblestones as the ma-chine guns popped and crackled behind them as if it were Chinese New Year.

Macbeth looked at Lady. She sat two seats away from him enthusiastically making conversation with her dinner partner, Jano-something-or-other. The property shark from Capitol. She had placed her hand on his arm. Last year one of the town's powerful factory owners had sat in the shark's chair and captured her attention. But this year the factory was closed and its owner was not invited.

"You and I should have a chat," Tourtell said.

"Yes," Macbeth said, turning to the mayor, who was pushing a heavily laden fork of veal into his open jaws. "What about?"

"What about? About the town, of course."

Macbeth watched with fascination as the mayor's many chins ex-panded and compressed as he chewed, like an accordion of flesh.

"About what's best for the town," Tourtell said with a smile. As though that was a joke. Macbeth knew he should concentrate on the conversation, but he couldn't keep his thoughts together, hold them here, down on the earth. Now for example he was wondering whether the calf's mother was still alive. And if so, if she could sense that now, right now, her child was being eaten.

"There's this radio reporter," Macbeth said. "Kite. He spreads malicious gossip and obviously has an unfortunate agenda. How do you neutralize a person like that?"

"Reporters," Tourtell said, rolling his eyes. "Now look, that's difficult. They answer only to their editors. And even if the editors in turn answer to owners who want to earn money, reporters are solemnly convinced that they're serving a higher purpose. Very difficult. You're not eating, Macbeth. Worried?"

"Me? Not at all."

"Really? With one chief commissioner dead, another missing and all the responsibility on your shoulders? If you aren't worried, *I'd* be worried, Macbeth!"

"I didn't mean it like that." Macbeth looked for help from Lady, who was sitting on the mayor's other side, but she was now engaged in conversation with a woman who was the town council's financial adviser or something.

"Excuse me," Macbeth said and stood up. Got a quizzical, slightly concerned look from Lady and strode quickly into reception.

"Give me the phone, Jack."

The receptionist passed him the phone, and Macbeth dialed the number of the HQ switchboard. It answered on the fifth ring. Was that a long or a short time to wait for an answer from the police? He didn't know, he had never considered it before. But now he would have to. Think about that sort of thing. As well. "Put me through to Patrols."

"OK."

He could hear he had been put through, and the phone at the other end began to ring. Macbeth looked at his watch. They were taking their time.

"I never see you in the gaming room, Jack."

"I don't work as a croupier anymore, sir. Not after . . . well, that night, you know."

"I see. It takes a while to get over."

Jack shrugged. "It's not just that. In fact, I think being a receptionist suits me better than being a croupier. So it's no tragedy."

"But don't you earn a good deal more as a croupier?"

"If you're a fish out of water, it doesn't matter how much you earn. The fish can't breathe and dies beside a fat bagful of money. That's a tragedy, sir."

Macbeth was about to answer when a voice announced that he had got through to Patrols.

"Macbeth here. I was wondering if you'd had any reports about a shooting in Gallows Hill during the last hour."

"No. Should we have done?"

"We have a customer here who said he'd just driven by and heard a loud bang. Must have been a puncture."

"Must have been."

"So there's nothing in District Two West?"

"Only a break-in at a jeweler's, sir. The closest patrol car was some distance away, but we're heading there now."

"I see. Well, have a good evening."

"You, too, Inspector."

Macbeth rang off. Stared down at the carpet, at the strange needle-work, the flowery shapes. He had never thought about them, but now it was as if they were trying to tell him something.

"Sir?"

Macbeth looked up. Jack had a worried expression on his face.

"Sir, you've got a nosebleed."

Macbeth put a hand to his top lip, realized the receptionist was right and hurried to the toilet.

Banquo accelerated down the main road. The wind howled outside the doorless passenger side. They passed the Obelisk. It wouldn't be long before they were at the central station now.

"Can you see them?"

Fleance said something.

"Louder!"

"No."

Banquo couldn't hear in the ear on Fleance's side, either because the auditory canal was blocked with blood or because the bullet had taken his hearing as well. However it wasn't that shot which bothered him. He looked at the petrol gauge—the indicator had dropped remarkably in the four or five minutes since they had left the shopping area. The machine guns might have *sounded* harmless, but they had holed the petrol tank. But it wasn't those shots that bothered him either; they had enough petrol to get to the Inverness and safety.

"Who are they, Dad? Why are they after us?"

There, in front of them, was the central station.

"I don't know, Fleance." Banquo concentrated on the road. And breathing. He had to breathe, get air into his lungs. Carry on. Carry on until Fleance was safe. That, and nothing else, was what mattered. Not the road that had begun to blur in front of him, not the shot that had hit him.

"Someone must have known we would come that way, Dad. The traffic lights, that wasn't normal. They knew exactly when we would pass Gallows Hill."

Banquo had worked that one out. But it meant nothing now. What did mean something was that they had passed the central station and that the lights of the Inverness lay before them. Park in front of the entrance, get Fleance inside.

"I can see them now, Dad. They're at least two hundred meters behind us."

More than enough if they didn't get held up. He should have had the blue light and the siren in the car. Banquo stared at the Inverness. Light. He could drive across Workers' Square at a pinch. The sirens. Something stuck in his throat. Stuck in his mind.

"Did you hear any sirens, Fleance?"

"Eh?"

"Sirens. Patrol cars. Did you hear them at the jeweler's?"

"No."

"Absolutely sure? There are always loads of patrol cars in District Two West."

"Absolutely sure."

Banquo felt the pain and darkness come. "No," he whispered. "No, Macbeth, my boy . . ." He held the wheel and turned left.

"Dad! This isn't the way to the Inverness."

Banquo pressed the horn, pulled the Volvo out from behind the car in front and accelerated. He could feel the paralyzing pain from his back spreading to his chest. Soon he wouldn't be able to keep his right hand on the wheel. The bullet probably hadn't made a big hole in the seat, but it had hit it. And that was the shot that worried him.

In front of them there was nothing. Only the container harbor, the sea and darkness.

But there was one last possibility.

Macbeth studied himself in the mirror above the sink. The bleeding had stopped, but he knew what it meant. That his mucous membranes couldn't take any more brew, and he should give it up for a while. It was different when he was young: then his body could take any amount of punishment. But if he continued now his nose would ache and bleed and his brain would spin until his head unscrewed itself from his neck. What he needed was a break. So why, thinking this, did he roll up a banknote and place it at the right-hand end of the line of powder on the sink? Because this was the exception. This was the critical point when he needed it. The point when he had to tackle the fat perverted mayor on the one side and the Norse Rider brigand who it seemed hadn't managed to keep to their agreement on the other. And Lady on the third. No, she wasn't a problem, she was the alpha and the omega, his birth, life and death. His reason for *being*. But just as their love could give him a tremulous joy, he could also feel the pain when he thought of what might be taken from him—her power now consisted in *not* loving him as much as loving him. He inhaled, sucked the brew up into his brain, hard, until it hit the inside of his scalp, or so it felt. Again looked at himself in the mirror. His face contorted and changed. He had white hair. A woman's red lips. A scar grew across his face. New chins extended under his chin. Tears filled his eyes and ran down his cheeks. He had to stop now. He had seen people who had sniffed so much they had ended up with prosthetic noses. Had to stop while there was still time, while there was something to save. He had to switch to a syringe.

The sergeant saw the rear lights of the Volvo gradually coming nearer. He opened the throttle knowing the others would find it difficult to keep up now even though his engine was only 450 cc. On wet oily tarmac experience and sensitivity were more important for road-holding than engine size. It was therefore with some surprise that he saw a bike approaching fast in his mirror. And with disbelief he recognized it. And the rider's helmet. The red Indian Chief passed so close to the sergeant that the point of a horn almost brushed against him. His headlight was reflected in the saber when the bike overtook him. Where had he come from? How did he know? How did he always know when they needed him? The sergeant slowed down. Let Sweno ride at the front and lead them.

Banquo drove the same way they had when they were following the Russian lorry, overtaking dangerously a couple of times and temporarily increasing their distance from the motorbikes. They would soon catch up again, but perhaps there was still time. There was a barrier in front of the tunnel and a sign to say the bridge was closed due to repairs. Splinters flew as the front of the Volvo smashed into the barrier and its headlights bored into the tunnel's darkness. He drove with one hand on the wheel; the other lay in his lap like a corpse. They could already see the exit when they heard the angry yapping of the motorbike engines entering the tunnel behind them.

Banquo braked approaching the sharp bend onto the bridge and then speeded up again.

And soon they were out on it, to a sudden silence beneath a clear sky and in the moonlight, which made the river glitter like copper below, far beneath them. All that could be heard was the Volvo's engine working as hard as it could. And then the whine of rubber on tarmac as Banquo braked suddenly in the middle of the bridge where the statue of Kenneth had once been and turned onto the shoulder where the breeze flapped the Highway Agency's red cordon tape, marking the spot the ZIS-5 had plunged down with the railing. Surprised, Fleance turned to his father, who had put the car into neutral. Banquo leaned over his son with a pocket-knife in his hand and cut his seat belt.

"What . . . ?"

"We've got a leak, son. Soon we won't have any petrol, so listen to me. I've never been much of a preacher, you know that, but I want to say this to you . . ." Banquo leaned against the door on his side, lifted his knees and swung round in his seat as Fleance had done.

"You can be whatever you want, Fleance. So don't be what I was. Don't be a lackey for lackeys."

"Dad . . ."

"And land on your feet."

He placed the soles of his shoes against his son's hip and shoulder, saw Fleance try to grab on to something, then shoved him with all his might. The son screamed in protest, in fear as he had done when he was born, but then he was out, the last umbilical cord severed, alone in the big wide world, in free fall toward his fate.

Banquo groaned with pain as he swung himself back, put the car in gear and accelerated toward his own fate.

When he ran out of petrol three kilometers after leaving the bridge they had almost caught him up. The car rolled the last meters, and Banquo could feel he was sleepy and laid his head back. A chill had spread down his whole back and into his stomach and was moving toward his heart. He thought about Vera. And when it finally rained on this side of the tunnel, it rained lead. Lead that pierced the car, seats and Banquo's body. He stared out of the side window, up the mountainside. There, almost at the top, he could see what looked like from the town side a tribute to evil. But here it was a Christian cross that shone in the light of the moon. It was so close. It showed the way. The gate was open.

"A planned rise," Banquo mumbled. "A plann—"

16

DUFF LISTENED TO CAITHNESS'S BREATHING as it slowly quietened. Then he freed himself from her embrace and turned to the bedside table.

"Well, Cinders?" she whispered. "Is it almost midnight?"

"We've got plenty of time, but I can't arrive late."

"You've been looking at the clock every half an hour ever since you got here. Anyone would think you were dying to leave."

He turned to her again. Put his hand behind her neck. "That's not why, my beautiful woman, it's just that I lose all concept of time when I'm here with you." He kissed her lightly on the lips.

She chuckled. "You can sweet-talk, you can, Romeo. But I've been thinking."

"Sounds scary."

"Stop it. I've been thinking I love you. And—"

"Scary."

"Stop it, I said. And I don't just want you here and now. I don't want you always disappearing like a half-dreamed dream."

"I don't want to either, my love, but—"

"No more buts, Duff. You always say you'll tell her about us, but then there's the constant but, which means you have to postpone doing it, which you say is out of consideration for her, for the children, for—"

"But there are considerations, Caithness. You have to understand that. I've got a family and with it come—"

"—*Responsibilities I can't run away from*," she mimicked. "What about some consideration for me? You never seem to have any problem running away from me."

"You know very well it's not like that. But you're young, you've got alternatives."

"Alternatives? What do you mean? I love *you*!"

"I only mean that Meredith and the children are vulnerable right now. If we wait until the children are a year older, it'll be easier, then I can—"

"No!" Caithness smacked her hand down on the duvet. "I want you to tell her now, Duff. And do you know what? That's the first time you've mentioned her by name."

"Caithness . . ."

"Meredith. It's a nice name. I've envied her that name for a long time."

"Why such a hurry all of a sudden?"

"I've realized something over the last few days. To get what you want you can't wait for someone to give it to you. You have to be tough, possibly inconsiderate, but a clean cut is best. Believe me, it isn't easy for me to ask you to do this, to sacrifice your family—it affects innocent people, and that's not in my nature."

"No, Caithness, it's not in your nature, so where have you got this from, this idea of a clean cut?"

"Duff." She sat up, cross-legged, in the middle of the bed. "Do you love me?"

"Yes! Jesus, yes."

"So will you do it? Will you do this for me?"

"Listen to me, Caithness—"

"I like Meredith better."

"Darling. I love you more than anything else. I would give my life for you. My very own life, yes, without hesitation. But others' lives?" Duff shook his head. Inhaled to speak but let his breath back out. A clean cut. Did it have to be now? The idea of it surprised him. Had he unwittingly been on his way there all the time? On his way from Caithness, on his way home to Fife? He took another deep breath.

"My mother—whom I never knew—sacrificed her life for me. Sacrificed hers so that I could live. So even if it's in my nature—as it was in my mother's nature—to sacrifice a life for love, love for a child is the greatest love. Just the *thought* of having to sacrifice anything smaller for my children—taking their family away from them for my selfish love for another woman—is like spitting on my mother's memory."

Caithness put her hand to her mouth and an involuntary sob escaped her as her eyes filled with tears. Then she stood up and left the bedroom.

Duff closed his eyes. Banged his head on the pillow behind him. Then he followed her. He found her in the sitting room, where she was standing by one of the attic windows and staring out. Naked and shimmeringly white in the neon light from outside, which made the trails of raindrops on the window look like tears running down her cheeks.

He stood behind her and put an arm around her naked body. Whispered into her hair. "If you want me to go now, I will."

"I'm not crying because I can't have all of you, Duff. I'm crying because of my own hard heart. While you, you're a man with a real heart, darling. A man a child can trust. I can't stop loving you. Forgive me. And if I can't have everything, give me what you can of your pure heart."

Duff didn't answer, just held her. Kissed her neck and held her. Her hips began to move. He thought of the time. Of Banquo. Their meeting by the locomotive. But it was still a long time to midnight.

"Inverness Casino, Jack speaking."

"Good evening, Jack. I'd like to talk to Macbeth."

"He's at a dinner. Can I give him a—"

"Get him, Jack. Come on."

Pause.

The sergeant looked at the motorbikes gathered around the telephone box. Their shapes were distorted by the thick snakes of water coiling down the outside of the glass, but still the sight was the most beautiful he knew—engines on two wheels. And the brothers who rode them.

"I can ask, sir. Who can I say is calling?"

"Just say this is the call he was expecting."

"I see, sir."

The sergeant waited. Shifting his weight from one foot to the other. Switching the blood-stained parcel from one arm to the other.

"Macbeth."

"Good evening. I'm just calling to say the fish has been caught and gutted, but the fry swam away."

"Where?"

"Now the chances of a single fry surviving are a thousand to one against, and I think in this case we can be satisfied that it's dead and lying at the bottom of the sea."

"Right. So?"

"The fish head's on its way. And I'd say you've won my respect,

Macbeth. There are few who have the palate or stomach for this kind of delicacy."

Macbeth put down the phone and held on to the counter as he breathed quickly in and out.

"Are you sure you're well this evening, sir?"

"Yes, thank you, Jack. Just a bit giddy."

Macbeth repressed his thoughts and images one by one. Then he adjusted his jacket and tie and went back to the dining room.

The guests at the long table were talking and toasting, but there wasn't a great atmosphere. Now perhaps these people didn't celebrate as loudly and passionately as they did in SWAT, but he wondered whether the shadow of Duncan's death didn't lie more heavily over the casino than Lady would have admitted. The mayor had seen Macbeth and waved him over. He saw that someone was sitting on his chair and assumed it was Tourtell's companion. But when Macbeth saw that he was wrong he came to a sudden halt. It felt as if his heart had stopped beating.

Banquo.

He was sitting there. Now.

"What is it, my love?" It was Lady. She had turned and was looking at him in surprise. "Sit down."

"My place is taken," he said.

Tourtell also turned. "Come on, Macbeth. Sit down."

"Where?"

"On your chair," Lady said. "What's the matter?"

Macbeth screamed as Banquo turned his head like an owl. Above his white collar ran a long, continuous wound that seemed to run completely around his neck. Blood ran from the wound, like from the rim of a full glass of wine someone was continuing to fill.

"Who . . . who did this to you?" Macbeth groaned and placed both hands around Banquo's neck. Squeezed to stop the blood, but it was thin and trickled between his fingers like diluted wine.

"What are you doing, my love?" Lady laughed in a strained voice.

Banquo's mouth opened. "It . . . was . . . you . . . my son." The words were delivered in a monotone, his face expressionless like a ventriloquist's doll.

"No!"

"I . . . saw . . . you . . . master . . . I . . . am . . . waiting . . . for . . . you . . . master."

"Be quiet!" Macbeth squeezed harder.

"You . . . are . . . strangling . . . me . . . Murdererbeth."

Macbeth, terrified, let go. He felt someone pull hard at his arm.

"Come on." It was Lady. He was about to tear his arm away when she hissed into his ear, "Now! While you're still chief commissioner."

She put her hand under his arm, as though she was following him, and like this they sailed out of the dining hall as if blown by the expressions of their guests.

"What's the matter?" she hissed when she had locked them in their suite.

"Didn't you see him? Banquo! He was sitting in my chair."

"My God, you're high. You're seeing things! Do you want the mayor to think he's got a lunatic as his chief commissioner?"

"*His?*"

"Where's your wretched brew? Where?" She thrust her hand into his trouser pocket. "This is going out now!"

Macbeth grabbed her wrist. "*His* chief commissioner?"

"Tourtell's going to appoint you, Macbeth. I put you two together because I thought at least you wouldn't destroy the impression that you were the right man for the job. Ow, let go!"

"Let Mayor Tourtell do what he likes. I've got enough on him to lock him up tomorrow. And if I don't, I can get it. I'm the chief commissioner, woman! Don't you understand what that means? I'm in command of six thousand people, two thousand of them armed. An army, darling!"

Macbeth saw her eyes were softening.

"All right, yes," she whispered. "Now you're talking sense again, love."

He was still gripping her fine, slender wrist, but her hand had started moving in his pocket.

"Now I can feel you again," she said.

"Come on, let's—"

"No, not now," she interrupted and pulled her hand away. "We've got guests. But I have something else for you. A present to celebrate your appointment."

"Oh?"

"Look in the bedside-table drawer."

Macbeth took out a case. Inside it was a bright, shiny dagger. He lifted it to the light. "Silver?"

"I was going to give it to you after the dinner, but I think you need it now. Silver, as is well known, is the only material that can kill ghosts."

"Thank you, my sweet."

"It's a pleasure. So tell me Banquo is dead."

"Banquo's dead. He's dead."

"Yes, and we'll mourn later. Now let's join the others. You tell them it was an inside joke between us. Come on."

It was ten minutes past eleven.

Caithness was still in bed, while Duff had got dressed and was standing by the kitchen worktop. He had made a cup of tea and found a lemon in the fridge, but the only clean knife was more suited to stabbing than slicing a lemon. He stuck the point in the peel and a fine spray came out. So late at night it would normally take half the usual time to get to the central station, find a parking spot and get to Bertha. He had no intention of being late. Banquo didn't seem as if he needed an excuse *not* to tell him what he knew. On the other hand, Duff had seen Banquo wanted to talk. Wanted to unburden himself of . . . of what? The guilt? Or just what he knew? Banquo was no bellwether, he was a sheep, no more than a link. And soon Duff hoped he would know who the others were. And armed with that he would . . . The silence was broken by the telephone on the wall beside the cork board.

"Phone!" he shouted.

"Heard it. I'll take it here," Caithness answered from the bedroom. She had a phone in every room, one of the things that could make him feel old when he was with her. They were perhaps a little old-fashioned, Meredith and him, but they thought that one phone per household was enough—it didn't hurt to have to run. He found a cloth and wiped his hand. Listened for her voice to determine what kind of conversation it was, who was ringing so late at night. Meredith? The thought came to him, and he rejected it at once. The second thought lingered for longer. A lover. Another lover, younger. No, an admirer, a potential lover. Someone standing in the wings, ready to step in if Duff hadn't given her the answer she wanted this evening. Yes, that was the reason for the sudden hurry. And Duff hadn't complied with her demands, while his ultimatum had been turned round to become her own. And she had chosen him. The moment he articulated the thought he half-wished it was an admirer. How strange are we humans?

"Could you repeat that?" he heard Caithness say from the bedroom. Her professional voice. Only more excited than usual. "I'm on my way. Call the others."

Definitely work. SOCO work.

He heard her rummaging around in her room. He hoped the job wasn't in Fife and she would suggest he drove her. His hand was sweaty. He licked it while looking down at the lemon. The juice had got into one of the cuts he had received when he fell on the tarmac at the quay. He was still for a second. Then he pulled the knife out and stabbed the lemon again. Hard and fast this time. Let go of the knife quickly and pulled his hand away, but it stung again. It was impossible. Impossible to stab and remove your hand before the spray.

Caithness rushed into the kitchen with a black doctor's bag in her hand.

"What is it?" Duff asked when he saw her expression.

"It was HQ. Macbeth's deputy from SWAT . . ."

"Banquo?" Duff felt his throat constrict.

"Yes," she said, pulling open a drawer. "He's been found on Kenneth Bridge."

"Found? Do you mean . . . ?"

"Yes," she said, rummaging angrily in the drawer.

"How?" The questions that accumulated were too numerous, and Duff helplessly grabbed his forehead.

"I don't know yet, but the police at the scene say his car's riddled with bullets. And his head's been removed."

"Removed? As in . . . cut off?"

"We'll soon see," she said, taking a pair of latex gloves from the drawer and putting them in the bag. "Can you drive me?"

"Caithness, I've got this meeting, so . . ."

"You didn't say where, but if it's a long detour . . ."

He looked at the knife again.

"I'll go with you," he said. "Of course I will. I'm head of the Homicide Unit, and this case is top priority."

Then he turned and threw the knife hard at the cork board. It spun one and a half times on its axis before hitting the board handle first and falling to the kitchen floor with a clatter.

"What are you trying to do?" she asked.

Duff stared at the knife. "Something you need a lot of practice at before you succeed. Come on."

17

"SO, SEYTON," MACBETH SAID, "What can I do for you?"

The rays of sunshine had found a break in the clouds and were now angled through the grimy windows of the chief commissioner's office and fell on his desk, on his photo of Lady, on the calendar showing it was a Tuesday, on the drawing of the Gatling gun and, sitting in front of Macbeth's desk, the polished, shiny pate of the lean, sinewy officer.

"You need a bodyguard," Seyton said.

"Do I? And what kind of bodyguard do I need?"

"One who can fight evil with evil. Duncan had two, and after this business with Banquo, God bless his soul, there's every reason to assume they're after you as well, Chief Commissioner."

"Who are *they?*"

Seyton looked at Macbeth with puzzlement in his eyes before answering. "The Norse Riders. My understanding is that they're behind this execution."

Macbeth nodded. "Witnesses in District Two say they saw bikers, some of them wearing Norse Rider jackets, shooting at a Volvo outside a jewelry shop the car had driven into. We presume it was Banquo's car."

"If Malcolm was involved, the threat to the chief commissioner may come from inside the force. I don't trust all our so-called leaders. In my opinion, Duff is someone who lacks spine and morality. Of the threats outside the force there's obviously Hecate."

"Hecate's a businessman. Being suspected of murder is rarely good for business. Sweno, on the other hand, has a motive which trumps business sense."

"Revenge."

"Good old-fashioned revenge, yes. Some of our economists seem to undervalue the human tendency to follow our basest instincts instead of the bank book. When the black widow's lover is lying on her back, sated and exhausted by lovemaking, he *knows* he'll soon be eaten. Yet he would never be able to make any other choice. And there you have Sweno."

"So you're less afraid of Hecate?"

"I've told you today that resources should be distributed more sensibly, the witchhunt aimed at Hecate has to be scaled down so that we can sort out other more pressing problems for the town."

"Such as?"

"Such as honest, hardworking people being openly cheated and robbed of their savings by one of our more dubious casinos. But back to the point. Former chief commissioners have had bad experiences with bodyguards, but I haven't forgotten how effective and brave you were when I was attacked by that dog at Cawdor's. So let me sleep on this, Seyton. Actually, I'd been thinking of giving you a different post, one which is not so different from the one you were requesting, actually."

"Oh?"

"Now that I'm chief commissioner and Banquo's gone, SWAT doesn't have a head. You, Seyton, are the oldest officer with the most experience."

"Thank you, Chief Commissioner. That is really an unexpected honor and statement of trust. The problem is that I don't know if I'm worthy of the trust. I'm not a politician, nor a leader of men."

"No, I know the type. You're a watchdog who needs a master and a mistress, Seyton. But SWAT is a kind of watchdog. You'd be surprised at the detail of the instructions you get. I barely needed to think about how to apprehend the bad guys. And given the murders over the last two days it's clear that the threat to someone sitting in my chair is such that SWAT will have to be used to actively protect the head of police HQ."

"Are you saying that SWAT will become the chief commissioner's personal bodyguard?"

"I can't imagine that an arrangement of that kind would meet any resistance that can't be quelled. In which case, we would be killing two birds with one stone. Your wishes and mine would be met. What do you say, Seyton?"

The sun was going down, and perhaps it was the sudden darkness falling in the room that made Seyton lower his voice so it sounded like a conspiratorial whisper: "As long as my orders come directly and in detail from you personally, Chief Commissioner."

Macbeth studied the man in front of him. *God bless his soul*, Seyton had said about Banquo. Macbeth wondered what kind of blessing it had been.

"My orders, loyal Seyton, will be unambiguous. As far as quelling protests is concerned, I've just ordered two of these Gatling guns." He passed Seyton the drawing. "Express delivery. Bit more expensive, but we'll get them in two days. What do you think?"

Seyton ran his eye over the drawing, nodding slowly. "Tasty," he said. "Beautiful in fact."

Duff yawned as he drove from a clear sky to dark clouds.

Ewan had woken him when he jumped up into the guest bed, with his sister hard on his heels.

"Daddy, you're home!"

They'd had breakfast in the kitchen with the morning sun low over the lake. Meredith had told the children to stop fighting to sit on Daddy's lap and eat; they had to go to school. She hadn't managed to put on the strict voice Duff knew she wanted to, and he had seen the smile in her eyes.

Now he passed the crime scene, where the bullet-riddled car had been towed away and the blood on the tarmac had been cleaned up. Caithness and her people had worked efficiently and found what evidence there was. And there hadn't been much for him to do apart from state the obvious: that Banquo had been shot and beheaded. There was no trace of Fleance, but Duff had noticed that the seat belt on the passenger seat had been cut. That could mean anything at all; for the time being all they could do was put out a general missing-person alert for Banquo's young son. It was a deserted stretch of road, as the bridge was closed, and it was unlikely there had been any witnesses in the vicinity, so after an hour Duff had decided that since he was halfway home he may as well sleep in Fife.

Where he had lain awake thinking to the accompaniment of the grass-hoppers' song outside. He had known. Known but hadn't understood. It wasn't that he had suddenly seen the bigger picture; it wasn't that all the interlocking pieces had suddenly fitted into the jigsaw puzzle. It had been one simple detail. The knife in Caithness's kitchen. But while he had been

brooding the other pieces had emerged and slowly fitted in. Then he had
fallen asleep and woken to the children's ambush at dawn.

Duff drove over the old bridge. It was narrow and modest in comparison with Kenneth Bridge, but solidly built, and many thought it would
stand for longer.

The problem was: who should he talk to?

It had to be someone who not only had enough power, influence and
dynamism, but also someone he could trust, who *wasn't* involved.

He drove down to the garage under HQ as the break in the clouds
closed and the sun's short visit was over.

Lennox looked up from his typewriter as Duff came in. "Lunch soon,
and you're yawning as if you've just got up."

"For the last time, is that thing genuine?" Duff asked, nodding at the
tarnished stick with a lump of rusty metal on the end that Lennox used as
a paperweight. Duff slumped down in a chair beside the door.

"And for the last time—" Lennox sighed "—I inherited it from my
grandfather, who had it thrown at his head in the Somme trenches. Fortunately, as you can see, the German forgot to pull the detonator pin. His
soldier pals laughed a lot at that story."

"Are you saying they laughed a lot in the Somme?"

"According to my grandfather the worse it got, the more they laughed.
He called it the laughter of war."

"I still think you're lying, Lennox. You're not the type to have a live
grenade on your desk."

Lennox smiled as he went on typing. "Granddad kept it in his house
all his life. He said it reminded him of the important things—the tran-
sience of life, the role of chance, his own mortality and others' incompe-
tence."

Duff motioned to the typewriter. "Haven't you got a secretary to take
care of that?"

"I've started writing my own letters and leaving the building to post
them myself. Yesterday I was told by the Public Prosecutor's Office that
one of my letters appeared to have been opened and resealed before they
received it."

"I'm not shocked. Thanks for receiving me at such short notice."

"*Receiving* me? That sounds very formal. You didn't say what this was
about on the phone."

"No. As I said, I'm not shocked that someone opens letters."

"The switchboard. Do you think—"

"I don't think anything, Lennox. I agree with you that there's no point taking risks with the situation as it is now."

Lennox nodded slowly and tilted his head. "And yet, good Duff, that's precisely why you've come here?"

"Maybe. I have some evidence concerning who killed Duncan."

Lennox's chair creaked as he straightened his back. He pushed himself away from the typewriter and rested his elbows on the desk. "Close the door."

Duff stretched out his arm and closed it.

"What kind of evidence? Tangible?"

"Funny you should use that word . . ." Duff took the letter opener from Lennox's desk and weighed it in his hand. "As you know, at both crime scenes, Duncan's and the bodyguards', everything was apparently kosher."

"The word *apparently* is used when something seems fine on the surface but isn't."

"Exactly." Inspector Duff placed the knife across his forefinger so that it balanced and formed a cross with his finger. "If you stabbed a man in the neck with a dagger to kill him, wouldn't you hold on to the dagger in case you missed the carotid artery and had to stab again?"

"I suppose so," Lennox said, staring at the letter opener.

"And if you hit the artery straightaway, as we know one dagger did, enormous quantities of blood would shoot out in a couple of brief spurts, the victim's blood pressure would fall, the heart would stop beating, and the rest would just trickle out."

"I follow. I think."

"Yet the handle of the dagger we found on Hennessy was completely covered in blood; his prints were in the blood, and the inside of his hand was also covered with Duncan's blood." Duff pointed to the handle of the letter opener. "That means the murderer wasn't holding the handle when the blood spurted from Duncan's neck, but grabbed the handle afterward. Or that someone pressed his hand around the handle later. Because someone—someone else—*threw* the dagger at Duncan's neck."

"I see," Lennox said, scratching his head. "But throw or stab, what's the difference? The result's the same."

Duff passed Lennox the letter opener. "Try and throw this knife so that it sticks in the noticeboard over there."

"I . . ."

"Come on."

Lennox stood up. The distance to the board was probably two meters.

"You have to throw it hard," Duff said. "It requires strength to pierce a man's neck."

Lennox threw. The knife hit the board and bounced off onto the floor with a clatter.

"Try ten times," Duff said, picking up the knife and letting it balance on his finger. "I bet you a bottle of good whiskey you can't get the point to stick in."

"You don't have much confidence in my ability or my luck?"

"If I'd given you a knife that wasn't balanced, with either a heavy handle or a heavy blade, I'd have made the odds better. But just like the dagger in Duncan's neck this is a balanced knife. You have to be an expert to throw one. And no one I've spoken to in this building has ever seen or heard anything to suggest Duncan's bodyguards were knife-throwers. To tell the truth, only one person I know was. Someone who actually almost ended up in a circus doing just that. And who was at Inverness Casino that evening."

"Who's that?"

"The man you gave Organized Crime. Macbeth."

Lennox stood stock-still gaping at a point on Duff's forehead. "Are you telling me . . . ?"

"Yes, I am. Chief Commissioner Duncan was killed by Macbeth. And the murder of those innocent bodyguards was cold-blooded murder carried out by the same man."

"God have mercy on us," Lennox said, sitting down with a bump. "Have you spoken to Forensics and Caithness about this?"

Duff shook his head. "They noticed there was blood on the handle, but they think that was down to quick reflexes when the dagger was let go, not that the dagger was thrown. Reasonable enough theory. After all, it's very rare for anyone to have that skill. And it's only Macbeth's closest colleagues who know he's one of them."

"Good. We mustn't mention this to anyone. *No one.*" Lennox clenched his hands and chewed his knuckles. "Are you aware of the situation this puts me in, Duff?"

"Yes. Now you know what I know, that can't be changed, and now your head's on the block with mine. I apologize for not giving you a choice, but what else could I do? Our moment of truth has come, Lennox."

"Indeed. If what you say is correct and Macbeth is the monster you believe, a wounding shot is not enough—that would make him doubly dangerous. He must be felled with a single, decisive shot."

"Yes, but how?"

"With cunning and caution, Duff. I'll have to give this some thought, and I'm no genius, so it will take time. Let's meet again. Not here where the walls have ears."

"At six," Duff said, getting up. "The central station. By Bertha."

"The old train? Why there?"

"That's where I was going to meet Banquo. He was going to tell me all I've worked out anyway."

"So that's a suitable meeting place. See you."

Macbeth stared at the telephone on his desk.

He had just put down the receiver after talking to Sweno.

His nerves were jerking and twitching under his skin. He needed *something*. Not *something*, he knew what. He snatched the big hat Lady had bought him. Priscilla smiled as Macbeth strode toward the anteroom. "How long will the chief commissioner be out?"

She had, at Macbeth's behest, been moved up from Lennox's office, the whole process taking less than two hours. He had wanted to give Duncan's old assistant the heave-ho, but instead had moved her down a floor after the head of admin explained to him that in the public sector not even a chief commissioner could dismiss employees at the drop of a hat.

"An hour," Macbeth said. "Or two."

"I'll say two to callers, then," she said.

"You do that, Priscilla."

He walked into the lift and pressed G for the ground floor. *To callers*. Not *if anyone calls*. Because people did call, non-bloody-stop. Unit heads, judges, council representatives. He didn't have the slightest clue what half of them did, apart from pester him with questions he couldn't fathom, and that meant a queue of callers. Journalists. Duncan's death, Malcolm's disappearance. And now another policeman, plus his son. Was everything spinning out of control? they asked. Could the chief commissioner assure them that . . . ? *No comment. May I refer you to the next press conference, which . . .*

And then there was Sweno.

The lift doors opened; two uniformed policemen on their way in stopped and backed out again. It was a rule Kenneth had introduced, and Duncan had abolished, that the chief commissioner should have the lift to himself. But before Macbeth could say they were welcome the lift doors had closed again and he continued down on his own.

On the pavement outside headquarters he bumped into a man in a gray coat reading a newspaper who mumbled, "Sorry, Macbeth." Not so strange because when Macbeth looked up he saw his own face on the front page. THIRD OFFICER TAKES THE HELM. Not a bad headline. Might have been Lady's suggestion. The editor was putty in her hands.

Macbeth pulled the big hat down over his face and walked with long strides. Now, in the middle of the day, the streets were so chock-a-block with traffic it was faster to walk than drive to the central station. And besides it was just as well no one saw the chief commissioner's limousine there.

God knows what Sweno had said to Priscilla to be put through. At any rate he hadn't said his name when Macbeth had him on the line, he hadn't needed to. If you heard his voice once you didn't forget it. The bass made the plastic in the receiver quiver. He said that Macbeth's promise had been the *immediate* release of the Norse Riders, and twelve hours had already passed. Macbeth had answered that it wasn't that simple: papers had to be signed by judges and lawyers as a prosecution had already been raised. But Sweno could safely prepare a welcome speech for the homecoming party in two days.

"That's two days too many," Sweno had said. "And the two last days you will ever get from me. The day after tomorrow, at eleven o'clock on the dot, one of our members will ring the home of one of the town's judges, I won't say which, and confess his involvement in Banquo's murder and how we knew exactly where Banquo and Fleance would be."

"One of your kamikaze pilots?"

"In addition, we have seven witnesses that saw you come to our club-house."

"Relax and think about your speech, Sweno. We'll drop your boys outside the club gate tomorrow afternoon at half past three."

And with that Macbeth rang off.

At the foot of the steps to the central station Macbeth scoured the area. Saw another gray coat, but not the same one. The hat hid his face, and he was after all only one of many smartly dressed men who ran up these steps every day to buy whatever they needed to function as surprisingly well as they did.

He stood where he had last stood, in the corridor, by the stairs down to the toilet. The young boy was nowhere to be seen. Macbeth hopped from foot to foot impatiently. It was many hours since he had felt the need, but it was only now, as he was about to satisfy his need, that it was really bad.

She appeared after what felt like an hour, but his watch told him only ten minutes had passed. She had a white stick in her hand, whatever that was supposed to mean.

"I need two bags," he said.

"You need to meet someone," Strega said. "Put these in your ears and wear these." She held out a pair of earplugs and some glasses that looked like a cross between swimming and welding goggles, the type he had seen blind people wear.

"Why should I?"

"Because if you don't you won't get any brew."

He hesitated. No, he didn't hesitate, he just took his time. He would have walked on his hands if that was what they demanded. The goggles were painted, so he could see nothing at all. Strega held him and whirled him round several times, evidently so that he would lose his sense of direction. Then she handed him the white stick and led him off. Ten minutes later he knew they had walked in the rain, people and traffic had been around them, the earplugs didn't shut out all sound. Strega had helped him up onto a cement edge a meter and a half high and from there they had walked on gravel or sand. Then up onto another cement edge and inside somewhere, he guessed—at least it was warmer and the air was drier. And he had been sat down on a chair where someone took out the earplugs and told him to keep the goggles on.

He heard someone approaching, and a *tap-tap* sound stopped right in front of him.

"I regret to have to bring you here in this way." The voice was unusually gentle and soft and sounded as if it belonged to an elderly man. "But I thought—all things taken into account—it was best to meet face-to-face. That is, you can't see mine of course, but if I were you, Macbeth, I would be glad of that."

"I understand. It means you intend to let me leave alive."

"You're not smart, but you're more smart than stupid, Macbeth. That was why we chose you."

"Why am I here?"

"Because we're concerned. We knew of course of your affection for stimulants before we chose you, but we weren't aware that it would take over so completely and so quickly. In short, we have to find out if you're trustworthy or we will have to swap you."

"Swap me for what?"

"Do you imagine you're unique? I hope the chief commissioner title hasn't gone to your head and that you realize it's only a front. Without me you're nothing. Duncan thought he could manage without me, indeed, that he could fight me. Do you believe that too, Macbeth?"

Macbeth gritted his teeth and swallowed his anger. He only wanted the bags and to get away. He took a deep breath. "As far as I can see, we have a form of collaboration we both profit from, Hecate. You may have triggered events that led to me becoming chief commissioner, and I will get rid of Sweno and ensure that the police don't bother you and your monopoly too much."

"Hm. So you have no moral scruples?"

"Of course I do, but I'm a pragmatist. In any town of this size there will be a market for dream sellers like you. If it isn't you or Sweno, it'll be someone else. Our cooperation will at least keep other and perhaps worse drug dealers away. I accept you as the means to the end of building a good future for this town."

The old man chuckled. "Sounds like words taken straight from Lady's mouth. Light and sweet to the taste but insubstantial. I'm at a crossroads here, Macbeth. And to decide my way I will have to make an assessment of your suitability. I see the newspapers are using metaphors about the third officer taking over the helm from the captain. Well, your ship is in a hurricane right now. Duncan, Banquo and a police cadet have been executed. Cawdor, Malcolm and two bodyguards are dead and assumed corrupt. Your ship is already a physical and moral wreck, Macbeth, so if I'm going to help you I have to know specifically how you're going to steer it into calmer waters."

"The guilty parties will of course be apprehended and punished."

"I'm glad to hear that. And who are the guilty parties?"

"That's obvious. The Norse Riders. They forced Malcolm and his guards to cooperate."

"Good. In which case we shall be acquitted, you and I. But what if Sweno can prove his innocence with respect to Duncan's murder?"

"I have a feeling he won't be able to."

"Hm. I hope you've got the energy to follow up what you've said, Macbeth."

"I have, Hecate. And I hope I can demand the same of you."

"What do you mean? I've carved out a path for you as chief commissioner, isn't that enough?"

"Not if I'm not protected. What I can see now is that everyone's out to get me: judges, journalists, criminals and probably colleagues too. With guns or words as weapons. The phone never stops. And look. I can be kidnapped or abducted like a blind man in the middle of the day."

"Haven't you got SWAT to keep an eye on you?"

"Who knows if I can rely on everyone there. I need more protection."

"I understand. And here's my answer. You already have my protection. You've already had it for some time. You just haven't seen it."

"Where is it?"

"Don't even think about it. You should know Hecate protects his investments. The person I am, what I stand for, is the guarantee that no one, absolutely no one in this town, can hurt you as long as you're mine, Macbeth."

"No one?"

"I promise you, the person isn't born that can harm a hair on your beautiful head. And old Bertha will roll again before anyone can push you out of office. Isn't that good enough for you, Macbeth?"

"Yes, I'm happy with both of those promises."

"Good. Because there's one last thing I have to say. And that is, watch out for Inspector Duff."

"Oh?"

"He knows it was you who killed Duncan."

Macbeth knew he should feel alarm. Fear. Panic. But all he had space for was the familiar, hated craving.

"Fortunately for you there is at the moment only one man who knows what Duff knows."

"Who's that?" Macbeth asked.

"The same man who launched and supported your candidature for head of Organized Crime, at my instruction. So discreetly that Duncan thought afterward it had been his idea."

"And who was that?"

"See for yourself."

A chair leg scraped as Macbeth was turned round. Then his goggles were removed. Macbeth's first thought was that he was looking into a soundproofed interview room. It had the same one-way window that meant the interrogee neither saw nor heard those outside. The difference was that this resembled a large laboratory with glass flasks, tubes and pipes leading to an enormous tank. The tank made an almost comical contrast with all the modern equipment and reminded Macbeth of cartoons showing cannibals boiling people alive. On the wall behind the tank hung a sign with the words NO SMOKING. In front of the tank in the harshly illuminated room, close to the glass, sat a pale red-haired man upright in a recliner. One shirtsleeve was rolled up, his face turned to the ceiling, his mouth half-open, his eyes half-shut. He sat so close to them that Macbeth could see the blue half-irises under the man's eyelids trembling. He recognized one of the Chinese sisters, who was holding a syringe with the needle sticking into Inspector Lennox's forearm.

The gentle voice behind Macbeth said, "Lennox sowed the idea in Duncan's mind, the idea that he should appoint someone who didn't belong to the elite, but a man people in the town felt was one of them."

"Lennox told Duncan he should appoint me head of Organized Crime?"

"Of course Lennox said the opposite. Duncan couldn't take you because you had no formal qualifications and were too popular. That's how you manipulate stubborn old mules with big egos."

"You said *jump* and Lennox jumped?"

"And Lennox didn't say *jump* and Duncan jumped." There came a gurgle of laughter from behind Macbeth, as though someone were pouring whiskey. "The labyrinths of the human mind, Macbeth. Broad avenues, above all, easy to navigate. Lennox has been mine for more than ten years. A loyal toiler, Inspector Lennox."

Macbeth tried to see the reflection of the man behind him, but he saw only Strega, as though Hecate himself could not be reflected. But he was standing there because Macbeth heard his voice by his ear:

"But when I say *jump*, it means jump."

"Oh?"

"Kill Duff."

Macbeth swallowed. "Duff's my friend. But you probably knew that."

"Banquo was a father to you, but that didn't stop you. Killing Duff is a necessity, Macbeth. Besides I have a better friend for you. Her name is power."

"I don't need any new friends."

"Yes, you do. Brew makes you unstable and quirky. You've had hallucinations, haven't you?"

"Maybe. Maybe this is a hallucination. What's power?"

"A new yet ancient product. Brew is a poor man's power. Power is seven times stronger and half as damaging. It sharpens and strengthens your mind. And that's what these times demand."

"I prefer brew."

"What you prefer, Macbeth, is to continue as chief commissioner."

"And this new drug, will it make me dependent?"

"I told you it was ancient. And power will replace everything you're already dependent on. So what do you think? Duff versus power?"

Macbeth saw Lennox's head tip forward. He heard Strega whisper something behind him. The sister laid Lennox back on the recliner and went to the tank.

"Give it to me."

"Sorry?"

Macbeth cleared his throat: "Give it to me, I said."

"Give him the bags," Hecate said.

Macbeth heard the *tap-tap* fade as his goggles were put back on and the world around him disappeared.

18

"SHE'S BEAUTIFUL, ISN'T SHE?" Lennox said, stroking the curves.

"No," Duff said. "Bertha is many things, but she isn't beautiful."

Lennox laughed and looked down at his hand, which was now covered with soot. "Everyone says Bertha, but her full name is Bertha Birnam. Named after a black-haired construction site cook, she was the only employee with them throughout the years it took to build the line from here to Capitol."

"How do you know that?"

"Because my grandfather worked on the line. From here to Capitol."

"So your grandfather swung a sledgehammer and dragged sleepers?"

"No, of course not, he helped to *finance* the railway."

"That sounds more likely." Duff looked across at Inverness Casino's welcoming lights in the afternoon darkness.

"Yep, we Lennoxes are really bankers. In fact, I'm a kind of black sheep. What about your origins, Duff?"

"The usual."

"Police."

"As far as the eye can see."

"I know lots of Duffs in town, but none of them is in the police."

"I took the name from my maternal grandfather when I moved here."

"And he's . . ."

"Dead. Orphanage after that. Then police college."

"If you're not from here why didn't you go to the police college in Capitol? It's better, and so are the weather and air."

"The big fish are here. The Norse Riders, Hecate . . ."

"I see. You really wanted Organized Crime, didn't you?"

"Yes, I probably did."

"Well, it's still free. And when we've arrested Macbeth as Duncan's murderer, you'll just have to point to which unit you want. We'll be hailed as the saviors of the town, Duff."

"Will we? Do you really think they care?" Duff nodded to the square, where people were scurrying to get out of sight as fast as possible, into the shadows to find shelter.

"I know what you mean, but it's a mistake to underrate the general public in this town."

"There are two ways to tackle a problem, Lennox. By solving it or ignoring it. Kenneth taught this town to do the latter. Apathy toward corruption and shoving responsibility for the community onto others. Watching them escape, like cockroaches when the light comes on."

"A contemptible town with contemptible inhabitants, and yet you're willing to risk everything?"

Lennox watched Duff shaking his head.

"My God, Lennox, what makes you think this is for the *town*? The town. It's just a way of speaking they use when they want to be elected to the town hall or become the chief commissioner. Tell me what you've turned up since we last met."

"OK. I've spoken to a judge in Capitol—"

"We shouldn't talk to *anyone*!"

"Take it easy now, Duff. I didn't say what or who it was about, only that it concerned corruption at a high level. The point is that this judge is reliable. He lives elsewhere, so he's out of Macbeth, Sweno or Hecate's control. As a judge in a federal court of law he can hook up with the federal police, so we can leapfrog HQ and prosecute in Capitol, where Macbeth can't pull any strings. The judge is coming here in three days and he's agreed to meet us in total secrecy."

"What's his name?"

"Jones."

Lennox saw Duff staring at him.

"Lars Jones," Lennox said. "Anything wrong?"

"You've got pupils like a junkie."

Lennox moistened his tongue and laughed. "That's how it is when you're born half-albino. Eyes sensitive to light. That's one reason my family prefers indoor jobs."

Duff shivered in his coat. Looked over at Inverness Casino again. "So, three days. What shall we do in the meantime?"

Lennox shrugged. "Keep our heads down. Don't rock the boat. And . . . I can't think of a third way to say that."

"I'm already dreading my next meeting with Macbeth."

"Why's that?"

"I'm no actor."

"You've never fooled anyone?"

"Yes, but people always see through me."

Lennox glanced at Duff. "Oh? At home?"

Duff shrugged. "Even my lad, who'll be nine in a couple of days, knows when his dad's telling fibs. And Macbeth knows me better than anyone."

"Strange," Lennox said, "that two people who are so different have been such close friends."

"We'll have to talk later," Duff said, looking to the west. "If I set off now I'll be in Fife by sunset."

Lennox stood looking in the same direction as Duff. And thought it was good that nature had arranged things in such a way that rain showers always hid the view from those who were behind so that you could always be optimistic about a quick improvement in the weather.

"I have a feeling we're over the worst," Macbeth said, stretching for the lighter on the bedside table and lighting his cigarette. "Everything will get better now, my sweet. We're back where we should be. This town is ours."

Lady rested a hand on her chest, felt her still-racing heart under the silk sheet. And talked between breaths: "If your newly acquired enthusiasm is an indicator of your strength, darling—"

"Mm?"

"—then we're unbeatable. Are you aware how much they love you out there? People in the casino talk about you, say you're the town's savior. And do you read the papers? Today *The Times* suggested in its leader that you should stand in the mayoral elections."

"Was that your friend, the editor?" Macbeth grinned. "Because you asked him?"

"No, no. The leader wasn't about you. It was a comment piece on

Tourtell not having a real rival and being re-elected despite being unpopular."

"You don't become popular by being Kenneth's lackey."

"So your name was mentioned as someone who theoretically could challenge Tourtell. What do you say to that?"

"To standing as mayor? Me?" Macbeth laughed and scratched his forearm. "Thank you, but no thank you. I've got a big enough office and now we have more than enough power to do what we want." His nail rasped over the little hole in his skin. Power. He had injected himself with a syringe, and the sales pitch hadn't exaggerated.

"You're right, darling," she said. "But muse on it a little anyway. When the idea matures it will perhaps feel different—who knows? By the way, Jack received a parcel for you this morning. A biker brought it. Heavy and very well packed."

Macbeth waited for the feeling of ice in his veins, but it didn't come. Must have been the effect of the new dope. "Where did you put it?"

"On the hat shelf in your wardrobe," she said, pointing.

"Thank you."

He slowly smoked his cigarette listening to her fall asleep beside him. Stared at the solid brown oak door of the wardrobe. Then he laid his head on the pillow and blew rings up into the beams of moonlight from the window, saw them twist and wreathe like an Arab belly dancer. He wasn't afraid. He had SWAT protecting him, he had Hecate protecting him, the gods of destiny were smiling on him. He lifted his head and stared at the wardrobe again. Not a sound came from it. The ghosts had made themselves scarce. And it was perfectly still outside, no drumming on the window. For sunshine did follow the rain. Love did purge you of the blood of battle. Forgiveness did come after sin.

19

"GOOD MORNING, EVERYONE," MACBETH SAID, meeting the eyes of everyone around the table. "Except that it isn't a good morning, but the second one Banquo has been dead and the thirty-sixth hour his murderer has been wandering around free and unpunished. Let's start with a minute's silence for Banquo."

Duff closed his eyes.

It was unusual to see Macbeth enter a room with such a serious expression; he used to greet every day and every person with a smile, come rain or come shine, whether he knew them or not. Like the first time they met at the orphanage. He must have looked at Duff, at his clothes and hair, how different the two of them were, but he had smiled as if they shared something that went deeper than such external matters, something that bound them together, that made them secret brothers. Perhaps he made everyone feel like that with this unconditional, white smile. It had conveyed a naive belief that the people around him wished one another the best and made Duff feel like a cold cynic even then. And what wouldn't Duff have given for a smile that could rub off on those around him.

"Duff?" Someone had whispered his name. He turned and looked into Caithness's clear green eyes. She nodded to the end of the meeting table, where Macbeth was looking at him.

"I asked if we could have an update on where we are in the investigation, Duff."

Duff sat up on his chair, coughed, blushed and knew it. Then he began. He talked about the witnesses who had seen members of the Norse Riders and—judging by the logos on their leather jackets—another bikers' club shoot at the Volvo outside the jewelers' shop, Jacobs & Sons. About the jacket and Fleance's wallet, which were found by the bank below Kenneth

Bridge, but no body as yet. Caithness had given a comprehensive account of the forensic evidence, which only confirmed what they already knew—that Sweno's gang had murdered Banquo and possibly Fleance.

"There's some evidence to suggest Sweno was personally present at the execution," Duff said. "The end of a cigarillo on the tarmac beside the car."

"Lots of people smoke cigarillos," Lennox remarked.

"Not Davidoff Long Panatellas," Duff answered.

"You *know* what Sweno smokes?" Lennox said with an arched eyebrow.

Duff didn't respond.

"We cannot allow this," Macbeth said. "The town cannot allow us to allow it. Killing a police officer is an attack on the town itself. For the heads of units sitting in this room to have the town's confidence tomorrow, something has to happen today. For that reason we cannot afford to hesitate, we have to strike with all the strength we have, even at the risk of losing police lives. This is a war and so we have to use the rhetoric of war. And, as you know, it doesn't consist of words but bullets. Accordingly I have appointed a new head of SWAT and given them extended powers regarding the use of weapons and also in their instructions for fighting organized crime."

"Excuse me," Lennox said. "And what are the instructions?"

"You'll see soon. They're being worked on as we speak."

"And who's writing them?" Caithness asked.

"Police Officer Seyton," Macbeth said, "SWAT's new head."

"He's writing his own instructions?" Caithness asked. "Without us—"

"It's time to act," Macbeth interrupted. "Not to polish formulations of instructions. You'll soon see the result, and I'm sure you'll be as happy as me. And the rest of the town."

"But—"

"Naturally, you'll be able to comment on the instructions when they're available. This meeting is terminated. Let's get down to work, folks!" And there it was. The smile. "Duff, can I have a few words with you?"

Chairs scraped back tentatively.

"You can go too, Priscilla," Macbeth said. "And please close the door after you. Thank you."

The room emptied. Duff braced himself.

"Come here. Sit closer," Macbeth said.

Duff stood up and moved to the chair beside him. Tried to be relaxed, breathe calmly and avoid involuntarily tensing his face muscles. Conscious that he was sitting within spitting distance of the man who killed Duncan.

"I've been thinking of asking you about something," Macbeth said. "And I want you to be absolutely honest."

Duff could feel his throat constrict and his heart race.

"I wanted to offer someone else the post of head of Organized Crime. I know your first reaction is disappointment—"

Duff nodded, his mouth was so dry he wasn't sure his voice would obey.

"—but only because I want you to be my deputy. How do you feel about that?"

Duff cleared his throat. "Thank you," he said hoarsely.

"Aren't you well, Duff?" Macbeth wore an expression of concern and placed a hand on Duff's shoulder. "Or just a wee bit disappointed? I know how much you wanted Organized Crime, and I can understand you'd prefer an operational post to helping an awkward bugger like me find his words and feet." He smiled the white smile as Duff did his best to answer.

"You're my friend, Duff, and I want you close by. How does that proverb go?"

Duff coughed. "Which proverb?"

"Proverbs are your domain, Duff, but never mind. If you insist on Organized Crime I'll give it some thought. I haven't said anything to Lennox yet. You look really dreadful. Shall I get you a glass of water?"

"No, thanks, I'm fine. I'm just a bit exhausted. I barely slept before the raid and I haven't had a wink of sleep since Duncan's murder."

"Only a *bit* exhausted?"

Duff pondered. Shook his head. "No, I'd actually been wondering whether I could have the next two days off. I know we're in the middle of an investigation, but Caithness can . . ."

"Of course, of course, Duff. No point riding a horse to death just because the rider's in a hurry. Go back home to Fife. Say hello to Meredith from me and tell her you have to stay in bed for two days at least. And those are, believe it or not, the chief commissioner's orders."

"Thank you."

"I warn you I'll come and check you're resting in Fife."

"Fine."

"And then you come back with an answer regarding the deputy position in three days."

"Deal."

Duff went straight to a toilet and threw up in the bowl.

His shirt was drenched with sweat and it was only an hour later, as he was finally driving over the old bridge, that his pulse dropped back to normal.

Lady walked through the restaurant and gaming room. She counted nine customers. Tried to tell herself that straight after lunch was the quietest time. She went to see Jack in reception.

"Any new clients today?"

"Not yet, ma'am."

"Not yet? Will there be any later today?"

He smiled apologetically. "Not that I know of."

"Did you pop into the Obelisk, as I asked?"

"Of course, ma'am."

"And there it was . . . ?"

"Quiet, I would say."

"You're lying, Jack."

"Yes, ma'am."

Lady had to laugh. "Jack, you're always a comfort to me. Is it the murders here, do you think?"

"Maybe. But someone also rang asking specifically for the room Duncan died in. At a pinch, the bodyguards' room."

"People are sick in the head. And talking about sick, I'd like you to do a bit of probing around this boy Tourtell had with him. Find out how old he is."

"So you think . . . ?"

"Let's hope for the boy's sake he's over sixteen. And for ours he's under."

"Any special reason for this information, ma'am?"

"Storing up ammo just in case, Jack. The mayor appoints the chief commissioner, and even if the mayor usually follows the pecking order, in a case like this we can never be too sure, can we?"

"That's all?"

"Well, we'd like to see Tourtell put more pressure on the Gambling and the Casino Board to scrutinize the Obelisk's business practices, of course. I've been patient and tried the kind approach, but if it doesn't produce any results soon, we'll have to take more drastic action."

"I'll see what I can find out."

"Jack?"

"Yes, ma'am?"

"Have I been sleepwalking recently?"

"Not on my shifts, ma'am."

"Are you lying again?"

"You might have popped down to reception last night, but I wasn't sure whether you were asleep or not."

She laughed. "Jack, Jack, if only everyone was as good as you. I had a suspicion. The key was in the lock on the outside of the door when I woke up."

"Anything in particular on your mind? You only sleepwalk when something's bothering you."

"Is there anything else but bother?" Lady sighed.

"And dreams? Do you have the same dream again and again?"

"I've told you, Jack. It isn't a dream, it's a memory."

"Sorry, but you can't *know* that, ma'am. You can't know it happened exactly like that if you see it every night. Then the dream becomes a memory. For all you know, the child died a natural death."

"The eternal comforter. But I don't need comfort. I don't need to forget. Quite the opposite, I need to *remember*. Remember what I've given up to be where I am, to put a price on my childless life every single morning when I wake up between silk sheets beside a man I've chosen to spend the night with, and can go downstairs to my place, to a life I've created for myself. Where I'm respected for what I am, Jack."

"None of us is respected for what we are, ma'am. We're respected for what we can do. Especially if there's something we can do *to* the person we want respect from—"

"You're too clever to be a receptionist, Jack."

"—and unfortunately that's why a receptionist's wisdom doesn't gain much respect. He's a harmless observer, a eunuch and occasionally a comfort to those who are respected."

"I'm glad you never had children, Jack. You're the only person I can talk to about neglecting your own baby without it arousing the shocked revulsion it would from parents. You're a clever, tolerant man who prefers understanding to condemnation."

"What is there to condemn? A young girl growing up in impoverished circumstances, who's raped when she's thirteen, becomes pregnant and— abandoned and without a roof over her head—gives birth to a child she cannot keep alive?"

"What if I didn't try hard enough?"

"What if you had died in the process, you mean? You were thirteen. Not an adult, but with a sharp mind. Should your future be sacrificed for a newborn baby, a seed which still isn't aware it's alive, which still doesn't feel longing, guilt, shame, true love, indeed is not really human, just a millstone around the neck of a young girl whom life has punished enough as it is? That this thirteen-year-old was unable to keep both of you alive, but survived herself, has to be called good luck within the bad luck. Because look what she achieved afterward. She set up a little brothel. Set up a bigger, more luxurious one, which catered to the needs of everyone from the police commissioner to the town's most important politicians. Sold it and established the town's best casino. And now—hey presto—she's the queen of the town."

Lady shook her head. "That's taking it too far, Jack. Embellishing my motives and granting me an amnesty for my misdeeds. What is a casino, what are the dreams of idiots against a real child's life? If I'd demanded less of my life I might have been able to save hers."

"Did you demand so much in reality?"

"I demanded acceptance from others. No, more—respect. Yes, and love. Those are gifts that are not granted to everyone, but I demanded to be one of the few. And the price is having to lose my child again and again, night after night."

Jack nodded. "And if you could choose again, ma'am?"

Lady looked at him. "Perhaps we're all, good or bad, only slaves of our desires, Jack. Do you believe that?"

"I don't know, ma'am, but with respect to slaves of desires I'll check out this boy of Tourtell's tomorrow."

Macbeth exited the lift in the basement and stood for a couple of seconds inhaling the smell of leather, gun oil and male sweat. Looked at SWAT's motto under a fire-breathing red dragon: LOYALTY, FRATERNITY, BAPTIZED IN FIRE, UNITED IN BLOOD. My God, it felt like a minor eternity since then.

He walked through the door to the SWAT common room.

"Olafson! Angus! Hey, what is this? Sit down, don't jump up like a couple of recruits. Where's Seyton?"

"In there," Angus said in his unctuous priest-like tone. "Sad to hear about Banquo. The lads are collecting money for a wreath, but you probably aren't—"

"One of the boys anymore? Of course I am." Macbeth pulled out his wallet. "Thought you were on sick leave, Olafson. Where's the sling?"

"Slung it." Olafson's lisp made him sound Spanish. "The doctor thought I'd destroyed all the tendons in my shoulder and would never be able to shoot again. But then Seyton looked at it and suddenly it was fine again."

"There you go. Don't trust doctors." Macbeth passed Olafson a wad of notes.

"That's too much, sir."

"Take it."

"It's enough for a coffin."

"Take it!"

Macbeth went into his old office. Which wasn't actually an office but a workshop with gun parts and ammunition on shelves and benches, where the typewriter had been moved unused to a chair.

"Well?" Macbeth said.

"The boys are briefed," Seyton said, sitting with a thick instruction manual in front of him. "And ready."

"And our two Gatling girls?" Macbeth nodded to the manual.

"The machine guns are coming at about eight, early tomorrow morning. You spoke to the harbor master, I take it, so that the boat could jump the queue?"

"We couldn't have the girls coming late to the party. And there'll be a little job for you lads later tomorrow."

"Fine. Where?"

"In Fife."

20

THURSDAY MORNING. FIFE WAS BATHED in sunshine.

Duff was swimming.

Full, muscular breaststroke, plowing a path through the cold, heavy water.

He had long preferred the saltwater of the river, it felt lighter to swim in. Which actually was strange because he had learned that saltwater gave you more buoyancy, which had to mean it had greater density, which in turn had to mean it was heavier than freshwater. Nevertheless, until recently he had preferred the river, which as well as being freezing cold was so polluted that he felt dirty every time he emerged from it. But now he was clean. He had got up early, done his exercises on the cold wooden floor beside the guest bed, made breakfast for the family, sung a little birthday song for Ewan, driven the children to school and afterward walked with Meredith the half a mile or so down to the lake. She had talked about how many apples there were on the trees this autumn, their daughter getting her first love letter—though Meredith was privately very disappointed it was from a boy who was three years younger than her—and Emily wanting a guitar for her twelfth birthday. Ewan had been in a fight in the school playground and had brought home a note for his parents. He had agreed with Mum that he would have to tell Dad himself, but it could wait until after his birthday party today—there would be plenty of time then. Duff asked if postponing the evil moment wouldn't mean Ewan would be dreading it for an unnecessarily long time.

"I don't know what he does most." Meredith smiled. "Look forward to something or dread it. The boy he had a fight with yesterday is in the class above him, and Ewan said the boy kicked little Peter first."

"Who?"

"Ewan's best friend."

"Oh, him," Duff lied.

"Ewan said he was sorry but he had to defend his pal; Dad would have done the same. So he's keen to hear what you have to say."

"I'll have to be balanced then. Condemn his behavior but praise his courage. Say something about taking the initiative to make up instead of waging war. Reconciliation, right?"

"I'd appreciate that."

And as he and Meredith glided out through the water Duff decided there and then that he would never swim anywhere except in their little lake in Fife.

"Here it is," Meredith panted behind him.

Duff turned onto his back so that he could watch her while he floated, moving his hands and kicking his feet. His body was pale with a greenish tint under the water whereas hers, even in this light, was golden brown. He spent too much time in town; he had to get more sun.

She swam past him and crawled ashore onto a large water-smoothed rock.

Not any rock. Their rock. The rock where their daughter was conceived one summer's day eleven years ago. They had come to Fife to escape the town and had found this lake almost by chance. They had stopped because they saw an abandoned little farm Meredith thought looked so sweet. And from there they saw the water glitter, walked for ten to fifteen minutes and found the lake. Although the only other creatures by the lake were a couple of cows, they had swum to this hidden rock across the water where it was unlikely anyone would see them. A month later Meredith had told him she was pregnant, and in total euphoria they went back, bought the house midway between the lake and the main road and, after their second child, Ewan, was born, the plot by the lake where the cabin now stood.

Duff clambered up next to her on the rock. From where they sat they could see over to the red cabin.

He lay on his back on the sun-warmed rock. Closed his eyes and felt waves of pleasure run through his body. Sometimes it was worth getting cold to enjoy warming up afterward, he thought.

"Are you home again now, Duff?"

When you lose something and find it again, the pleasure is greater than before you lost it.

"Yes," he said.

Her shadow fell over him.

And when they kissed he wondered why he now—and not before—thought a woman's lips wetted by freshwater tasted better than wetted by saltwater, but concluded that it must be the body at some point telling you that freshwater can be drunk but not saltwater.

Afterward when they lay entwined and sweaty from the sun and making love, he said he had to go to town.

"Right. It's broth at the usual time."

"I'll be back in good time before. I just have to pick up Ewan's present. It's in the desk drawer in my office."

"He wanted the undercover cop outfit, didn't he?"

"Yes, and there's one other thing I have to sort out ASAP."

She stroked a finger down his forehead and nose. "Something come up?"

"Yes and no. I should have sorted it out ages ago."

"In which case—" her finger, which knew him so well, caressed his lips "—you do whatever you think you have to do. I'll wait for you here."

Duff sat up on his elbows and looked down at her. "Meredith."

"Yes?"

"I love you."

"I know, Duff. You just forgot for a while."

Duff smiled. Kissed her freshwater lips again and stood up. Went to dive in, then stopped. "Meredith?"

"Yes?"

"Did Ewan say who won the fight?"

"Did the chief commissioner say why they have to be driven to their clubhouse?" the driver asked.

The prison warder looked down at the bunch of keys to find the right one for the next cell. "Not enough evidence to keep them in custody."

"Not enough evidence? Bloody hell, the whole town *knows* it was the Norse Riders who picked up the dope at the harbor. And they *know* it was the Norse Riders who killed that policeman and his son. But I didn't ask why they were being set free—I'm used to that malarkey—I was wondering why we don't just let them go. When I drive prisoners it's usually from one prison to another, not as a bloody taxi service so they don't have to walk home."

"Don't ask me," the warder said, unlocking the cell. "Hey, Sean! Off your bed and home to your missus and daughter!"

"All hail Macbeth!" came a cry from inside the cell.

The warder shook his head and turned to the driver. "You'd better bring the bus to the exit and we'll assemble there. We'll send two armed officers with you."

"Why? Aren't these boys free?"

"The chief commissioner wants to be sure they're delivered where they're going with no trouble."

"Can I put leg shackles on them too?"

"Not according to the book, but do as you like. Hey! Do up your shoes. We haven't got all day."

"Do you mean it? Are the good times back, like under Kenneth?"

"Heh, heh. It's a bit early to say, but Macbeth's shaping up well, they say."

"His problem is the unsolved police murders. If you don't fix things smartish you're soon out on your arse."

"Maybe. Kite said on the radio today that Macbeth's a catastrophe." He repeated "catastrophe," exaggerating the rolled "r," and the driver laughed. And gave a shudder when he saw the tattoo on the forehead of the prisoner who came out.

"Livestock transport," he mumbled as the warder pushed the prisoner in the direction they were going.

Duff popped into his office, stuffed the parcel for Ewan in his jacket and hurried out. At Forensics on the second floor he was told that Caithness was in the darkroom in the garage. He took the lift down and let himself in. At some point when Caithness was sharing a flat with a girlfriend Duff had persuaded the caretaker that as head of Narco it would be useful if he had a key to the garage where Forensics had a firing range for ballistic analysis, a chemistry room, a darkroom to develop crime-scene photographs, plus an open area inside the garage door facing the street where they could keep larger objects, such as cars, that had to be examined for evidence. After work hardly anyone did overtime in the cold damp basement; they went up to the offices on the second floor. For a year Duff and

Caithness had had a regular rendezvous after work in the basement, as well as their weekly lunchtime meeting in Room 323 under the name of Mittbaum at the Grand Hotel. After Caithness had acquired her attic flat, strangely enough, Duff had missed these rushed trysts.

And opening the door and feeling the raw air hit him, he thought they must have been very much in love. In the middle of the garage stood Banquo's bullet-ridden Volvo. It was covered with a tarpaulin, presumably because the door on the passenger side had been torn off and they wanted to protect possible evidence in the car from the rats that roamed the basement at night. Duff stopped outside the darkroom and took a deep breath. The decision was made. Now it was just the deed that needed doing. The deed. He pressed down the door handle and went into the darkness. Closed the door after him. Stood inhaling the ammonia smell from the fixer liquid, waiting for his pupils to expand.

"Duff?" he heard from the darkness. The same friendly, slightly tentative voice that had woken him in the meeting room yesterday morning. The same friendly, slightly tentative voice that had woken him on so many mornings in her attic flat. The friendly, tentative voice he wouldn't hear anymore, not in the same way, not there.

"Caithness, we can't—"

"Roy," she said, "can you leave us alone for a while?"

Duff's eyes got used to the darkness in time for him to see the forensic photographer leave.

"Have you seen these?" asked Caithness, pointing a red light at the three recent dripping exposures hanging on a line.

One showed Banquo's car. The second, Banquo's headless body on the tarmac outside the car. The third was a close-up of the skin of Banquo's neck where it had been severed. She pointed to the last one. "We think it was cut by a large blade, like the saber you said Sweno has."

"I see," Duff said, staring at the picture.

"We found traces of other blood on the spine. Isn't that interesting?"

"What do you mean?"

"Sweno, or whoever it is, clearly hasn't been very particular about washing his saber, so as the saber cut through the spine here—" she pointed "—it scraped old dried blood off the blade. If we can determine which blood group it is, it might help us in other murder cases."

Duff's stomach was on the point of turning, and he clutched the bench.

"Still feeling ill?" Caithness asked.

Duff took some deep breaths. "Yes. No. I just had to get away. We have to talk."

"What about?" He could hear in her voice she already knew. She had probably already known when he burst in; talking about the photos had been a kind of panic reaction.

"About meeting," he said. "It won't work any longer."

He tried to see her face, but it was too dark.

"Is that all we've done?" she said. Her voice was tearful. "Meet?"

"No," he said. "No, you're right of course—it was more than meeting. And all the more reason for it to stop."

"You want to stop, dump me, here, at work?"

"Caithness—"

Her bitter laugh interrupted him. "Well, that's very fitting. A relationship that has taken place in a dark room is concluded in a darkroom."

"I'm sorry. It's out of consideration for—"

"You. You, Duff. Not the children, not the family, but you. You're the most selfish person I've ever met, so don't try to tell me it's out of consideration for anyone else but you."

"As you like. It's out of consideration for me."

"And out of *which* consideration are you dumping me, Duff? Is there an even younger, even more naive girl out there, who you know won't nag you to commit, to sacrifice something? Not *yet* anyway."

"Does it help if I say I'm only thinking about the personal, selfish well-being I hope to feel when I imagine I'm doing the right thing for those I have obligations toward? If I'm breaking up with you because I'm scared stiff not to be included among the saved souls on the Day of Judgment?"

"Do you think you will be?"

"No. But the decision has been taken, Caithness, so just tell me how you want me to pull the tooth, slowly or all in one go?"

"Why should the torment stop now? Come to my flat at four."

"What's the point?"

"To hear me cry, curse and beg. I can't do that here."

"I've promised to eat with the family at five."

"If you don't come, first of all I'll throw all your possessions out on the street, then I'll ring and tell your wife about your escapades—"

"She knows already, Caithness."

"—and your parents-in-law. Tell them how you deceived their daughter and grandchildren."

Duff gulped. "Caithness—"

"Four o'clock. If you're nice and listen you'll get to your bloody meal."

"OK, OK, I'll come. But don't think this will change anything."

The crime photographer was leaning against the garage door and smoking when Duff came out.

"Nasty?" he asked.

"Sorry?"

"Cutting off his head like that."

"Murder's always nasty," Duff said, making for the exit.

Lady was in the bedroom, standing in front of the door to Macbeth's wardrobe. Listening to the sound of wet rats scurrying across the wooden floor. She told herself the sounds were only in her imagination; the floor was thickly carpeted. Sounds in her imagination. Soon it would be voices. The voices her mother had talked about that wouldn't leave her in peace, the same voices her mother's mother had heard—their forefathers speaking, commanding them to sleepwalk at night, to hurtle toward death. She had been so afraid when she saw Macbeth hallucinating at the table during the dinner. Had she infected her only true love with this illness?

The scurrying rat feet had been in her imagination a long time now and they didn't want to disappear.

All she could do was scurry herself. Away from the sounds, away from her imagination.

She opened the wardrobe door.

Pulled out the drawer under the shelf. There was a little bag of powder inside. Macbeth's escape. Did it work? Would she escape if she went to the same place he went? She didn't think so. She closed the drawer again.

Looked up at the hat shelf. At the parcel Jack had been given. It was wrapped in paper, tied with twine and with transparent plastic on top. It was only a parcel. And yet it was as though it was staring down at her.

She opened the drawer again and took out the bag. Sprinkled a tiny bit of powder on the table in front of the mirror, rolled up a banknote and— unsure of how you actually did it—put one end in one nostril and held the other above the powder and breathed in, half with her nose, half with her mouth. As that didn't work, and after a couple more attempts, she arranged the powder in a line, inserted the note in her nostril and inhaled hard while running the note along the line, vacuuming it up. She sat for a while studying herself in the mirror. The sound of scurrying rats disappeared. Then she went to the bed and lay down.

"Here they come!" the sarge shouted. He stood in the Norse Riders gateway watching the yellow prison bus come up the road. It was half past three, bang on time. He glanced over at those who had gathered outside the clubhouse in the drizzle. Everyone in the club was duty-bound to welcome back the injured they'd had to leave to the police that night. The women had also turned up—the girls who had a boyfriend among the released prisoners and those who did the rounds. The sergeant smiled at the laughing baby in Betty's arms; Betty was looking for her Sean. Even their cousins from the south had decided to join them again for this party, which already promised to be legendary. Sweno had given orders that there should be enough booze and dope to entertain the average village because they were celebrating more than just the release of their comrades. The Norse Riders had avenged the losses they had suffered with the dispatching of Banquo and—even more important—gained a new and gold-plated alliance. As Sweno had said, by making a personal appearance at the clubhouse and ordering a hit job, Macbeth had sold his soul to the devil, and there was no right of cancellation on that. Now he was in their pocket just as much as they were in his.

The sarge went into the street and signaled to the bus to pull up outside the gate. No one except one-hundred-percent-ID'd members were allowed inside, that was the new club rule.

And then they trooped off the bus as the stereo in the clubhouse was turned up. "Let's Spend the Night Together." Some walked and some danced to the gate, where they were received with clapping and raised fists by comrades and hugs and wet kisses by the women.

"This is fun," shouted the sergeant, "but the booze is inside."

Calls and laughter. They moved inside. But the sarge stood at the doorway, scanning their surroundings one more time. The bus on its way down the road again. Chang, who had been joined by two men, guarding the gate. The empty factory buildings around, which they had checked to make sure no one was watching the club. The sky to the west, where it actually seemed that a little blue was on the way. Now perhaps he could relax a little. Perhaps Sweno was right: perhaps better times really were coming their way.

The sergeant went in, refused spirits and put a mug of beer to his mouth. Party or not, these were critical times. He looked around. Sean and Betty were smooching in the corner with the baby squeezed between them, and the sarge thought it would be a bizarre way to end a young life. But there were plenty of things a lot bloody worse than being suffocated by undiluted love.

"Norse Riders!" he shouted. The music was turned down, and conversations died away.

"This is a day of happiness. And a day of sadness. We haven't forgotten the fallen. But there's a time to cry and a time to laugh, and today we're partying. Cheers!"

Cheering and raised glasses. The sergeant took a huge swig and wiped the foam from his beard.

"And this is a new start," he continued.

"To the speech?" shouted Sean, and everyone laughed.

"We lost a few men; they lost a few men," the sergeant said. "The drugs from Russia are water under the bridge." No laughter. "But as a man whose name you all know said to me today, 'With this head case as the chief commissioner better times are coming our way.'"

More cheering. The sarge felt as if he could talk for quite some time yet, say a few things about the club, about comradeship and sacrifice. But he had taken up enough time and space. No one but the sergeant knew that Sweno was waiting in the wings somewhere right now. It was time for the evening's grand entrance.

"And with these words," he said, "let me pass you over—"

In the dramatic pause that followed he heard something. The deep growl of a lorry with a powerful engine and in too low a gear. Well, there were lots of poor drivers out there.

"—to—"

He heard a roar. And knew the gate had flown off its hinges. And that the evening's grand entrance had a rival.

Duff stood outside the gray five-story block of flats. He looked at his watch. Five minutes to four. He could still make it to the birthday party by quite a margin. He rang the bell.

"Come up," said Caithness's voice from the intercom.

After their conversation in the darkroom he had gone to the Bricklayers Arms, sat in one of the booths and had a beer. He could of course have spent the time working in his office, but Macbeth's orders had been to stay at home in Fife. And then he had another. Giving himself time to think.

Now he walked up the stairs, not with the plodding, heavy steps of someone going to the scaffold, but with the quick, light steps of someone wanting to get a scene over with and survive. And who had another life he wanted to get back to.

The flat door was open.

"Come in," he heard Caithness shout from somewhere. He gave a sigh of relief when he saw she had collected all his possessions on the table in the hall. A toilet bag. A shaver. A couple of shirts and underwear. The tennis racket she had bought him as they both played, though it had never been used. A necklace and pearl earrings. Duff's fingers caressed the jewelry he had bought her. It had been worn often.

"In here," she shouted. From the bedroom.

The stereo was on. Elvis. "Love Me Tender."

Duff walked toward the open bedroom door, hesitating, not so light-footed now. He could smell her perfume from where he was.

"Duff," she said with a sniffle when he appeared in the doorway. "I'm giving you back what you gave me, but I expect a farewell present."

She lay on the bed in a black corset and nylons. Also bought by him. At the bedhead there was a champagne cooler containing an open bottle, which she was obviously well into. He absorbed the sight of her. She was the most beautiful, most gorgeous woman he had ever been with. Every single time he saw her he was struck by her beauty, as though it were the first time. And he could feel every caress they had exchanged, every wild ride they'd had. And now he was renouncing this. Now and forever.

"Caithness," Duff said, feeling his throat thicken. "My dear, dear, beautiful Caithness."

"Come here."

"I can't . . ."

"Of course you can. You've been able to for so long, so many times, this is just the last. You owe me that."

"You won't enjoy it. Neither of us will."

"I don't want to enjoy it, Duff. I want closure. I want *you* to crawl, for once. I want you to swallow your virtue and do as *I* want. And now this is what I want. Just this. And afterward you can go to hell and home to the meal with the wife you no longer love. Come on now. I can see from here you're ready for—"

"No, Caithness. I can't. You said you'd be satisfied with what you could have of my heart. But I can't just give you a bit of that, Caithness. Then I would be cheating twice, both you and the mother of my children. And what you said about me not loving her anymore isn't true." He inhaled. "Because I'd forgotten. But then I remembered. That I love her and I always have. And I've been unfaithful to you with my own wife."

He saw the words hit home. Saw the thin, false veneer of seduction melt into deep shock. Then tears sprang from her eyes, and she curled up, pulled up the sheet and covered herself.

"Goodbye, Caithness. Hate me as I should be hated. I'm leaving now."

At the front door Duff took the clothes and toiletries under his arm. The racket could stay. You don't play tennis on a smallholding. He stood looking at the earrings and necklace. Heard Caithness's pained sobs from the bedroom. It was expensive jewelry—it had cost him more than strictly speaking he could afford—but now, in his hand, it had no value. There was no one he could give it to anyway, except a pawnbroker. But could he bear the thought of this jewelry being worn by a stranger?

He hesitated. Looked at his watch. Then he put down the other things, took the jewelry and went back to the bedroom.

She stopped crying when she saw him. Her face was wet with tears, black with makeup. Her body shook with a last sob. One stocking had slipped down, also a shoulder strap.

"Duff . . ." she whispered.

"Caithness," he said with a gulp. Sugar in his stomach, blood rushing in his head. The jewelry fell on the floor.

The sergeant grabbed the rifle from behind the bar and ran to the window; the rest of the club members were already on their way to the arms cupboard. Outside there was a lorry standing side on to the clubhouse. The engine was running and the club gate was still hanging off its front bumper. As was Chang. The sergeant put the rifle to his shoulder as the tarpaulin over the back of the lorry dropped. And there were SWAT in their ugly black uniforms, their guns raised. But there was something even uglier on board, something which made the blood in the sergeant's veins turn to ice. Three monsters. Two of them made of steel and on stands, with ammunition feeds, rotating barrels and cooling chambers. The third stood between them, a bald, lean, sinewy man the sergeant had never seen before but knew he had always known, had always been close to. And now this man raised his hand and shouted, "Loyalty, fraternity!"

The others responded: "Baptized in fire, united in blood!"

Then a single command: "Fire." Of course. Fire.

The sergeant got him in his sights and pulled the trigger. One shot. The last.

The raindrop fell from the sky, through the mist, toward the filthy port below. Heading for an attic window beneath which a couple were making love. The man was silent as his hips went up and down, slowly but with force. The woman beneath him clawed the sheet as, sobbing and impatient, she received him. The gramophone record had stopped playing its sweet melody some time ago, and the stylus kept bumping monotonously, like the man, against the record label with the command *Love Me Tender*. But the lovers didn't appear to notice, didn't appear to notice anything apart from the repetitive motion they were caught up in, didn't even notice each other as they banged away, banging out demons, banging out reality, the world around them, this town, this day, for these few minutes, this brief hour. But the raindrop never reached the window pane above them. A cold gust from the northwest drew the drop east of the river that split the town lengthways and south of the disused railway line dividing the town diagonally. It fell on the factory district, past Estex's extinguished chimneys and farther east toward the fenced-in low timber building between the closed factories. There the drop ended its passage through the air and hit the shiny skull of a lean man, ran down his forehead, stopped for an instant in his short eyelashes, then fell like a tear down one cheek that had never known real tears.

Seyton didn't notice he had been hit. Not by a random raindrop, nor by the sergeant's bullet. He stood there, legs planted wide, his hand raised, feeling only the vibrations through the lorry as the Gatling guns opened up, feeling them spread from the soles of his shoes up to his hips, feeling the sound pound evenly on his eardrums, a sound that rose from a chattering mumble to a roar and then to a concerted howl as the barrels spat out bullets faster and faster. And as time passed, as the clubhouse in front of them was shot to pieces, he felt the heat from the two machines. Two machines from hell with one function, to swallow the metal they were fed and spit it out again like bulimic robots, but faster than anything else in the world. So far the machine gunners hadn't seen much damage, but gradually it became apparent as windows and doors fell off and parts of the walls simply dissolved. A woman appeared on the floor inside the door. Sections of her head were missing, while her body was shaking as if from electric shocks. Seyton sensed he had an erection. Must be the vibrations of the lorry.

One machine gun stopped firing.

Seyton turned to the gunner.

"Anything wrong, Angus?"

"The job's done now," Angus shouted back, pulling his blond fringe to the side.

"No one stops until I say so."

"But—"

"Is that understood?" Seyton yelled.

Angus swallowed. "For Banquo?"

"That's what I said! For Banquo! Now!"

Angus's machine gun opened up again. But Seyton could see that Angus was right. The job was done. There wasn't a square decimeter in front of them that wasn't perforated. There was nothing that wasn't destroyed. Nothing that wasn't dead.

He still waited. Closed his eyes and just listened. But it was time to let the girls have a rest.

"Stop!" he shouted.

The machine guns fell silent.

A cloud of dust rose from the obliterated clubhouse. Seyton closed his eyes again and breathed in the air. A cloud of souls.

"What's up?" lisped Olafson from the end of the lorry.

"We're saving ammo," Seyton said. "We've got a job this afternoon."

"You're bleeding, sir! Your arm."

Seyton looked down at his jacket, which was stuck to his elbow where blood was pouring from a hole. He placed a hand on the wound. "It'll be all right," he said. "Handguns at the ready, everyone. We'll go in and do a body count. If you find Sweno, tell me."

"And if we find any survivors?" Angus asked.

Someone laughed.

Seyton wiped a raindrop from his cheek. "I repeat. Macbeth's order was that none of Banquo's murderers should survive. Is that a good enough answer for you, Angus?"

21

MEREDITH WAS HANGING SHEETS ON the line over the veranda by the front door. She loved this house, the rural, unpretentious, traditional, sober but practical essence of it. When people heard that she and Duff lived on a farm in Fife they automatically assumed it was a luxurious estate and probably thought she was being coy when she described how simply they lived. What would a woman with her surname be doing on a disused smallholding, they must have thought.

She had washed all the bedlinen in the house so that Duff wouldn't think she had only done the sheets of the marital bed. Where they would sleep tonight. Forget the bad stuff, repress what had been. Reawaken what they'd had. It had been dormant, that was all. She felt her stomach grow warm at the thought. The intimacy they had shared on the rock this morning had been so wonderful. As wonderful as in the first years. No, more wonderful. She hummed a tune she had heard on the radio—she didn't know what it was—hung up the last sheet and ran her hand over the wet cotton, inhaled the fragrant perfume. The wind blew the sheet high in the air, and the sunshine swept over her face and dress. Warm, pleasant, bright. This is how life should be. Making love, working, living. This was what she had been brought up to do, this was still her credo.

She heard a seagull scream and shaded her eyes. What was it doing here, so far from the sea?

"Mum!"

She had hung the washing over several lines, so she had to move between them, skip her way to the front door.

"Yes, Ewan?"

Her son was sitting on a bench, his chin propped on one hand, looking into the distance. Squinting into the low afternoon sun. "Won't Dad be here soon?"

"Yes, he will. How's the soup doing, Emily?"

"It was ready eons ago," the daughter said, dutifully stirring the big pot. Broth. Simple, nutritious peasant food.

Ewan stuck out his lower lip. "He said he'd be here *before* the meal."

"You hang him up by his toes for breaking his promise," Meredith said, stroking his fringe.

"Should people be hung for lying?"

"Without exception." Meredith looked at her watch. There might be holdups in the rush-hour traffic, now that only the old bridge was open.

"Who by?" the boy asked.

"What do you mean who by?"

"Who should hang people who lie?" Ewan's eyes had a faraway look, as though he were talking to himself.

"The honest joes of course."

Ewan turned to his mother. "Then liars are stupid because there are lots more of them than there are honest joes. They could beat the joes and hang them instead."

"Listen!" Emily said.

Meredith pricked up her ears. And now she could hear it too. The distant rumble of an engine getting closer.

The boy jumped down from the bench. "Here he comes! Emily, let's hide and give him a fright."

"Yes!"

The children disappeared into the bedroom while Meredith went to the window. Tried to shade her eyes from the sun. She felt an unease she couldn't explain. Perhaps she was afraid the Duff who came home wouldn't be the same one who had left that morning.

Duff put his car in neutral and let it roll the last part of the gravel track to the house. The gravel murmured and fretted like subterranean trolls beneath the wheels. He had driven like a man possessed from Caithness, had broken a principle he had always adhered to, never to misuse the blue light he kept in the glove compartment. With the light on the roof he had managed to jump the queue on the road to the old bridge, but once there the carriageway was so narrow that even with the light he'd had to grit his teeth as they moved forward at a snail's pace. He braked hard and the subterranean voices died. Switched off the engine and got out. The sun was shining on the white sheets on the veranda welcoming him home with a wave. She had done the washing. All the bedlinen so that he wouldn't think she had only done the sheets on the marital bed. And even though he was sated with lovemaking, the notion warmed his heart. Because he had left Caithness. And Caithness had left him. She had stood in the door, wiping a last tear, given him a last goodbye kiss and said that now the door was closed to him. She could do this now that she had made up her mind. One day maybe someone else would come through the door he was leaving. And he replied that he hoped so, and the "someone else" would be a very lucky man. On the street he had leaped in the air with relief, happiness and freedom regained. Yes, imagine that—free. To be with his wife and children! Life is strange. And wonderful.

He walked toward the veranda. "Ewan! Emily!" Usually when he came home they ran out to meet him. But sometimes they also hid to launch a surprise attack on him.

He dodged between the lines of sheets.

"Ewan! Emily!"

He stopped. He was hidden between the sheets, which cast long shadows that moved across the veranda floor. He inhaled the soap's perfume and the freshwater in which they had been washed. There was another smell too. He smiled. Broth. His smile became even broader as he remembered the good-natured discussion they'd had when Ewan insisted on having the beard glued on *before* he ate his soup. It was perfectly still. The ambush could come at any second.

There were tiny dots of sunshine in the shadows the sheets cast.

He stood staring at them.

Then down at himself. At his sweater and trousers covered with tiny dots of sunshine. He felt his heart skip a beat. Ran a finger over a sheet. It found a hole at once. And another. He stopped breathing.

Pulled the sheet at the back to the side.

The kitchen window was gone. The wall was holed so badly it looked more like a hole than a wall. He looked in through where the window had been. The pot on the hotplate looked like a sieve. The stove and the floor around were covered with a steaming yellowish-green broth.

He wanted to go inside. He *had* to go inside. But he couldn't; it was as if his feet were frozen to the veranda floor and his willpower was deactivated.

But there's no one in the kitchen, he told himself. Empty. Perhaps the rest of the house was empty too. Destroyed but empty. Perhaps they had escaped to the cabin. Perhaps. Perhaps he hadn't lost everything.

He forced himself to pass through the opening where the door had been. He went into the children's rooms. First Emily's, then Ewan's. Checked the cupboards raked with machine-gun fire and under the beds. No one. Nor in the guest room. He went toward the last room, his and Meredith's bedroom, with the broad soft double bed where on Sunday mornings they made room for all four of them, lay on their sides, tickled bare toes to the children's loud shrieks, gently scratched one another's backs, talked about all sorts of weird and wonderful things and fought to decide who should get up first.

The bedroom door hadn't been shot away, but the gaps between the bullet holes were the same as elsewhere in the house. Duff took a deep breath.

Perhaps not all was lost yet.

He gripped the handle. Opened the door.

Of course he knew he had been lying to himself. He had become good at it: the more he had practiced self-deception the easier it had been to see what he wanted to see. But in the last few days the scales had fallen from his eyes and now he was there and couldn't not see what lay before his eyes. The feathers from the mattress were everywhere, as though snow had been falling. Perhaps that was why everything seemed so peaceful. Meredith looked as if she had tried to keep Ewan and Emily warm as they sat on the floor in the far corner with her arms around them. Red feathers were stuck to the walls around them.

Duff's breathing came in gasps. And then came a sob. One single, bitter, raging sob.

Everything was lost.

Absolutely everything was lost.

22

DUFF REMAINED STANDING IN THE doorway. Saw the blanket on the bed. He knew it wouldn't help if he waded into the feathers; all he would do was contaminate the crime scene and potentially destroy the evidence. But he had to cover them up. Cover them up for a last time, they couldn't stay like that. He stepped inside, then stopped.

He had heard a sound. A shout.

He backed out and strode into the sitting room, over to the smashed window facing southeast, toward the lake. There was the cry again. So far away he couldn't see who was shouting, but sound carried well out there in the afternoon. The voice sounded angry. It had repeated the same word, but Duff couldn't make out what it was. He pulled out the remains of a chest drawer, took out the binoculars kept there, focused on the cabin. One lens of the binoculars was pierced, but the other was good enough for him to see a fair-haired man hurrying toward the house on the narrow road. Behind him, in front of the cabin, stood a lorry, on the back of which was a man whose face he recognized. Seyton. He was standing between what looked like two enormous meat mincers on stands. Duff remembered Macbeth's words. *Stay in bed for two days at least . . . an order.* Macbeth had known. Known that Duff was about to reveal that he had killed Duncan. *Lennox.* Lennox, the traitor. There was no judge from Capitol coming to town tomorrow.

Duff saw Seyton's mouth moving before the sound reached him. The same furious word: "Angus!"

Duff moved back from the window so that the glass in the binoculars wouldn't reflect the sun and give him away. He had to escape.

As darkness fell over the town, news of the massacre at the Norse Riders' clubhouse was already spreading. And at nine o'clock most of the town's journalists, TV and radio crews were gathered in Scone Hall. Macbeth stood in the wings listening to Lennox welcome them to the press conference.

"We would ask you not to use flash until the chief commissioner has finished, and please ask questions by raising a hand and speaking. And now here is this proud town's chief commissioner, Macbeth."

This introduction—and possibly the rumors of the victory over the Norse Riders in the battle at the clubhouse—were cause enough for a couple of the less experienced journalists to clap when Macbeth appeared on the podium, but the thin applause died under the eloquent gazes of the more seasoned members of the audience.

Macbeth walked up to the lectern. No, he *took the lectern by force*, that was how it felt. It was strange that this—speaking to an audience—was what he had feared most; now he didn't just like it, he longed for it, he *needed* it. He coughed, looked down at his papers. Then he started.

"Today the police carried out two armed operations against those behind the recent murders of our officers, among them Chief Commissioner Duncan. I'm pleased to say that the first operation, given the circumstances, was one-hundred-percent successful. The criminal gang known as the Norse Riders has ceased to exist." A single hurrah from the audience broke the silence. "This was a planned action based on new information that emerged after the release of some Norse Rider members. The circumstances were that the Norse Riders fired shots at SWAT, and we had no choice but to hit back hard."

A shout from the back of the hall: "Is Sweno among the dead?"

"Yes," said Macbeth. "He is indeed one of the bodies that cannot be identified because of the comprehensive nature of his injuries, but I think you all recognize this . . ." Macbeth held up a shiny saber. More hurrahs, and now some of the more experienced journalists joined in the spontaneous applause. "And with it an era is over. Fortunately."

"There are rumors that women and children are among the dead."

"Yes and no," Macbeth said. "Adult women who had chosen to associate with the club, yes. Many of them have what we might call a sullied record and none of them did anything to stop the Norse Riders firing at us. As for children, that's just nonsense. There were no innocent victims here."

"You mentioned a second operation. What was that?"

"It took place out of town, in Fife, straight after the first, in a relatively deserted area, so you may not have heard about it, but this was an attempt to arrest someone we now know had been working with the Norse Riders for some time. It is of course regrettable that such an officer could be found within our ranks, but it also proves that Chief Commissioner Duncan was not infallible when he handed the Narcotics Unit and later the Homicide Unit to this man, Inspector Duff. And we're not infallible either. We considered his family and assumed he would do the same and give himself up. So when we arrived, Police Officer Seyton, the head of SWAT, went toward the house and asked Duff to come out alone and give himself up. Duff responded by shooting at Seyton."

He nodded toward Seyton, who was standing under the light by the door at the front of the hall so that everyone could see him with his arm in a sling.

"Luck would have it that the shot wasn't fatal. Police Officer Seyton soon received medical attention and there's every chance that he'll escape permanent injury. However, despite the seriousness of his injury, Police Officer Seyton led the attack. Unfortunately, Duff, in his desperation and cowardice, chose to use his family as a shield, with the tragic result that they paid with their lives, while Duff managed to escape from the back of the house and make a getaway in his car. He's a wanted man, and we have commenced a search. I promise to you here and now that we *will* find and punish Duff. Incidentally, let me use this opportunity to announce that we'll soon be able to address Police Officer Seyton as Inspector Seyton."

More joined in the applause this time. Once it had died down there was a cough, and a voice with rolled "r"s said, "This is all very well, Macbeth, but where is the evidence—" the questioner pronounced "*evidence*" slowly with ultra-clear diction as though it were a difficult foreign word "—against the people you have mown down?"

"As far as the Norse Riders are concerned, we have witnesses who saw them shooting at Banquo's car, and we have fingerprints on and inside the car, also blood on Banquo's seat identical to the types of some of those found dead in the clubhouse this evening. Forensics can also confirm that fingerprints found on the inside of the windscreen, on the driver's side, match those of—" Macbeth paused "—Inspector Duff."

A ripple went through the hall.

"At this juncture I'd like to praise the SOC officers. Duff went to the crime scene just after the murder. This was odd as no one at Homicide had been able to get hold of Duff to inform him of the murder. Obviously he turned up with the intention of erasing his fingerprints and other clues he must have known he'd left behind. But the Forensic Unit didn't let anyone, no one at all, go near the body and contaminate the evidence. Personally, I can add that my suspicion that Duff was working with the Norse Riders grew during the raid on the container harbor. Both the Narcotics Unit and we at SWAT had received such a clear tip-off that Duff couldn't have ignored it without arousing suspicion that he was protecting them. Duff cleverly set up a raid that was doomed to fail, with inexperienced officers from his own unit in insufficient numbers, without seeking the assistance of SWAT, which is the normal procedure in such cases. Luckily the raid came to our attention, so SWAT reacted independently, and I think I can say without blowing our own trumpet that this was the start of the Norse Riders' and Duff's downfall. The Norse Riders and Inspector Duff dug their own graves when they avenged the loss of the drugs consignment and five of their members by killing first Duncan and then Banquo and his son. And this is, incidentally, the last time I will mention Duff by rank, which in our police force is considered an honor regardless of whether it is the highest or the lowest." Macbeth noticed to his dismay that the slightly tremulous indignation in his voice was genuine, completely genuine.

"Do you really mean to say, Macbeth—"

"Hand up before you . . ." Lennox started to say, but Macbeth raised his palms and nodded for Kite to continue. He was ready to take on this insubordinate querulous bastard now.

"Do you really mean to say, Macbeth, that you, the police, cannot be criticized for *anything* during these operations? In the course of one afternoon you killed seven people you'd released from prison an hour earlier, nine other gang members, most of whom had no record, plus six women who, as far as we know, had nothing to do with any crimes committed by the Norse Riders. Then you tell us there's also a family in Fife who are by definition innocent victims. And you consider that you didn't make a single error?"

Macbeth observed Kite. The radio reporter had dark hair surrounding a bald head and a mustache that formed a sad mouth around his own. Always bad news. Macbeth wondered what fate awaited such a man. He shuffled his papers. Found the page he had drafted and to which Lady, later Lennox, had added detail. Breathed in. Knew he was in perfect equilibrium. Knew his medication was perfect. Knew he had received the perfect serve.

"He's right," Macbeth said, looking across the assembled journalists. "We've made mistakes." Waited, waited until it was even quieter than quiet, until the silence was unbearable, you couldn't breathe, until the silence demanded *sound*. He looked down at his speech. He had to bring it alive, make it seem as if he wasn't just quoting the text he had in front of him.

"In a democracy," he began, "there are rules which determine when suspects must be released from custody. We obeyed them." He nodded as an amen to his declaration. "In a democracy there are rules which state that the police can and must arrest suspects when there is *new* evidence in a case. We obeyed them." More nodding. "In a democracy there are rules which set out how the police should react if suspects resist arrest and, as in this case, shoot at the police. And we obeyed them." He could of course have continued like this, but three instances of "We obeyed them" were enough. He raised a forefinger. "And that's all we've done. Some have already called what we did heroic. Some have already called it the most effective and eagerly awaited police operation in the history of this town's suffering. And some have called it a turning point in the fight against crime on our streets." He saw how his nodding had rubbed off on the listeners, he even heard a couple of mumbled yesses. "But the way I see it as chief commissioner is that we were only doing the job we'd been given. Nothing more than you can ask of us as police officers."

In the empty gallery he saw Lennox standing ready by the projector while following the speech in his copy of the manuscript.

"But I have to admit it makes me feel good this evening," Macbeth said, "to be able to say *police officers* and do so with pride. And now, goodness me, folks, let's put the formalities to one side for a moment. The fact is we had a big cleanup today. We paid Sweno and his murderers back in their own coin. We showed them what they can expect if they take our best men from us . . ."

The light shone brighter around him, and he knew the slide of Duncan had come up on the screen behind him; soon it would shift to Banquo and Fleance in uniform under the apple tree in the garden behind their house.

"But, yes, we made errors. We made an error by not starting this cleanup *before*! Before it was too late for Chief Commissioner Duncan. Before it was too late for Inspector Banquo, who served this town all his life. And his son, Police Cadet Fleance, who was looking forward to doing the same." Macbeth had to take deep breaths to control the tremor in his voice. "But this afternoon we showed that this is a new day. A new day when criminals are no longer in charge. A new day when the citizens of this town have stood up and said no. No, we won't allow this. And now this is the evening of the first of these new days. And in the days to come we will continue to clean up the streets of this town because this big cleanup isn't over."

When Macbeth had finished and said, "Thank you," he stayed on his feet. Stood there in the storm of applause that broke out as chairs scraped and people rose and the ovation continued with undiminished vigor. And he could feel his eyes going misty at the cynical journalists' genuine response to his falsehoods. And when Kite also stood up and clapped, albeit in a rather more sedate tempo, he wondered if that was because the guy knew what was good for him. Because he saw that Macbeth had won their love now. Won power. And he could see and hear that the new chief commissioner was a man who was unafraid to use it.

Macbeth strode down the corridor behind Scone Hall.

Power. He could feel it in his veins; the harmony was still there. Not as perfect as a while ago—the unease and restlessness were already on the verge of returning—but he had more than enough medicine for the moment. And he would just enjoy tonight. Enjoy the food and drink, enjoy Lady, enjoy the view of the town, enjoy everything that was his.

"Good speech, sir," Seyton said, who seemed to have no problem keeping up with Macbeth's pace.

Lennox ran up alongside him.

"Fantastic, Macbeth!" he exclaimed, out of breath. "There are some journalists here from Capitol to see you. They'd like to interview you and—"

"Thank you but no," Macbeth said without slowing down. "No victory interviews, no laurels until we've achieved our goal. Any news of Duff?"

"His car's been found in the town, parked beside the Obelisk. The roads out of town, the airport, passenger boats—everything has been under surveillance since half an hour after we saw him driving toward the town from Fife, so we know he's still here somewhere. We've checked Banquo's house, his parents-in-law, and he's not there. But in this weather a man *has* to have a roof over his head at night, so we'll go through every hotel, every boarding house, pub and brothel with a toothcomb. Everyone, absolutely everyone is chasing Duff tonight."

"Chasing's good, catching's better."

"Oh, we'll catch him. It's just a question of time."

"Good. Could you leave us alone for a minute?"

"OK." Lennox stopped and was soon far behind them.

"Something bothering you, Seyton? The wound?"

"No, sir." Seyton took his arm out of the sling.

"No? The sergeant shot you in the arm, didn't he?"

"I have unusually good healing tissue," Seyton said. "It's in the family."

"Indeed?"

"Good healing tissue?"

"Family. There's something else eating you then?"

"Two things."

"Out with it."

"The baby we found and removed from the club house after the shooting."

"Yes?"

"I don't really know what to do with it. I've got it locked in my office."

"I'll take care of it," Macbeth said. "And the other thing?"

"Angus, sir."

"What about him?"

"He didn't obey orders in Fife. He refused to fire and in the end left before the op was finished. He called it slaughter. He hadn't joined SWAT to take part in *this kind of thing*. I think there's a risk he might blab. We have to do something."

They stopped in front of the lift.

Macbeth rubbed his chin. "So you think Angus has lost the belief? If so, it won't be the first time. Has he told you he studied theology?"

"No, but I can smell it. And he walks about with this bloody ugly cross around his neck."

"You're in charge of SWAT now, Seyton. What do you think should be done?"

"We have to get rid of him, boss."

"Death?"

"You said yourself we're at war, sir. In war traitors and cowards are punished with death. We'll do what we did with Duff: we'll leak that he's corrupt and make it look like he resisted arrest."

"Let me chew on it. Right now we're in the spotlight and we need to show loyalty and unity. Cawdor, Malcolm, Duff and now Angus. It's too many. The town likes dead criminals better than duplicitous policemen. Where is he?"

"He's sitting alone moping in the basement. He won't talk to anyone."

"OK. Let me have a chat with him before we make a move."

Macbeth found Angus in the SWAT common room. He was sitting with his head in his hands and barely reacted when Macbeth put a large shoe-box before him on the table and sat down in the chair directly opposite.

"I heard what happened. How are you?"

No answer.

"You're a principled lad, Angus. That's part of what I like about you. Principles are important to you, aren't they?"

Angus raised his head and looked at Macbeth with bloodshot eyes.

"I can see them burning in your eyes right now," Macbeth said. "Righteous indignation, it warms your heart, doesn't it? Makes you feel like the person you want to be. But when the brotherhood demands a real sacrifice it's sometimes exactly that that we want, Angus. Your principles. For you to renounce the cozy warmth of a good conscience, for you to be wakened by the same nightmares as us, for you to give up what is most valuable to you, the way your former god demanded that Abraham give up his son."

Angus cleared his throat, but his voice was still hoarse. "I can give. But for what?"

"For the long-term goal. For the community's good. For the town, Angus."

Angus snorted. "Can you explain to me how killing innocent people is for the community's good?"

"Twenty-five years ago an American president dropped the atom bomb on two Japanese towns populated by children, civilians and innocents. It stopped a war. That's the kind of paradox God torments us with."

"That's easy to say. You weren't there."

"I know what it costs, Angus. Recently I cut the throat of an innocent person for the good of the community. I don't sleep well at night. The doubt, the shame, the sense of guilt, they're part of the price we have to pay if we really want to do something good and not just bathe in the cozy, safe warmth of self-righteousness."

"God doesn't exist and I'm no president."

"That's correct," Macbeth said, taking the lid off the shoebox. "But as I'm both in this building I'll give you a chance to make up for the mistake you made in Fife."

Angus peeped into the box. And recoiled in his chair in shock.

"Take this and burn it in the furnace at Estex tonight."

Angus swallowed, as pale as death. "That's the b-b-baby from the club-house . . ."

"Front-line soldiers, like you and me, know that innocent lives have to be lost in war, but they don't know that at home—the people we fight for. That's why we keep such things hidden from them, so they don't get hysterical. Do you get hysterical, Angus?"

"I-I . . ."

"Listen. I'm showing my confidence in you by giving you this assignment. You can go to Estex or you can use this to report your brothers here in SWAT. I'm giving you the choice. Because I need to know that I can trust you."

Angus shook his head, a sob escaped him. "You need to make me an *accessory* to know you can trust me!"

Macbeth shook his head. "You're already an accessory. I only need to know that you're strong enough to take and carry the guilt without those at home finding out the price we pay to defend them. Only then will I know if you're a real man, Angus."

"You make it sound as if we, and not the child, are the victims. I can't do it! I'd rather be shot."

Macbeth looked at Angus. He didn't feel any anger. Perhaps because he liked Angus. Perhaps because he knew Angus couldn't hurt them. But mostly because he was sorry for him. Macbeth put the lid back on the shoebox and stood up.

"Wait," Angus said. "H-how are you going to punish me?"

"Oh, you'll punish yourself," Macbeth said. "Read what it says on our flag. It's not the child's screaming you'll hear when you wake up sweaty after a nightmare, but the words: *Loyalty, fraternity, baptized in fire, united in blood.*"

He took the shoebox and left.

There was still more than an hour to midnight when Macbeth let himself into the suite.

Lady was standing by the window with her back to him. The room was sparsely illuminated by a single wax candle, and she was dressed in a nightdress. He put the shoebox on the table under the mirror, went over to her and kissed her neck.

"The electricity went when I arrived," he said. "Jack's checking the fuse box. Hope none of the customers are using the opportunity to make off with the kitty."

"The electricity has gone in over half the town," she said, leaning back and resting her head on his shoulder. "I can see from here. What have you got in the shoebox?"

"What do you normally have in a shoebox?"

"You're carrying it as if it were a bomb."

At that moment a huge streak of lightning flashed like a white luminous vein across the sky, and they caught a glimpse of the town. Then it was dark again and thunder rolled in.

"Isn't it beautiful?" he said, inhaling the scent of her hair.

"I don't know what it is, you know."

"I meant the town. And it will be more beautiful. When Duff's no longer in it."

"It will still have a mayor who makes it ugly. Won't you tell me what's in the box?" Her voice was thick, as though she had just woken up.

"Just something I have to burn. I'll ask Jack to take it up to the furnaces at Estex tomorrow."

"I want to be burned too, darling."

Macbeth stiffened. What had she said? Was she sleepwalking? But sleepwalkers couldn't hold conversations, could they?

"So you haven't found Duff yet?" she said.

"Not yet, but we're looking everywhere."

"Poor man. Losing his children and now he's all alone."

"Someone's helping him. Otherwise we'd have found him. I don't trust Lennox."

"Because you know he serves Hecate and brew?"

"Because Lennox is basically weak. He might be getting soft and con-spiratorial, the way Banquo became. Perhaps he's hiding Duff. I should arrest him. Seyton tells me that under Kenneth they used to give arrestees an electric shock in the groin if they didn't talk. And another one to *stop* them talking."

"No."

"No?"

"No. Arresting one of your own unit commanders would look bad now. For the time being the general impression is that you've nabbed two rotten apples in Duff and Malcolm. Three would make it look like a purge. Purges raise questions not only about the unpurged but also the leader, and we don't want to give Tourtell any reason to hesitate in appointing you. And as for electric shocks, right now there's no electricity in this part of town."

"So what do I do?"

"You wake the electrician and ask him to fix it."

"You're difficult this evening, my love. This evening you should be uniting with me, acclaiming me as a hero."

"And you me as a heroine, Macbeth. Have you checked out Caith-ness?"

"Caithness? What makes you think she's involved?"

"During the dinner that night Duff said he was staying with a cousin."

"Yes, he mentioned that."

"And you weren't surprised that an orphanage boy had an uncle in town?"

"Not all uncles can take on . . ." Macbeth frowned as he stood behind her. "You mean Duff and Caithness . . . ?"

"Dear Macbeth, my hero, you are and will always be a simple man without a woman's eye for how two secretly enamored people look at each other."

Macbeth blinked into the darkness. Then he put his arms around her, closed his eyes and pulled her to him. How would he have survived with-out her? "Only when we two stand in front of the mirror," he whispered in her ear. "Thank you, darling. Go to bed now and I'll tell Lennox to go to Caithness's at once."

"It's back," she said.

"What is?"

"The electricity. Look. Our town is lit up again."

Macbeth opened his eyes and looked at her illuminated face. Looked down at both of their bodies. They glowed red from the neon Bacardi lights on the building across Thrift Street.

"Lennox?" Caithness was already so frozen that her teeth were chattering as she stood with her arms crossed in the doorway to her flat. "Police Officer Seyton?"

"*Inspector* Seyton," the lean policeman said, pushed her aside and went in.

"What's this about?" she asked.

"I'm sorry, Caithness," Lennox said. "Orders. Is Duff here?"

"Duff? Why on earth would he be here?"

"And why on earth would you say yes?" Seyton said, directing the four machine-gun-toting men in SWAT uniforms to the four rooms in the flat. "If he's here it's because you're hiding him. You know very well he's a wanted man."

"Feel free," she said.

"Thank you so much for your permission," Seyton said acidly. Studying her in a way that made her wish she had more on than her thin nightdress. Then he smiled. Caithness shuddered. His mouth arced up behind his slightly slanting eyes, making him look like a snake.

"Are you trying to hold us up?" he said.

"Hold you up?" she said, hoping he didn't notice the fear in her voice.

"Sir?" It was one of the men. "There's a door to a fire escape here."

"Oh, is there?" Seyton intoned without taking his eyes off Caithness. "Interesting. So when we rang your doorbell down on the street you let the cat out through the flap, did you?"

"Not at all," she said.

"You are of course familiar with the penalty for lying to the police—in addition to that for hiding a criminal?"

"I am *not* lying, Police Officer Seyton."

"*Inspec*—" He paused, regained his smile. "This is SWAT you're dealing with, Miss Caithness. We know our job. Such as examining the drawings of buildings before we enter." He lifted his walkie-talkie to his mouth. "Alpha to Charlie. Any sign of Duff by the fire escape door? Over."

The brief sibilance when he pressed the button of the walkie-talkie made her think of waves lapping on a beach somewhere far far away.

"Not yet, Alpha," came the answer. "Conditions for a controlled arrest are good here, so can we confirm that the object should be shot on sight? Over."

Caithness saw Seyton's eyes harden and heard his voice sharpen. "Duff's dangerous. The order comes straight from the chief commissioner and must be followed to the letter."

"Roger. Over and out."

The four men came back into the sitting room. "He's not here, sir."

"Nothing?"

"I found this lying on the bedroom floor by the door to the fire escape." One of them held up a tennis racket and jewelry.

Seyton took the racket and leaned over the hand holding the jewelry. To Caithness it looked as if he was sniffing them. Then he turned back to her holding the handle of the racket in an obscene way.

"Big racket for a little hand like yours, Miss Caithness. And do you make a habit of throwing your earrings on the floor?"

Caithness straightened. Breathed in. "I think it's a common habit, Police Officer. Casting pearls before swine. But in time one learns, hopefully. If you've finished looking and the cat on the stairs has been executed, I'd like to go back to sleep. Good night, gentlemen."

She saw Seyton's eyes go black and his mouth open, but he held his tongue when Lennox placed a hand on his shoulder.

"We apologize for the disturbance, Caithness. But as a colleague you will understand that absolutely no stone must be left unturned in this case."

Lennox and the rest headed toward the front door, but Seyton stood his ground. "Even if we don't always like the filth we find under them," he said. "So he didn't buy you a wedding ring then, I suppose?"

"What do you want, Seyton?"

His repulsive smile returned. "Yes, what do we want?"

Then he turned and left.

She closed the door behind him. Pressed her back against it. Where was Duff? Where was he last night? And what did she wish for him? The hell he had to be in or the redemption he didn't deserve?

Lennox stared through the rain pouring down the windscreen. The re-
fracted light made the red traffic lights blur and distort. God, how he
longed to get these hours, this shift, this night over and done with. God,
how he longed to relax in his sitting room, pour himself a glass of whiskey
and inject some brew. He wasn't addicted. Not to the extent that it was a
problem anyway. He was a user, not a misuser; *he* was in control, not the
dope. One of the lucky few who could take drugs and still function in a
demanding job as well as be a father and a husband. Yes, dope did actually
help him to function. Without the breaks at work he wasn't sure he would
have managed. Balancing everything, watching his step. Making compro-
mises where he had to, eating shit with a smile, not rocking the boat, understanding who was in charge, bending with the wind. But one day it
would probably be his turn to take charge. And if it wasn't, other things
were more important. His family—that was who he was working for. So
that he and Sheila could have a spacious house in a safe neighborhood in
the west of town, send their three lovely kids to a good school with healthy
values, take a well-deserved Mediterranean holiday once a year, cover the
health insurance, dentist and all that kind of thing. God, how he loved his
family. Sometimes he would put down the newspaper and just look at
them sitting in the lounge, all of them busy, and then he would think, *This
is a gift I never thought I would have the good fortune to receive.* The love of
others. He, the one they called Albert Albino, was beaten up in every
school break until he got a doctor's note saying he couldn't tolerate daylight and had to stay in the classroom alone during breaks. White, small
and delicate he may have been, but he had a big mouth on him. That was
how he had got Sheila—he talked loudly and volubly for both of them.
And even more when he had tried cocaine for the first time. It was coke
that had made him a better version of himself, energetic, dogged and unafraid. At least for a while. Later it had become a necessity so that he
wouldn't become a bad version of himself. Then he had changed drug in
the hope that there was another way other than the dead-end street that
cocaine was. Maximum one shot a day. No more. Some needed five. The
dysfunctional. He was a long way from that. His father was wrong, he did
have a spine. He had control.

"Everything under control?"

Lennox started. "Eh?"

"Your list," Seyton said from the back seat. "What's left?"

Lennox yawned. "HQ. That's the last stop."

"Police HQ's massive."

"Yes, but according to the caretaker Duff has only three keys. One for Narco and one for Homicide."

"And the third?"

"The Forensics garage. But I hardly think he'd want to catch pneumonia in the cellar if he can hide under a table in a warm dry office."

The police radio crackled, and a nasal voice informed them that all the rooms at the Obelisk, including the penthouse suite, had been searched without success.

The caretaker stood waiting for them with a big bunch of keys outside the staff entrance to HQ. It took Lennox, Seyton and eight officers less than twenty minutes to search the Narco rooms. Less to trawl through Homicide. And they had even checked behind the ceiling boards and the pipes in the ventilation system.

"That's that, then." Lennox yawned. "That's it, folks. Grab a few hours' sleep. We'll continue tomorrow."

"The garage," Seyton said.

"As I said—"

"The garage."

Lennox shrugged. "You're right. Won't take long. Lads, you go home, and Seyton, Olafson and I will check the garage."

The three of them took the lift down to the basement floor with the caretaker, who let them in and switched on the lights.

In the silence as the electricity worked to get the phosphates in the neon tubes to fluoresce Lennox heard something.

"Did you hear that?" he whispered.

"No," the caretaker said. "But it'll be rats if it's anything."

Lennox had his doubts. It hadn't been a rattling or a scurrying, it had been a creak. As if from shoes.

"A plague," the caretaker sighed. "Can't get rid of 'em, not down here."

The large cellar room was empty apart from a trolley carrying various tools and Banquo's Volvo covered with a tarpaulin by the garage door. Ranged along the wall there were five closed doors.

"If you want to get rid of rats," Seyton said, releasing the safety catch on his machine gun, "just contact me. Olafson, let's start from the left."

Lennox watched as the bald man moved quickly and nimbly across the room with Olafson hard on his heels. They took the doors one by one as if in a precisely choreographed and practiced dance. Seyton opened, Olafson went in with his gun to his shoulder, sank to his knees while Seyton followed and passed him. Lennox counted the minutes. It was getting late for his shot, he could feel. There, the final room at last. Seyton pressed the handle.

"Locked!" he shouted.

"Oh yes, the darkroom is always locked," the caretaker said. "Photos are considered evidence. Duff hasn't got a key for this room. At least, he didn't get it from me."

"Let's go then," Lennox said.

Seyton and Olafson came toward them with the short barrels of their machine guns lowered as the caretaker held the door open.

At last.

Seyton held out his hand. "The key."

"What?"

"To the darkroom."

The caretaker hesitated, glanced at Lennox, who sighed and nodded. The caretaker removed a key from his bunch and gave it to Seyton.

"What's he doing?" asked the caretaker as they watched Seyton and Olafson walk past the Volvo to the darkroom door.

"His job," growled Lennox.

"I mean with his nose. Looks like he's sniffing, like an animal."

Lennox nodded. Thinking he wasn't alone in noticing that Seyton could assume the shape of a . . . he didn't know what. Something that wasn't human anyway.

Seyton could smell him now. That smell. The same as the one in the house in Fife and Caithness's flat. Either he was here or he had been here recently. Seyton unlocked the door and opened it. Olafson went in and sank to his knees. When the caretaker had turned on the switch at the front door all the lights in the garage and the side rooms had come on as well, but in here it was still dark. Of course. A darkroom.

Seyton went in. The stench of chemicals drowned the smell of the prey, of Duff. He found the light switch on the inside of the door, twisted it on, but still no light came. Maybe the fuse had gone during the power cut. Or someone had removed the bulb. Seyton switched on his torch. The wall above the table was covered with big photos hanging from a line. Seyton shone his torch across them. They showed a dagger with a bloodstained blade and handle. Duff had been here. Seyton was absolutely sure.

"Hey! What's going on?" It was Lennox. The little albino wimp wanted to go home. He was sweating and yawning. The bloody old woman.

"Coming," Seyton shouted, switching off the torch. "Come on, Olafson."

Seyton let Olafson pass. Shut the door hard after him and stood inside the door. Listened in the darkness. Until Duff thought the coast was clear and relaxed. Seyton lifted his gun to the photos. Pressed the trigger. The weapon shook in his hands, the sound reverberated against his eardrums. He drew a cross with the burst. Then he switched on his torch again, walked over to the perforated photos and pulled them aside.

Stared at the bullet holes in the wall behind.

No Duff.

The explosions were still ringing in his ears. He noted that one of the holes was extra-deep—must have been two bullets hitting the same spot. Chance.

Of course.

Seyton marched out toward the others.

"What was that?" Lennox asked.

"I didn't like the photos," Seyton said. "There's one place we've forgotten."

"Yes," Lennox groaned. "Our beds."

"Duff thinks like they did during the bomb attacks in the war. He hides in a bomb crater because he believes two bombs can't hit exactly the same place."

"What the hell . . . ?"

"He's back in his house in Fife. Come on!"

The rat darted out of its hiding place after the light in the garage had gone off; it had heard the door slam and the steps fade away. It padded over to the damp brick floor to the car in the middle. There was blood on the driver's seat, which attracted it. Sweet, nutritious and days old. It just had to get through the tarpaulin spread over the car. The rat had almost got through before when it was disturbed. But now it gnawed through the last part and was inside. It ran across the floor on the passenger side, past the gear stick and down onto the rubber mat on the driver's side. Over a pair of leather shoes. Recoiled when one leather shoe creaked and rose. It reared up onto its legs and hissed. The lovely bloodstained driver's seat was occupied.

Duff heard the rustle of the fleeing rat. Then he loosened his tensed grip on the wheel. He could feel his heart wasn't pounding anymore, only beating. It had been hammering so hard while Seyton and his men were in the garage he was sure they must have heard. He looked at his watch. Still five hours to daybreak. He tried to shift position, but his trousers were stuck to the blood on the seat. Banquo's blood. It glued him to this place. But he had to get away. Move on.

But where? And how?

When he fled his idea had been that it would be easier to drive to town and disappear in the crowds there than escape along a country road. He had abandoned his car in a street not far from the Obelisk and gone into the casino, which was the only place besides the Inverness he knew stayed open all night. He couldn't rent a room of course; overnight accommodation would be the first place Macbeth would check. But he could sit among the great swath of one-armed bandits, as lonely and undisturbed as the person on the nearest machine, feeding it with coins and slowly allowing himself to be robbed. And he had done that while thinking—*trying* to think—about how he could escape and staring at the images of the odds spinning round in the three small windows. A heart. A dagger. A crown. After a few hours he went to the bar for a beer to see if that could brighten his mood and saw on the muted TV above the barman the press conference at police HQ, and suddenly a familiar face appeared on the screen, with a white scar running diagonally across it like a traffic sign. A close-up of himself, with the word WANTED written over it. Duff made for the exit with his collar turned up and head bent. And the cold night air cleared his brain enough for him to remember their old love nest, the garage, which was his best overnight option.

But soon Friday would dawn, a working day, and he would have to get out before the staff arrived, and outside the newsstands would be adorned with his face.

Duff put his hand into his jacket pocket. Felt the glossy paper under his fingers. Pulled out the package. Couldn't stop himself, imagined Ewan's face when he saw that he had been given what he asked for. Duff heard his own wild sobbing. Stop! He mustn't! He had promised himself he wouldn't think about them now. Grieving was a privilege he could grant himself later if he survived. He switched on the Volvo's inside light, dried his tears, removed the wrapping paper, took out the false beard, opened the glue tube and squeezed out the shiny glue, which he spread over his chin, around his lips and inside the beard. Used the rearview mirror to stick it on. Pulled the tight woolen hat over his forehead so that the upper part of his scar was hidden. Then he put on the glasses. The comically wide frames covered the scar on his cheek above the beard. In the mirror he saw he had glue on his cheek. Searched in vain through his pockets for something to wipe it off with, opened the glove compartment, found a notebook, took it out and was about to tear off the top page. Stopped. In the light he saw depressions in the paper. Someone had recently written in the notebook. So what? He tore off the sheet, wiped the glue from his cheek. Scrunched up the paper and put it in his jacket pocket. Put the notebook back in the glove compartment.

So.

Leaned back in the seat. Closed his eyes.

Five hours. Why had he put on the beard so early? It already itched. He started thinking again. Fought to keep his mind off Fife. He had to find himself a place to hide in town. All the roads out would be closed. Besides he didn't have any bolt-holes outside town or in Fife, no hostels or hotels that wouldn't be warned, no one out of town who would hide a wanted cop-killer. And then it struck him. He didn't know anyone who would help him. Not here, not anywhere. He was the type of person people got on with; they didn't necessarily actively dislike him. They just didn't like him. And why would they? What had he ever done to help them that hadn't also helped himself? He had alliances, not friends. And now, when Duff really needed help, a friend, a shoulder to cry on, Duff was a man with no creditworthiness, a lost cause. He examined his pathetic, stiff, hirsute reflection. The fox. The hunters were closing in on him, Macbeth's new chief hound, Seyton, already barking at his heels. He had to get away. But where, where could the fox find a foxhole?

Five hours to daybreak. To Friday. To Ewan's birth . . .

No! Don't cry! Survive! A dead man can't avenge anything.

He had to stay awake until it became light, then find himself somewhere else. One of the disused factories perhaps. No, he had already rejected that idea. Macbeth knew as well as he did where he would try to hide. Shit! Now he was going round in circles, crossing his own tracks, the way people did when they got lost.

He was so tired, but he had to stay awake until it was light. Ewan had never turned ten. Shit! He tried to find something to distract himself. He read all the gauges in front of him. Took the crumpled sheet from his jacket pocket, uncrumpled it and smoothed the page. Tried to read. Rummaged through the glove compartment until he found a pencil. Held it sideways over the paper and shaded over the depressions. What had been written on the paper, on the sheet above, which had been taken, shone white against black: *Dolphin. 66 Tannery St., District 6. Alfie. Safe haven.*

An address. There was a Tannery Street in town, but no District 6. And there was only one other town that was divided into districts. Capitol. When could this note have been written? He had no idea how long it took for an impression made by a pencil to disappear. And what did it mean by *Safe haven*?

Duff switched off the light and closed his eyes. A little nap maybe?

Capitol. Friday. He had seen this combination somewhere quite recently.

Duff was slipping into a dream with associations to the two words when he woke with a start.

He switched the light back on.

23

"MEREDITH AND I ARE GETTING MARRIED," Duff said. A sun seemed to be shining out of his eyes.

"Really? That was . . . erm quick."

"Yes! Will you be my best man, Macbeth?"

"Me?"

"Of course. Who else?"

"Erm. When . . . ?"

"Sixth of July. At Meredith's parents' summer place. Everything's sorted. Invitations were sent out today."

"It's kind of you to ask, Duff. I'll give it some thought."

"Thought?"

"I've . . . planned a longish trip in July. July's difficult for me, Duff."

"Trip? You didn't say anything about this to me."

"No, I might not have done."

"But then we haven't spoken for a while. Where have you been? Meredith was asking after you."

"Was she? Oh, here and there. Been a bit busy."

"And where will this trip take you?"

"To Capitol."

"Capitol?"

"Yes, I've . . . erm never been there. Time to see our capital, isn't it? It's supposed to be so much nicer than here."

"Listen to me now, my dear Macbeth. I'll pay for a return air ticket from Capitol. Can't have my best pal not being there when I get married. It'll be the party of the year! Imagine all Meredith's single girlfriends . . ."

"And from Capitol I'm going abroad. It's a long trip, Duff. I'll probably be away all July."

"But . . . Has this got anything to do with the little flirtation you and Meredith had once?"

"So if we don't see each other for a bit, all the best with the wedding and . . . well, everything."

"Macbeth!"

"Thanks, Duff, but I won't forget I owe you dragon blood. Say hello to Meredith and thank her for the little flirtation."

"Macbeth, sir!"

Macbeth opened his eyes. He was lying in bed. A dream. Nevertheless. Were those the words they had used then? *Dragon blood*. Lorreal. Had he really said that?

"Macbeth!?"

The voice came from the other side of the bedroom door and now it was accompanied by frenetic banging. He looked at the clock on the bedside table. Three o'clock in the morning.

"Sir, it's Jack!"

Macbeth turned the other way. He was alone. Lady wasn't there.

"Sir, you have to—"

Macbeth tore open the door. "What's up, Jack?"

"She's sleepwalking."

"So? Aren't you keeping an eye on her?"

"It's different this time, sir. She . . . You've got to come."

Macbeth yawned, switched on the light, donned a dressing gown and was about to leave the room when his gaze fell on the table under the mirror. The shoebox was gone.

"Quick. Show me the way, Jack."

They found her on the roof. Jack paused on the threshold of the open metal door. It had stopped raining, and all that could be heard was the wind and the regular rumble of the traffic that never slept. She was standing right on the edge, in the light of the Bacardi sign, with her back to them. A gust of wind caught her thin nightdress.

"Lady!" Macbeth said and was about to rush over to her, but Jack held him back. "The psychiatrist said she mustn't be woken up when she's sleepwalking, sir."

"But she could fall over the edge!"

"She often comes up here and stands just there," Jack said. "She can see even if she's asleep. The psychiatrist says sleepwalkers rarely come to harm, but if you wake them they can become disoriented and hurt themselves."

"Why has no one told me she comes up here? I've been given the impression she basically strolls up and down the corridor."

"She told me in no uncertain terms that I was not to say what she does in her sleep, sir."

"And what does she do?"

"Sometimes she strolls up and down the corridor as you say. Otherwise she goes into the washroom and uses the strong soap there. Scrubs her hands, occasionally until her skin goes red. Then she comes up on the roof."

Macbeth looked at her. His beloved Lady. So exposed and vulnerable out in the wind-blown night. So alone in the darkness of her mind, the darkness she had told him about but where she couldn't take him. There was nothing he could do. Just wait and hope she would choose to come back in from the night. So near and so out of reach.

"What makes you think she might take her life tonight?"

Jack glanced at Macbeth in surprise. "I don't think she will, sir."

"So what was it then, Jack?"

"What was what, sir?"

"What made you so worried that you called me?"

At that moment the moonlight broke through a gap in the cloud. And as if at an agreed signal Lady turned and walked toward them.

"That, sir."

"God help us," Macbeth whispered and hurriedly took a step back.

She was holding a bundle in her arms. She had pulled her nightdress to expose one breast, which she held to the open end of the bundle. Macbeth saw the back of a baby's head. He counted four black holes in it.

"Is she asleep?" Macbeth asked.

"I think so," Jack whispered.

They had followed her closely off the roof, down the stairs and into the suite. Now they were standing by her bed, where she lay with the blanket pulled up over her and the child.

"Shall we take it off her?"

"Let her keep it," Macbeth said. "What harm can it do? But I want you to sit here and watch over her tonight. I have an important radio interview early tomorrow morning and have to sleep, so just give me a key for another room."

"Of course," Jack said. "I'll ring for someone to take over at reception."

While Jack was away Macbeth stroked the baby's cheek. Cold, stiff, a destroyed baby. What Lady and he had been. But they had managed to repair themselves. No. Lady had managed to repair herself. Macbeth had had help. From Banquo. And before that, at the orphanage, from Duff. Had Duff not killed Lorreal, Macbeth would probably have committed suicide sooner or later. Even when he escaped from the home he still had four black holes in his heart. Four holes that had to be filled with something. Brew was the quickest and easiest available sealant. But at least he kept himself alive. Thanks to Duff, the bastard.

And then there was Lady of course. Who had shown him that hearts can be sealed with love, and pain can be eased with lovemaking. He stroked her cheek. Warm. Soft.

Were there ways back or had they forgotten to plan for a possible retreat? Had they planned only for victories? Yes, and they'd had victories. But what if the victory leaves a bitter taste, what if it comes at too great a cost and you would prefer a cheap defeat? What do you do then? Do you abdicate, renounce the royal trappings, ask humbly for forgiveness and return to your daily chores? When you step off the edge of the roof, and the cobbles of the red-light district rush toward you, do you ask gravity if you can retrace your ill-considered step? No. You take what's coming. Make the best of it. Make sure you land on your feet and perhaps break a leg or two. But you survive. And you become a better person who has learned to tread more carefully the next time.

Jack came in. "I've found someone for reception," he said and handed Macbeth a key.

Macbeth looked at it. "Duncan's room?"

Jack put a hand to his mouth in horror. "I thought it was the best room, but you might prefer . . ."

"That's fine, Jack. I'm close by in case there is anything. Besides I don't believe in ghosts. And as everyone knows I have nothing to fear from Duncan's ghost."

"No, nothing."

"Indeed, nothing at all. Good night."

They came as soon as he closed his eyes.

Duncan and Malcolm. They were lying under the duvet on either side of him.

"There isn't room for us all," Macbeth screamed and kicked them out onto the floor, where they hissed until rat tails rustled alongside the wall and they were gone.

But then the door opened, and in crept Banquo, Fleance and Duff, each with a dagger in hand, poised to strike.

"What do you want?"

"Justice and our sleep back."

"Ha, ha, ha!" Macbeth laughed, writhing in his bed. "The person who can hurt me hasn't been born! Only Bertha can unseat me as chief commissioner! I am immortal! Macbeth is immortal! Out, you dead mortals!"

24

FRED ZIEGLER YAWNED.

"Fred, you need a cup of coffee." The captain of MS *Glamis* chuckled. "We can't have a harbor pilot falling asleep in this weather. Tell me, are you always tired?"

"Busy days, not enough sleep," Fred said. He could hardly tell the captain the reason he was always yawning was that he was frightened. Fred had seen the same symptom in his dog, but fortunately yawning was usually regarded as indicating that you were totally at ease. Bored. Or, indeed, you hadn't slept enough. The captain pressed the intercom, and his order for coffee went down the cable to the galley, deck after deck after deck. MS *Glamis* was a big ship. A tall ship. And that was what bothered Fred Ziegler.

He stifled another yawn and stared across the river. He knew every reef, every shallow and every tiny paragraph in the port authority rule-book about sailing into and out of the harbor—where the current flowed strong, where the waves broke, where you could lie in shelter and where every bollard on the quay was. That didn't bother him. The river was gray; he could guide ships in and out blindfolded, and often had, or as good as. The weather didn't bother him either. A near gale was blowing, and the glass in front of them was already white with spray and salt. But he had guided bigger and smaller ships in hurricanes and worse without needing a beacon, a spar buoy or a lookout. The trip in the little pilot boat that would take him ashore didn't trouble him, even though it was as seawor-thy as a cow—a fresh breeze and it took in water, the hint of a gale and it could turn round if the coxswain didn't hit the waves right.

Fred Ziegler yawned because he dreaded the ship lowering the red and white flag that showed they had a pilot on board. Or to be more precise, having to leave the ship. Going down the rope ladder.

For twelve years he had worked as a pilot and still he hadn't got used to going up and down the side of a ship. It didn't bother him that he might end up in the drink, although he knew he ought to have been afraid because he couldn't swim.

No, what bothered him was the height.

The paralyzing fear when he would have to step out backward from the ship's side. Even in this weather the ship was so big that climbing down the ladder on the leeward side wasn't difficult from a purely technical point of view. However, seeing or just knowing that there was fifteen meters of thin air between him and the abyss bothered him. It had always been like this and always would be. Every bloody working day was bound up with this minor hell: it was the first thing on his mind when he woke up in the morning and the last before he went to sleep. But what the heck, there was nothing unusual about it—all around him he saw people who lived their whole lives doing jobs or in positions they weren't cut out for.

"You must have come out of the harbor so many times now that you could ask the coast guard just to let you go," Fred said.

"Let me go?" the captain said. "I wouldn't have your company then, Fred. What is it? Don't you like me?"

I don't like your ship, Fred thought. *I'm a small man who doesn't like big ships.*

"By the way, you're going to see less of me in the future," the captain said.

"Oh?"

"Not enough cargo. Last year we lost Graven when they went bankrupt and then Estex closed down. What we have on board now is the last remaining stock."

Fred had noticed by the way the ship lay in the water there was less cargo than usual.

"Shame," Fred said.

"No, makes no odds," the captain said gloomily. "Knowing this toxic stuff we've been transporting for all these years is paid for with our fellow citizens' lives . . . Believe me, I haven't always slept well and I've sometimes wondered what it must have been like being the captain of a

slave ship. You have to be creative to find good enough excuses for yourself. Perhaps we know the difference between right and wrong even
without using this wonderful big brain of ours. But with it we can assemble some really sophisticated arguments which, individually, sound
good and, as a whole, can lead us to exactly where we want to go, regardless of how steeped in insanity this all is. No, Fred, I don't want to ask
the coast guard for permission to navigate these contaminated waters
without a pilot. On Wednesday we were queueing up to come in when a
message came from the harbormaster himself saying that we had top
priority. Free of charge."

"That must have been a nice surprise."

"Yes. Then I took a closer look at the bill of lading. Turned out we'd
been transporting two Gatling guns. This is beginning to resemble how it
was under Kenneth. Hey, careful! Are you trying to scald our pilot, son?"

The man in the checkered galley outfit had lost his balance as the ship
pitched into a wave and had spilled coffee on the pilot's black uniform.
The guy mumbled an apology into his beard, put down the cups and hurried out.

"Sorry, Fred. Even here, where half the town is unemployed, it's hard
to find crew with sea legs. This bloke came to us this morning claiming
he'd worked in a galley before but had lost his papers."

Fred slurped from the cup. "He's not been on board a boat before and
he can't make coffee either."

"Oh well," the captain sighed. "We'll manage as we're only going to
Capitol. That's the Isle of Hanstholm behind us and now we're over the
worst. I'll call up your boat and tell them to throw out the ladder."

"OK," Fred said, swallowing. "Then we're over the worst."

Macbeth was sitting on a chair in the corridor wringing his hands and
staring at the door to the suite. "What's he actually doing in there?"

"I don't know much about psychiatry," Jack said. "Shall I get some
more coffee, sir?"

"No, stay where you are. But he's good, you say?"

"Yes, Dr. Alsaker's supposed to be the best in town."

"That's good, Jack. That's good. Terrible, terrible." Macbeth leaned
forward on the chair and hid his face in his hands. There was still an hour
to go to the radio interview. He had woken before dawn to screams from

Lady's room. And when he dashed in she had been standing beside the bed pointing at the dead baby.

"Look!" she shrieked. "Look what I've done!"

"But it wasn't you, my love." He tried to hold her, but she tore herself away and fell to her knees sobbing.

"Don't call me *my love*! I can't be loved, a child killer *shouldn't* be loved!" Then she turned to Macbeth and looked at him through those crazed gray eyes of hers. "Not even a child killer should love a child killer. Get out!"

"Come and lie down with me, darling."

"Get out of my bedroom! And don't *touch* the child!"

"This is insanity. It's going to be burned today."

"Touch the child and I'll kill you, Macbeth, I swear I will." She took the body in her arms and rocked it.

He swallowed. He needed his morning shot. "I'll take some clothes and leave you in peace," he said, going to the wardrobe. Pulled out a drawer. Stared.

"Sorry," she said. "You'll have to go and get some more. We need it, both of us."

He left and instead of going for some more power he had got Jack to call for psychiatric assistance.

Now Macbeth looked at his watch again. How long could it take to fix the little short circuit she'd obviously had?

In response the door opened and Macbeth jumped up from his chair. A little man with a wispy gray beard and eyelids that appeared to be one size too large came out.

"Well?" Macbeth asked. "Doctor . . . er . . ."

"Dr. Alsaker," Jack said.

"I've given her something to calm her down," the psychiatrist said.

"What's wrong with her?"

"Hard to say."

"Hard? You're supposed to be the best."

"That's nice to hear, but not even the very best know all the labyrinths of the mind, Mr. Macbeth."

"You *have* to cure her."

"As I said, with the little we really know about the human mind that's a lot to ask . . ."

"I'm not *asking*, Doctor. I'm giving you an ultimatum."

"An ultimatum, Mr. Macbeth?"

"If you don't make her normal again, I'll have to arrest you as a charlatan."

Alsaker looked at him from under his oversized eyelids. "I can see that you have slept badly and you're beside yourself with worry, Chief Commissioner. I recommend you take a day off work. Now as for your wife—"

"You're mistaken," Macbeth said, taking a dagger from his shoulder holster. "And the punishment for not doing your job is draconian during the present state of emergency."

"Sir . . ." Jack started to say.

"Surgery," Macbeth said. "That's what's needed, that's what a real doctor does: he cuts away what is pernicious. He excludes any thought of the patient's pain because that only makes him vacillate. You remove and destroy the offending item, a tumor or a rotting foot, to save the whole. It's not that the tumor or the foot are evil in themselves, they simply have to be sacrificed. Isn't that so, Doctor?"

The psychiatrist tilted his head. "Are you sure it's your wife who needs to be examined and not yourself, Mr. Macbeth?"

"You have your ultimatum."

"And I'm leaving now. So you'd better stab me in the back with that thing if you need to."

Macbeth watched Alsaker turn his back and set off toward the stairs. He stared at the dagger in his hand. What on earth was he doing?

"Alsaker!" Macbeth ran after the psychiatrist. Caught up with him and knelt down before him. "Please, you *have* to, you have to help her. She's all I have. I must have her back. *You* must get her back. I'll pay whatever it costs."

Alsaker held his beard between his thumb and forefinger. "Is it brew?" he asked.

"Power," Macbeth said.

"Naturally."

"You know it?"

"Under a variety of sobriquets, but the chemicals are the same. People think it's an antidepressant because it acts as an upper the first few times until the episodes become psychotic."

"Yes, yes, that's what she takes."

"I asked what *you* take, Mr. Macbeth. And now I can see. How long have you been taking power?"

"I . . ."

"Not long evidently. The first thing to go is your teeth. Then your mind. And it's not easy to escape from the prison of psychosis. Do you know what they call you when you're completely hooked on power? A POW."

"Now listen here—"

"A prisoner of war. Neat, isn't it?"

"I'm not your patient now, Alsaker. I beg you not to leave until you've done all you can."

"I promise to return, but I have other patients to attend to now."

"Jack," Macbeth said without moving or taking his eyes off the psychiatrist.

"Yes, sir."

"Show him."

"But . . ."

"He's bound by the Hippocratic oath."

Jack unwound the cloth from the bundle and held it out for the doctor. He took a step back covering his nose and mouth with his hand.

"She thinks it's hers," Macbeth said. "If not for my sake and hers, then for the town's, Doctor."

Macbeth felt a strange pressure in his ears as the door closed behind him. Finally, he thought, I'm in the nuthouse. The walls of the little square room, where three people sat observing him, were padded, although there was a window.

"Don't be afraid," said the man at the table in front of him. "I'm just going to ask a few questions. It'll all be over soon."

"It's not the questions I'm frightened of," Macbeth said, sitting down, "it's the answers."

The man smiled, the music from the speaker above the window died, and he put a finger to his mouth as a red light on the wall came on.

"This is *Rolling News* with Walt Kite," the man trilled, turning to the mike in front of him. "We have a visit from the town's new favorite, Chief Commissioner Macbeth, who after wiping out one of the town's most notorious drug gangs, the Norse Riders, is now tirelessly chasing their corrupt collaborators inside the police's own ranks. He has won the hearts of the people and lifted their hopes with inspiring speeches in which he says we're entering new times. Chief Commissioner Macbeth, isn't this just rhetoric?"

Macbeth cleared his throat. He was up for this. He was a new man. Once again he was perfectly medicated. "I'm a simple man and I don't know much about rhetoric, Walt. I've only said what was on my mind. And that is that if this town has the will it has the muscle power to raise itself. But neither the chief commissioner nor politicians can lift a town; its citizens have to do that themselves."

"But they can be inspired and led?"

"Naturally."

"You're already being touted as mayor material. Is this something that might tempt you, Chief Commissioner Macbeth?"

"I'm a police officer and I wish only to serve the town in the job I have been appointed to."

"As a humble servant of the people, in other words. Your predecessor, Duncan, also saw himself as a servant of the people, though he wasn't so humble. He promised to catch the town's most powerful criminal, Hecate, also known as the Invisible Hand, within a year. Now, you've dealt with the Norse Riders. What deadline have you set yourself for Hecate?"

"First, let me say there is a reason for the name 'the Invisible Hand.' We know very little about Hecate, only that he's *probably* behind the manufacturing of the drug called brew. But given its widespread production and distribution it's equally probable that we're talking about a network or a shared supply chain."

"Do I hear you saying you're not going to prioritize the arrest of Hecate as highly as Duncan did?"

"What you hear is a chief commissioner refusing to use all his resources on arrests that might make headlines, bring honor to the police and lead to clinking champagne glasses in the town hall, but in reality do little for people's everyday lives. If we arrest a man by the name of Hecate others will take over his market unless we tackle the town's real problem."

"Which is?"

"Jobs, Walt. Giving people work. That's the best and the cheapest initiative against crime. We can fill our prisons, but as long as we have people walking the streets without food . . ."

"Now you really sound as if you're considering standing for election."

"I don't care what it sounds like. I only want this town back on an even keel."

"And how will you do that?"

"We can do that by ensuring this becomes a town where we take account of both investors and workers. Investors mustn't get away with not paying taxes into the common pot or bribing their way to privileges. But the town can give them the sure knowledge that rules are being followed. And workers should know that their workplace isn't poisoning them. Our recently deceased hero Banquo lost his wife, Vera, several years ago. She had breathed in poisonous fumes at the factory where she worked for many years. Vera was a lovely hardworking wife and mother. I knew her personally and loved her. As chief commissioner I *promise* the town that none of its future workplaces will take the lives of any more Veras. There are other ways of finding employment for people. *Better* ways. Which will give them a *better* life."

Macbeth could see from Walt Kite's grin that he was impressed. Macbeth was impressed himself. He had never been so clear-thinking. It had to be the new powder, delivering the words, so concise and logical, from the brain to the tongue.

"Your popularity has grown quickly—exponentially—Chief Commissioner. Is that why you dare to make statements that, if I were Mayor Tourtell, I would regard as a challenge? Formally speaking, he is your boss and has to endorse your appointment to the post of chief commissioner. Otherwise you don't have a job."

"I have more bosses than the mayor, Walt, among them my own conscience and the citizens of this town. And for me my conscience and this town are above a comfy chair in the chief commissioner's office."

"In four months there are elections for a new mayor, and the closing date for nominations is in three weeks."

"If you say so, Walt."

Walt Kite laughed and raised an arm above his head. "And with that we say thank you to Chief Commissioner Macbeth. I'm not so sure he's telling us the truth when he says he knows *nothing* about rhetoric. And now here's Miles Davis . . ." He dropped his arm and pointed to the window. The red light went out, and the sound of a soft, dry trumpet filled the speakers.

"Thank you." Kite smiled. "*No one will take the lives of any more Veras?* You are aware that you could be elected as mayor on that sound bite alone, aren't you?"

"Thanks for the interview," Macbeth said without moving.

Kite glanced at him questioningly.

"Did I hear you aright?" Macbeth said slowly in a low voice. "Did you accuse me of lying at the end there?"

Kite blinked, taken aback. "Lying?"

"*I'm not so sure he's telling us the truth when he . . .*"

"Oh, but that—" the reporter's Adam's apple jumped "—was just a joke of course, a . . . erm, way of speaking, a . . ."

"I was just teasing." Macbeth smiled and got up. "See you."

As Macbeth left the radio building in the rain he felt that Walt Kite wouldn't be a problem anymore. And as he sat in the back of the limousine he felt that the Obelisk, Duff and Lady's illness weren't going to be problems anymore either. Because he was thinking more clearly than ever.

"Drive a bit more slowly," he said.

He wanted to enjoy the trip through the town. *His* town.

True enough, it wasn't his yet, but it soon would be. Because he was invincible. And perfectly medicated.

While they were waiting at some red lights his gaze fell on a man waiting by the crossing, although the pedestrian light was green. His upper body and face were hidden by a large black umbrella, so all Macbeth could see was his light-colored coat, brown shoes and the big black dog he was holding on a lead. And a thought struck Macbeth. Did the dog wonder why he was owned, why he was on a lead? He gets a little food, his allotted portion, just enough for him to prefer security to insecurity, to be kept in check. That is all that stops the dog from trotting over to the owner while he is asleep, tearing out his throat and taking over the house. For that is all he has to do. Once you realize how to open the pantry door it is actually the natural response.

PART THREE

25

"OUR FINEST-QUALITY WOOL," THE ASSISTANT said, respectfully stroking the material of the black suit on the clothes hanger.

Outside the windows of the outfitters it was drizzling and on the river the waves had started to settle after the gales of the previous days.

"What do you think, Bonus?" Hecate said. "Would it fit Macbeth?"

"I thought you were going for a dinner jacket, not a dark suit."

"You never wear, as of course you know, a dinner jacket in church, and Macbeth has many funerals to attend this week."

"So no dinner jacket today?" the assistant asked.

"We need both, Al."

"I'd just like to point out that if this is for the gala banquet, full evening dress is de rigueur, sir."

"Thank you, Al, but this isn't the royal palace, just the local town hall. What do you say, Bonus, aren't tails a bit—" Hecate clicked his tongue "—pretentious?"

"Agreed," Bonus said. "It's when the new rich dress themselves in old-money attire that they really look like clowns."

"Good, a dark suit and a dinner jacket. Will you send a tailor to Inverness Casino, Al? And put everything on my account."

"It will be done, sir."

"And then we need a dinner jacket for this gentleman."

"For me?" Bonus said in astonishment. "But I've already got a wond—"

"Thank you. I've seen it and, believe me, you need a new one."

"Do I?"

"Your position requires an impeccable appearance, Bonus, and you're working for me, what's more."

Bonus didn't answer.

"Will you run and get me some more dinner jackets, Al?"

"Right away," said the assistant, and dutifully ran a few bowlegged steps to the stairs down to the shop.

"I know what you're thinking," Hecate said. "And I admit that dressing you up is a way of displaying my power, the way kings dress up their soldiers and servants. But what can I say? I like it."

Bonus had never been one-hundred-percent sure if the abnormally white, even teeth in the old man's smile were his own. If they were dentures, they were quite eccentric because they came equipped with three big gold crowns.

"Speaking of displayed power," Hecate said, "that attractive young boy who was at the dinner at the Inverness, is his name Kasi?"

"Yes."

"How old is he?"

"Fifteen and a half," Bonus said.

"Hm. That's young."

"Age is—"

"I have no moral scruples, but neither do I have your taste for young boys, Bonus. I'm just pointing out that that's *illegally* young. And that it could potentially cause great harm. But I see this makes you uncomfortable, so let's change the topic of conversation. Lady is sick, I understand?"

"That's what the psychiatrist says. Serious psychosis. It can take time. He's afraid she might be suicidal."

"Don't doctors take an oath?"

"Dr. Alsaker may also soon be in need of a new dinner jacket."

Hecate laughed. "Just send me the bill. Can he cure her?"

"Not without hospitalization, he says. But we don't want that, do we?"

"Let's wait and see. I believe it's well known that Lady is one of the chief commissioner's most important advisers, and during these critical days there would be unfortunate consequences if it became public knowledge that she'd gone mad."

"So psychosis is . . . ?"

"Yes?"

Bonus swallowed. "Nothing." What was it about Hecate that always made him feel like a dithering teenager? It was more than the display of real power; there was something else, something that terrified Bonus but he couldn't quite put his finger on. It wasn't what he could see in Hecate's eyes, it was more what he *couldn't* see. It was the blood-curdling certainty of a nothingness. Wasteland and numbingly cold nights.

"Anyway," Hecate said, "what I wanted to discuss was Macbeth. I'm concerned about him. He's changed."

"Really?"

"I fear he's hooked. Not so strange; maybe, after all it is the world's most addictive dope."

"Power?"

"Yes, but not the type that comes in powder form. Real power. I didn't think that he would be hooked quite so quickly. He's already managed to divest himself of any emotions that tie him to morality and humanity; now power is his new and only lover. You heard the radio interview the other day. The brat wants to be mayor."

"But in practice the chief commissioner has more power."

"As chief commissioner he will of course make sure that real power is returned to the town hall before he occupies the mayoral office. Truly, Macbeth is dreaming of taking over this town. He thinks he is invincible now. And that he can challenge me too."

Bonus looked at Hecate in surprise. He had folded his hands over the golden top of his stick and was studying his reflection.

"Yes, Bonus, it should be the other way round: it should be you telling me that Macbeth is after me. That's what I pay you for. And now your little flounder brain is wondering how I can know this. Well, just ask me."

"I . . . er . . . How do you know?"

"Because he said so on the radio program you also listened to."

"I thought he said the opposite, that pursuing Hecate *wouldn't* have the same priority as under Duncan."

"And when did you last hear anyone with political ambitions say on radio what they *weren't* going to do for the electorate? He could have said he was going to arrest Hecate *and* create jobs. Sober politicians always promise everything under the sun. But what he said wasn't meant for voters, it was meant for me, Bonus. He didn't need to, yet he committed himself publicly and pandered to me. And when people pander you have to watch out."

"You think he wants to gain your confidence—" Bonus looked at Hecate to see if he was on the right track "—because he hopes that way you will let him in close and he can then dispose of you?"

Hecate pulled a black hair from a wart on his cheek and studied it. "I could crush Macbeth under my heel this minute. But I've invested a lot in getting him where he is now, and if there's one thing I hate it's a bad investment, Bonus. Therefore I want you to keep your eyes and ears open to find out what he's planning." Hecate threw up his arms. "Ah! Look, here's Al with more jackets. Let's find one to fit your long tentacle arms."

Bonus gulped. "What if I don't find out anything?"

"Then I have no more use for you, dear Bonus."

It was said in such a casual way and made even more innocuous with a little smile. Bonus's eyes searched behind the smile. But he found nothing there except night and chill.

"Look at the watch," Dr. Alsaker ordered and let his pocket watch swing in front of the patient's face. "You're relaxing, your arms and legs are feeling heavy, you're tired and you're falling asleep. And you won't wake until I say *chestnut*."

She was easy to hypnotize. So easy that Alsaker had to check a couple of times that she wasn't pretending. Whenever he came to the Inverness he was followed up to the suite by the receptionist, Jack. There she sat ready in her dressing gown—she refused to wear anything else. Her hands were red from compulsive daily scrubbing, and even if she insisted she wasn't taking anything, he could see from her pupils that she was under the influence of some drug or other. It was one of several disadvantages of being refused permission to admit her to a psychiatric ward, where he could have kept an eye on her medication, sleep and meals and observed her behavior.

"Let's begin where we left off last time," Alsaker said, looking at his notes. Not that he needed them to remember; the details were of such a brutal nature they had seared themselves into his memory. He needed his notes to *believe* what she had actually told him. The first lines were not unusual; on the contrary they were a common refrain in many similar cases. "Unemployed, alcoholic father and depressive and violent mother. You grew up by the river in what you call a hovel or a rats' nest. Literally. You told me your first memories were watching rats swimming toward your house when the sun set, and you remember thinking it was the rats' house. You slept in their bed, you had eaten their food, when they came up into your bed you understood why they bit you."

Her voice was soft and low. "They just wanted what was theirs."

"And your father said the same when he got into your bed."

"He just wanted what was his."

Alsaker skimmed his notes. It wasn't the first abuse case he had treated, but this one had some details that were particularly disturbing.

"You became pregnant when you were thirteen and gave birth to a child. Your mother called you a whore. She said you should chuck the misbegotten child into the river, but you refused."

"I just wanted to have what was mine."

"So you and the child were thrown out of the house, and you spent the next night with the first man you met."

"He said he'd kill the baby if it didn't stop screaming, so I took it into the bed. But then he said it ruined his concentration because it was *watching*."

"And while he was sleeping you stole money from his pockets and food from the kitchen."

"I just took what was mine."

"And what is yours?"

"What everyone else has."

"What happened then?"

"The river ran dry."

"Come on, Lady. What happened then?"

"More factories were built. More workers came to town. I earned a bit more money. Mum came to see me and told me Dad was dead. His lungs. It had been a painful death. I told her I'd have liked to have been there to see his pain."

"Don't skirt around it, Lady. Get to the *point*. What happened to the baby?"

"Have you seen how babies' faces change, almost from one day to the next. Well, suddenly, one day it had his face."

"Your father's."

"Yes."

"And what did you do then?"

"I gave it extra milk so that it was smiling blissfully at me when it fell asleep. Then I smashed its head against the wall. A head smashes easily, you know? How fragile a human life is."

Alsaker swallowed and cleared his throat. "Did you do it because the child's face was like your father's?"

"No. But it finally made it possible."

"Does that mean you'd been thinking about it for a while?"

"Yes, of course."

"Can you tell me why you say *of course*?"

She was silent for a moment. Alsaker saw her pupils twitch, and this reminded him of something. Frog spawn. A tadpole trying to break free from a sticky egg.

"If you want to achieve your aims you have to be able to renounce what you love. If the person you climb with to reach the peak weakens, you have to either encourage him or cut the rope."

"Why?"

"Why? If he falls he'll drag both of you down. If you want to survive, your hand has to do what your heart refuses to do."

"Kill the person you love?"

"The way Abraham sacrificed his son. Let the blood flow. Amen."

Alsaker shivered and took notes. "What is there at the peak that you want?"

"The peak is the top. Then you're up. Higher than everything and everyone."

"Do you *have* to go there?"

"No. You can crawl around in the lowlands. On the rubbish heap. In the muddy riverbed. But once you've started climbing there's no way back. It's the peak or the abyss."

Alsaker put down his pen. "And for this peak you're willing to sacrifice everything—also what you love? Is survival above love?"

"Naturally. But recently I've seen that we can live without love. So all this survival will be the death of me, Doctor."

Her eyes had a sudden clarity which for an instant made Alsaker think she wasn't psychotic after all. But it may have been just the hypnosis or a temporary awakening. Alsaker had seen this many times before. How a patient in deep psychosis or depression can apparently perk up, like a drowning person coming to the surface with an effort of will, giving both relatives and an inexperienced psychiatrist hope. They can stay afloat for several days, only to use this last effort of will to do what they had been threatening or just sink back into the darkness whence they came. But no, it must have been the hypnosis because now the frog-spawn membrane was over her eyes again.

"It says in the paper here that after the radio interview people are waiting for you to announce you're standing in the mayoral election," Seyton said. He had spread the newspaper over a coffee table and was dropping his fingernail clippings onto it.

"Let them write," Macbeth said, looking at his watch. "Tourtell should have been here ten minutes ago."

"But will you, sir?" There was a loud, clear snip as the long, pointed nail on his forefinger was cut.

Macbeth shrugged. "You have to ponder something like that. Who knows? When the idea matures it might feel different."

The door creaked. In the narrow opening Priscilla's sweet over-made-up face appeared. "He's here, sir."

"Good. Let him in." Macbeth stood up. "And get us some coffee."

Priscilla smiled, and her eyes disappeared into her chubby cheeks, then she disappeared too.

"Shall I go?" Seyton asked, making a move to rise from the sofa.

"You stay," Macbeth said.

Seyton resumed his nail-cutting.

"But stand up."

Seyton rose to his feet.

The door opened wide. "Macbeth, my friend!" roared Tourtell, and for a moment Macbeth wondered whether the doorway would be wide enough. Or his ribs strong enough, when the mayor slapped his chunky hand against his back.

"You've really got things buzzing here, Macbeth."

"Thank you. Please, take a seat."

Tourtell nodded briefly to Seyton and sat down. "Thank you. And thank you, Chief Commissioner, for receiving me at such short notice."

"You're my employer, so it's me who should feel honored that you've made the time. And, importantly, that you've come here instead of the other way round."

"Oh, that. I don't like to give people the feeling they've been summoned."

"Does that mean I've been summoned?" Macbeth asked.

The mayor laughed. "Not at all, Macbeth. I only wanted to see how things were going. Whether you were finding your feet. I mean it is a bit of a transition. And with all that's happened in the last few days . . ." Tourtell rolled his eyes. "That could have been a mess."

"Do you mean it has? Been a mess?"

"No, no, no. Not at all. I think you've tackled everything beyond all expectation. After all, you're new to this game."

"New to the game."

"Yes. Things move fast. You have to react on the hoof. Comment. And then you can say things you don't even think."

Priscilla came in, put a tray on the table, poured coffee, curtseyed awkwardly and left.

Macbeth sipped his coffee. "Hm. Is that a reference to the radio interview?"

Tourtell reached for the bowl of sugar lumps, took three and put one in his mouth. "Some of what you said could be interpreted as criticism of the town council and me. And that's fine—we appreciate a chief commissioner who calls a spade a spade—no one wears a muzzle here. The question is of course whether the criticism came across as a bit harsher than it was meant. Or what?"

Macbeth placed his forefinger under his chin and stared into the air pensively. "I didn't consider it overly harsh."

"There you go. That's exactly what I thought. You didn't mean to be harsh! You and I, we want the same things, Macbeth. What's best for the town. To get the wheels moving, to bring down unemployment. A lower jobless rate we know from experience will bring down crime and hit the drug trade, which in turn reduces property crime. Soon prisoner numbers are drastically down, and everyone asks themselves how Chief Commissioner Macbeth has achieved what none of his predecessors managed. As you know, a mayor can only serve two terms of office. So after I've been elected, hopefully, and then finished my second term, it's a new man's turn. And then perhaps the town will feel this is the kind of man they need, someone who has produced results as a chief commissioner."

"More coffee?" Macbeth poured the brown liquid into Tourtell's already full cup until it ran over into the saucer. "Do you know what my friend Banquo used to say? Kiss the girl while she's in love."

"Which means?" Tourtell said, staring at the saucer.

"Feelings change. The town loves me now. And four years is a long time."

"Maybe. But you have to choose your battles, Macbeth. And your decision now is whether to challenge the incumbent mayor—which historically seldom leads to success—or wait for four years and be supported in the election by the departing mayor—which historically very *often* leads to success."

"That kind of promise is easily made and more easily broken."

Tourtell shook his head. "I've based my long political career on strategic alliances and cooperation, Macbeth. Kenneth made sure that the chief commissioner's office had such extensive powers that I as mayor was—and am—completely dependent on the chief commissioner's goodwill. Believe me, I *know* a broken promise would cost me dear. You're an intelligent man and you learn quickly, Macbeth, but you lack experience in the complicated tactical game called politics. Instant popularity and a couple of juicy sound bites on radio aren't enough. My support isn't enough either, but it's more than you can hope to achieve on your own."

"You wouldn't have come here to persuade me not to throw my hat in the ring for the upcoming elections if you didn't see me as a serious challenger."

"You might think so," Tourtell said, "because you still don't have enough experience of politics to see the bigger picture. And the bigger picture is that when I continue as mayor and you as chief commissioner over the next four years, then the town will have a problem if its two most powerful men have had an agonizing electoral struggle which makes it difficult for them to work together. And it would also make it impossible for me to support your candidature later. I'm sure you understand."

I'm sure you understand. Ever so slightly condescending. Macbeth opened his mouth to object, but the thought that was supposed to form the words didn't come.

"Let me make a suggestion," Tourtell said. "Don't stand for election, and you won't have to wait four years for my support."

"Oh?"

"Yes. The day you arrest Hecate—which will be an immense victory for us both—I'll go public and say I hope you'll be my successor at the elections in four years. What do you say to that, Macbeth?"

"I think I said on the radio that Hecate isn't our top priority."

"I heard you. And I interpreted that as you saying you didn't want the pressure that Duncan put on himself and the police by making such optimistic and all-too-specific promises. Now, the day you arrest him will simply be a bonus. That's what you've planned, isn't it?"

"Of course," Macbeth said. "Hecate's a difficult man to arrest, but if the opportunity should offer itself—"

"My experience, I'm afraid to say, is that opportunities don't offer themselves," Tourtell said. "They have to be created and then grasped. So what's your plan for arresting Hecate?"

Macbeth coughed, played with his coffee cup. Tried to collect his thoughts. He had noticed he could suddenly have difficulty doing this, as though it were too much: there were too many balls to keep in the air at once, and when one ball fell, they all fell, and he had to start anew. Was he taking too much power? Or too little? Macbeth's eyes sought Seyton's, who had sat down at the coffee table, but there was no help to be found there. Of course not. Only she could help him. Lady. He would have to give up the drugs, talk to her. Only she could blow away the fog, clarify his thinking.

"I want to lure him into a trap," Macbeth said.

"What kind of trap?"

"We haven't got the details worked out yet."

"We're talking about the town's number-one enemy, so I would appreciate it if you keep me informed," Tourtell said and stood up. "Perhaps you could give me the plan in broad outline at Duncan's funeral tomorrow? Along with your decision regarding the election."

Macbeth took Tourtell's outstretched hand without getting up. Tourtell nodded to the wall behind him. "I've always liked that painting, Macbeth. I'll find my own way out."

Macbeth watched him. Tourtell seemed to have grown every time he saw him. He hadn't touched the coffee. Macbeth swiveled on his chair to face the picture. It was big and showed a man and a woman, both dressed as workers, walking hand in hand. Behind them came a procession of children and behind that the sun was high in the sky. The bigger picture. He guessed Duncan had hung it; Kenneth had probably had a portrait of himself. Macbeth angled his head to one side but still couldn't work out what it meant.

"Tell me, Seyton. What do *you* think?"

"What do I think? To hell with Tourtell. You're more popular than he is."

Macbeth nodded. Seyton was like him, not a man with an eye for the bigger picture. Only she had that.

Lady had locked herself in her room.

"I need to talk to you," Macbeth said.

No answer.

"Darling!"

"It's the child," Jack said.

Macbeth turned to him.

"I took it from her. It was beginning to smell, and I didn't know what else to do. But she thinks you ordered me to take it."

"Good. Well done, Jack. It's just that I needed her advice on a case and . . . well . . ."

"She can hardly give you the advice you need in the state she's in right now, sir. May I ask—no. Sorry, I was forgetting myself. You aren't Lady, sir."

"Did you think I was Lady?"

"No, I just . . . Lady usually airs her thoughts with me and I help in any way I can. Not that I have much to offer, but sometimes hearing yourself say something to someone can clear your mind."

"Hm. Make us both a cup of coffee, Jack."

"At once, sir."

Macbeth went to the mezzanine. Looked down into the gaming room. It was a quiet evening. He saw none of the usual faces. Where were they?

"At the Obelisk," Jack said, passing Macbeth a cup of steaming coffee.

"What?"

"Our regulars. They're at the Obelisk. That was what you were wondering, wasn't it?"

"Maybe."

"I was in the Obelisk yesterday and I counted five of them. And spoke to two of them. Turns out I'm not the only one spying. The Obelisk's got its people here too. And they've seen who our regular customers are and have offered them better deals."

"Better deals?"

"Credit."

"That's illegal."

"Unofficially, of course. It won't appear in any of the Obelisk's ledgers and if they're confronted they'll swear blind they don't give credit."

"Then we'd better offer the same."

"I think the problem runs deeper than that, sir. Can you see how few there are in the bar downstairs? In the Obelisk there are queues. Beer and cocktails cost thirty-percent less, and that not only increases the number of customers and the turnover in the bar, it makes people less guarded in the gaming rooms."

"Lady thinks we appeal to a different, more quality-conscious clientele."

"The people who go to casinos in this town can be divided broadly into three groups, sir. You have the out-and-out gamblers who don't care about the quality of the carpets or expensive cognac; they want an efficient croupier, a poker table with visiting country cousins they can fleece and—if it's possible—credit. The Obelisk has this group. And then you have the country folk I mentioned, who usually come here because we have the reputation of being the *real* casino. But now they've discovered they prefer the simple, more fun-filled sinful atmosphere at the Obelisk. These are people who tend to go to bingo rather than the opera."

"And we're the opera?"

"They want cheap beer, cheap women. What's the point of an outing into town otherwise?"

"And the last group?"

Jack pointed down to the room. "West Enders. The ones who don't want to mingle with the dregs. Our last loyal customers. So far. The Obelisk plans to open a new gaming room next year with a dress code, higher minimum stakes and more expensive brands of cognac in the bar."

"Hm. And what do you suggest we do?"

"Me?" Jack laughed. "I'm just a receptionist, sir."

"And a croupier." Macbeth looked down at the blackjack table where he, Lady and Jack had first met. "Let me ask you for some advice, Jack."

"A croupier just watches people placing bets, sir. They never give advice."

"Fine, you'll have to listen then. Tourtell came to tell me he didn't want me to stand as mayor."

"Had you planned to do that, sir?"

"I don't know. I've probably half-thought about doing it and half-rejected it and then half-thought about it again. Especially after Tourtell so patronizingly explained to me what politics was *really* about. What do you think?"

"Oh, I'm sure you'd be a brilliant mayor, sir. Think of all the things you and Lady could do for the town!"

Macbeth studied Jack's beaming face—the undisguised happiness, the naive optimism. Like a reflection of the person he had once been. And a strange thought struck him: he wished he were Jack, the receptionist.

"But I have a lot to lose as well," Macbeth said. "If I don't stand now Tourtell will support me next time. And Tourtell's right about the sitting mayor invariably being elected."

"Hm," Jack said, scratching his head. "Unless there's a scandal just before the elections, that is. A scandal so damaging that the town can't possibly let Tourtell continue."

"For example?"

"Lady asked me to check out the young boy Tourtell brought to the dinner. My sources tell me Tourtell's wife has moved to their summer cottage in Fife, while the boy has moved in. And he's underage, sexually. What we need is concrete evidence of indecent behavior. From employees in the mayor's residence, for instance."

"But, Jack, this is fantastic!" Excitement at the thought of skewering Tourtell warmed Macbeth's cheeks. "We gather the evidence, and I get Kite to set up a live election debate, and then I can throw this unseemly relationship straight in Tourtell's face. He won't be prepared for that. How about that?"

"Maybe."

"Maybe? What do you mean?"

"I was just thinking, sir, that you yourself moved into the house of a childless man when you were fifteen. The mayor would be able to come back with that."

Macbeth felt the blood rising in his face again. "What? Banquo and I . . . ?"

"Tourtell won't hesitate if you throw the first stone, sir. All's fair in love and war. At the same time it would be unfortunate if it looked as if you'd used your position to spy on Tourtell's private life."

"Hm, you're right. So how would you do it?"

"Let me mull it over." Jack took a sip of coffee. And another. Then he put his cup down on the table. "The information about the boy must be leaked via roundabout means. But if you're standing against Tourtell you'll still be suspected of being the source. So the leak should happen before you announce your candidature. In fact, to be sure you avoid suspicion you should perhaps announce you're *not* standing, at least not for four years. You've got a job to do as chief commissioner first. Then, when the scandal disqualifies Tourtell, you'll say rather reluctantly that as the town needs a leader at short notice you'll put yourself at its disposal. You'll refuse to comment on the Tourtell scandal when journalists ask, showing that you're above that kind of behavior, and only focus on how to get the town . . . er . . . You used such a good expression on the radio, sir, what was it again?"

"Back on an even keel," Macbeth said. "Now I understand why Lady uses you as an adviser, Jack."

"Thank you, sir, but don't exaggerate my significance."

"I'm not, but you have an unusually lucid eye for these matters."

"It may be easier to be a croupier and observer than a participant, with all the risk and strong emotions involved, sir."

"And I think you're one hell of a croupier, Jack."

"And as a croupier I'd advise you to study your cards even more carefully to see if they can be employed better than this."

"Oh?"

"Tourtell promised you his support at the next election if you didn't stand now, but that won't be worth much if he's outed as a pedophile, will it?"

Macbeth stroked his beard. "True enough."

"So you should ask for something else now. Tell Tourtell you're not even sure you'll stand at the next election. And that you'd rather have something specific he can give you now."

"For example?"

"What would you like, sir?"

"What would I . . . ?" Macbeth saw Jack motion toward the gaming room. "Erm, more customers?"

"Yes. The Obelisk's clientele. But as chief commissioner you don't have the authority to close the Obelisk even if you had proof of illegal credit being given."

"Don't I?"

"As a croupier I happen to know that the police can charge individuals, but it's only the Gambling and Casino Board that can close a whole casino, sir. And they're subject to the jurisdiction of . . ."

"The town hall. Tourtell."

Macbeth could see it clearly now. He didn't need power; he should flush what he had down the toilet. A bell rang somewhere.

"Sounds like we've got customers, sir." Jack got up.

Macbeth grabbed his arm. "Just wait till Lady hears what we've cooked up. I'm sure it'll make her feel better in a flash. How can we thank you, Jack?"

"No need, sir." Jack smiled wryly. "It's enough that you saved my life."

26

DUFF SWALLOWED HIS VOMIT. IT was his fourth day on board, but there was
no sign of improvement yet. One thing was the sea, quite another the stale
smell in the galley. Inside, behind the swing door, it was a mixture of ran-
cid fat and sour milk; on the other side, in the mess where the men sat
eating, it was sweat and tobacco. The steward had left breakfast to Duff,
saying he ought to be able to manage that on his own. Put out bread and
assorted meats and cheese, boil eggs and make coffee, even a seasick first-
timer could cope with that.

Duff had been woken at six, and the first thing he did was to throw up
in the bucket beside his bed. He still hadn't had two nights in the same
cabin as lack of berths meant he had had to borrow the beds of those who
were on duty. Luckily he had only had lower bunks, so he didn't have to
actually sleep with the bucket. He had just got his sweater over his head
when the next wave of nausea came. On his way down to the galley he'd
had pit stops to vomit in the toilet beside the first mate's cabin and in the
sink before the last steep staircase.

Breakfast had been served, and those of the crew who were on duty
had finished, it seemed. Time to clear away before they started making
lunch.

Duff inhaled three stomachfuls of dubious air, got up and went out
into the mess.

Four people were sitting at the nearest table. The speaker was a loud,
slightly overweight engineer with hairy forearms, an Esso T-shirt stained
with oil and sweat rings under his arms and a striped Hull City Tigers cap
on his head. When he spoke he sniffed before and afterward, like a form
of inverted commas. What came between them was always denigration of
those lower on the ladder. "Hey, Sparks," the engineer shouted to be sure

everyone realized he was referring to the young boy with glasses at the end of the table, "hadn't you better ask the new galley boy if he can heat you up some fish pie so you can stuff your dick in and enjoy the closest you'll ever get to cunt." He sniffed before starting to laugh. This raised no more than short-lived, forced laughter from the others. The young radio-telegrapher smiled fleetingly and ducked his head even lower into his plate. The engineer, whom Duff had heard the others call Hutch, sniffed. "But judging by today's breakfast I doubt you know how to heat up a fish pie, do you, lad?" Another sniff.

Duff kept his head down, like the telegrapher. That was all he had to do until they reached the docks in Capitol. Keep a low profile, mouth shut, mask on.

"Tell me, galley boy! Do you call this scrambled egg?"

"Anything wrong?" Duff said.

"Wrong?" The engineer rolled his eyes and turned to the others. "The greenhorn asks me if something's wrong. Only that this scrambled egg looks and tastes like vomit. *Your* vomit. From your green, seasick gills."

Duff looked at the engineer. The guy was grinning, and there was an evil glint in his shiny eyes. Duff had seen it before. Lorreal, the director of the orphanage.

"I'm sorry the scrambled egg didn't live up to your expectations," Duff said.

"*Didn't live up to your expectations*," the engineer mimicked, and sniffed. "Think you're at some posh fuckin' restaurant, do you? At sea we want food, not muck. What do you reckon, guys?"

The men around him chuckled their agreement, but Duff saw two of them keep their heads down in embarrassment. Presumably they played along so as not to become targets.

"The steward's on duty at lunch," Duff said, putting plates of food and milk cartons on a tray. "Let's hope it's better then."

"What isn't any better," the engineer said, "is the way you look. Have you got lice? Is that why you wear that hat? And what about those cunt pubes that pass for a beard? What happened, galley boy? Get your moth-er's cunt where others got a face?"

The engineer looked around expectantly, but this time all the others were studying the floor.

"I've got a suggestion," Duff said. Knowing he shouldn't speak.

Knowing he had promised himself he wouldn't. "Sparks can stuff his wanger under your arm. That way he can feel what a cunt's like and you finally get some dick."

The table went so quiet all that could be heard was the noise of Duff putting the plates of cheese, sausage and cucumber onto the tray. No sniff this time.

"Let me repeat the bit that might interest you most," Duff said, putting down the tray. "You finally get some dick." He stressed the consonants so that no one would be in any doubt as to what he had said. Then Duff turned to the table. The engineer had risen to his feet and was coming toward him.

"Take off your glasses," he said.

"Can't see fuck all without them," Duff said. "See a fuckwit with them."

The engineer wound back his arm, announcing where the blow would come from, and swung. Duff retreated a step, swayed and, when the engineer's oil-black fist had passed, took two steps forward, grabbed the engineer, who was now off-balance, by his other hand, forced it back against his wrist, grabbed the engineer's elbow and let his momentum take him forward while Duff slipped behind. The engineer screamed, automatically bending forward to relieve the painful pressure on his wrist as Duff steered him into a wall head first. Duff pulled the engineer back. Rammed him forward again. Against the bulkhead. Duff pushed the helpless engineer's arm higher, knowing that soon something would have to give, something would break. The engineer's scream rose to a whine, and his fingers lunged desperately at Duff's hat. Duff rammed his head against the wall for the third time. Was steadying himself for a fourth when he heard a voice.

"That's enough, Johnson!"

It took Duff a second to remember that was the name he had given when he signed on. And to realize the voice was the captain's. Duff looked up. The captain was standing right in front of them. Duff let go of the engineer, who fell to his knees with a sob.

"What's going on here?"

Duff noticed only now that he was panting. The provocation. The anger. "Nothing, Captain."

"I know the difference between nothing and something, Johnson. So what is this? Hutchinson?"

Duff wasn't sure, but it sounded like the man on his knees was crying.

Duff cleared his throat. "A friendly bet, Captain. I wanted to show that the Fife grip is more effective than a Hull haymaker. I might have got carried away." He patted the engineer's shaking back. "Sorry, pal, but we agree that Fife beat Hull on this occasion, don't we?"

The engineer nodded, still sobbing.

The captain took off his hat and studied Duff. "The Fife grip, you say?"

"Yes," Duff answered.

"Hutchinson, you're needed in the engine room. You others have got jobs to do, haven't you?"

The mess cleared quickly.

"Pour me a cup of coffee and sit down," the captain said.

Duff did as he said.

The captain raised his cup to his mouth a couple of times. Looked down at the black liquid and mumbled something. Just as Duff was beginning to wonder whether the captain had forgotten he was there, he raised his head.

"Generally I don't consider it worth the effort to delve into individuals' backgrounds, Johnson. Most of the crew are simple, with limited intellects; they have pasts best left unprobed and futures that won't be on board MS *Glamis*. As they won't be under my command or be my problem for long, I know it's not worth getting too involved. All that concerns me is how they function as a group, as my crew."

The captain took another sip and grimaced. Duff had no idea if this was due to the coffee, pain or the conversation.

"You seem like a man with education and ambition, Johnson, but I won't ask how you ended up here. I doubt I would hear the truth anyway. But my guess is you're someone who knows how groups function. You know that there'll always be a pecking order, and everyone will have their role in that order, their place. The captain at the top, the rookie at the bottom. As long as everyone accepts their own and others' positions in the order we have a working crew. Exactly as I want it. At the moment, however, we have some confusion at the lower end of the pecking order on MS *Glamis*. We have three potential chickens at the bottom. Sparks because he's the youngest. You because it's your first time. And Hutchinson because he's the most stupid and very difficult to like."

Another sip.

"Sparks will survive this trip as the bottom chicken. He's young, intelligent enough and he'll learn. And you, Johnson, have moved up the order, I've just seen, after what you did to Hutchinson. For all I know, it was a situation you initiated to achieve just this. But if I know Hutch, he started it. Like the stupid idiot he is, he set himself up for another fall. And that's why he's looking for someone to be under him. It'll probably be some poor soul who signs on in Capitol, where we're going to need a couple of new men as people sign off all the time. Do you understand?"

Duff shrugged.

"And this is my problem, Johnson. Hutch is going to keep trying, but he is the permanent bottom chicken. And I would prefer another bottom chicken, one who would quietly accept his fate. But as Hutch is an ill-natured troublemaker who considers he's been given enough beatings in life and now it's someone else's turn, he's going to continue to create a bad atmosphere on board. He's not a bad engineer, but he makes my crew work worse than it would be without him."

A loud slurp.

"So why don't I get rid of him, you say. And you say that because you're not a seaman and know nothing about Seafarers' Union employment contracts, which mean I'm stuck with Hutch until I can get something on him that would give me a so-called objective reason to off-load him. Physically attacking a colleague would be one such objective reason . . ."

Duff nodded.

"So? All I need from you is a yes and a signature for the Seafarers' Union. I can get the rest from the witnesses."

"We were only playing, Captain. It won't happen again."

"No, it won't." The captain scratched his chin. "As I said, I don't make a habit of delving into my crew's backgrounds unnecessarily. But I have to say I've only seen the grip you had on Hutch used twice before: by the military police and the port police. The common denominator is police. So now I'd like to hear the truth."

"The truth?"

"Yes. Did he attack you?"

Duff eyed the captain. He presumed he had known from the start his real name wasn't Cliff Johnson and that the galley boy hadn't worked in any restaurant. All he was asking for was a yes and a false signature. If and when there was ever any discussion of the real identity of this Johnson he would be over the hills and far away.

"I see. Here's the truth," Duff said, watching the captain lean across the table. "We were only playing, Captain."

The captain leaned back. Put the coffee cup to his mouth. His gaze above the cup was firmly fixed on Duff. Not on Duff's eyes but higher, on his forehead. The captain's Adam's apple went up and down as he swallowed. Then he brought the empty cup down hard on the table.

"Johnson."

"Yes, Captain?"

"I like you."

"Captain?"

"I have no reason to believe you like Hutch any more than the rest of us. But you're no snitch. That's bad news for me as a captain, but it shows integrity. And I respect that, so I won't mention this matter again. You're seasick and you're lying, but I could use more people like you in my crew. Thanks for the coffee."

The captain got up and left.

Duff remained seated for a couple of seconds. Then he took the empty cup to the galley and put it in the sink. Closed his eyes, placed his hands on the cold shiny metal and swallowed his nausea. What was he doing? Why hadn't he told him the truth, that Hutch was a bully?

He opened his eyes. Saw his reflection in the saucepan hanging from the shelf in front of him. His heart skipped a beat. His hat had ridden up to his hairline without him noticing. Hutchinson must have clipped it when he swung. The scar shone against his skin like a thick white vapor trail after a plane in the sky. The scar. That was what the captain had been staring at before he put down his cup.

Duff closed his eyes, told himself to relax and think through the whole business.

Their departure had been so early the newspapers wouldn't have been out on the streets the day they left, so the captain couldn't have seen any WANTED pictures of him. Unless he had seen Duff's face on the TV broadcast of the press conference the evening before. But had there been any sign of shock in the captain's eyes when he saw the scar—*if* he had seen it? No. Because the captain was a good actor and didn't want to show that he had recognized him until they set upon him later? As there was little he could do about that, he decided the captain hadn't realized, but what about the others? No, he had been standing with his back to them until the captain had ordered them out. Apart from Hutchinson, lying in front of him. If he had seen the scar he didn't strike Duff as the type to scour the news.

Duff opened his eyes again.

In two days, on Wednesday, they would dock.

Forty-eight hours. Stay low for two days. He must be able to do that.

The organ music started, and standing between the rows of benches in the cathedral he could feel the hairs rise all over his body. It wasn't because of the music, nor the priest's or the mayor's eulogies, nor Duncan's coffin being borne down the aisle by six men, nor was it the fact that he hadn't taken any power. It was because of the dreadful new uniform he was wearing. Whenever he moved, the coarse wool rubbed against his skin and gave him the shivers. His old one had been cheaper material and was more worn-in and comfortable. He could of course have chosen the new black suit delivered to police HQ, which could only have come from Hecate. The quality of the wool cloth was much better, but strangely enough it itched even more than the uniform. Besides, it would have been a breach of tradition to turn up to a police funeral in anything but a uniform.

The coffin passed Macbeth's row. Duncan's wife and two sons followed it with lowered heads, but when one son happened to look up and met his eyes, Macbeth automatically looked down.

Then they all filed out into the aisle and joined the cortège. Macbeth positioned himself in such a way that he was walking beside Tourtell.

"Fine speech," Macbeth said.

"Thank you. I'm really sorry the town hall didn't agree to the town paying for the funeral. With closed factories and falling tax revenues, I'm afraid such demonstrations of honor are way down the list. Still pretty uncivilized, if you ask me."

"The town hall has my sympathy."

"I don't believe Duncan's family feels the same way. His wife rang me and said we should have driven his coffin through the streets and given people the opportunity to show how much they cared. They wanted what Duncan wanted."

"Do you think people would have done that?"

Tourtell shrugged. "I honestly don't know, Macbeth. My experience is that people in this town don't care about so-called reforms unless they see them putting food on the table or providing enough for an extra beer. I thought change was beginning to take place in the town, but if so the murder of Duncan would have made people seething mad. Instead it seems as if people have accepted that in this town good always loses. The only person who's opened his mouth is Kite. Are you going to Banquo and his son's funeral tomorrow?"

"Of course. Down in the Workers' Church. Banquo wasn't particularly religious, but his wife, Vera, is buried there."

"But Duff's wife and children are going to be buried in the cathedral, I've been informed."

"Yes. I won't be there personally."

"Personally?"

"We're going to have officers posted here in case Duff decides to pitch up."

"Oh yes. You should accompany your children to their graves. Especially if you know you're partly responsible."

"Yes, it's funny how guilt marks you for life, while honor and glory come out in the wash the same night."

"Now, for a second there, Macbeth, you sounded like a man who knows a bit about guilt."

"So let me confess right here and now that I've killed my nearest and dearest, Tourtell."

The mayor stopped for a moment and looked at Macbeth. "What was that you said?"

"My mother. She died in childbirth. Let's keep walking."

"And your father?"

"He ran away to sea when he heard Mum was pregnant and was never seen again. I grew up in an orphanage. Duff and I. We shared a room. But you've probably never seen a room in an orphanage, have you, Tourtell?"

"Oh, I have opened an orphanage or two."

They had come out onto the cathedral steps, where the wet northwesterly gale met them. On the gravel path Macbeth saw the coffin teeter dangerously.

"Well, well," Tourtell said. "The sea is also a way to escape."

"Are you criticizing my father, Tourtell?"

"Neither of us knew him. I'm just saying the sea is full of them—men who don't accept the responsibilities nature has placed on them."

"So men like you and me should take even more responsibility, Tourtell."

"Exactly. So what have you decided?"

Macbeth cleared his throat. "I can see that for the good of the town it's best the chief commissioner continues to be chief commissioner and carries on his good, close cooperation with the mayor."

"Wise words, Macbeth."

"So long as this cooperation functions, of course."

"And you're referring to?"

"The rumors that the Obelisk is running a prostitution racket under the auspices of the casino and giving credit illegally to some gamblers."

"The former is an old accusation, the latter new. But, as you know, it's difficult to get to the bottom of such rumors, so they tend to stay that way and don't go anywhere."

"I have specific suspicions relating to at least two gamblers, and with effective interviewing methods and the promise of an amnesty I'm sure I can establish whether the Obelisk has offered them credit or not. Thereafter the Gambling and Casino Board will presumably have to close the place while the extent of the irregularities is examined more closely."

The mayor pulled at the lowest of his chins. "You mean close down the Obelisk in return for not standing?"

"I mean only that the town's political and administrative leaders have to be consistent in their enforcement of laws and regulations. If they don't want to be suspected of being bought and paid for by those who evade them."

The mayor clicked his tongue. Like a child with an olive, Macbeth thought. The kind of food that takes you years to like. "We're not talking about a series of possible irregularities," Tourtell said as if to himself. "And, as I said, it's difficult to get to the bottom of such rumors. It can take time."

"A long time," Macbeth said.

"I'll prepare the board by saying there's some information on its way which may necessitate closing the casino down. Where's Lady, by the way? I would imagine, as she and Duncan . . ."

"She doesn't feel well, I'm afraid. Temporary."

"I see. Say hello and wish her well. We'd better go down and offer our condolences to the family."

"You go first. I'll follow."

Macbeth watched Tourtell waddle down the stairs and grasp Mrs. Duncan's hand in both of his, watched his lips move as he inclined his head in the deepest sympathy. He really did look like a turtle. But there was something Tourtell had said. The sea was full of them. Men who had run off.

"Everything OK, sir?" It was Seyton. He had been waiting outside. He couldn't stand churches, he said, and that was fine; those who had it in for the chief commissioner would hardly be inside.

"We checked all the passenger boats leaving town," Macbeth said, "but did anyone think of checking the other ships?"

"For stowaways, you mean?"

"Yes. Or simply people who'd got a job on board."

"Nope."

"Send a precise description of Duff to all the boats which have left since yesterday. Now."

"Right, sir." Seyton took the steps in two strides and disappeared around the corner.

Meredith. Meredith had ceased to exist. But the scar on his heart was still there. And yet Macbeth wasn't going to the funeral. Because it was a long time since she had ceased to exist, so long that he had forgotten who she was. So long that he had forgotten who he himself had been then.

He shifted his weight, felt the material against the inside of his thigh, smelled wet wool. And shivered.

27

DUFF STOOD IN THE GALLEY looking at the men in the mess. They had eaten lunch and now they were rolling cigarettes and talking in low voices, laughing, lighting their cigarettes, drinking their coffee. Only one man sat on his own. Hutchinson. A big skin-colored plaster on his forehead told those who hadn't been present about the beating he had been given. Hutchinson tried to look as though he were thinking about something that required concentration as he puffed on his roll-up, but his acting ability wasn't good enough for him to look anything but lost.

"We'll be docking tomorrow," the steward said, who himself had lit a cigarette and was leaning against the cooker. "You've learned fast. Fancy some more peggy?"

"Sorry?"

"Are you staying on for the next trip?"

"No," Duff said. "But thank you for asking."

The steward shrugged. Duff watched someone who was late for lunch balance his soup dish and make for Hutchinson's table, look up, see who was sitting there and instead squeeze onto a full table. And Duff saw that Hutchinson had registered this and was now concentrating on his fag even harder while blinking furiously.

"Any of that cheesecake left from yesterday?"

Duff turned. It was the first engineer; he was standing in the doorway with a hopeful expression on his face.

"Sorry," the steward said. "All gone."

"Hang about," Duff said. "I think I wrapped up a small slice." He went into the freezer room, found a plate wrapped in foil and came back. Passed it to the first engineer. "It's a bit cold."

"That's OK," said the first engineer, licking his lips. "I like it cold."

"One thing . . ."

"Yes?"

"Hutchinson . . ."

"Hutch?"

"Yes. He looks a bit . . . erm downcast. I was wondering about something the captain said to me. He said he was a good engineer. Is that right?"

The first engineer rocked his head from side to side looking at Duff a little uncertainly. "He's good enough."

"Perhaps it'd be a good idea to tell him."

"Tell him what?"

"He's good enough."

"Why?"

"I think he needs to hear it."

"I don't know about that. If you build people up they just want more money and longer breaks."

"When you were a young engineer did you have a first engineer who gave you the feeling you were doing a good job?"

"Yes, but I was."

"Try and remember how good you *really* were then."

The first engineer stood with his mouth ajar.

At that moment the boat rolled. Screams came from the mess, and there was a loud bang behind Duff.

"Fuckin' Ada!" the steward shouted, and when Duff turned he saw the big soup tureen had fallen on the floor. Duff stared at the thick, green pea soup oozing out. Without warning his stomach lurched, he felt the nausea in his throat and just managed to grab the doorframe as it spurted from his mouth.

"Well, rookie," said the first engineer, "any other good advice?" He turned and left.

"Bloody hell, Johnson. Haven't you finished with all that?" the steward groaned, handing Duff a kitchen roll.

"What happened?" Duff asked, wiping his mouth.

"Hit a swell," the steward said. "It happens."

"Have a breather. I'll clean up here."

When Duff had finished scrubbing the floor, he went into the mess to collect the dirty crockery. Only three guys were sitting at one table, plus Hutch, who hadn't stirred from his place.

Duff listened to their chitchat as he piled dishes and glasses on a tray.

"That breaker must have come from an earthquake or a landslide or something," one of them said.

"Perhaps it was a nuclear test," suggested one of the others. "The Soviets are supposed to have some shit going on in the Barents Sea and shock waves apparently go all the way round the world."

"Any messages about that, Sparks?"

"No." Sparks laughed. "The only excitement is a search for a guy with a white scar right across his face."

Duff stiffened. Kept piling dishes as he listened.

"Yeah, it's gonna be good to get ashore tomorrow."

"Is it, hell. Missus says she's pregnant again."

"Don't look at me."

Good-natured laughter around the table.

Duff turned with the tray in his hands. Hutchinson had lifted his head and suddenly sat bolt upright. The few times they had met after their skirmish Hutchinson had looked down and avoided Duff's face, but now he was staring at Duff with wide-open eyes. Like a vulture that has unexpectedly and happily spotted a helpless, injured animal.

Duff shoved open the door to the galley with his foot and heard it clatter behind him. Put the tray down on the worktop. Damn, damn, damn! Not now, not with less than twenty-hours to land.

"Not too fast here," Caithness said, looking through the windscreen.

The taxi driver took his foot off the accelerator, and they drove slowly past the Obelisk, where people were streaming into the street from the main entrance. Two police cars were parked on the pavement. The blue lights rotated idly.

"What's going on?" Lennox said and thrust his blue face between the two front seats. He was—like Caithness—still wearing his uniform, as the taxi had collected them from outside the church straight after Duncan's funeral. "Has the fire alarm gone off?"

"The Gambling and Casino Board closed the place today," Caithness said. "Suspicion of breaching the Casino Act."

They saw one of the policemen leading out an angrily gesticulating man in a light suit and flowery shirt with impressive sideburns. It looked as if the man was trying to explain something to the policeman, who was obviously turning a deaf ear.

"Sad," the driver said.

"What's sad?" Lennox asked. "Law enforcement?"

"Sometimes. At the Obelisk you could at least have a beer and a game of cards without dressing up and coming home ruined. By the way, do you know that the factory you want to go to is closed?"

"Yes," Caithness answered. Thinking that was all she knew about it. Police Officer Angus had rung that morning and implored her to bring Inspector Lennox from the Anti-Corruption Unit with her to Estex. They would find out the rest when they got there. It was about corruption at the highest level and for the moment they mustn't mention their meeting to anyone. When she said she didn't know any Police Officer Angus, he had explained to her that he was the guy in SWAT with the long hair who she smiled at and said hello to in the lift. She remembered him. He was cute. Looked more like an affable, unworldly hippie than a SWAT man.

They glided through the streets. She saw the unemployed men leaning against the walls sheltering from the rain, fags in mouths, wet coats, hungry, weary eyes. Hyenas. Not because they were born like that; it was the town. Duncan had said if carrion was all there was on the menu, you ate carrion, whoever you thought you were. And irrespective of what they did at police HQ the best way to reduce crime was to get the town's citizens back to work.

"Are you opening Estex again?" the driver asked, squinting at Caithness.

"What makes you think that?"

"I think Macbeth is smarter than Duncan, the blockhead."

"Oh?"

"Closing a great factory just because it's leaking some gunge? Christ, everyone who worked there smokes. They'll die anyway. That was five thousand jobs. Five thousand jobs this town needed! Only some upper-class twit from Capitol could be so snobbish. Macbeth, on the other hand, is one of us—he understands and he does something. Let Macbeth take charge for a bit and maybe people will be able to afford a taxi again in this town."

"Talking of Macbeth," Caithness said, turning to the back seat. "He's canceled the morning meeting two days in a row and he looked very pale in church. Is he ill?"

"Not him," Lennox said, "but Lady. He's barely been at HQ."

"Of course it's good of him to look after her, but he's the chief commissioner and we have a town in our charge."

"Good job he has us there." Lennox smiled.

The taxi stopped in front of the gate, from which hung a chain with a padlock. The CLOSED sign had fallen onto the potholed tarmac. Caithness got out, stood by the driver's open window and scanned the abandoned industrial wasteland while waiting for her change. No telephone boxes, and the telephones at Estex had probably been cut off.

"How will we get hold of a taxi when we want to go back?" she asked.

"I'll park here and wait," the driver said. "There's no work in town anyway."

Inside the factory gate was a rusty forklift and a tower of rotting wooden pallets. The pedestrian entrance beside the big retractable door was open.

Caithness and Lennox stepped into the factory building. It was cold outside, even colder under the high vaulted roof. The furnaces stood like gigantic pews inside the rectangular hall as far as the eye could see.

"Hello?" Caithness called, and the echo sent shivers down her spine.

"Here!" came the answer from up on the wall where the foreman's office and surveillance platform were located. Like a watchtower in a prison, Caithness thought. Or a pulpit.

The young man standing up there pointed to a steel staircase.

Caithness and Lennox went up the steps.

"Police Officer Angus," he said shaking hands with them. His open face displayed his nervousness, but also determination.

They followed him into the foreman's office, which smelled of a marinade of dried sweat and tobacco. The large windows facing the factory floor had a strange yellow frosted glaze which looked as if it had been burned into the glass. On the tables there were open files that had clearly been taken from the shelves along the walls. The young man was unshaven and wearing tight faded jeans and a green military jacket.

"Thank you for coming at such short notice," Angus said, indicating the peeling wooden chairs.

"I don't want to pressurize you, but I hope this is important," Lennox said, taking a seat. "I had to leave an important meeting."

"As you haven't got much time, indeed as none of us has got much time, I'll get straight to the point."

"Thank you."

Angus crossed his arms. His jaws were working, and his eyes roamed, but there was a determination about him—he was like a man who *knows* he is right.

"Twice I've been a believer," Angus said, swallowing, and Caithness knew he was memorizing something he had written and rehearsed for the occasion. "And twice I've lost that belief. The first was in God. The second in Macbeth. Macbeth is no savior, he's a corrupt murderer. I wanted to say that first so that you know why I'm doing this. This is to rid the town of Macbeth."

In the ensuing silence they could hear the deep sighs as drops of water hit the floor of the factory. Angus breathed in.

"We were—"

"Stop!" Caithness said. "Thank you for your honesty, Angus, but before you say anymore, Inspector Lennox and I have to decide whether we want to hear."

"Let Angus finish," Lennox said. "Then we can discuss it later without anyone else present."

"Wait," Caithness said. "There's no way back if we receive information which—"

"We were sent to the clubhouse to kill everyone," Angus said.

"I don't want to hear this," Caithness said and stood up.

"No one was going to be arrested," Angus said in a louder voice. "We started shooting at the Norse Riders, and they managed to fire off one—" he held up a forefinger which trembled as much as his voice "—one single bloody shot in self-defense! Unlike at—"

Caithness stamped on the floor to drown out Angus's voice, opened the door, was about to step outside and leave when she heard his name and froze.

"—Duff's place in Fife. Not a single shot was fired there. Because he wasn't at home. When we entered the house after we'd shot it to pieces we found a girl and a boy and their mother—" Angus's voice failed him.

Caithness turned to him. The young man leaned against the table and squeezed his eyes shut, "—who had tried to cover them with her own body in the bedroom."

"Oh, no, no, no," Caithness heard herself whisper.

"Macbeth gave the order," Angus said, "and Seyton ensured it was carried out to the letter by SWAT, including—" he coughed "—me."

"Why on earth would Macbeth give orders for these . . . liquidations?" Lennox asked with disbelief in his voice. "He could have just arrested them, both Duff and the Norse Riders."

"Maybe not," Angus said. "Maybe they had something on Macbeth, something that made him need to silence them."

"Such as what?"

"Haven't you asked yourselves why the Norse Riders took their revenge on Banquo? Why not kill the person who gave the orders, Macbeth himself?"

"Simple," Lennox snorted. "Macbeth is better protected. Have you any proof at all?"

"These eyes," Angus said, pointing.

"They're yours, and the same applies to your accusations. Give me one reason why we should believe you."

"There's one reason," Caithness said, walking slowly back to her chair. "It's easy enough to get Angus's accusations confirmed or denied by the other SWAT officers, and if they're false, he'll lose his job, find himself on a charge and, to put it mildly, his future prospects will be poor. And he knows that."

Angus laughed.

Caithness raised an eyebrow. "Excuse me, did I say something stupid?"

"It's SWAT," Lennox said. "Loyalty, brotherhood, baptized in fire, united in blood."

"Sorry?"

"You'll never get anyone in SWAT to say a word that will harm Macbeth," Angus said. "Or Seyton. Or any of the brothers."

Caithness dropped her hands to her sides. "So you come to us with these claims of executions even though you know there's no way to prove them?"

"Macbeth asked me to burn the body of a baby killed in the clubhouse massacre," Angus said. He fidgeted with his necklace. "Here, in one of the furnaces."

Caithness shuddered. And regretted staying. Why hadn't she turned on her heel? Why wasn't she already sitting in the taxi leaving this behind her?

"I said no," Angus continued. "But that means someone else has done it. Perhaps he did it himself. I've looked through the furnaces and one of them has been used recently. I thought that if you got your Forensics people to examine the furnace you might find clues. Fingerprints, remains of bones, what do I know? And if you did, the Anti-Corruption Unit could take the case further."

Lennox and Caithness exchanged glances.

"The police can't investigate their own chief commissioner," Lennox said. "Didn't you know?"

Angus frowned. "But . . . the Anti-Corruption Unit, isn't it . . . ?"

"No, we can't do internal inquiries," Lennox said. "If you want to go after the chief commissioner you'll have to present your case to the town council and Tourtell."

Angus shook his head desperately. "No, no, no, they're bought and paid for, the whole bunch of them! We have to do this off our own bat. We have to bring Macbeth down from the inside."

Caithness didn't answer. Confirming only that Angus was right. No one on the town council, Tourtell included, would dare to come out into the open against Macbeth. Kenneth had made sure that the chief commissioner had the legal authority to stamp down hard on that kind of political rebellion.

Lennox looked at his watch. "I have a meeting in twenty minutes. I recommend you drop the matter until you've got something concrete, Angus. Then you can take your chances with the town council, can't you."

Angus blinked in disbelief. "*My* chances?" he said in a thick voice. He turned to Caithness. Despair, supplication, fear and hope flitted across his face like a narrative. And instantly she realized that Angus hadn't only asked her to come along because he needed Forensics to examine the furnaces. Angus needed a witness, a third person to ensure that Lennox couldn't pretend he hadn't received the information and, regardless of the outcome, then make his life uncomfortable. Angus had chosen Caithness simply because she had smiled at him in the lift. Because she looked like someone he could trust.

"Inspector Caithness?" he begged in a low voice.

She took a deep breath. "Lennox is right, Angus. You're asking us to attack a bear and all we have is a cardboard sword."

Angus's eyes were watery. "You're frightened," he stuttered. "You believe me. Otherwise you wouldn't still be here. But you're frightened. You're frightened *because* you believe me. Because I've shown you what Macbeth is capable of."

"Let's agree that this meeting never took place," Lennox said, making for the door. Caithness was about to follow when Angus grabbed her arm.

"A baby," he whispered, close to tears. "It was in a shoebox."

"It was an innocent victim in the fight against a crime syndicate," she said. "It happens. Macbeth wanting to hide it from the press to avoid a police scandal doesn't make him a murderer."

Caithness saw Angus let go of her arm as if he had burned himself. He took a step back and stared at her. Caithness turned and left.

On the steel staircase to the factory floor the chill hit her warm cheeks.

As she made for the exit she stopped by one of the furnaces. There were stripes and marks made of gray dust.

Lennox stood in the factory doorway waving to the taxi to drive through the gate so that they wouldn't have to walk through the driving rain. "What do you think Angus is after?" he asked.

"After?" Caithness turned and looked up at the foreman's shed-like office.

"He must know he's too young for a management post," Lennox said. "Hey! Over here! Is it about honor and fame?"

"Perhaps it's what he said. Someone has to stop Macbeth."

"Duty calls?" Lennox chuckled, and Caithness heard the crunch of tires on gravel. "Everyone wants something, Caithness. Are you coming?"

"Yes." Caithness could just make out the shape of Angus behind the window—he hadn't moved since they left him. He was just standing there. Waiting for something, it seemed.

How long would it be before Lennox informed Macbeth about this attempted mutiny?

What was she going to do with what Angus had told them?

She put her hand to her cheek. She knew why it was warm. She was blushing. Blushing with shame.

Lennox took the short cut through the station concourse. He liked short cuts. Always had. He had bought sweets to make friends, lied about diving off the crane on the harbor quay and about paying for a hand job from the girl working at the Indigo kiosk. He had worn higher platform shoes than anyone else, cheated in exams and still had to blag up his grade when the results came out. His father used to say—generally at family gatherings and without any attempt to conceal who he was referring to—that only a man with no spine would take short cuts. When his father had given a smallish gift to the town's private university, thereby saving himself and Lennox the disgrace of his son studying in the public sector, Lennox had also forged his degree certificate. Not to show potential employers but his father, who had asked to see it. Of course this was a fiasco because Lennox didn't have the spine to resist his father's suspicious looks and questions, and his father told him he didn't know how a mollusk like Lennox could stand up straight; he didn't have a single bone in his body!

Fair enough, but he definitely had enough spine to ignore the drug dealers who came up to him mumbling their offers. They recognized a user when they saw one. However, this wasn't how he got his brew; he had it sent in anonymous brown envelopes. Or when he occasionally asked for special treatment, they blindfolded him and led him—like a prisoner of war to a firing squad—to the secret kitchen, where he got his shot straight from the pot.

He passed Bertha Birnam, where Duff had fallen for his bluff about the judge from Capitol. But Hecate hadn't said anything about Macbeth killing Duff's wife and children. Lennox stepped up his tempo across Workers' Square, as though he had to hurry before something happened. Something inside him.

"Macbeth's busy," said the little receptionist at Inverness Casino.

"Say it's Inspector Lennox. It's important and will only take a minute."

"I'll ring up, sir."

While Lennox waited he looked around. He couldn't put his finger on what, but there was something missing. Some final touch. Perhaps it was only the atmosphere that had changed; perhaps it was that some less well-dressed guys were laughing too loudly as they walked into the gaming room. This type of customer was new.

Macbeth came down the stairs.

"Hello, Lennox."

"Hello, Chief Commissioner. The casino's busy today."

"Daytime gamblers straight from the Obelisk. The Gambling and Casino Board closed down their place a few hours ago. I haven't got much time. Shall we sit here?"

"Thank you, sir. I just wanted to inform you about a meeting that took place today."

Macbeth yawned. "Oh yes?"

Lennox breathed in. Hesitated. Because there were millions of ways to start. Thousands of ways to formulate the same message. Hundreds of first words. And yet only two options.

Macbeth frowned.

"Sir," the receptionist said. "Message from the blackjack table. They're asking if we can provide them with another croupier. There's a queue."

"I'm coming, Jack. Sorry about the interruption, Lennox. Lady usually deals with this. Well?"

"Yes. The meeting . . ." Lennox thought about his family. Their house. The garden. The safe neighborhood, where the kids hadn't got involved in any nastiness. The university they would go to. The paycheck that made all this possible. Plus the cash on the side that had now become a necessity to make ends meet. This wasn't for him; it was for the family, the family, the family. *His* family, not a house in Fife, not . . .

"Yes?"

The front door went.

"Sir!"

They turned. It was Seyton. He was out of breath. "We've got him, boss."

"We've found . . . ?"

"Duff. And you were right. He's on board a boat that sailed from here. The MS *Glamis*."

"Fantastic!" Macbeth turned to Lennox. "This will have to wait, Inspector. I'll have to be off now."

Lennox remained seated as the other two went through the door.

"A busy man," the receptionist said, smiling. "A coffee, sir?"

"No, thanks," Lennox said, staring ahead. Darkness had already started to fall, but there were still several hours before his next shot. An eternity. "I think I'll take you up on that coffee. Yes, please." An eternity for a man with no spine.

28

"WHERE ARE YOU GOING?" WHISPERED Meredith.

"I don't know," Duff said, trying to stroke her cheek, but he couldn't reach. "I've got an address, but I don't know whose it is."

"So why are you going there?"

"It was written down just before Banquo and Fleance died. It says *Safe haven*, and if they were on the run it might be safe for me too. I don't know. It's all I have, love."

"In that case . . ."

"Where are you?"

"Here."

"Where's *here*? And what are you doing?"

Meredith smiled. "We're waiting for you. It's still the birthday."

"Did it hurt?"

"A bit. It was soon over."

Duff felt his throat thicken. "Ewan and Emily, were they frightened?"

"Shh, darling, we're not talking about that now . . ."

"But—"

She laid a hand over his mouth. "Shh, they're asleep. You mustn't wake them."

Her hand. He couldn't breathe. He tried to move it, but she was too strong. Duff opened his eyes.

In the darkness above him he saw a figure, and the figure was pressing a hand against his mouth. Duff tried to scream and grab the hairy wrist, but the other person was too strong. Duff knew who it was when he heard the sniff. It was Hutchinson. Who leaned over him and whispered in his ear.

"Not a sound, Johnson. Or to be more accurate, Duff."

His cover was blown. Was there a price on his head, dead or alive? Hutchinson's moment for revenge had come. Knife? Bradawl? Hammer?

"Listen to me, Johnson. If we wake the guy in the bunk above, you're done for. OK?"

Why had the engineer woken him? Why hadn't he killed him?

"The police will be waiting for you when we dock in Capitol." He removed his hand from Duff's mouth. "Now you know and we're quits."

The cabin was lit up for a moment as the door opened. Then it closed, and he was gone.

Duff blinked in the darkness, thinking for a moment that Hutchinson had also been part of his dream. Someone coughed in the bunk above. Duff didn't know who it was. The steward had explained the lack of bunks was because they had transported "some very important boxes of ammo" on the last trip. They'd had to remove some bunks and use two of the cabins as the regulations only allowed them to store a certain quantity of explosives in one place on a boat. Only crew with stripes on their uniform had cabins of their own. Duff swung his legs onto the floor and hurried into the corridor. Saw the back of a dirty Esso T-shirt on its way down the ladder to the engine room.

"Wait!"

Hutchinson turned.

Duff trotted up to him.

The engineer's eyes were shiny now too. But the evil glint was gone.

"What are you talking about?" Duff said. "Police? Quits?"

Hutchinson crossed his arms. Sniffed. "I went in to see Sparks to . . ." another sniff " . . . to apologize. The captain was talking on the radio. They had their backs to me and didn't hear me."

Duff felt his heart stop and crossed his arms. "Carry on."

"The captain said he had a Johnson who matched the description. You had a scar on your face and had signed up on the relevant date. The voice on the radio said the captain shouldn't do anything, as Duff was dangerous and the police would be ready when we came ashore. The captain answered he was glad to hear that after seeing you in action in the mess." Hutchinson ran two fingers across his forehead.

"Why are you tipping me off?"

The engineer shrugged. "The captain told me to apologize to Sparks.

He said the only reason I still had a job was that you'd refused to squeal on me. And I'd like to keep this job . . ."

"And you will?"

The engineer sniffed. "Probably. It's the only thing I'm any good at, according to the first engineer."

"Oh? Did he say that?"

Hutchinson grinned. "He came over to me this evening and said I shouldn't go getting any airs. I was a pimple on the arse of this boat, but I was a good engineer. Then he walked off. Pretty weird fellas on this boat, eh?" He laughed. Almost looked happy. "I'd better go where I'm needed."

"Wait," Duff said. "What good is it if you tell a doomed man he has a noose around his neck? I can't escape until we've docked."

"That's not my problem, Johnson. We're quits."

"Are we? This boat transported the machine guns that killed my wife and children, Hutchinson. No, it's not your problem, and it wasn't my problem when the captain asked me to give him a reason to fire you."

Sniff. "Jump in the sea then and swim away. It's not far. ETA in nine hours, Johnson." Sniff.

Duff stood watching the engineer disappear into the belly of the ship.

Then he went to a porthole and looked at the sea. Day was dawning. Eight hours until they were in harbor. The waves were high. How long would he survive in such weather, in such cold water? Twenty minutes? Thirty? And when they were approaching land the captain was sure to have someone keeping an eye on him. Duff leaned his brow against the glass.

There was no way out.

He went back into the cabin. Looked at his watch. A quarter to five. There were still fifteen minutes until he had to turn out, as they said. He lay on his bunk and closed his eyes. He could see Meredith: she was waving from the rock, across the water. Waving to him to join her.

"We're waiting for you."

As if in a dream, Macbeth thought. Or like swimming in a grotto under the water. That must be roughly what it was like sleepwalking. He held the torch in one hand and Lady with the other. Shone the light across the roulette table and the empty chairs. Shadows moved like ghosts across the walls. The false crystal above them gleamed.

"Why's no one here?" Lady asked.

"Everyone's gone home," Macbeth said, shining the torch on a half-full glass of whiskey on a poker table, and instinctively his mind went to dope. The absence of it had begun to make itself felt, but he was holding firm. He *was* strong, stronger than ever. "It's just you and me, my love."

"But we never close, do we?" She let go of his hand. "Have you closed the Inverness down? And you've changed everything. I don't recognize anything! What's that?"

They had come into another room, where the cone of light caught a line of one-armed bandits. There they were, standing in a row down the room. Like an army of small, sleeping robots, Macbeth thought. Mechanical boxes that would never wake again.

"Look, children's coffins," Lady said. "And so many, so many . . ." Her voice faded, and soundless sobbing took over.

Macbeth drew her close, away from the machines. "We're not in the Inverness, darling, this is the Obelisk. I wanted to show you what I've done for you. Look, it's closed. They've even cut off the electricity. Look, this is our victory. This is the foe's handsome battlefield, darling."

"It's ugly, it's hideous! And it stinks. Can you smell it? It stinks of bodies. The stench is coming from the wardrobe!"

"Darling, darling, it's from the kitchen. The police threw everyone out at one so that no one could spoil the evidence. Look, there are still steaks on plates."

Macbeth shone the torch over the tables: white cloths, burned-down candles and half-eaten meals. He stiffened when the light was reflected in two luminous yellow eyes staring at them. Lady screamed. He reached inside his jacket, but only glimpsed a lean, sinewy body before it was gone in the darkness. And discovered that he was holding a silver dagger in his hand.

"Relax, darling," he said. "It was only a dog. It must have smelled the food and got in somehow. There, there, it's gone now."

"I want to go! Get me out! I want to go away!"

"OK, we've seen enough. We'll go back to the Inverness now."

"Away, I said!"

"What do you mean? Away where?"

"Away!"

"But . . ." He didn't complete the sentence, only the thought. They had nowhere else to go. They never had, but it hadn't struck him until now. Everyone else had a family, a childhood home, relatives, a summer cottage, friends. They only had each other and the Inverness. But it had never occurred to him that this wouldn't be enough. Not until now, after they had challenged the world and he was about to lose her. She had to come back; she had to wake up; he had to get her out of this dark place where she was trapped—that was why he had brought her here. But even their triumph was unable to jolt her back to reality. And he needed her now, needed her clear brain, her firm hand, not this woman crying silent tears who had no sense of what was happening around her.

"We've found Duff," he said leading her quickly through the darkness toward the exit. "Seyton's flown to Capitol, and at two MS *Glamis* will be docking." There was light outside, but at the Obelisk all the windows had blinds, it was eternal night and party time. Gambling tables he didn't remember from when they had passed through before appeared suddenly in the torchlight and blocked their way. The sound of their footsteps was muffled by the carpet and he thought he heard the snarling and snapping of dogs' jaws behind them. *Shit! Where is it?* Where was the exit?

Lennox stood in the green grass. He had parked his car up on the main road and put on his sunglasses.

This was one of the reasons he would never settle in Fife. The light was too bright. He could already feel the sun burning his pale pink skin, as though he were going to be set alight like some damn vampire.

But he wasn't a vampire, was he. Some things you didn't see until you got close. Like the white farmhouse in front of him. It wasn't until you got close that you saw the whiteness was peppered with small black holes.

29

"**WELCOME ABOARD," SAID THE CAPTAIN** of MS *Glamis* as the pilot entered the bridge. "I'd like us to be on time today. We've got someone waiting for us."

"No problem," the pilot said, shook the captain's hand and took up a position beside him. "If the engines are working."

"Why wouldn't they be?"

"One of your engineers asked to go back on my boat. He had to get hold of a part the first engineer wants."

"Oh?" the captain said. "I hadn't been told that."

"Probably a minor detail."

"Who was the engineer?"

"Hutch-something-or-other. There they are." The pilot pointed to the boat rapidly moving away from them.

The captain took his binoculars. On the aft deck he saw a striped cap over the back of an Esso T-shirt.

"Anything wrong?" the pilot asked.

"No one leaves the ship without my permission," the captain said. "At least not today." He pressed the intercom button for the galley. "Steward!"

"Captain," came the response from the other end.

"Send Johnson up with two cups of coffee."

"I'm coming, Captain."

"Johnson, I said."

"He's got stomach cramps, Captain, so I let him rest until we dock."

"Check he's in his cabin."

"Righty-ho."

The captain took his finger off the button.

"Three degrees port," the pilot said.

"Aye-aye," said the first mate.

Inspector Seyton had said the safest option was for the captain and the telegrapher to remain the only ones in the know so that Duff didn't realize his cover had been blown. Seyton and two of his best men would be ready on the quay when they docked, board the boat and overpower Duff. And Seyton had stressed that when it happened he wanted the crew well clear so that no one would be hurt if shots were fired. Although to the captain it sounded like *when* shots were fired.

"Captain!" It was the steward. "Johnson's sleeping like a baby in his bunk. Shall I wake—"

"No! let him sleep. Is he alone in his cabin?"

"Yes, Captain."

"Good, good." The captain looked at his watch. In an hour everything would be over and he could go home to his wife. Soon have a couple of days off. Just that summons to the shipping line tomorrow concerning the insurance company report about a suspiciously high number of cases of the same type of illness in the crew who had worked in the hold over the last ten years. Something to do with blood.

"Course is fine," the pilot said.

"Let's hope so," the captain mumbled. "Let's hope so."

Ten minutes past one. Ten minutes ago a large elk head had come out of an elk clock and mooed. Angus looked around. He regretted the choice of place. Even if it was only unemployed layabouts and drunks at the Bricklayers Arms during the day now, it was the SWAT local, and if someone from police HQ saw him and the reporter talking it would soon get to Macbeth's ears. On the other hand, it was less suspicious than sitting in some bar hidden in the back streets.

But Angus didn't like it. Didn't like the elk. Didn't like it that the journalist still hadn't arrived. Angus would have gone long ago if this hadn't been his last chance.

"Sorry for being late."

The rolled "r"s. Angus looked up. It was only the voice that reassured him the man standing there in yellow oilskins was Walter Kite. Angus had read that this radio reporter consistently said no to TV and being pictured in newspapers and celeb magazines, as he considered a person's appearance a distraction from the story. The word was everything.

"Rain and traffic," Walt Kite said, undoing his jacket. Water ran from his thin hair.

"It's always rain and traffic," Angus said.

"That's the excuse we use anyway," the radio reporter said and sat down opposite him in the booth. "The truth is the chain came off my bike."

"I thought Walter Kite didn't lie," Angus said.

"Kite, the radio reporter, never lies," Kite said with a wry smile. "Walter, the private person, is a long way behind."

"Are you alone?"

"Always. Tell me what you didn't say on the phone."

Angus drew a deep breath and began to speak. He experienced nothing of the nerves he had felt when he had presented his information to Lennox and Caithness. Perhaps because the die was already cast; there was no way back. He used more or less the same words he had at Estex the day before, but also told Kite about the meeting with Lennox and Caithness. He gave Kite everything. The names. The details about the clubhouse and Fife. The order to burn the baby's body. While they were speaking Kite took a serviette from the box on the table and tried to wipe the black oil off his hands.

"Why me?" Kite asked, taking a second serviette.

"Because you're considered to be a brave reporter with integrity," Angus said.

"Nice to hear people think so," Kite said, studying Angus. "Your language is more elevated than other young police officers'."

"I studied theology."

"So that explains both the language and why you want to expose yourself to this. You believe in salvation for good deeds."

"You're mistaken, Mr. Kite. I don't believe in either salvation or divinity."

"Have you spoken to any other journalists—" he smirked "—with or without integrity?"

Angus shook his head.

"Good. Because if I work on this case I need total exclusivity. So not a word to other journalists, not to anyone. Are we in agreement?"

Angus nodded.

"Where can I get hold of you, Angus?"

"My phone number—"

"No phones. Address."

Angus wrote it down on Kite's oil-stained serviette. "What happens now?"

Kite heaved a sigh. Like a man who knew there was an immense amount of work in front of him.

"I have to check a few things first. This is a big case. I wouldn't like to be caught presenting false information or be suspected of being part of someone's agenda."

"My only agenda is that the truth should come out and that Macbeth is stopped."

Angus knew he had raised his voice when Kite looked around the sparse clientele to make sure no one had heard. "If it's true, you're lying when you say you don't believe in divinity."

"God doesn't exist."

"I'm thinking about divinity in *humans*, Angus."

"You mean the humanity in humans, Kite. Wanting goodness is as human as sinning."

Kite nodded slowly. "You're the theologian. Although I have to confess I believe you, I'll have to check out the story—and you as a person. I think that's what's called—" he got to his feet and buttoned up his oilskin jacket "—integrity."

"When do you think this can appear in print?" Angus breathed in and then let it out again. "I don't trust Lennox. He'll go to Macbeth."

"I'll prioritize the story," Kite said. "It should be mainly finished in two days." He took out his wallet.

"Thank you. I'll pay for my own coffee."

"Right." Kite put his wallet back in his jacket. "You're a rare bird in this town, you know."

"Definitely in danger of extinction." Angus smiled weakly.

He watched the reporter until he was out the door. Looked around the pub. No one conspicuous. Everyone seemed occupied with their own business. Two days. He had to try and stay alive for two days.

Seyton didn't like Capitol. Didn't like the broad avenues, the magnificent old parliamentary buildings and all the other shit—the green parks, the libraries and the opera house, the street artists, the tiny Gothic churches and the ridiculously extravagant cathedral, the smiling people in the pavement restaurants and the expensive national theatre with its pompous plays, incomprehensible dialogue and megalomaniac kings who die in the last act.

That was why he preferred to stand like this, with his back to the town and his eyes across the sea.

They were inside the harbor office and could see MS *Glamis* now.

"Sure you don't want any help?" asked the policeman with the CAPITOL POLICE patch on his uniform. There had been a discussion about jurisdiction before they arrived, but Capitol's chief commissioner had been cooperative, partly, he had said, because they felt the murder of a policeman in another town affected them, partly because you can make exceptions on board vessels.

"Thank you again, but I'm very sure," Seyton said.

"Fine, but when he's been arrested and brought ashore, we take over."

"Absolutely. As long as you keep an eye on the gangway and the ship."

"He won't get away, Inspector." The Capitol policeman pointed to the plainclothes policemen in two rowing boats fifty meters from the quay. The officers were pretending to fish, but were ready to catch Duff if he jumped overboard.

Seyton nodded. It wasn't so long since he had been standing waiting in another harbor office. That time it had been Duff who had refused help, the stupid idiot. But the roles were changed now. And he would make sure Duff knew. He would make him *feel* it. For some endlessly long seconds. The Capitol police knew nothing of Macbeth's orders, of course: Duff was not to be brought but carried ashore. In a body bag.

The *Glamis* reversed, and the sea was whipped white below the surface, then the white water rose and bubbled like champagne. Seyton loaded his MP-5. "Olafson. Ricardo. Ready?"

The two SWAT men nodded. They had drawings of the boat showing the cabin where Duff was.

Hawsers were thrown from the *Glamis* onto the quay, one from the bow and one from the stern, coiled around bollards and tightened. The side of the boat pushed gently against screaming tires. A gangway was lowered.

"Now," Seyton said.

They ran out across the quay and up the gangway. The crew stared at them openmouthed; the captain had obviously managed to keep the secret. They rushed down an iron ladder past what was labeled the first mate's cabin. Farther down. And farther down. Stopped outside the door of cabin 12.

Seyton listened but heard only his own breathing and the rumble of the engines. Ricardo had taken up a position farther down the corridor where he could keep an eye on the nearby doors, in case Duff was in a different cabin, heard them and tried to make a getaway.

Seyton switched on his torch and nodded to Olafson. Then he went in. The torch was redundant; there was enough light inside. Duff was lying on the lower bunk, turned to the wall with a blanket over him. He was wearing the green hat the captain said "Johnson" never took off and always kept pulled down to his big glasses. Apart from once when it had ridden up and the captain had seen the scar. Seyton took out the gun that would be placed in Duff's hand and fired two shots into the wall behind them. The explosions temporarily deprived him of hearing, and for a couple of seconds all Seyton heard was a high-pitched squeak. Duff had gone rigid in his bunk. Seyton put his mouth to Duff's ear.

"They screamed," he said. "They screamed, and it was wonderful to hear. You can scream a little too, Duff. Because I've decided to shoot you in the stomach first. For old acquaintance's sake, you arrogant prick."

A strong smell rose from Duff. Seyton breathed it in. But it wasn't the delicious scent of fear. It was . . . sweat. Stale, old masculine sweat. Older than the few days that Duff had been missing.

The man in the bunk turned his face to him.

It wasn't Duff's face.

"Eh?" said the man, and the blanket fell off revealing a naked chest and a hairy forearm.

Seyton put the barrel of his machine gun to the man's forehead. "Police. What are you doing here and where's Duff?"

The man sniffed. "I'm *sleeping*, as you can see. And I have no idea who Duff is."

"Johnson," Seyton said, pressing the muzzle into the man's brow so hard his head fell back onto the pillow.

Another sniff. "The galley boy? Have you checked the galley? Or the other cabins? We just take any bunk that's free on this trip. What's Johnson done, eh? Something serious by the look of it. If you're gonna make a dent in my head you'd better shoot, arsehole."

Seyton pulled his gun away.

"Olafson, take Ricardo and search the boat." Seyton studied the bloated face in front of him. Smelled him. Was the man really so unafraid or was it the composite stench of other body functions that drowned the smell of fear?

Olafson was still standing behind him.

"Search the boat!" Seyton yelled. And heard Olafson and Ricardo's boots pounding down the corridor and the sound of cabin doors being pulled open.

Seyton stretched. "What's your name and why are you wearing Johnson's hat?"

"Hutchinson. And you can have the hat. You look like you need something to wank in."

Seyton hit out. The gun opened the skin on the man's cheek and blood leaked out. But the guy didn't turn a hair even though his eyes filled with tears.

"Answer me," Seyton hissed.

"I woke up cold and was going to put on my T-shirt. I left it on the chest over there. Both my T-shirt and cap were gone; instead there was this hat. It was cold, so I took it, OK?" Hutchinson's voice shook, but the hatred shone through the tears. Fear and hatred, hatred and fear, it was always the same, Seyton thought, wiping the blood off the muzzle of his MP-5.

Angry voices came from the corridor. Seyton already knew. They would search the whole boat, every nook and cranny, in vain. Duff had already gone.

30

DUFF HURRIED DOWN BROAD AVENUES past magnificent old buildings, through parks, passing street musicians and portrait painters. A smiling couple at a pavement restaurant pointed him in the right direction when he showed them the address on the slip of paper. Stared at his beard, which had started to come unstuck on one side. Duff, trying not to run, passed Capitol Cathedral.

Hutchinson had turned round.

Turned round as he was on his way down the ladder. Came back up. Had listened to Duff's story. And even when Duff told him details he himself would not have believed if someone else had told him, Hutchinson had kept nodding as if in recognition. As though nothing was alien to him with regard to what humans were capable of doing to one another. And when Duff had finished, the engineer presented an escape plan. Without any hesitation, so simple and obvious Duff assumed the engineer must have hatched it for himself at some point. Duff would put on Hutchinson's clothes and stand by the railing ready.

"Just make sure you have your back to the bridge so the captain can't see your face and thinks it's me. The boatman will leave the ladder to you if you're standing ready. Throw it out early, climb down and stand at the bottom when the pilot's boat comes alongside. Tell him you need to be ashore before the *Glamis* docks because you have to pick up a spare part at the shipping office which we need for the winch that tightens the hawsers on the quay."

"Why?"

"Eh?"

"Why are you doing this for me?"

Hutchinson shrugged his shoulders. "I was on the detail to load up the ammo boxes. There was a skinny, bald police bloke with his arms crossed who looked as if he wanted to spit on us as we loaded them onto his truck."

Duff waited. For the rest of his explanation.

"People do things for each other," Hutchinson said and sniffed. "It seems." Sniff. "And if I've understood you right, you're alone against—" he pointed to the decks above them "—them. And I know a bit about how that feels."

Alone. Them.

"Thank you."

"No worries, Johnson." The engineer shook Duff's hand. Briefly, almost shyly. And then he ran his hand over the plaster on his forehead. "Next time I'll be ready, and it'll be your turn for a beating."

"Of course."

Duff was east of the center now.

"Sorry. District Six?"

"Over there."

He passed a kiosk with a newsstand. The houses were becoming smaller, the streets narrower.

"Tannery Street?"

"Down to the lights and the second or third left."

A police siren rose and sank. They had a different sound here in the capital, not so harsh or sharp. And a different tune. Not as gloomy, not so piercingly disharmonious.

"Dolphin?"

"The nightclub? Isn't it closed? Anyway, do you see that café there? Right next to it." But the eyes lingered too long on the scar, trying to remember something.

"Thank you."

"Not at all."

Number 66 Tannery Street.

Duff studied the names next to the bells by the rotting big wooden door. None of them meant a thing to him. He pulled at the door. Open. Or to be more precise, a smashed lock. It was dark inside. He stood still until his pupils began to widen. A staircase. Wet newspaper, smell of urine. Sound of tuberculous coughing from behind a door. A sound like a hard wet slap. Duff set off up the stairs. There were two front doors on every floor, as well as a low door on every landing. He rang one of the doorbells. From inside came the angry barking of a dog and shuffling steps. A small, almost comical, wrinkled lady opened the door. No safety chain.

"Yes, love?"

"Hello, I'm Inspector Johnson."

She eyed him skeptically. Duff assumed she could smell Hutchinson from the Esso T-shirt. The scent appeared to have quietened the little fluffball of a dog anyway.

"I'm looking for—" Yes, what was he looking for? "—someone a friend of mine, Banquo, gave me an address for."

"Sorry, young man. I don't know any Banquo."

"Alfie?"

"Oh, Alfie. He lives on the second floor, right-hand side. Excuse me, but you . . . erm . . . you're losing your beard."

"Thank you."

Duff tore off the beard and glasses as he went up to the second floor. The door to the right had no name on it, just a bell with a button hanging from a spiral metal spring.

Duff knocked. Waited. Knocked again, harder. Another wet slap from the ground floor. He pulled at the door. Locked. Should he wait and see if anyone came? It was a better alternative than showing his face on the street.

Low cough. The sound came from behind the low door on the landing. Duff walked down the five steps and turned the doorknob. It moved a little, as though someone was holding on to it on the inside. He knocked.

No answer.

"Hello? Hello, is anyone there?"

He held his breath and put his ear to the door. He heard something which sounded like the rustle of paper. Someone was hiding in there.

Duff went down the stairs with loud, heavy footsteps, took off his shoes on the floor below and tiptoed back.

He grabbed the doorknob and gave it a sharp pull. Heard something go flying as the door swung open. A piece of string.

He stared at himself.

The picture wasn't particularly big and positioned to the right at the bottom of the page underneath the headline.

The newspaper was lowered, and Duff stared into the face of an old man with a long, unkempt beard. He was sitting leaning forward with his trousers around his ankles.

A splash box. Duff had seen them before, in the old workers' blocks of flats along the river. He assumed they got their name from the sound made when shit from the upper floors hit the container on the ground floor. Like a wet slap.

"Sorry," Duff said. "Are you Alfie?"

The man didn't answer, just stared at Duff. Then he slowly turned the page of the newspaper, looked at the photo and back up at Duff. Moistened his lips. "Louder," he said, pointing to his ear with one hand.

Duff raised his voice. "Are you Alfie?"

"Louder."

"Alfie!"

"Shh. Yes, he's Alfie."

Perhaps it was because of the shouting that Duff didn't hear someone come. He just felt a hard object being pressed against the back of his head, and there was something vaguely familiar about the voice that whispered in his ear: "And yes, this is a gun, Inspector. So don't move; just tell me how you found us and who sent you."

Duff made to turn, but a hand pushed his face forward again, to face Alfie, who clearly regarded the situation as resolved and had resumed his reading.

"I don't know who you are," Duff said. "I found the impression of an address on a notepad in Banquo's car. And no one sent me. I'm alone."

"Why have you come here?"

"Because Macbeth's trying to kill me. I'm fairly sure he had Banquo and Fleance killed. So if Banquo had an address he thought was a safe haven, it might be good for me too."

A pause. For thought, it seemed.

"Come with me."

Duff was turned, but in such a way that the person with the gun was still behind him. Then he was prodded up the stairs to the door where he had rung the bell. It was now open, and he was pushed into a big room that smelled stale even though the windows were wide open. The room contained a large table with three chairs, a kitchen counter with a sink, a fridge, a narrow bed, a sofa and a mattress on the floor. And one other person. He was sitting on a chair with his forearms and hands on the table and staring straight at Duff. The glasses were the same, also the long legs protruding from under the table. But there was something different about him. Perhaps it was the beard. Or his face had become thinner.

"Malcolm," Duff said. "You're alive."

"Duff. Sit down."

Duff sat down on the chair opposite the deputy chief commissioner.

Malcolm took off his glasses. Cleaned them. "So you thought I drowned myself after I took Duncan's life, did you?"

"At first I thought so. Until I realized that Macbeth was behind Duncan's murder. Then I also realized that he had probably drowned you to clear his path to the chief commissioner's office. And that the suicide letter was a forgery."

"Macbeth threatened to kill my daughter if I didn't sign it. What do you want, Duff?"

"He says—" the voice behind Duff started.

"I heard you," Malcolm interrupted. "And I see that the newspapers are making out that Macbeth is after you, Duff. But of course you could be working with him, and the scribblings are a plant so you can infiltrate us."

"Killing my family was a cover operation?"

"I read about that too, but I don't trust anything any longer, Duff. If Macbeth and the police really were so keen to catch you they would already have done so."

"I was lucky."

"And then you came here." Malcolm drummed his fingers on the table. "Why?"

"Safe haven."

"Safe?" Malcolm shook his head. "You're a police officer, Duff, and you know that if you can find us that easily then so can Macbeth. A moderately intelligent wanted person sits tight. He doesn't visit other people also on the wanted list. So give me a better answer. Why here?"

"What do you think?"

"Let me hear you say it. The gun's pointing at where you have, or don't have, a bleeding heart."

Duff gulped. Why had he come here? It had been a lot to hope for. But it had also been the only hope he had. The odds had been poor, but the calculation simple. Duff took a deep breath.

"Banquo was supposed to meet me to tell me something the night he died. And he was the last person to see you the day you disappeared. I thought there was a chance I might find you here. And we could help each other. I have proof Macbeth killed Duncan. Macbeth knows and that's why he's trying to kill me."

Malcolm arched an eyebrow. "And how can we help each other? You don't imagine the police here in Capitol can help us, do you?"

Duff shook his head. "They've been instructed to arrest us and send us back to Macbeth at once. But we can bring Macbeth down together."

"To avenge your family."

"Yes, that was my first thought."

"But?"

"There's something bigger than revenge."

"The chief commissioner's job?"

"No."

"What then?"

Duff nodded toward the open window. "Capitol is an elegant town, isn't she? It's difficult not to like her. To fall in love with her even—such a smiling blond beauty with sunshine in her eyes. But you and I can never love her, can we? For we've given our hearts to the foul, rotten city up on the west coast. I've disowned her, thought she didn't mean anything to me. Me and my career were more important than the town that has done nothing but darkened our moods, corrupted our hearts and shortened our lives. Absurd, wasted love, I thought. But that's how it is. Too late we realize who we really love."

"And you're willing to sacrifice yourself for a town like that?"

"It's easy." Duff smiled. "I've lost everything. There's not much left to sacrifice other than my life. What about you, Malcolm?"

"I have my daughter to lose."

"And you can only save her if we bring Macbeth down. Listen. You're the man who can carry on Duncan's work. And that's why I'm here to follow you, if you're willing to take over as chief commissioner and rule justly."

Malcolm eyed him cautiously. "Me?"

"Yes."

Malcolm laughed. "Thank you for the moral support, Duff, but let me make a few things clear first."

"Yes?"

"The first is I've never liked you."

"Understandable," Duff said. "I've never paid a thought to anyone else but myself. I'm not saying I'm a changed man, but what has happened has definitely given me new insights. I'm still not a clever man, but perhaps a little less stupid than I was."

"Possibly, although you may only be saying what you want me to hear. But what I don't want to hear is any conversion nonsense. You might be slightly changed, but the world is the same."

"What do you mean?"

"I'm pleased you regard me as relatively decent. But if I'm going to have you as part of my team I have to know your angel wings don't prevent you from keeping your feet on the ground. Surely you don't think you can get to me without turning a blind eye to some things? Accepting some . . . established practices for who gets away with something and who doesn't, and who gets the brown envelopes. If you take everything from a badly paid policeman overnight, how are you going to get his loyalty? And isn't it better to win a few small battles now and then rather than to insist on always losing the big ones?"

Duff looked at the man with the beard as if to make sure this really was Malcolm. "You mean, don't go after Hecate but his small competitors?"

"I mean, be realistic, my dear Duff. No one gains anything with a chief commissioner who doesn't know how things work in this world. We have to make a better and cleaner town than those who came before us, Duff, but for this job we damn well have to be paid."

"Take payment, you mean?"

"We can't win against Hecate, Duff. Not yet. In the meantime we can let him pay some of our wages so that we're equipped to fight all the other crime in the town. God knows there's enough of it."

At first Duff felt a weariness. And a strange relief. The fight was over; he could give in, could rest now. With Meredith. He shook his head. "I can't accept that. You aren't the person I'd hoped you were, Malcolm, so that's my last hope gone."

"Do you think there are better men? Are *you* a better man?"

"Not me, but I've met men in the belly of a boat who are better than you or me, Malcolm. So now I'm going to leave. You'd better make up your mind whether you're going to let me go or shoot me."

"I can't let you go now as you know where I am. Unless you swear not to reveal my whereabouts."

"A promise between traitors wouldn't be worth much, Malcolm. I still won't swear though. Please shoot me in the head—I have a family waiting for me."

Duff got up, but Malcolm did too, put both hands on his shoulders and forced him back down onto the chair.

"You've asked me quite a few questions, Duff. And in an interview the questions are often truer and more revealing than the answers. I've been lying to you, and your questions were the right ones. But I wasn't sure if your righteous indignation was genuine until now, when you were willing to take a bullet for a clean police force and town."

Duff blinked. His body was so heavy all of a sudden, he was close to fainting.

"There are three men in this room," Malcolm said. "Three men willing to sacrifice everything to carry on what Duncan stood for." He put on the glasses he had been cleaning. "Three men who may not be better than any others—perhaps we've already lost so much that it doesn't cost us much to sacrifice the rest. But this is the seed and the logic of the revolution, so let's not get carried away by our own moral excellence. Let's just say we have the will to do the right thing irrespective of whether the fuel powering our will is a sense of justice—" he shrugged "—a family man's lust for revenge, a traitor's shame, the moral exaltation of a privileged person or a God-fearing horror of burning in hell. For this *is* the right path and what we need now is the will. There are no simple paths to justice and purity, only the difficult one."

"Three men," Duff said.

"You, me and . . . ?"

"And Fleance," Duff said. "How did you manage it, lad?"

"My father kicked me out of the car and off the bridge," the voice said behind him. "He taught me how to do what he never succeeded in teaching Macbeth. How to swim."

Duff looked at Malcolm, who sighed then smiled. And to his surprise Duff felt himself smiling too. And felt something surge up his throat. A sob. But he realized it was laughter, not tears, only when he saw Malcolm also burst into laughter and then Fleance. The laughter of war.

"Wozzup?"

They turned to see old Alfie standing in the doorway with a bewildered expression on his face and the newspaper in his hand, and they laughed even louder.

31

LENNOX WAS STANDING BY THE window staring out. Weighing the grenade in his hand. Angus, Angus. He still hadn't told anyone about the meeting at Estex. Why, he didn't know. He only knew he hadn't done a thing all day. Or yesterday. Or the day before. Whenever he tried to read a report he lost concentration. It was as though the letters moved and made new words. *Reforming* became *informing* and *portrayal* became *betrayal*. Whenever he lifted the phone to make a call the receiver weighed a ton and he had to cradle it again. He had tried to read the newspaper and found out that old Zimmerman was standing for mayor. Zimmerman was neither controversial nor charismatic; he was respected for his competence, as far as that went, but he was not a serious challenger to Tourtell. Lennox had also started reading an article about the increase in drug trafficking, which according to the UN had turned into the biggest industry after arms dealing, before realizing he was only looking at sentences, not reading them.

Eight days had gone by since Duff had evaded capture in Capitol. When Lennox and Seyton had stood before him in the chief commissioner's office Macbeth had been so furious that he was literally foaming at the mouth. White bubbles of saliva gathered at the corners of his mouth as he ranted on about what an idiot he had been made to look like in the capital. And if Lennox and Seyton had done their jobs and caught Duff while he was still in town then this would never have happened. And yet Lennox felt this paradoxical relief that Duff was still alive and free.

There wasn't much light left outside, but his eyes smarted. Perhaps he needed an extra shot today. Just to get through this one day; tomorrow everything would be better.

"Is that really a hand grenade or is it supposed to be an ashtray?"

Lennox turned to the voice at the door.

Macbeth was in an odd pose, leaning forward with his arms down by his sides as though he were standing in a strong wind. His head was bowed, his pupils at the top of his eyes as he stared at Lennox.

"It was thrown at my grandfather in the First World War."

"Lies." Macbeth grinned, coming in and closing the door behind him. "That's a German Model 24 *Stielhandgranate*, stick grenade. It's an ash-tray."

"I don't think my grandfather—"

Macbeth took the grenade out of Lennox's hand, grasped the cord at the end of the handle and began to pull.

"Don't!"

Macbeth raised an eyebrow and eyed the frightened head of the Anti-Corruption Unit, who continued: "It will d-detonate—"

"—your grandfather's story?" Macbeth put the cord back into the handle and placed the grenade on the table. "We can't have that, can we. So what were you thinking about, Inspector?"

"Corruption," Lennox said, putting the grenade in a drawer. "And anti-corruption."

Macbeth pulled the visitor's chair forward. "What is corruption actually, Lennox? Is a solemnly committed revolutionary paid to infiltrate our state machinery corrupt? Is an obedient but passive servant who does nothing but receive his regular and somewhat unreasonably high salary in a system he knows is based on corruption corrupt?"

"There are many gray areas, Chief Commissioner. As a rule you know yourself if you're corrupt or not."

"You mean it's a matter of feelings?" Macbeth sat down, and Lennox followed suit so as not to tower over him.

"So if you don't *feel* corrupt because the family you're providing for is dependent on your income, you're *not* corrupt? If the motive is good—for the family or town's benefit—we can just paraphrase the word *corruption*—say, well, *pragmatic politics*, for instance."

"I think it's the other way round," Lennox said. "I think when you know that greed and nothing else is at the root, then you resort to para-phrases for yourself. While the morally justified crime requires no para-phrase. We can live with it going by its right name. Corruption, robbery, murder."

"So this is what you do? Spend your time in here thinking," Macbeth said, holding his chin in his fingertips. "Wondering whether you're corrupt or not."

"Me?" Lennox chuckled. "I'm talking about the people we investigate of course."

"And yet we always talk about ourselves. And I'd still maintain that desperate situations make people call their own corruption by another name. And the payment you receive to take advantage of your position is not money but charity. Life. Your family's life, for instance. Do you understand?"

"I don't know . . ." Lennox said.

"Let me give you an example," Macbeth said. "A radio reporter who is known for his integrity is contacted by a young police officer who thinks he has a story to tell that could bring down a chief commissioner. What this perfidious officer, let's call him Angus, doesn't know is that this radio reporter has a certain . . . relationship with the chief commissioner. The reporter, with good reason, fears for his family if he doesn't do as this chief commissioner wishes. So the reporter informs said chief commissioner about the officer's seditious plans. The reporter promises to get back to the young officer, and the chief commissioner tells the reporter to meet the officer where no one can see or hear them. Where the boss or his people can . . . well, you know."

Lennox didn't answer. He wiped his hands on his trousers.

"So the boss is safe. But he wonders, naturally enough, who the corrupt person is here: the young officer, the radio reporter or . . . or who, Lennox?"

Lennox cleared his throat, hesitated. "The chief commissioner?"

"No, no, no." Macbeth shook his head. "The third person. The one who should have informed the chief commissioner right from the start. The third person who knew about Angus's plans, who isn't part of them yet still is, indirectly, for as long as he fails to go to his boss and fails to save him. Which he hasn't done yet. Because he has to think. And think. And while he's thinking, he's becoming corrupt himself, or isn't he?"

Lennox tried to meet Macbeth's eyes. But it was like staring at the sun.

"The meeting at Estex, Lennox. I don't know when you were considering telling me about it."

Lennox couldn't stop blinking. "I . . . I've been thinking."

"Yes, it's difficult to stop. Thoughts just come, don't they? And no matter how free we think our will is, it's governed by thoughts, bidden or unbidden. Tell me who came to you, Lennox."

"This person—"

"Say the name."

"He's—"

"Say the name!"

Lennox took a deep breath. "Police Officer Angus."

"Carry on."

"You know Angus. Young. Impulsive. And with all that's happened recently anyone can react a little irrationally. I thought that before I came to you with these serious accusations I'd try to talk some common sense into him. Let him cool down a bit."

"And in the meantime keep me in ignorance? Because you assumed that your judgment of the situation was better than mine? That I wouldn't let Angus, whom I employed in SWAT, have another chance? That I would have his overheated, though otherwise innocent, head chopped off straight-away?"

"I . . ." Lennox searched for words to complete his sentence.

"But you're wrong, Lennox. I always give my subordinates two chances. And that rule applies to both you and Angus."

"I'm pleased to hear that."

"I believe in magnanimity. So I would have forgotten the whole business if Angus had shown signs of regret and refused to meet the reporter when he rang to set up a second meeting. I wouldn't have given it another thought. Life would have gone on. Unfortunately Angus didn't do that. He accepted. And I don't have a third cheek."

Macbeth got up and walked to the window.

"Which brings me to *your* second chance, Lennox. My reporter has been informed that you and Seyton are going to this meeting. It'll take place at the Estex factory this evening, where Angus believes there will also be a photographer to take pictures of a furnace where he believes a child's body has been burned. And there you will personally punish the traitor."

"Punish?"

"I'll leave you to mete out the punishment at your own discretion. My only demand is that death should be the outcome." Macbeth turned to Lennox, who was breathing through his mouth.

"And afterward Seyton will help you dispose of the body."

"But—"

"Third chances probably exist. In heaven. How's your family by the way?"

Lennox opened his mouth, and a sound emerged.

"Good," Macbeth said. "Seyton will pick you up at six. Depending on the punishment you choose it should all be over within an hour and a half, so I suggest you ring your charming wife to say you'll be a little late for tea. I've been told her shopping indicates she's giving you black pudding."

Macbeth closed the door quietly behind him as he left.

Lennox put his head in his hands. A mollusk. A creature without a bone in his body.

A fix. He had to have a shot.

Macbeth crashed his heels down on the floor as he strode along the corridor. Trying to drown the voice shouting he had to have power. Or brew. Or anything. He had managed to stay clean for more than a week now. It would get worse before it got better, but it *would* get better. He had done it before and would do it again. There was just the awful sweat—it stank, stank of displeasure, fear and pain. But it would pass. Everything would pass. *Had* to pass. He walked into the anteroom to his office.

"Chief Commissioner—"

"No messages, no phone calls, Priscilla."

"But—"

"Not now. Later."

"You've got a visitor."

Macbeth pulled up sharp. "You let someone in—" he pointed to the office door "—there?"

"She insisted."

Macbeth looked at Priscilla's desperate expression.

"It's your wife."

"What?" came his astonished response. He did up the lowest button on his uniform and went into his office.

She was standing behind his desk examining the painting on the wall. "Darling! You really have to do something about the art in here."

Macbeth stared at Lady in disbelief. She was wearing a plain, elegant outfit under a fur coat; she had obviously come straight from the hairdresser's and looked relaxed and energetic. He approached her with caution. "How . . . are you, darling?"

"Excellent," she said. "I can see this picture is propaganda, but what's it trying to say actually?"

Macbeth couldn't take his eyes off her. Where was the crazy woman he had seen yesterday? Gone.

"My love?"

Macbeth gazed at the painting. Saw the workers' coarse features. "It was put there by someone else. I'll get it changed. I'm so glad you feel better. Have you . . . taken your medicine?"

She shook her head. "No medicine. I've stopped my medicine. All of it."

"Because there's none left?"

She smiled fleetingly. "I saw the drawer was empty. You've stopped too." She sat in his chair. "This is a bit . . . cramped, isn't it?"

"Maybe." Macbeth sat down on one of the visitor's chairs. Perhaps her madness had just been a labyrinth and she had found her way out.

"Glad you agree. I had a chat with Jack this morning. About the plan you made regarding the mayoral elections."

"Yes. Well, what do you think?"

She pouted and waggled her head. "You've done the best you can do, but you've forgotten one thing."

"What's that?"

"Your thinking is that we should leak information about Tourtell's relationship with this boy just before the elections. And then you, the Sweno-killer, will quickly fill the vacuum before people go to the ballot box."

"Yes?" said Macbeth, full of enthusiasm.

"The problem is that the vacuum was filled when Zimmerman announced that he was standing."

"That bore? No one cares about him."

"Zimmerman doesn't have great appeal, it's true, but people know him and know what they can expect. So they feel safe with him. And it's important for people to feel safe in these dramatic times. That's why Tourtell will be re-elected."

"Do you really think Zimmerman could beat me?"

"Yes," Lady said. "Unless you're officially supported by a Tourtell who has not been damaged by scandal and you've also dealt with Hecate. Get those two things organized and you're unbeatable."

Macbeth felt a wearied relief. She was out of the labyrinth. She was here, back with him.

"Fine, but how?"

"By giving Tourtell an ultimatum. He can either voluntarily withdraw, giving advancing age and poor health as reasons, and lend you his unreserved, official support. Or we can force him to withdraw by threatening to unmask him as the perverted pig he is, after which he'll be arrested and thrown into jail, where he knows what happens to pederasts. Shouldn't be the most difficult decision to make."

"Hm." Macbeth scratched his beard. "We'll have made an enemy."

"Tourtell? On the contrary. He understands power struggles and will be grateful we gave him a merciful alternative."

"Let me think about it."

"No need, darling. There's nothing to consider. Then there's the puppeteer, Hecate. It's time he was got rid of."

"I'm not so sure that's wise, darling. Remember he's our guarantor and will support us if we come up against opponents."

"Hecate still hasn't demanded his pound of flesh for making you chief commissioner," Lady said. "But soon the day of reckoning will come. And then you'll do this." She raised an elbow as though it were attached to a string. "And this." A foot shot out. "Do you want to be Hecate's puppet, my love? Curtailing the campaign against him won't be enough; he'll want more and more, and in the end everything—that's what people such as him are like. So the question is whether you want to let Hecate control the town through you? Or—" she placed her elbows on the desk "—do you want to be the puppeteer yourself? Be the hero who caught Hecate and became mayor?"

Macbeth fixed her with his eyes. Then he nodded slowly.

"I'll invite Tourtell to a private game of blackjack," Lady said, getting up. "And you send a message to Hecate telling him you wish to meet him face-to-face."

"And why do you think he'll say yes?"

"Because you'll hand him a suitcase full of gold as thanks for him getting us the chief commissioner's job."

"And he'll swallow the bait, do you think?"

"Some people are blinded by power, others by money. Hecate belongs to the latter group. You'll get the details later."

Macbeth accompanied her to the door. "Darling," he said, laying a hand on her back, stroking the thick fur, "it's good to have you back."

"Likewise," she said, letting him kiss her on the cheek. "Be strong. Let's make each other strong."

He watched her as she sailed through the anteroom, wondering if he would ever fully understand who she was. Or if he wanted to. Wasn't it that which made her so irresistible to him?

Lennox and Seyton had parked in the road on the opposite side from Estex. It was so dark that Lennox couldn't see the drizzle; he only heard it as a whisper on the car roof and windscreen.

"There's the reporter," Seyton said.

The light from a bike wobbled across the road. Turned in through the gate and was gone.

"Let's give him two minutes," Seyton said, checking his machine gun.

Lennox yawned. Luckily he had managed to get a shot.

"Now," Seyton said.

They stepped out, ran through the darkness, through the gate and into the factory building.

Voices were coming from the foreman's office high up on the wall.

Seyton sniffed the air. Then he motioned toward the steel staircase.

They tiptoed up, and Lennox felt a wonderful absence of thought and the steel of the railing, which was so cold it burned the palms of his hands. They stood just outside the door. The high gave him that sense of sitting in a warm safe room and watching himself. The buzz of voices inside reminded him of his parents in the sitting room when he was small and had gone to bed.

"When will it appear in print?" Angus was speaking.

The answer came with drawled arrogance and long rolled "r"s: "Disregarding the fact that on radio we don't refer to *print*, I hope—"

When Seyton opened the door it was as if someone had pressed the stop button on a cassette player. Walt Kite's eyes behind his glasses were large. With fear. Excitement. Relief? Not surprise anyway. Lennox and Seyton had been punctual.

"Good evening," Lennox said, feeling a warm smile spread across his face.

Angus stood up and knocked his chair over as he reached for

something inside his jacket. But froze when he caught sight of Seyton's machine gun.

In the silence that followed Kite buttoned up his yellow oilskin jacket. It was like being in a gentlemen's toilet: no looks were exchanged, no words were said; he just left them quickly with his head lowered. He had done his bit. Left the others with the stench.

"What are you waiting for, Lennox?" Angus asked.

Lennox became aware of his outstretched arm and the gun on the end of it. "For the reporter to be so far away he won't hear the shot," he said.

Angus's Adam's apple went up and down. "So you're going to shoot me?"

"Unless you have another suggestion. I've been given a free hand as to how this should happen."

"OK."

"OK as in *I understand* or as in *Yes, I want to be shot?*"

"As in—"

Lennox fired. In the enclosed space he felt the physical pressure of the explosion on his eardrums. He opened his eyes again. But Angus was still standing in front of him, openmouthed now. There was a hole in the file on the shelf behind him.

"Sorry," Lennox said, walking two steps closer. "I thought a sudden shot to the head would be the most humane solution here. But heads are very small. Stand still, please . . ." An involuntary giggle escaped his lips.

"Inspector Lennox, without—"

The second shot hit the target. And the third.

"Without wishing to criticize," Seyton said, looking down at the dead body, "it would have been more practical if you'd ordered him down to the furnaces and done it there. Now we'll have to carry him."

Lennox didn't answer. He was studying the growing pool of blood seeping out of the young man's body toward him. There was something strangely beautiful about the shapes and colors, the sparkling red, the way it extended in all directions, like red balloons. They carried Angus down to the factory floor and then picked up the empty shell casings, washed the floor and dug the first bullet out of the wall. Downstairs they removed his watch and a chain with a gold cross and maneuvered the body into a furnace, closed it and fired it up. Waited. Lennox stared at the gutter that went from the bottom of the furnace to a tub on the floor. A low hissing sound came from the furnace.

"What happens to . . . ?"

"It evaporates," Seyton said. "Everything evaporates or turns to ash when the temperature's more than two thousand degrees Celsius. Except metal, which just melts."

Lennox nodded. He couldn't take his eyes off the gutter. A gray trembling drop appeared with a membrane over it, like a coating.

"Lead," Seyton said. "Melts at three hundred and fifty."

They waited. The hissing inside had stopped.

Then a golden drop came.

"We've topped a thousand now," Seyton said.

"What . . . what's that?"

"Gold."

"But we removed—"

"Teeth. Let's wait until it's over sixteen hundred, in case there's any steel in the body. After that all we have to do is hoover up the ash. Hey, are you OK?"

Lennox nodded. "Bit dizzy. I've never . . . erm . . . shot anyone before. You have, so I'm sure you remember what it felt like the first time."

"Yes," Seyton said quietly.

Lennox was going to ask what it had felt like, but the glint in Seyton's eyes made him change his mind.

32

MACBETH STOOD ON THE ROOF of Inverness Casino looking to the east through a pair of binoculars. It wasn't easy to distinguish in the darkness, but wasn't that smoke coming from the top of the brick chimney at Estex? If so, the matter had been dealt with. And they would have two more men in their spider's web, two men with blood on their hands. Kite and Lennox. Kite could be useful to have around in the mayoral elections. If there were any other candidates standing. And Lennox would soon need someone else to get him dope. Before much longer Hecate would be no more than a saga as well.

Macbeth had waited by the stairs to the toilet in the central station for fifteen minutes before Strega turned up. At first he had rejected the bags of power and said he only wanted to pass on a message to Hecate. He wanted to meet him as soon as possible, inform him about his future plans and also give him a present as a token of Macbeth and Lady's gratitude for what Hecate had done for them. A present he was sure that Hecate—if the rumors about him liking gold were true—would appreciate.

Strega had said he would hear from her. Perhaps.

Yes, there was smoke coming from the chimney.

"Darling, Tourtell's here."

Macbeth turned. Lady was standing in the doorway. She had put on her red dress.

"I'm coming. You look pretty, did I say?"

"You did. And that's all you'll say for a while, my love. Let me do the talking so we follow the plan."

Macbeth laughed. Yes, she was back all right.

The gaming room and the restaurant were so full of customers that they literally had to force their way through to the gaming table they'd had set up in the separate small room at the end of the restaurant where Tourtell was waiting.

"Alone this evening?" Macbeth said, pressing the mayor's hand.

"Young ones have to study for exams." Tourtell smiled. "I saw there was a queue outside."

"Since six o'clock," Lady said, sitting down beside him. "We're so full I had to persuade Jack here to be our croupier."

"Which tells me there ought to be room for two casinos in this town," Tourtell said, fidgeting with his black bow tie. "You know how unhappy voters get when they aren't allowed to go out and waste their money."

"Agreed," Lady said, beckoning a waiter. "Has the mayor had a lucky evening, Jack?"

"Bit early to say," Jack said, smiling from where he stood in his red croupier's jacket. "Another card, Mr. Mayor?"

Tourtell looked at the two cards he had been given. "Nothing ventured, nothing gained. Isn't that right, Lady?"

"You are so right. And that's why I've decided to tell you about a consortium which is keen to invest its capital by not only taking over the Obelisk but also renovating and reopening it as the most attractive casino in the country. It is of course a financial risk given that the Obelisk's reputation is being dragged through the mud right now, but we're willing to put our faith in a new owner and a new profile changing that."

"We, Lady?"

"I'm in the consortium, yes. Together with Janovic, a property investor from Capitol. It's important, as you said, for the town to have the Obelisk up and running again. Just think of all the taxable income it will bring in from the neighboring counties. And when we open the newly renovated, spectacular Obelisk in a few months' time it will be a tourist attraction. People will travel from Capitol to gamble in our town, Tourtell."

Tourtell looked at the card Jack had given him and sighed. "Doesn't look like this is going to be my night."

"It still could be," Lady said. "The shares in the consortium haven't all been taken up, and we've considered you as a potential investor. You also need something to fall back on after your mayoralty is over."

"Investor?" He laughed. "As mayor I'm afraid I don't have the legal ability or the money to buy shares in companies, so the undoubted share-fest will have to take place without me."

"Shares can be paid for in a variety of ways," Lady said. "For example, with services rendered."

"What are you suggesting, my beautiful duchess?"

"That you publicly support Macbeth's candidature for mayor."

Tourtell looked at his cards again. "I've already promised I would and I'm famous for keeping my promises."

"We mean in *this* election."

Tourtell glanced up from his cards, at Macbeth. "This election?"

Lady placed a hand on the mayor's arm and leaned against him. "Yes, because you won't be standing."

He blinked twice. "I won't be?"

"It's true you intimated you would, but then you changed your mind."

"And why was that?"

"Your health isn't the best, and the job of mayor requires an energetic man. A man of the future. And as soon as you're not the mayor you'll be free to join a consortium which in practice will have a monopoly over the casinos in this town and, unlike the cards you have in your hand, will make you a very rich man."

"But I don't want to—"

"You recommend the voters elect Macbeth as your successor because he's a man *of* the people, who works *for* the people and leads *with* the people. And because he, in his role as chief commissioner, has brought down both Sweno and Hecate and shown that he gets things *done*."

"Hecate?"

"Macbeth and I are anticipating events here a little, but Hecate's a dead man. We're going to propose a meeting with Hecate, which he won't leave alive. This is a promise, and I'm famous for keeping promises too, my dear Mr. Mayor."

"And if I don't go along with this—" he spat the words out like a rotten grape "—*share deal*?"

"That would be a shame."

Tourtell pushed his chair back, took one of his chins between his forefinger and middle finger. "What else have you got, woman?"

"Sure we shouldn't stop there?" Lady asked.

Jack coughed, tapped his forefinger on the pack. "Enough cards, Mr. Mayor?"

"No!" Tourtell snarled without taking his eyes off Lady.

"As you wish," she sighed. "You'll be arrested and accused of unseemly behavior with an underage boy." She nodded to the card Jack had placed in front of him. "See, you went too far. Bust."

Tourtell stared at her with his heavy cod-eyes. His protruding wet lip twitched. "You won't get me," he hissed. "Do you hear me? You won't get me!"

"If we can get Hecate, we can certainly get you."

Tourtell stood up. Looked down at them. His chins, his scarlet face, indeed his whole body was shaking with fury. Then he spun on his heel and marched out, the inside thighs of his trousers rubbing against each other.

"What do you think?" Macbeth said after he had gone.

"Oh, he'll do what we want," Lady said. "Tourtell's no young fool. He just needs a bit of time to work out the odds before he makes his play."

Caithness dreamed about Angus. He had rung her, but she didn't dare lift the receiver because she knew someone had been tampering with her phone and it would explode. She woke up and turned to the alarm clock on the bedside table beside the ringing telephone. It was past midnight. It had to be a murder. She hoped it was a murder, an everyday murder and not . . . She lifted the receiver.

"Hello?" She heard the click which had been there ever since the meeting at Estex.

"Sorry for ringing so late." It was an unfamiliar, young man's voice. "I just wanted to confirm that you're coming to three twenty-three at the usual time tomorrow, Friday?"

"I'm doing what?"

"Sorry, perhaps I have the wrong number. Is that Mrs. Mittbaum?"

Caithness sat up in bed, wide awake. She moistened her lips. Imagined the reels of the tape recorder in a room somewhere, perhaps the Surveillance Unit on the first floor of HQ.

"I'm not her," she said. "But I wouldn't worry. People with German surnames are generally punctual."

"My apologies. Good night."

"Good night."

Caithness lay in bed, her heart pounding.

323. The room in the Grand Hotel where she and Duff used to have their lunchtime trysts, booked in the name of Mittbaum.

33

HECATE SWUNG THE TELESCOPE ON its stand. The morning light leaked between the clouds and descended like pillars into the town. "So Macbeth said he was planning to kill me during the meeting?"

"Yes," Bonus said.

Hecate looked through the telescope. "Look at that. Already a queue outside the Inverness."

Bonus looked around. "Are the waiters here today?"

"The boys, you mean? I book them only when I need them, same as with this penthouse suite. Owning things is tying yourself to them. And people, Bonus. But when you notice your car is so full of junk that it's slowing you down, you get rid of the junk, not the car. That's what Macbeth hasn't realized. That I'm the car, not the junk. Did you ring Macbeth, Strega?"

The tall man-woman, who had just entered the room, stepped out of the shadows.

"Yes."

"And what did you arrange?"

"He'll come here alone tomorrow at six to meet you."

"Thank you."

She merged back into the shadows.

"I wonder how he dares," Bonus said.

"Dares?" Hecate said. "He can't stop himself. Macbeth has become like a moth drawn helplessly to the light, to power."

"And like a moth he'll burn."

"Maybe. What Macbeth has most to fear is—like the moth—himself."

Caithness looked at her watch. Twelves minutes to twelve. Then she directed her gaze at the hotel door in front of her. She would never forget the brass numbers, however long she lived and however many men she met, loved and shared days and nights with.

323.

She could still turn back. But she had come here. Why? Because she thought she would meet Duff again and something had changed? The only thing that had changed was that now she knew she would be able to manage perfectly well without him. Or was it because she suspected that behind the door there could be another chance, a chance to do the right thing? Which she had failed to do when she walked away from Angus at Estex. She had got hold of his private phone number but there had been no answer.

She raised her hand.

The door would explode if she knocked.

She knocked.

Waited. Was about to knock again when the door opened. A young man stood there.

"Who are you?" she asked.

"Fleance, son of Banquo." The voice was the same as on the phone. He stepped aside. "Please come in, Mrs. Mittbaum."

The hotel room was as before.

Malcolm was as before.

But not Duff. He had aged. Not only in the months and years since she had last seen him sitting on the plush-covered hotel bed waiting for her like now, but in the days that had passed since he had left her flat for the last time.

"You came," Duff said.

She nodded.

Malcolm coughed and cleaned his glasses. "You don't seem particularly surprised to see us here, Caithness."

"I'm most surprised that *I'm* here," she said. "What's going on?"

"What are you hoping is going on, Caithness?"

"I'm hoping we're going to remove Macbeth."

Seyton pushed down the lever on the iron door and opened it. Macbeth stepped inside and twisted the switch. The neon tubes blinked twice before casting a cold blue light on the shelves of ammunition boxes and various weapons. On the floor in the square room were a safe and two half-dismantled Gatling guns. Macbeth went over to the safe, twirled the dial and opened it. Pulled out a zebra-striped suitcase. "The ammo room was the only place with thick enough walls where we dared to keep it," he said. "And even then, in a safe."

"So it's a bomb?"

"Yep," said Macbeth, who had crouched down and opened the suitcase. "Disguised as a case of gold." He lifted out the bars covering the bottom. "The bars are actually iron with a gold coating, but the bomb in the space beneath—" he opened the lid to the false bottom "—is genuine enough."

"Look at that," Seyton said with a low whistle. "Your classic IED time bomb."

"Ingenious, eh? The gold means no one will be suspicious about the weight. This was designed to blow up the Inverness."

"Aha, it's that case. And why wasn't the bomb destroyed?"

"My idea," Macbeth said, studying the clockwork machinery. "It's a fantastically intricate piece of work and we had it fully disarmed. I thought we at SWAT might find a use for it one day. And now we have . . ." He touched a matchstick-size metal pin. "You just have to pull this, and the clock counts down. It looks easy, but it took us almost forty minutes to defuse it, and there are only twenty-five minutes and fifty-five seconds left on the clock, so if I pull this out there's no way back."

"Your discussions with Hecate will have to be quick, then."

"Oh, it won't be a long meeting. I'll say that the gold is proof of my gratitude for what he's already done and there'll be more if he helps me to be elected as mayor."

"Will he, do you think?"

"I don't know, and he'll be dead ten minutes later anyway. The point is that he mustn't suspect anything, and he knows that in this town you don't get anything for nothing. I'll ask him to think about it, look at my watch, say I have a meeting with a management group—which is true—and go."

"Sorry . . ." They turned to the door. It was Ricardo. "Telephone."

"Tell them I'll ring back," Seyton said.

"Not for you, for the chief commissioner."

Macbeth heard the almost imperceptible coldness in the voice. He had felt it when he came to SWAT before. How the men had dutifully mumbled a greeting but had looked away seemingly busy with other things.

"For me?"

"Your receptionist has put it through. She says it's the mayor."

"Show me the way."

He followed the SWAT veteran. Something about Ricardo's narrow, aristocratic face, the shiny blackness of his skin and the suppleness of his majestic gait had always made Macbeth think the officer must be descended from a lion-hunting tribe. What was it called again? A loyal man of honor. Macbeth knew Ricardo would be willing to follow his brothers to the death if necessary. A man worth his weight in gold. Genuine gold.

"Anything wrong, Ricardo?"

"Sir?"

"You seem quiet today. Anything I should know?"

"We're a bit worried about Angus, that's all."

"I heard he'd been off-color. This job isn't for everyone."

"My worry is he hasn't appeared for work, and no one knows where he is."

"He'll turn up soon enough. He probably needed some time out for a think. But, yes, I can see you're concerned he might have done something drastic."

"Something drastic has happened to . . ." Ricardo stopped by the open office door. Inside a telephone receiver lay on a desk. "I don't think Angus has done anything."

Macbeth stopped and looked at him. "So what do you think?"

Their eyes met. And Macbeth saw nothing of the admiration and happiness directed at him that he was used to from his men in SWAT. Ricardo lowered his eyes. "I don't know, sir."

Macbeth closed the office door behind him and took the phone.

"Yes, Tourtell?"

"I lied about being the mayor so I'd be put through. The way you lied. You promised me no one would die."

Macbeth thought it was strange how fear trumped arrogance. There wasn't a trace left of the latter in Walt Kite's voice.

"You must have misunderstood," Macbeth said. "I meant no one *in your family* would die."

"You—"

"And they won't. If you continue to do as I say. I'm busy, so if there was nothing else, Kite."

All he heard at the other end was an electric crackle.

"Good job we cleared that up," Macbeth said and rang off. Looked at the photograph pinned to the wall above the desk. Showing the whole of the SWAT gang at the Bricklayers Arms. The broad smiles and the raised beer mugs testifying to the celebration of another successful mission. There was Banquo. Ricardo. Angus and the others. And Macbeth himself. So young. Such a stupid smile. So ignorant. So blissfully powerless.

"So that's the plan," Malcolm said. "And apart from you, we three are the only ones who know about it. What do you say, Caithness? Are you with us?"

They sat close to one another in the cramped hotel room, and Caithness looked from one face to the next. "And if I say the plan's crazy and I won't have anything to do with it, will you let me stroll away, so that I can blab to Macbeth?"

"Yes," Malcolm said.

"Isn't that naive?"

"Well. If you were thinking of running to Macbeth I assume you would have first told us it was a brilliant plan and that you were in. And *then* you would have blabbed. We know asking you is a calculated risk. But we refuse to believe there aren't good people out there, people who care, who put the town before their own good."

"And you think I'm one of them?"

"Duff thinks you're one of them," Malcolm said. "He puts it stronger than that in fact: he says he *knows* you are. He says you're better than him."

Caithness looked at Duff.

"It's a brilliant idea and I'm in," she said.

Malcolm and Fleance laughed, and yes, even in Duff's sad, lifeless eyes she saw a brief glimpse of laughter.

34

AT FIVE MINUTES TO SIX Macbeth entered the reception area at the Obelisk hotel. The spacious lobby was empty apart from a doorman, a couple of bellboys and three receptionists in black suits talking in low voices, like undertakers.

Macbeth headed straight for the lift, which was open, went in and pressed the button for the nineteenth floor. Clenched his teeth and blew out to equalize the pressure. The fastest lift in the country—they had even advertised it, probably to appeal to the country cousins. The handle of the suitcase felt slippery against his hand. Why had Collum, the unlucky gambler, chosen zebra stripes to disguise a bomb?

The lift door slid open and he walked out. He knew from drawings of the building that the stairs to the penthouse suite were to the left. He trotted up the fifteen steps and along a short corridor to the only door on the floor. Raised his hand to knock. But stopped and studied his hand. Did he detect a tremble, the tremble veterans said they got after around seven years at SWAT? The seven-year tremble. He couldn't see one. They said it was worse if there *wasn't* one; then it was definitely time to get out.

Macbeth knocked.

Heard footsteps.

His own breathing.

He didn't have any weapons on him. He would be searched, and there was no reason to make anyone jumpy, after all this was supposed to resemble a business meeting. Repeated to himself that he was only going to say he was standing for mayor and hand over the suitcase as thanks for services rendered and future favors. That explanation should be plausible.

"Mr. Macbeth, sir?" It was a young boy. He was wearing jodhpurs and white gloves.

"Yes?"

The boy stepped to the side. "Please come in."

The penthouse suite had views in all directions. It had stopped raining, and in the west, behind the Inverness, the thin cloud cover was colored orange by the afternoon sun. Macbeth's eyes roamed farther, over the harbor in the south and the factory towers to the east.

"Mr. Hand said he would be a little delayed, but not by much," the boy said. "I'll bring you some champagne."

The door closed gently and Macbeth was alone. He sat down in one of the leather chairs by the round Plexiglas table. "Mr. Hand. Right."

Macbeth looked at his watch. It was precisely three minutes and thirty-five seconds since he had been sitting with Seyton in the SWAT car and had pulled out the pin to activate the countdown. Twenty-two minutes and twenty seconds to detonation.

He got up, went over to the big brown fridge standing by one wall and opened it. Empty. Same with the wardrobe. He peered into the bedroom. Untouched. No one lived here. He went back to the leather chair and sat down.

Twenty minutes and six seconds.

He tried not to think, but thoughts came anyway.

They said that time ran out.

That darkness thickened.

That death drew closer.

Macbeth breathed deeply and calmly. And what if death came now? It would of course be a meaningless end, but isn't that the case with all ends? We're interrupted in mid-sentence in the narrative about ourselves, and the end hangs in the air, with no meaning, no conclusion, no unraveling final act. A short echo of the last, semi-articulated word and you're forgotten. Forgotten, forgotten, not even the biggest statue can change that. The person you were, the person you *really* were, disappears faster than concentric rings in water. And what was the point of this short, interrupted guest appearance? Of playing along as best you can, seizing the pleasures and happiness life has to offer while it lasts? Or leaving a mark, changing the direction of things, making the world a slightly better place before you yourself have to leave it? Or perhaps the point is to reproduce, to put more suitable small creatures on the earth in the hope that humans will at some point become the demigods they imagine they are? Or is there simply no meaning? Perhaps we're just detached sentences in an eternal chaotic babble in which everyone talks and no one listens, and our worst premonition finally turns out to be correct: you are alone. All alone.

Seventeen minutes.

Alone. Then Banquo had come along and taken him to his heart, made him part of his family. And now he had got rid of him. Got rid of everyone. And was alone again. Him and Lady. But what did he want with all this? *Did* he want it? Or did he want to give it to someone? Was it for her, for Lady?

Fourteen minutes.

And did he really think it would last? Wasn't it all as fragile as Lady's mind, wasn't it doomed to crash to the ground, this empire they were building, wasn't it just a question of time? Perhaps, but what else do we have but time, a little time, the frustratingly temporary nature of impermanence?

Eleven minutes.

Where was Hecate? It was already too late to take the suitcase to the harbor and heave it into the sea. The alternative was to dump it under a manhole cover in the street, but it was bright daylight, and the chances of Macbeth being recognized were high after the recent news programs and press exposure.

Seven minutes.

Macbeth made up his mind. If Hecate wasn't here in two minutes he would go. Leave the suitcase. Hope Hecate arrived before the bomb went off.

Five minutes. Four minutes.

Macbeth got up and went to the door. Listened.

Nothing.

Time to withdraw.

He gripped the door handle. Pulled. Pulled harder. Locked. He was locked in.

"Do you mean you were cheated, sir?" Lady was standing by the roulette table. She had been called because a customer was beginning to cause trouble. The man wasn't completely sober, nor was he drunk, though. Creased tweed jacket. She didn't have to guess even: ex-Obelisk customer from bumpkin land.

"Of course I was," the man said as Lady surveyed the room. It was just as full this evening. She would have to take on more staff, they needed at least two more in the bar. "The ball lands on fourteen three times in a row. What are the chances of that, eh?"

"Exactly the same as they are for three, twenty-four and then sixteen," Lady said. "One in fifty thousand. Exactly the same as for any combination of numbers."

"But—"

"Sir." Lady smiled, lightly touching his arm. "Has anyone ever told you that during a bombing raid you should hide in a bomb crater because lightning never strikes twice in the same place? That was when you were cheated. But now you're in Inverness Casino, sir." She passed him a ticket. "Have a drink at the bar at my expense. Please consider the logic of what I've just said and we can talk afterward, OK?"

The man leaned back and scrutinized her. Took the ticket and was gone.

"Lady."

She turned. Above her towered a tall broad-shouldered woman. Or man.

"Mr. Hand would like to speak to you." The man-woman nodded toward an elderly man standing a few meters away. He wore a white suit, had dyed dark hair and was leaning on a gilded walking stick while examining the chandelier above him with interest.

"If this could wait for a couple of minutes . . ." Lady smiled.

"He also has a nickname. Starting with H."

Lady stopped.

"He prefers Hand." The man-woman smiled.

Lady walked over to the old man.

"Baccarat crystal or Bohemian?" he asked without taking his eyes off the chandelier.

"Bohemian," she said. "It is, as you can see, a slightly smaller copy of the chandelier in Dolmabahçe Palace in Istanbul."

"Unfortunately I've never been there, ma'am, but I was once in a chapel in a small place in Czechoslovakia. After the Black Death they had so many skeletons lying around there wasn't enough room for them. So they employed this one-eyed monk to tidy up and stack the remains. But instead of doing that he used them to decorate the chapel. They have an attractive chandelier there made out of skulls and human bones. Some might think that shows little respect to the dead; I would maintain the opposite." The old man shifted his gaze from the chandelier to her. "What greater gift can mankind receive than the touch of immortality inherent in retaining a function even after death, ma'am? Like becoming a coral reef. A chandelier. Or a symbol and guiding star, a chief commissioner who dies so prematurely that people still have this notion of a good person, a selfless leader, so blessedly prematurely that there was never time to unmask him as another megalomaniacal corrupt king. I'm of the opinion that we need such deaths, ma'am. I hope the one-eyed monk received the gratitude he deserved."

Lady swallowed. Usually she could see something in a person's eyes which she could interpret, understand and then use. But behind this man's eyes she saw nothing—it was like looking into the eyes of a blind man. "How may I be of assistance, Mr. Hand?"

"As you know, I should be at a meeting with your husband. He's sitting in a hotel suite waiting to kill me."

Lady felt her windpipe contract and knew that if she spoke now her voice would be high and squeaky. So she refrained.

"But as I can't see that I'd be serving any good purpose dead, I thought instead I'd talk sense with the sensible one of you two."

Lady looked at him. He nodded and smiled a sad, gentle smile, like a wise grandfather. Like someone who understood her and told her that excuses were unnecessary and pointless anyway.

"I see," Lady said with a hefty cough. "I think I need a drink. What can I offer you?"

"Well, if your bartender knows how to make a dirty martini . . . ?"

"Come with me."

They went to the bar, where people were queueing. Lady plowed her way to behind the bar counter, grabbed two martini glasses, poured from the gin bottle and then the Martini bottle, mixed the cocktails on the worktop beneath the counter. Less than a minute later she was back and handing the old man his glass. "I hope it's dirty enough."

He tasted. "Definitely. But unless I'm mistaken it has an extra ingredient."

"Two. It's my own recipe. This way?"

"And what are the ingredients?"

"That's a business secret of course, but let me put it this way: I think drinks should have a local touch." Lady led the old man and the tall man-woman into the empty room behind the restaurant.

"Naturally, a man in my position has some sympathy with you wanting to protect your business secrets," Hecate said, waiting for the man-woman to pull out a chair for him. "So please excuse me if I've revealed your intentions to take over my town. I respect ambition, but I have other plans."

Lady sipped her martini. "Are you going to kill my husband?"

Hecate didn't answer.

She repeated the question.

Macbeth stared at the door and felt his mouth go dry. Locked in. He imagined he could *hear* the bomb ticking behind him now. There was no other way out—exits were one of the things he always checked when he examined drawings of buildings. Outside the windows the smooth wall dropped twenty floors to the tarmac.

Locked in. Trapped. Hecate's trap. His own trap.

He breathed through his mouth and tried to shut out the mounting panic.

His eyes swept the room. There was nowhere to hide, the bomb was too powerful. His eyes fell on the door again. On the thumb turn lock under the handle.

The thumb turn. He let his breath out in a long, relieved hiss. Shit, what was wrong with him? He laughed. A hotel door is *supposed* to lock when it closes. He lived in a hotel himself, for Christ's sake. All you had to do was turn the lock to open the door.

He reached out a hand. Hesitated. Why was something telling him it couldn't be so easy? That it never was, that where he was it would be impossible to get out, and that he was doomed to blow himself sky-high?

He could feel his fingers slippery with sweat as they closed round the lock. Turned.

The lock turned.

He pressed the handle.

Pushed open the door.

Went out. Rushed down the stairs and along the corridor, cursing quietly.

Stood in front of the lift and pressed the button.

Saw on the wall display it was on its way up from the ground floor.

Looked at his watch. Two minutes and forty seconds.

The lift was approaching. Could he hear something? A clinking, voices? Were there people in the lift? What if Hecate was there? There was no time to go back to the suite and talk now.

Macbeth ran. According to the drawings the fire escape was round the corner to the left.

It was.

He pushed open the door as he heard a *pling* signaling that the lift had arrived. Held his breath and the door as he waited.

Voices. High-pitched, boys' voices.

"I don't quite understand what—"

"Mr. Hand isn't coming. We've just been told to delay the man in there for half an hour. Hope he likes champagne."

The sound of trolley wheels.

Macbeth closed the door behind him and ran down the stairs.

On every floor there was a number.

He stopped at seventeen.

Lady nodded. Breathed. "But you're going to kill him another day?"

"That depends. Did you put apple juice in?"

"No. Depends on what?"

"If this is just temporary confusion. You both seem to have stopped using my products, and that's perhaps best for all parties."

"You won't kill him because you need him as chief commissioner. And now you've exposed Macbeth's plans once, you reckon he's learned his lesson. A dog isn't trained until it's been disobedient and has received its punishment."

The old man turned to the man-woman. "Do you now see what I mean when I say she's the smart one of the two?"

"So what do you want from me, Mr. Hand?"

"Ginger? No, the recipe's a secret you said, so your answer won't be reliable. I just wanted to make you aware of the choice you have. Obey and I'll protect Macbeth against anything that can harm him. He'll be your Tithonos. Disobey and I'll kill both of you the way you do with dogs which turn out to be untrainable. Look around, Lady. Look at all you stand to lose. You have everything you've ever dreamed of. So you don't have to dream anymore. As for recipes, if your dreams are too big they're a recipe for disaster." The old man knocked back the rest of the drink and put the glass on the table. "Pepper. That's one of the two ingredients."

"Blood," Lady said.

"Really?" He laid his hands on the walking stick and levered himself into a standing position. "Human blood?"

Lady shrugged. "Is that so important? You believe it is, and you seemed to like the recipe."

The old man laughed. "You and I could be very good friends if circumstances were different, Lady."

"In another life," she said.

"In another life, my little Lily." He banged his stick twice on the floor. "Stay where you are. We'll find our way out."

Lady retained her smile until he was out of sight. Then she gasped for breath, felt the room whirling, had to hold on to the chair arm. *Lily.* He knew. How *could* he know?

Seventeenth floor.

Macbeth looked at his watch. One minute left. So why had he stopped? They must be carrying the trolley up the steps. They would be there when the bomb went off. So what? They were Hecate's boys. They had to be part of the whole setup, so what was the problem? No one in this town was innocent. So why had this *something* come into his mind right now? Was it something from a speech? Written by Lady, given by him? Or was it from even longer ago, an oath they had sworn when they graduated from police college? Or before that too, something Banquo had said to him? Something, there was something, but he couldn't remember what. Just that . . .

Shit, shit, shit!
Fifty seconds.
Macbeth ran.
Up the stairs.

35

"COME WITH ME!" MACBETH SCREAMED.

The two young boys stared at the man who had suddenly appeared in the doorway to the penthouse suite. One of them was holding a bottle of champagne and had started loosening the wire from the cork.

"Now!" Macbeth shouted.

"Sir, we—"

"You've got thirty seconds if you don't want to die!"

"Calm down, sir."

Macbeth grabbed the champagne cooler and hurled it at the window. The ice cubes bounced and ricocheted with a crackle across the parquet floor. He lowered his voice in the following silence: "A bomb will go off inside here in twenty-five seconds."

Then he turned and set off at a run. Down the stairs. With the clatter of footsteps in his ears. Sprinted past the lift. Held the door to the stairs open for the two boys.

"Run! Run!"

Closed the door behind them and charged after them.

Fifteen seconds. Macbeth had no idea how big the blast would be, but if the bomb had been made to destroy a building as solid as the Inverness they would need to get as far away as possible. Sixteenth floor. He noticed a headache coming on as though he could already feel the pressure of the explosion on his eardrums, eyeballs, inside his mouth. Fourteenth. He checked his watch. It was fifteen seconds over.

Eleventh floor. Still nothing. The countdown mechanism might not have been quite accurate or a deliberate delay had been built in. The two boys in front of him began to slow down. Macbeth yelled and they sped up again.

On the eighth floor they burst through the fire escape door into a corridor, but Macbeth continued downward, using the main stairs. The lift was a death trap. When he reached the ground floor the bomb was almost three minutes overdue.

He walked into reception. The same members of staff were there, hovering over the counter as though nothing had happened, unaware of him. He went out into the rain. Looked up. Stood like that until his neck hurt. Then he started across the deserted square toward Seyton and the waiting car. What the hell had happened? Or rather, what hadn't happened? Had the bomb got damp in the police HQ basement? Had someone managed to stop the countdown after he left the penthouse suite? Or had it detonated, but with much less power than SWAT's bomb expert had given him to believe? And what now? He pulled up. What if Hecate or his people went to the suite and discovered he had left a bomb there? He had to go back and fetch the suitcase.

Macbeth turned. Took two paces. Saw his shadow outlined on the cobbles and heard a dull boom like thunder. For a moment he thought it was hail. White granules hit him on the face and hands, pitter-pattered on the cobbles around him and danced on the parked cars. A showerhead smacked to the ground a few meters from him. He glanced upward, then was sent flying as he heard something crash beside him. Macbeth raised his arms to protect himself, but the man who had tackled him had already got up, brushed down his gray coat and run off. Macbeth saw a smashed brown fridge where he had been standing a second ago.

He rested his head on the cool cobbles.

Flames rose from the top of the Obelisk, and black smoke billowed into the sky. Something bounced over the cobbles toward him and came to rest beside his head. He picked it up. It was still wrapped in its wire cage.

"What the hell happened?" Seyton said as Macbeth got in the car.

"Tourtell," Macbeth said. "He warned Hecate. Drive."

"Tourtell?" Seyton said, pulling away from the pavement as the wipers swept small fragments of white glass from the windscreen.

"Tourtell's the only person who knew about our plan, and he must have informed Hecate hoping that he would kill me instead."

"And Hecate didn't try to kill you?"

"No. Quite the contrary. He saved me."

"How come?"

"He needs his puppets."

"What?"

"Nothing, Seyton. Drive to the Inverness."

Macbeth scanned the pavement, scanned the people gawping up. He searched for gray coats. How many were there? Did they all wear gray coats or only some of them? Were they always there? He closed his eyes. Immortal. As immortal as a wooden puppet. The pressure inside his head rose. And a strange thought whirled past. Hecate's promise to make him invulnerable was not a blessing but a curse. He could feel the wire on his skin as he rolled the cork from the champagne bottle between his fingers and heard the first police siren.

Seyton had stopped in front of the Inverness and Macbeth was about to get out of the car when he heard Tourtell's voice.

"Turn up the radio," Macbeth said and got back in.

". . . and to counter the rumors and out of respect for you, my dear fellow citizens, and your right to know about your elected representatives, I have today decided to tell you that fifteen years ago I had a brief extramarital affair which led to the birth of a son. In agreement with the relevant parties—that is, my son's mother and my wife—it was decided to keep this out of the public eye. I've always stayed in close contact with my son and his mother and maintained them using my own means. Not going public at that time was a judgment, taking several parties into consideration. The town was not one of them as at that juncture I wasn't in office and didn't need to answer to anyone except those closest to me and to myself. Now, however, things are different, and now is the right time to disclose this information. My son's mother is seriously ill, and with her consent two months ago he came to live with me. Since then I have taken Kasi with me to public events, where I have introduced him as my son, but paradoxically it seems my honesty has led to other rumors. The truth, as we know, is the last thing to be believed. I am not proud of being unfaithful fifteen years ago, but beyond having sought the forgiveness of those closest to me, there's little I can do about it. Just as little as I can do about people judging my abilities as a leader on the basis of my private life. All I can do is ask you for your trust as indeed I trust you now by making public details which are extremely painful and precious to me. I may not have always acted in ways that make me feel proud; however, I am proud of my fifteen-year-old son, Kasi. Last night I had a long talk with him, and he told me to do what I'm doing now. To tell the whole of this town that I'm his father." Tourtell took a deep breath before concluding with a clear vibrato in his voice, "And that he's my son." He coughed. "And to win the coming mayoral election."

Pause. A woman's voice, also clearly moved.

"That was an announcement from Mayor Tourtell. Now back to the news. There has been a major explosion in District Four, to be precise at the top of the Obelisk Casino. No one has been reported dead or injured, but—"

Macbeth switched off the radio.

"Damn," he said. Then he burst into laughter.

36

LADY LAY BACK AGAINST THE pillows and stretched a foot out from under her dressing gown. Toward Macbeth, who was sitting on a low stool by the end of the bed. She had hung up two red dresses. He stroked her slim ankle and her smooth shaved leg.

"So Hecate knew about our plans," he said. "Did he say who had told him?"

"No," Lady said. "But he said you would be my Tithonos if we behaved."

"Who's Tithonos?"

"A handsome Greek who was granted eternal life. But he also said that if we don't obey he'll kill us like dogs that don't respond to training."

"Hm. It could only have been Tourtell who told him."

"That's the third time you've said that, darling."

"And not only did the slippery bugger blab. The boy really is his son. The question is now whether people in this town want a lecher as their mayor."

"One single affair fifteen years ago?" Lady said. "Which Tourtell admitted at the time, begged forgiveness for and has since paid for by looking after mother and son? And now when she's ill St. Tourtell takes his son in? People will love him for it, darling. He's made a mistake most people will understand and shown shame and kindness afterward. Tourtell has become *of* the people. This announcement is a stroke of genius. They're going to turn out in full force to vote for him."

"Tourtell's going to stand and win. So what can we do?"

"Yes, what can we do? Well, first things first. Which dress, Jack?"

"The Spanish one," Jack said, taking a cup of tea from the tray and placing it on Lady's bedside table.

"Thank you. What about Tourtell and Hecate, Jack? Shall we do something or is it too risky?"

"I'm no strategist, ma'am. But I've read that when you have enemies on two fronts there are two classic strategies. One is to negotiate an armistice with one enemy, then concentrate your forces to knock out the other and attack without warning. The second is to set the two enemies against each other, wait until they are both weakened and then strike."

He gave a cup of coffee to Macbeth.

"Remind me to promote you," Macbeth said.

"Oh, he's already been promoted," Lady said. "We're fully booked for the next two weeks, so Jack now has an assistant. An assistant who'll address him as 'sir.'"

Jack laughed. "This wasn't my idea."

"It's mine," Lady said. "And it's not an idea. It's only sensible to have rules for forms of address. It reminds everyone about the hierarchy so that misunderstandings can be avoided. If a mayor declares a state of emergency, it's important for example to know who runs the town. And who does?"

Jack shook his head.

"The chief commissioner," Macbeth said, sipping his coffee. "Until the chief commissioner suspends the state of emergency."

"Really?" Jack said. "And what if the mayor dies? Does the chief commissioner take over then too?"

"Yes," Macbeth said. "Until a new mayor is elected."

"These are rules Kenneth introduced right after the war," Lady said. "At that time they placed a lot of emphasis on dynamic, assertive leadership in crises."

"Sounds sensible," Jack said.

"The great thing about a state of emergency is that the chief commissioner runs absolutely everything. He can suspend the justice system, censor the press, defer elections indefinitely; he is in brief . . ."

"A dictator."

"Exactly, Jack." Lady stirred her tea. "Unfortunately, Tourtell will hardly agree to declare a state of emergency, so we'll have to make do with the next-best option."

"Which is?"

"Tourtell dying, of course." Lady sipped her tea.

"Dying? As in . . . ?"

"An assassination," Macbeth said, squeezing her calf muscle gently. "That's what you mean, isn't it, my love?"

She nodded. "The chief commissioner announces that he's taking over the running of the town while the assassination is investigated. Could there be political motives behind it? Hecate? Did it have anything to do with Tourtell's infidelity? The investigation drags on of course."

"I can only rule temporarily," Macbeth said, "until a new mayor is elected."

"But, darling, look, there's blood on the streets. Police officers murdered and politicians assassinated. The chief commissioner, who now functions as mayor, would probably decide to declare a state of emergency. And postpone the election indefinitely until things have calmed down. And it's the chief commissioner who determines when things have calmed down."

Macbeth felt the same childish pleasure as when he and Duff had been kings of the castle in the school playground at the orphanage, and even the tough older kids had to accept it. "In practice we'd have limitless power for as long as we wanted. And you're sure Capitol can't intercede?"

"Darling, I've had a long and interesting conversation with one of our Supreme Court judges today. Capitol has few or no sanctions, provided that the measures Kenneth introduced don't conflict with federal laws."

"I see." Macbeth rubbed his chin. "Interesting indeed. So all that's needed is for Tourtell to die or declare a state of emergency himself."

Jack coughed. "Anything else, ma'am?"

"No, thanks, Jack." Lady cheerfully waved him away.

Macbeth heard the hollow bass from the ground floor as Jack opened the door to the corridor and the wailing siren of an ambulance that followed after he closed it.

"Tourtell's making plans to stop us," Lady said. "The assassination will have to be soon."

"What about Hecate? If this snake is Tourtell and Hecate, then Tourtell is the tail and Hecate the head. And cutting off the tail only makes it more dangerous. We have to tackle the head first!"

"No."

"No? He says he'll kill us if we don't obey. Do you want to be his trained dog?"

"Sit still and listen to me now, darling. You heard Jack. Arrange an armistice with one party and attack the other. This is not the moment to challenge Hecate. What's more, I'm not sure that Hecate and Tourtell actually work together. If so, Hecate would have said we should stay away from Tourtell and the mayoral office. But he hasn't, not even after the speculation that you would stand. As long as Hecate thinks we've been taught a lesson and we're now his obedient dogs he'll only applaud us— and indirectly himself—taking political control of the town. Do you understand? We take care of one enemy now and get what we want. Then we decide what we have to do about Hecate afterward."

Macbeth ran his hand up her leg, past her knee. She fell quiet, closed her eyes, and he listened to her breathing. The breathing that with non-verbal commands determined what his hand should and shouldn't do.

Through the afternoon and night the rain continued to wash the town that was never clean. Hammered down on the roof of the Grand Hotel, where Fleance, Duff, Malcolm and Caithness had agreed they would stay until it was over. It was two o'clock in the morning when Caithness was woken by knocking on the door to her room. At once she knew who it was.

It wasn't the number of knocks, the interval between them or the force of them. It was the style. He knocked with a flat hand. And she knew the hand, every crease and cranny of it.

She opened the door a fraction.

Rain dripped from Duff's clothes and hair, his teeth were chattering and his face was so pale the scar was barely visible. "Sorry, but I need a really hot shower."

"Haven't you . . . ?"

"Fleance and I share a room with bunk beds and a sink."

She opened the door a bit more, and he slipped in.

"Where have you been?" she asked.

"To the cemetery," he said from inside the bathroom.

"In the middle of the night?"

"Not so many people out and about." She heard the water being switched on. She stood close to the bathroom door. "Duff?"

"Yes."

"I just wanted to say I'm sorry."

"What?" he shouted.

She cleared her throat and raised her voice. "About your family."

She listened to the beating of the water, which muffled her words, and stared into the steam that hid him from her.

When Duff came out again in the dressing gown that hung in the bathroom and with his wet clothes over one arm Caithness was dressed and lying on the broad bed. He pulled a soggy packet of cigarettes from the pocket of his wet trousers. She nodded, and he lay beside her. Caithness rested her head on his arm and looked up at the domed yellow glass ceiling light. The bowl was dotted with dead insects.

"That's what happens when you get too close to the light," he said. So he still had the ability to guess what she was thinking.

"Icarus," she said.

"Macbeth," he said and lit a cigarette.

"I didn't know you'd started smoking again," she said.

"Well, it's a little strange. I've actually never liked this shit." He grimaced and blew a big fat smoke ring up at the ceiling.

She sniggered. "So why did you start?"

"Have I never told you?"

"There's a lot you've never told me."

He coughed and passed her the cigarette. "Because I wanted to be like Macbeth."

"I'd have thought he wanted to be like you."

"He looked so damned good. And was so . . . free. In harmony with himself and happy, so happy in his own skin. I never was."

"But you had intellect." She inhaled and passed the cigarette back. "And the ability to persuade people you were right."

"People don't like to realize they're wrong. And I didn't have the ability to persuade them to like me. He did."

"Cheap charm, Duff. Look who he is now. He duped everyone."

"No." Duff shook his head. "No, Macbeth didn't dupe anyone. He was straight-talking and upfront. No saint, but no ulterior motives—what you saw was what you got. Perhaps he didn't impress everyone with his wit or originality when he spoke, but you trusted every word. And rightly so."

"Trust? He's an unfeeling murderer, Duff."

"You're wrong. Macbeth is full of feelings. That's why he can't hurt a fly. Or to be accurate, especially not a fly. An aggressive wasp, yes, but a defenseless fly? Never, regardless of how annoying it is."

"How can you defend him, Duff? You who have lost—"

"I'm not defending him. Of course he's a murderer. All I'm saying is he can't kill anyone who can't defend himself. It's happened only once. And he did it to save me."

"Oh yes?" she said. "Are you going to tell me about it?"

He sucked hard on the cigarette. "It was when he killed the Norse Rider on the country road out by Forres. A young guy who'd just seen me kill his comrade, who I'd mistaken for Sweno."

"So they didn't pull guns on you?"

Duff shook his head.

"But then Macbeth's no better than you," Caithness said.

"Yes, he was. I killed for my own sake. He did it for someone else."

"Because that's what we do in the police. We take care of each other."

"No, because he thought he owed it to me."

Caithness sat up on her elbows. "Owed it to you?"

Duff held his cigarette up to the ceiling, pinched one eye shut and aimed above the glow with the other. "When Grandad died and I ended up in the orphanage, I was almost too old—I was fourteen. Macbeth and I were the same age, but he'd been there since he was five. Macbeth and I shared a room and became friends straightaway. In those days Macbeth stammered. And especially when Saturday night approached, which was when he disappeared from the room in the middle of the night and returned an hour later. He would never tell me where he'd been; it was only when I jokingly threatened to report him to the home's feared director, Lorreal, that he said he doubted that would do much good." Duff pulled hard on the cigarette. "Because that was where he'd been."

"You mean . . . the director—"

"—had been abusing Macbeth for as long as he could remember. I couldn't believe my ears. Lorreal had done things to him . . . you can't imagine anyone would do to another person or find any enjoyment in. The one time Macbeth had stood up against him Lorreal had half-killed him and kept him locked up for two weeks in the so-called correction room in the cellar, a genuine cell. I was so furious I cried. Because I knew every word was true. Macbeth never lies. So I said we had to kill Lorreal. I would help him. And Macbeth agreed."

"You planned to *kill* him?"

"No," Duff said, passing her the cigarette. "We didn't plan so much. We just killed him."

"You . . ."

"We went to his room one Thursday. Checked at the door that Lorreal was snoring. Went in. Macbeth knew the room inside out. I kept watch inside the door while Macbeth went to the bed and raised a knife. But time passed, and when my eyes had got used to the darkness I saw he was standing there as rigid as a pillar of salt. Then he crumpled and came over to me, whispering that he c-c-couldn't do it. So I took the knife, went over to Lorreal and thrust it hard into his snoring mouth. Lorreal twitched one more time, then he stopped snoring. There wasn't much blood. We left straight after."

"My God." Caithness was curled up in the fetal position. "What happened afterward?"

"Not much. There were two hundred young suspects to choose from. No one noticed that Macbeth was stammering more than before. And when he did a runner a couple of weeks later, no one connected that with the murder. Kids ran away all the time."

"And then you and Macbeth met up again?"

"I saw him a couple of times down by the central station. I wanted to talk to him, but he legged it. You know, like a bankruptee from a creditor. Then we met several years later at police college. By then he was clean and had completely stopped stammering—he was a very different boy. The boy *I* wanted to be."

"Because he was a clean-living kindhearted man without a murder on his conscience like you?"

"Macbeth has never seen being able to murder in cold blood as a virtue but a weakness. In all his time at SWAT he killed only if he, or any of his men, was attacked."

"And all these murders?"

"He ordered others to carry them out for him."

"Killing women and children. I think he's become a different man from the one you knew, Duff."

"People don't change."

"*You've* changed."

"Have I really?"

"If not, you wouldn't be here. Fighting this fight. Spoken as you have about Macbeth. You're a total egoist. Ready to ride roughshod over everything and everyone who's in your way. Your colleagues, your family. Me."

"I can only remember really wanting to change once, and that was when I wanted to be like Macbeth. And when I realized that was impossible I had to become something better. Someone who could take what he wanted, even if it had less value for me than for who it belonged to, the way Hecate took that boy's eye. Do you know when I fell in love with Meredith?"

Caithness shook her head.

"When all four of us were sitting there—Macbeth, me, Meredith and her girlfriend—and I saw the way Macbeth was looking at Meredith."

"Tell me this isn't true, Duff."

"I regret to say it is."

"You're a petty man, Duff."

"That's what I'm trying to tell you. So when you say I'm fighting this fight for others, I don't know if it's true or if I only want to take something away from Macbeth that I know he wants."

"But he doesn't want it, Duff. The town, power, wealth—he couldn't care less about them. He wants only her love."

"Lady."

"Everything's about Lady. Haven't you realized?"

Duff blew a deformed smoke ring up to the ceiling. "Macbeth's driven by love while I'm driven by envy and hatred. Where he has shown mercy, I've killed. And tomorrow I'm going to kill the person who was once my best friend—ambush him—and mercy and love will have lost again."

"That's just cynicism and your self-loathing talking, Duff."

"Hm." He stubbed out the cigarette in the ashtray on the bedside table. "You forgot self-pity."

"Yes, I did. And self-pity."

"I've been an arrogant egoist all my life. I can't understand how you could have loved me."

"Some women have a weakness for men they think can save them, others for men they think they can save."

"Amen," Duff said, getting up. "You women don't understand that we men don't change. Not when we discover love, not when we realize we're going to die. Never."

"Some use false arrogance to cover up their lack of confidence, but your arrogance is genuine, Duff. It's down to total confidence."

Duff smiled and pulled on his wet trousers. "Try to sleep now. We have to have our wits about us tomorrow."

After he had left, Caithness got up, pulled the curtain to one side and looked down at the street. The swish of tires through pools of water. Faded adverts for Joey's Hamburger Bar, Peking Dry-Cleaners and the Tandrella Bingo Hall. A cigarette glowing for a second in an alleyway.

In a few hours day would break.

She wouldn't be able to go back to sleep now.

37

SATURDAY ARRIVED WITH MORE RAIN. The front pages of both the town's newspapers carried Tourtell's announcement and the explosion on top of the Obelisk. *The Times* commented in its leader that Macbeth's radio interview had to be understood as him not categorically rejecting standing for mayor. And said Tourtell wasn't available for comment as he was at his son's mother's bedside in St. Jordi's Hospital. Late that morning the rain cleared.

"You're home early," Sheila said, wiping her hands on her apron in the hall and looking at her husband with a little concern.

"I couldn't find anything to do. I think I was the only person at work," Lennox said, putting his bag by the chest of drawers, taking a clothes hanger from the wardrobe and hanging up his coat. Two years had passed since the town council had adopted the five-day week for the public sector, but at police HQ it was an unspoken rule that if you wanted to get on you had to show your face on Saturdays as well.

Lennox kissed his wife lightly on the cheek, noticed a new, unfamiliar perfume and a hitherto unthought notion fluttered through his brain: what if he had caught her in bed with another man? He rejected this at once. First because she wasn't the type. Second because she wasn't attractive enough—after all there was a reason why she had ended up with a diminutive albino. The third and strongest reason for rejecting the notion was, however, simple: it was too hard to bear.

"Is there anything wrong?" she asked and followed him into the sitting room.

"Not at all," he said. "I'm just tired. Where are the kids?"

"In the garden," she said. "Finally some decent weather."

He stood by the big window. Watching his children as they romped around screaming and laughing and playing a game the point of which he couldn't work out. Escaping, it seemed. Good skill to learn. He looked up at the sky. Decent? A little break before the piss came hammering down again. He slumped into an armchair. How long could he carry on like this?

"Lunch won't be ready for an hour," she said.

"That's fine, love." He looked at her. He genuinely liked her, but had he ever been in love with her? He couldn't remember and perhaps it wasn't that important. She hadn't said a word one way or the other, but he was fairly sure she hadn't been in love with him either. Generally Sheila didn't say much. Perhaps that was why she had given in to his persuasion and in the end said yes to being his girlfriend and eventually his wife. She had found someone who could talk for them both.

"Sure there's nothing wrong?"

"Absolutely sure, sweetheart. That smells good. What is it?"

"Erm, cod," she said, her frown framing a question.

He was going to explain that he meant her perfume, not the lunch she had barely started, but she went to the kitchen and he swung his chair round to face the garden. His elder daughter saw him, beamed and shouted something to the other two. He waved to them. How could two such unattractive people have such beautiful children? And that was when the notion struck him again: *If they really were his.*

Infidelity and treachery.

Now his son was calling to him—what, he couldn't hear—but when he saw he had caught his father's attention he did a cartwheel on the grass. Lennox applauded with his hands raised high in the air, and now all three of them were doing cartwheels. Impress their daddy, impress the daddy they still admired, the daddy they thought was worth emulating. Shouting, laughter and frolics. Lennox thought of the silence out in Fife, the sunshine, the curtains fluttering in a window that had been shot to pieces, the gentle breeze whistling a barely audible doleful note through one of the holes in the wall. All the unbearable thoughts. There were so many ways to lose those you loved. What if one day they found out, realized, what kind of person their husband or father really was? Would the wind sing the same lament then?

He closed his eyes. Bit of a rest. Bit of decent weather.

He sensed someone was there, standing over him and breathing on him. He opened his eyes. It was Sheila.

"Didn't you hear me shouting?" she said.

"What?"

"There's a phone call for you. Some Inspector Seyton."

Lennox went into the hall, picked up the receiver from the table. "Hello?"

"Home early, Lennox? I'll need some help this evening."

"I'm not well. You'd better try someone else."

"The chief commissioner said to take you."

Lennox swallowed. His mouth tasted of lead. "Take me where?"

"To a hospital. Be ready in an hour. I'll pick you up." There was a click. Lennox had rung off. Lead.

"What is it?" Sheila called from the kitchen.

A pale metal shaped by its environment, which poisons and kills, a heavy but unresisting material that melts at three hundred and fifty degrees Celsius.

"Nothing, sweetheart. Nothing."

Macbeth woke from a dream about death. There was a knock at the door. Something about the knocking told him it had been going on for a long time.

"Sir!" It was Jack's voice.

"Yes," Macbeth grunted, looking around. The room was flooded with daylight. What was the time? He had been dreaming. Dreaming he had been standing over the bed with a dagger in his hand. But whenever he blinked the face on the pillow changed.

"It's Inspector Caithness on the phone, sir. She says it's urgent."

"Put her through," Macbeth said, rolling over toward the bedside table. "Caithness?"

"Sorry to ring you on a Saturday, but we've found a body. I'm afraid we'll have to ask you to help." She sounded out of breath.

"Why's that?"

"Because we think it could be Fleance, Banquo's son. The body is in a bad way, and as he has no close relatives in town it seems you're the best person to identify him."

"Oh," Macbeth said, feeling his throat tighten.

"Sorry?"

"Yes, I suppose I am," Macbeth said and pulled the duvet tighter around him. "When a body's been in seawater for so long . . ."

"That's the point."

"What's the point?"

"We didn't find the body in the sea but in an alleyway between Fourteenth and Fifteenth Streets."

"What?"

"That's why we want to be absolutely sure it's Fleance before we go any further."

"Fourteenth and Fifteenth, you say?"

"Go to Fourteenth and Doheney. I'll wait for you outside Joey's Hamburger Bar."

"OK, Caithness. I'll be there in twenty minutes."

"Thank you, sir."

Macbeth rang off. Lilies. The flowers in the carpet were lilies. Lily. That was the name of Lady's child. Why hadn't he made the connection before? Dead. Because he hadn't seen, tasted, eaten and slept so much death before. He closed his eyes. Recalled the changing faces from the dream. Orphanage Director Lorreal's unknowing face as he snored with his mouth open became Chief Commissioner Duncan's, eyes that opened and stared at him, knowing. Then Banquo's stiff, brutal glare. No bodies, only the head on the pillow. Then the nameless young Norse Rider's panic-stricken expression as he knelt on the tarmac staring at his already dead comrade and Macbeth coming toward him. He looked at the ceiling. And remembered all the times he had woken from a nightmare and breathed a sigh of relief. Relieved to find in reality he wasn't drowning in quicksand or being eaten by dogs. But sometimes he *thought* he had woken from a nightmare but was still dreaming, still drowning, and he had to break through several layers before he reached consciousness. He shut his eyes tight. Opened them again. Then he got up.

The buxom black woman in reception at St. Jordi's Hospital looked up from the ID card Lennox showed her.

"We've been told that no one has access . . ." She checked the card again. "Inspector."

"Police matter," he said. "Top priority. The mayor has to be informed at once."

"If you leave a message I can—"

"Confidential matter, urgent."

She sighed.

"Room two-oh-four, first floor."

Mayor Tourtell and the young boy sat side by side on wooden chairs next to one of the beds in the large ward. The older man held the boy around the shoulder and they both looked up as Lennox stood behind them and coughed. In the bed lay a wan, thin-haired, middle-aged woman, and Lennox saw at once the likeness with the boy. "Good evening, sir. You won't remember me, but we met at the dinner at Inverness Casino."

"Inspector Lennox, isn't it? Anti-Corruption Unit."

"Impressive. I apologize for bursting in like this."

"How can I help, Lennox?"

"We've had a credible tip-off of an imminent assassination attempt against you."

The boy gave a start, but Tourtell didn't bat an eyelid. "More details, Inspector."

"We don't have any more for the present, but we're taking it seriously and I'm to escort you from here to a safer place."

Tourtell raised an eyebrow. "And what could be safer than a hospital?"

"The newspapers say you're here, Mr. Mayor. Anyone has access here. Let me accompany you to your car and follow you until you're safe within your own four walls. Then I hope we'll have time to delve deeper. So if you wouldn't mind coming with me . . ."

"Right now? As you see—"

"I can see and I apologize, but it's your duty and mine to protect the person of the mayor."

"Stand by the door and keep watch, Lennox, so—"

"These aren't my orders, sir."

"They are now, Lennox."

"Go." The whispered, barely audible word came from the woman in the bed. "Go, and take Kasi with you."

Tourtell laid a hand on hers. "But Edith, you—"

"I'm tired, my dear. I want to be alone now. Kasi's safer with you. Listen to the man."

"Are you—"

"Yes, I'm sure."

The woman closed her eyes. Tourtell patted her hand and turned to Lennox. "OK, let's go."

They left the room. The boy a few steps in front of them.

"Does he know?" Lennox asked.

"That she's dying? Yes."

"And how's he taking it?"

"Some days are harder than others. He's known for a while." They went down the stairs toward the kiosk and the exit. "But he says it's fine. It's fine as long as he has one of us. I'm just going to get some cigarettes. Will you wait for me?"

"There she is," Macbeth said, pointing.

Jack pulled in to the curb opposite the Grand Hotel, between a dry-cleaner's and a hamburger bar. They both got out, and Macbeth ran his eye up and down the empty street.

"Thanks for coming so quickly," Caithness said.

"No problem," Macbeth said. She smelled of strong perfume. He couldn't remember having noticed that before.

"Show me," Macbeth said.

Macbeth and Jack followed her down the street. Saturday evening was just warming up. Under a flashing neon sign that read NUDE WOMEN a suited doorman gave Caithness the once-over, then threw his cigarette end to the tarmac and ground it in with his heel.

"I thought you would bring Seyton with you," Caithness said.

"He had to go to St. Jordi's this evening. Is it here?"

Caithness had stopped by the entrance to a narrow alley cordoned off with orange Homicide Unit tape. Macbeth peered down. It was so narrow that the dustbins outside the back doors on both sides were close. And it was too dark to see anything at all.

"I was here first. The rest of the SOC team is coming later. That's the way it is at the weekend. They're scattered to the four winds." Caithness pushed up the tape and Macbeth ducked underneath. "If you could go in and have a look at the body alone, sir. I've covered it with a sheet, but please don't touch anything else. We want as few prints as possible in there. Your driver can wait here while I go back to Joey's and meet the pathologist. He's supposed to be just around the corner."

Macbeth looked at her. He saw nothing in her face. Yet. She had thought Seyton would be coming. Strong perfume. Which camouflaged any other smell she might be secreting.

"OK," he said and set off down the alley.

He hadn't walked more than ten meters before all the sounds from the main street disappeared and all that could be heard was the whirr of fans, coughing from an open window and the drone of a radio: Todd Rundgren, "Hello, It's Me." He sneaked between the dustbins, creeping forward without quite knowing why. Habit, he supposed.

The body lay in the middle of the alley, half inside the cone of light from a wall lamp. He could make out 15th Street at the other end, but it was too far away for him to see if the alley was taped off there as well.

A pair of feet stuck out from under the white sheet. He immediately recognized the winklepickers.

He went over to the sheet. Took a deep breath. The air contained the sweet smell of dry-cleaning chemicals coming from a noisy extractor fan above the door right behind him. He grasped the sheet in the middle and pulled it away.

"Hi, Macbeth."

Macbeth stared into the muzzle of the shotgun raised toward him by the man lying on his back in the darkness. The scar shone on his face. Macbeth released the air from his lungs.

"Hi, Duff."

Duff studied Macbeth's hands as he spoke. "Macbeth, you are hereby arrested. If you move a finger I'll shoot you now. Your choice."

Macbeth looked toward 15th Street. "I'm the chief commissioner in this town, Duff. You can't arrest me."

"There are other authorities."

"The mayor?" Macbeth laughed. "I don't think you can rely on him living that long."

"I'm not talking about anyone in this town." Duff got to his feet without the shotgun veering a centimeter from Macbeth.

"You've been arrested for involvement in the murders committed in

Fife, and you will be transported there to stand trial. We've spoken with them. You will be charged with the murder of Banquo, which took place in Fife. Hold your hands above your head and face the wall."

Macbeth did as instructed. "You've got nothing on me and you know it."

"With Inspector Caithness's statement about what Angus told her, we have enough to keep you in custody in Fife for a week. And a week without you at the helm will give us enough time to indict you here too. For the murder of Duncan. We have forensic evidence." Duff took out his handcuffs. "Turn round, put your hands behind— You know the drill."

"Are you really not going to shoot me, Duff? Come on, you're a man who lives for revenge."

Duff waited until Macbeth had turned his back and linked his hands behind his head, then approached.

"I know it affected you finding out the man you killed wasn't Sweno, Duff. But now that you're sure you have the right man in front of you, aren't you going to avenge Meredith and the children? Or did your mother mean more to you than them?"

"Stand still and shut your mouth."

"I've kept my mouth shut for years, Duff. I know the female officer Sweno killed in Stoke was your mother. What year was the business in Stoke? You can't have been very old."

"I was young." Duff closed the handcuffs around Macbeth's wrists.

"And why did you take your maternal grandfather's surname instead of your parents' name?"

Duff turned Macbeth so that they stood face-to-face.

"You don't need to answer," Macbeth said. "You did it so that no one in the police or the Norse Riders could link your name to the Stoke Massacre. No one would know that you didn't become an officer to serve the town and all that shit we swear to. It was all about catching Sweno, about you getting your revenge. Hatred drove you, Duff. At the orphanage when you killed Lorreal, it was easy, wasn't it? You saw Sweno in front of you. Lorreal was another man who had destroyed a childhood."

"Maybe." Duff was so close he could see his reflection in Macbeth's brown eyes.

"So what's happened, Duff? Why don't you want to kill now? I'm the man who took your family, and now this is your chance."

"You'll have to take responsibility for what you've done."

"And what have I done?"

Duff cast a quick glance in the direction of 15th Street, where the car with Malcolm and Fleance was waiting. Caithness was on her way there. "You've killed innocent people."

"It's our damned *duty* to kill innocent people, Duff. As long as it serves a greater purpose we have to overcome our sentimental, compliant natures. The man whose throat I cut out on the country road, that wasn't for you, it wasn't repayment for you killing Lorreal for me. I made myself a murderer so that no one would drag the police force through the mud. It was for the town, against anarchy."

"Come on. Let's go."

Duff grabbed Macbeth's arm, but Macbeth twisted away. "Has your lust for power become greater than your lust for revenge, Duff? Do you think you're going to get Organized Crime by arresting the chief commissioner himself?"

Duff pressed the muzzle of the shotgun under Macbeth's chin. "I could of course tell them you resisted arrest."

"Difficult decision?" Macbeth whispered.

"No," Duff said, lowering the gun. "This town doesn't need more bodies."

"So you didn't love them, eh? Meredith, the children? Oh no, I forgot, you can't love—"

Duff hit out. The shotgun barrel struck Macbeth in the mouth. "Remember I've never had your problem about killing a defenseless man face-to-face, Macbeth."

Macbeth laughed and spat blood. What must have been a tooth bounced into the darkness. "Then prove it. Shoot the only friend you've ever had. Come on. Do it for Meredith!"

"Don't even say her name."

"Meredith! Meredith!"

Duff heard the blood throbbing in his ears, felt his heart pounding, heavy and painful. He mustn't— Macbeth's forehead hit Duff's nose with a crunch. But they were standing too close for Macbeth to have the momentum and power to knock him down. Duff stepped back two paces and raised the shotgun to his shoulder.

At that moment the door behind Macbeth flew open.

A silhouette in the doorway. The arm of a gray coat shot out, grabbed the handcuffs behind Macbeth's back and pulled. The force was so great that Macbeth's feet left the ground as he disappeared through the door into the darkness behind.

Duff fired.

The explosion met his eardrums and quivered between the walls of the alley.

Half-deafened, Duff stepped over the threshold into the darkness.

Something whirled in the air which he breathed in and spat out. People seemed to be lined up in front of him. The smell of perchlorethylene was overwhelming. His free hand found a light switch on the wall by the door. The people lined up were stands holding jackets and coats, each under a plastic cover with a note stating a name and date. In front of him a hole had been blasted in a plastic cover and a brown fur coat, and Duff realized he had been spitting out animal hair. He stood listening but heard only the drone of the green Garrett dry-cleaning machine by the wall. Then a ringing, like a bell above a shop door. He threw himself against the wall of clothes, plowed past stand after stand through a door to the rear of a counter where a Chinese couple stared at him, scared out of their wits. He ran past them and onto the street. Looked up and down. The Saturday evening rush had started. A man bumped into him and for a moment Duff lost his balance. He cursed as the man apologized and continued down the pavement.

He heard laughter behind him. Turned and saw a guy in rags, filthy, a few stumps of teeth in an open mouth.

"You been robbed, mister?"

"Yes," Duff said, lowering the shotgun. "I have been robbed."

38

LENNOX STOOD OUTSIDE THE HOSPITAL entrance with Kasi. Glanced toward the kiosk where Tourtell was queueing to buy cigarettes, then focused on the car park. A light came on inside Tourtell's limousine. The distance was probably a hundred meters. Around the same distance as up to the roof of the multistory car park to the left. Lennox shivered. Clear weather often came with a rare northeasterly wind, but also the cold. And if it blew a bit more now the sky would be free of clouds. In moonlight Olafson could probably have shot Tourtell from anywhere, but in the darkness the plan was that it would happen in the car park, under one of the lights.

He checked his watch again. The cold was eating into his body, and he coughed. His lungs. He couldn't stand the sun and he couldn't stand the cold. What did God actually mean by sending someone like him to earth, a lonely suffering heart without armor, a mollusk without a shell?

"Thanks for helping us."

"Sorry?" Lennox turned to the boy.

"Thank you for saving my father."

Lennox stared at him. Kasi was wearing the same kind of denim jacket as his own son wore. And Lennox couldn't prevent the next thought coming. Here was a boy, not much older than his own, about to lose his mother. And his father. *He says it's fine as long as he has one of us.*

"Let's go, shall we?" Tourtell said as he came out puffing a cigarette he had just bought.

"Yes," Lennox said. They crossed the road and went into the car park. Lennox moved to the left of Tourtell. Kasi was a few steps in front of them. All Lennox had to do was to stop as they went through the light under the first lamp so that he was out of the line of fire, and then the rest was up to Olafson.

Lennox felt a strange numbness in his tongue, fingers and toes.

"They're coming," Seyton said, lowering the binoculars.

"I can see them," Olafson lisped. He stood with one knee on the concrete of the car-park roof. One eye was shut, the other wide open behind the telescopic sights of the rifle resting on the parapet in front of them. Seyton scanned the roof behind them to make sure they were still alone. Their car was the only one up there. People didn't seem to visit the sick on a Saturday evening. He could hear the music from the streets below them and smell the perfume and testosterone from right up there.

Down in the car park the boy was walking in front of Tourtell and Lennox and out of the line of fire. Good. He could hear Olafson take a deep breath. The two men walked into the light under a lamp.

Seyton felt his heart give a leap of joy.

Now.

But there was no shot.

The two men walked out of the circle of light and became vague outlines in the darkness again.

"What happened?" Seyton asked.

"Lennox was in the line of fire," Olafson said.

"I suppose he'll get out of the way when they pass under the next light."

Seyton raised his binoculars again.

"Any idea who could be after me, Lennox?"

"Yes," Lennox said. There were two lamps left before they reached the limousine.

"Really?" Tourtell said in surprise and slowed down. Lennox made sure to do the same.

"Don't look up at the multistory behind me, Tourtell, but on the roof there's an expert marksman and right now we're in his sights. To be more precise, *I* am. So walk at the exact same speed as me. If not, you'll be shot in the head."

He could see from Tourtell's look that the mayor believed him. "The boy . . ."

"He's not in any danger. Keep walking. Don't let on."

Lennox saw Tourtell open his mouth as though it were the only way his big body could get enough oxygen as his heart rate increased. Then the mayor nodded and walked faster, taking short steps.

"What's your role in this, Lennox?"

"The rogue," Lennox said, and saw the driver, who must have been keeping his eye on them, get out of the car to open the rear door. "Is it bulletproof?"

"I'm the mayor, not the president. Why are you doing this if you're the rogue?"

"Because someone has to save this town from Macbeth. I can't, so you'll have to, Tourtell."

"What the fuck's Lennox up to?" Seyton said, snatching the binoculars from his eyes to check that what he had seen through them tallied with the reality down in the car park. "Is he *intentionally* standing in front of Tourtell?"

"Don't know, boss, but this is becoming critical. They'll soon be by the car."

"Your bullets, would they go through Lennox?"

"Boss?"

"Will they go through Lennox and kill Tourtell?"

"I use FMJ bullets, boss."

"Yes or no?"

"Yes!"

"Then shoot the traitor."

"But—"

"Shh," Seyton whispered.

"What?" Sweat had broken out on the young officer's brow.

"Don't talk and don't think, Olafson. What you just heard was an order."

The driver had walked around the car and smiled as he opened the rear door. A smile which disappeared when he saw Tourtell's expression. The boy walked to the rear door on the left-hand side.

"Get in and duck," Lennox hissed. "Driver, get out of here. Now!"

"Sir, what—"

"Do as he says," Tourtell said. "It—"

Lennox felt the shot to his back before he heard the *thwack*. His legs withered beneath him, he collapsed and automatically put his arms around Tourtell, who was dragged down as he fell.

Lennox registered the tarmac coming up to meet them. He didn't feel it as it hit them, but he smelled it all: dust, petrol, rubber, urine. He couldn't move and couldn't produce a sound, but he could hear. Hear the panting of Tourtell from underneath him on the tarmac. The driver's shocked "Sir, sir?"

And Tourtell's "Run, Kasi, run!"

They had almost made it. One more meter and they would have been covered by the car. Lennox tried to say something, the name of an animal, but still nothing came from his mouth. He tried in vain to move his hand. He was dead. Soon he would be floating up and looking down on his own body. One meter. He registered the sound of running feet quickly distancing themselves and the driver bending over them and trying to drag him off Tourtell. "I'll get you in the car, sir!" Another *thwack* and Lennox was blinded by something wet in his eyes. He blinked, so at least his eyelids could move. The driver lay beside them staring vacantly into the air. His forehead was gone.

"Turtle," Lennox whispered.

"What?" Tourtell gasped from underneath him.

"Crawl. I'm your shell."

"That's got the driver," Olafson said, pushing another cartridge into the chamber.

"Hurry. Tourtell's crawling behind the car," Seyton said. "And the boy's run off."

Olafson loaded. He rested the butt against his shoulder and shut one eye.

"I've got the boy in my sights."

"I don't give a fuck about the boy!" Seyton snarled. "Shoot Tourtell!"

Seyton watched Olafson's rifle barrel swing back and forth, saw him blink a bead of sweat from his eyelashes.

"I can't see him, boss."

"Too late!" Seyton slapped his hand against the parapet. "They're behind the car. We'll have to go down and finish the job."

Lennox heard Tourtell groan as he extricated himself. Lennox rolled onto the wet tarmac. He was lying on his stomach, helpless, his legs sticking out past the rear of the car. Until Tourtell grabbed his arms and pulled him to safety.

Rubber screamed on tarmac. A car was heading for them. Lennox looked under the car, but all he saw was the body of the driver on the other side. Tourtell had sat down with his back to the side of the car. Lennox tried to open his mouth to tell Tourtell to get in the car and escape, to save himself, but it was no use. It was the same old story, as though his whole life could be summed up in one sentence: he was unable to do what his brain and heart wanted.

A car stopped and doors opened.

Footsteps on the tarmac.

Lennox tried to move his head but couldn't. From the corner of his eye he saw the barrel of a gun parallel with a pair of trouser legs.

They were goners. In some strange way it felt like a relief.

The trouser legs came a step closer. A hand gripped his neck. He was going to be killed silently, strangulation. Lennox held his gaze on the shoes. They went out of fashion a while ago. Winklepickers.

"This one's dead," said a familiar voice from the other side of the car.

"Tourtell's unhurt," said the man holding him in a stranglehold. "Lennox isn't moving, but he's got a pulse. Where did they shoot from?"

"The top of the multistory," Tourtell sobbed. "Lennox saved my life."

Saved?

"Get over to this side, Malcolm!"

The hand removed itself, and a face came into Lennox's field of vision. Duff stared him in the eye.

"Is he conscious?" asked a woman behind him. Caithness.

"Paralyzed or in shock," Duff said. "His eyes are moving, but he can't move or talk. We need to get him into the hospital."

"Car," a voice said. A young boy. "Coming out of the multistory car park."

"Looks like a SWAT car," Duff said, getting up and putting the shotgun to his shoulder.

There was silence for a couple of seconds. The sound of the car engine faded away.

"Let them go," Malcolm said.

"Kasi." Tourtell's voice.

"What?"

"You've got to find Kasi."

Kasi ran. His heart was beating in his throat and his feet pummeling the wet tarmac, faster and faster. Until they were running as fast as the song that used to play in his head when he was afraid. "Help." He had been getting in the car when he heard the thud and saw the shot hit the pale-faced policeman in the back. He had fallen over Dad and Dad had told him to run.

He automatically took the road down toward the area where he had grown up, by the river. There was a burned-out house where they used to play, the rat house they called it.

The burned-out house was white with patches of soot around the door and windows, like a decrepit over-made-up whore. Down by the river the small houses lay huddled together as if searching for shelter with one another. Apart from one, which was on its own, as though the others were shunning it. It was timber-framed and painted blue; and around it the grass had grown high. Kasi ran up the steps into the doorless hall to what once had been a kitchen but now was an empty, urine-stinking shell with names and dirty words scribbled on the walls. He continued up the narrow stairs to the bedrooms. A moldy mattress lay on the floor of one. He'd had his first kiss on it among empty spirit bottles and the stiff carcasses of river rats scattered around the floor. One afternoon when he was ten or eleven he and two friends had sat on it and tasted their first cigarette—in between coughing fits—in the sunset, and watched rats come toward the house, padding across the cracked and litter-strewn mud of the dry riverbed. Perhaps they came here to die.

Should he go back? No, Dad had said he should get away. And the other man, Lennox, was from the police, and there must be more of them there if they knew of plans to assassinate the mayor.

He would hide until it was all over, then go home.

Kasi opened the big wardrobe in the corner. It was empty, stripped of everything. He huddled inside and closed the door. Leaned his head back against the wood. Softly hummed the song in his mind. "Help!" Thought

of the film where the Beatles were running around helter-skelter and having fun in comic fast-forward motion, a world where nothing really horrible happened. And no one could find him here. Not unless they knew
where he was. And anyway, he wasn't the mayor, only a boy who hadn't
done anything bad in his life apart from smoke a few cigarettes on the
quiet, share half a bottle of diluted whiskey and kiss a couple of girls who
had boyfriends.

His heart gradually slowed.

He listened. Nothing. But he would have to wait some time. He had
got his breath back, enough to inhale through his nose now. He didn't
know how many years it was since clothes had hung here, but he could
still smell them. The smell, the ghosts of lives unknown. God knows
where they were now. Mum said it had been an unhappy house, with alcohol, beatings and much worse. He should thank his lucky stars he had a
father who loved him and had never laid a hand on him. And Kasi *had*
thanked his lucky stars. No one had known his father was the mayor, and
he didn't tell anyone either, neither those who called him a brat, nor the
other brats who never saw their fathers or even knew who they were. He
felt sorry for them. He had told his father that one day he would help
them. Them and all the others in difficulty after Estex closed. And Dad
had patted him on the head and laughed, as other fathers would have
done. He had listened attentively and said that if Kasi really wanted to do
something, when the time came he would help him. He had promised.
And who knows, one day Kasi might become mayor, greater wonders had
come to pass, Dad had said, and called him Tourtell Junior.

"Help!"

But the world wasn't like that. The world hadn't been made for good
deeds and funny pop singers in films. You couldn't help anyone. Not your
father, not your mother, not other children. Only yourself.

Olafson braked as the bus in front of them stopped. Young people, mostly
women, streamed onto the pavement. Looking their best. Saturday night.
That was what he would have done tonight: had a beer and danced with a
girl. Drunk and danced away the sight of the driver. Beside him Seyton
stretched out a hand and turned off the radio and Lindisfarne's "Meet Me
on the Corner."

"Where the hell did they come from? Duff. Malcolm. Caithness. And the young guy I could have sworn was Banquo's son."

"Back to HQ?" Olafson asked. It still wasn't too late for a decent Saturday night.

"Not yet," Seyton said. "We've got to catch the boy."

"Tourtell's son?"

"I don't want to go back to Macbeth empty-handed, and the boy can be used. Turn left here. Drive even more slowly."

Olafson swung the car down the narrow street and glanced at Seyton, who had opened the window and was inhaling the air, his nostrils opening and closing. Olafson was about to ask if Seyton could sniff out where the boy had run to, but refrained. If this man could heal a shoulder by touching it he was probably capable of smelling his way to where someone had gone. Was he afraid of his new commander? Maybe. He had definitely asked himself whether he preferred his predecessor. But he hadn't known it could come to this. All he knew was that the surgeon at the hospital had pointed to an X-ray of his shoulder and explained that the bullet had destroyed the joint; he was an invalid and would have to get used to never working as a marksman for SWAT again. In a few moments the surgeon had deprived Olafson of all he had ever dreamed about doing. Then it had been easy to agree when Seyton said he could fix it if Olafson agreed to a deal. He hadn't even meant it because who could fix something like that in a day? And what did he have to lose? He had already sworn allegiance to the brotherhood that was SWAT, so what Seyton wanted from him was in many ways something he already had.

No, there was no point having regrets now. And just look what had happened to his best pal, Angus. He had betrayed SWAT, the idiot. Betrayed the most precious thing they had, all they had. *Baptized in fire and united in blood* wasn't an empty phrase, it was how they had to be, there were no alternatives. He wanted this. To know there was some meaning in what he did, that he meant something to people. To his comrades. Even when he couldn't see any meaning in what they did. That was a job for other people. Not for Angus, the bloody fool. He must have lost the plot. Angus had tried to persuade him to join him, but he had told him to go to hell, he didn't want anything to do with someone who betrayed SWAT. And Angus had stared at him and asked him how his shoulder had healed so quickly—a gunshot wound like that didn't heal in a couple of days. But Olafson hadn't answered. He just showed him the door.

The street ended. They had reached the riverbed.

"We're getting warmer," Seyton said. "Come on."

They got out and walked by the hovels between the road and the riverbed. Passing house after house as Seyton sniffed the air. At a red building he stopped.

"Here?" Olafson asked.

Seyton sniffed in the direction of the house. Then he said aloud, "Whore!" And walked on. They passed a burned-out house, a garage with a wrought-iron gate and came to a blue timber house with a cat on the steps. Seyton stopped again.

"Here," he said.

"Here?"

Kasi looked at his watch. He had been given it by his father and the hands shimmered green in the darkness, the way he imagined wolves' eyes did in the night, from the light of a fire. More than twenty minutes had passed. He was fairly sure no one had followed him when he ran from the car park; he had looked back several times and hadn't seen anyone. The coast ought to be clear now. He knew the area like the back of his hand, that was why he had run straight here. He could go down to Penny Bridge and take the 22 bus from there, go west. Back home. Dad would be there. He *had* to be there. Kasi stiffened. Had he heard something? The staircase creaking? That was the only wood that had survived the fire, he didn't know why, just that it creaked when the wind blew or there was a change in the weather. Or if someone came. He held his breath. Listened. No. Probably the weather changing.

Kasi counted slowly to sixty.

Then he pushed the door open with his foot.

Stared.

"You're frightened," said the man standing outside and looking at him. "Smart thinking, hiding in a wardrobe. It keeps in the smell. Almost." He stretched his arms out to the side with his palms up. Inhaled. "But the air here is wonderful and full of your fear, boy."

Kasi blinked. The man was lean, and his eyes were like the hands on

Kasi's watch. Wolf eyes. And he had to be old. Not that he looked that old, but Kasi just knew that this man was very, very old.

"Hel—" Kasi started to shout, before the man's hand shot out and grabbed him by the throat. Kasi couldn't breathe, and now he knew why he had come here. He was like the river rats. He had come here to die.

39

DUFF LOOKED AT HIS WATCH, yawned and slumped even deeper in the chair. His long legs stretched almost across the hospital corridor, to Caithness and Fleance. Duff's eyes met Caithness's.

"You were right," she said.

"We were both right," he said.

It was less than an hour since he had jumped into the car in 15th Street, cursing, and said Macbeth had got away. And that something was afoot. Macbeth had said the mayor wouldn't live that long.

"An assassination," Malcolm had said. "A takeover. He's gone completely insane."

"What?"

"The Kenneth Laws. If the mayor dies or declares a state of emergency, the chief commissioner takes over until further notice and in principle has unlimited power. Tourtell has to be warned."

"St. Jordi's," Caithness had said. "Seyton's there."

"Drive," Duff had shouted, and Fleance stamped on the accelerator.

It had taken them less than twenty minutes, and they heard the first shot from the car park when they stopped in front of the hospital's main entrance and were on their way up the steps.

Duff closed his eyes. He hadn't slept, and this should have been over now. Macbeth should have been behind lock and key in Fife.

"Here they are," Caithness said.

Duff opened his eyes again. Tourtell and Malcolm were walking down the corridor toward them.

"The doctor says Lennox will live," Malcolm said and sat down. "He's fully conscious and can talk and move his hands. But he's paralyzed from the middle of the back down, and it'll probably be permanent. The bullet hit his spine."

"It was *stopped* by his spine," Tourtell said. "Otherwise it would have gone through him and hit me."

"His family are in the waiting room," Malcolm said. "They've been in to see him, and the doctor said that's enough for today. He's had morphine and needs to rest."

"Heard anything from Kasi?" Caithness asked.

"He hasn't come home yet," Tourtell said. "But he knows his way around. He may have gone to friends or hidden somewhere. I'm not worried."

"You're not?"

Tourtell pulled a grimace. "Not yet."

"So what do we do now?" Duff asked.

"We wait a few minutes until the family has gone," Malcolm said. "Tourtell persuaded the doctor to give us two minutes with Lennox. We need a confession as soon as possible from Lennox so that we can get Capitol to issue a federal arrest warrant for Macbeth."

"Aren't our witness statements good enough?" Duff asked.

Malcolm shook his head. "None of us has received death threats directly from Macbeth or personally heard him give an order to murder."

"What about blackmail?" Caithness asked. "Tourtell, you just said that when you were playing blackjack in the private room at the Inverness Macbeth and Lady tried to force you to withdraw from the elections, dangling the bait of shares in the Obelisk and threatening to go public with a story of indecent behavior with an underage boy."

"In my line of work we call that kind of blackmail 'politics,'" Tourtell said. "Hardly punishable."

"So Macbeth's right?" Duff said. "We've got nothing on him."

"We hope Lennox has something," Malcolm said. "Who should talk to him?"

"Me," Duff said.

Malcolm regarded him pensively. "Fine, but it's just a question of time before someone here recognizes you or me, and raises the alarm."

"I know how Lennox looks when he lies," Duff said. "And he knows I know."

"But can you persuade him to reveal his cooperation and thus . . . ?"

"Yes," Duff said.

"Don't persuade him the way you did the Norse Rider patient, Duff."

"That was a different person who did that, sir. I'm not him anymore."

"Aren't you?"

"No, sir."

Malcolm held Duff's gaze for a few seconds. "Good. Tourtell, could you please take Duff?"

"Out of curiosity," Duff said when he and Tourtell had got some way down the corridor, "when Macbeth gave you his ultimatum why didn't you tell him Kasi was your son?"

Tourtell shrugged. "Why tell the person pointing a gun at you it isn't loaded? They'll only start looking around for another weapon."

The doctor was waiting for them outside a closed door. He opened it.

"Just him," Tourtell said, pointing to Duff.

Duff stepped inside.

Lennox was as white as the sheets he was lying between. Tubes and wires led from his body to drip bags on a stand and machines emitting beeps. He looked like a surprised child, staring up at Duff with wide-open eyes and mouth. Duff took his hat and glasses off.

Lennox blinked.

"We need you to go public and say Macbeth is behind this," Duff said. "Are you willing to do that?"

Thin, shiny saliva ran from one corner of Lennox's mouth.

"Listen, Lennox. I've got two minutes, and—"

"Macbeth's behind this," Lennox said. His voice was hoarse, husky, as though he had aged twenty years. But his eyes cleared. "He ordered Seyton, Olafson and me to execute Tourtell. Because he wanted to take over the reins of the town. And because he thinks Tourtell is Hecate's informant. But he isn't."

"So who is the informant?"

"I'll tell you if you do me a favor."

Duff breathed hard through his nose. Concentrated on controlling his speech. "You mean I might have to owe you a favor?"

Lennox closed his eyes again. Duff saw a tear forced out. Pain from his wound, Duff assumed.

"No," Lennox whispered in a fading voice.

Duff leaned forward. There was a nauseous, sweet smell coming from

Lennox's mouth, like the acetone breath of a diabetic, as he whispered, "*I'm* Hecate's informant."

"You?" Duff tried to digest the information, tried to make it fit.

"Yes. How do you think Hecate slipped through our fingers all these years, how he was always a step ahead?"

"You're a spy for both—"

"—Hecate and Macbeth. Without Macbeth knowing. But that's how I know Tourtell's not in Hecate's pocket. Or Macbeth's. But it wasn't me who warned Hecate, so there must be another informant as well. Someone close to Macbeth."

"Seyton?"

"Maybe. Or perhaps not a man."

"A woman? Why do you think that?"

"I don't know. Something invisible, something that's just *there*."

Duff nodded slowly. Raised his eyes and looked into the darkness outside the window.

"How does it feel?"

"How does what feel?"

"To say it out loud finally. That you're a traitor. Is it a relief or does it weigh more heavily on you when the words make you realize it's true, the damage is your fault?"

"Why do you want to know?"

"Because I was wondering about it myself," Duff said. The sky outside was dark, covered, giving no answer or sign. "How it would feel to tell my family everything."

"But you didn't," Lennox said. "We don't. Because we'd rather destroy ourselves than see the pain in their faces. But you didn't have the chance to choose."

"Yes, I did. I chose. Every day. To be unfaithful."

"Will you help me, Duff?"

Duff was torn out of his thoughts. Blinked. He needed to sleep soon. "Help?"

"A favor. The pillow. Put it over my face and hold it there. It'll look as if I died of my wounds. And will you tell my children that their father, murderer and traitor that he was, repented?"

"I . . ."

"You're the only person I know who might understand me, Duff. That you can love someone so much and still betray them. And when it's too late, it's too late. All you can do is . . . what is right, but it's too late."

"Like saving the life of the mayor."

"But that isn't enough, is it, Duff?" Lennox's dry laughter turned into a bout of coughing. "A last desperate act which, seen from the outside, is a sacrifice, but which deep down you hope will be rewarded with the forgiveness of your sins and the opening of heaven's gates. But that's too much, Duff. You don't think you can ever make amends for everything, do you."

"No," Duff said. "No, I can't make amends. But I can start by forgiving you."

"No!" Lennox said.

"Yes."

"No, you can't! Don't do that, don't . . ." His voice crumbled away. Duff looked at him. Small shiny tears rolled down his white cheeks.

Duff took a deep breath. "I'll consider not forgiving you on one condition, Lennox."

Lennox nodded.

"That you agree to give a radio interview this evening in which you tell everything and clear Malcolm."

Lennox raised a hand with difficulty and wiped his cheeks. Then he placed his tear-wet hand round Duff's wrist. "Ring Priscilla and ask her to come here."

Duff nodded, got up and freed his wrist. Looked down at Lennox for a last time. Wondering if he saw a man who had changed or was just taking the easiest way out.

"Well?" Tourtell said, getting up from a chair against the corridor wall when Duff came out.

"He's confirmed that Macbeth was trying to kill you and he'll do the interview," Duff said. "But Hecate has an informant, an infiltrator close to Macbeth. It could be anyone at police HQ . . ."

"Anyway," Tourtell boomed as they hurried down the corridor, "with Lennox's statement Macbeth's finished! I'll ring Capitol and have a federal arrest warrant issued."

A nurse came toward them. "Mr. Mayor, sir?"

"Yes?"

"We've had a call from Agnes, your maid. She says Kasi still hasn't come home."

"Thank you," Tourtell said. They continued walking. "You'll see, he's gone to some friends and is waiting until the coast is clear."

"Probably," Duff said. "Your maid . . ."

"Yes?"

"I've never had servants, but I assume that after a while they become part of the furniture. You speak freely and don't think they'll repeat stuff that shouldn't go beyond your four walls, isn't that right?"

"Agnes? Yes. Yes, at least when I was sure I could trust her. But that took time."

"And yet you can never know for sure what another person thinks and feels, can you?"

"Hm. You're wondering if Macbeth has a personal secretary at HQ who might . . ."

"Priscilla?" Duff said. "Well, as you said, it takes time to trust someone."

"And?"

"You said you played blackjack in a private room as Macbeth and Lady made plans to kill Hecate. But doesn't it need a fourth person?"

"Sorry?"

"Blackjack. Don't you need a croupier?"

"Jack?"

"Yes, Lady?" Jack took his hand away. It had been casually placed on Billy's arched back as the two of them stood over the guestbook and Jack had explained how new customers should be entered.

"I have to talk to you about something, Jack. Let's go upstairs."

"Of course. Will you hold the fort, Billy?"

"I'll do my best, Mr. Bonus."

Jack smiled and knew he held the newly employed boy's eyes a moment too long. Then he dashed up the stairs after Lady.

"What do you think of the new boy?" she asked after he had caught her up.

"Bit early to say, ma'am. A little young and inexperienced, but he doesn't seem impossible."

"Good. We need two waiters for the restaurant. The two who came today were utterly hopeless. How are young people going to survive in this world if they can't take things seriously and *learn* something? Do they think everything's going to be served to them on a silver platter?"

"True," Jack said and went into the suite, Lady holding the door open for him. Turning, he saw she had closed the door and collapsed in tears on a chair.

"Lady, what's the matter?"

"Lily," she sobbed. "Lily. He said her name."

"Lily? As in the flower, ma'am?"

Lady hid her face in her hands, and sobs racked her body.

Jack was at a loss to know what to do. He went toward her but then stopped. "Would you like . . . to talk about it?"

"No!" she exclaimed. Took a tremulous breath. "No, I don't want to talk about it. Dr. Alsaker wanted to talk about it. He's crazy, did you know that? He told me himself. But that doesn't make him a bad psychiatrist, he says, more the opposite. I don't need words, Jack, I've heard them all. My own and those of others, and they don't soothe anymore. I need medicine." She sniffed and wiped under her eyes carefully with the back of her hand. "Quite simply, medicine. Without it I can't be the person I have to be."

"And who's that?"

"Lady, Jack." She looked at the mascara smeared on her hand. "The woman who lives and lets die. But Macbeth has stopped using medicine and so there's nothing here. Imagine. He's stronger than me. You wouldn't have guessed that, would you? So you'll have to go and buy some for me, Jack."

"Lady . . ."

"Otherwise everything will collapse here. I hear a child crying all the time, Jack. I go into the gaming room and smile and talk." Tears started rolling again. "Talk loudly and laugh to drown out the sound of the crying child, but now I can't do it any longer. He knew the name of my child. He said my final words to her."

"What do you mean?"

"Hecate. He knew. The words I said before I smashed the head with the questioning blue eyes. *In another life, my little Lily.* I've never told that to a living soul. Never! At least not in a conscious state. But perhaps when I've been dreaming. Perhaps when I've been sleepwa—" She stopped. Frowned as if she had realized something.

"Hypnosis," Jack said. "You said it during the hypnosis. Hecate knows it from Dr. Alsaker."

"Hypnosis?" She nodded slowly. "Do you think so? Do you think Alsaker betrayed me? And was paid for it, you mean?"

"People are greedy, that's their nature, ma'am. Without greed man wouldn't have won the fight on earth. Just look what you've created, ma'am."

"You mean it's down to *greed*?"

"Not for money, ma'am. I think different people are greedy for different things. Power, sex, admiration, food, love, knowledge, fear . . ."

"What are you greedy for, Jack?"

"Me?" He shrugged. "I like happy, satisfied customers. Yes, I'm greedy for the happiness of others. Such as your own, ma'am. When you're happy, I'm happy."

She fixed him with her gaze. Then she got up, went over to the mirror and grabbed the hairbrush lying on the table beneath. "Jack . . ."

He didn't like the sound of her voice but met her eyes in the mirror. "Yes, ma'am."

"You ought to know something about loneliness."

"You know I do, ma'am."

She started to brush her long flame-red hair, which men had been attracted by or had taken as a warning, according to circumstances. "But do you know what is lonelier than never having anyone? It is believing you had someone, but then it turns out that the person you thought was your closest friend never was." The brush got stuck, but she forced it through the thick unruly hair. "That you've been deceived the whole time. Can you imagine how lonely that is, Jack?"

"No, I can't, ma'am."

Jack looked at her. He didn't know what to do or say.

"Be happy you haven't been deceived, Jack." She put down the brush and passed him some notes. "You're like a suckerfish: you're too small to be deceived, you can only deceive. The shark lets you hang on because you clean off other, worse parasites. In return, it takes you across the oceans of the world. And that's how you travel, to the mutual benefit of both, and the relationship is so intimate and close that it can be confused with friendship. Until a bigger, healthier shark swims by. Go on, Jack. Go and buy me some brew."

"Are you sure, ma'am?"

"Say you want something that works. Something strong. That can take you up high and far away. So high that you would crush your skull if you fell. For who wants to live in a cold, friendless world like this one?"

"I'll do my best, ma'am."

He closed the door behind him without a sound.

"Oh, I'm sure you know where to find it, Jack Bonus," she whispered to the reflection in the mirror. "Say hello to Hecate, by the way." A tear ran down her cheek, in the salty trail of the previous one. "My good, dear Jack. My poor little Jack."

"Mr. Lennox?"

Lennox opened his eyes. Looked at his watch. An hour and a half to midnight. His eyelids went again. He had begged for more morphine. All he wanted was sleep, even the tormented sleep of the guilty.

"Mr. Lennox."

He opened his eyes again. The first thing he saw was a hand holding a microphone. Behind it he glimpsed something yellow. Slowly it came into focus. A man in a yellow oilskin jacket sitting on a chair beside a hospital bed.

"You?" he whispered. "Of all the reporters in this world they sent you?"

Walt Kite straightened his glasses. "Tourtell, Malcolm and the others know that I . . . that I . . ."

"That you're in Macbeth's pocket?" Lennox lifted his head from the pillow. They were alone in the room. He squirmed to reach the alarm button by the bedhead, but the radio reporter placed his hand over it.

"No need," Kite said calmly.

Lennox tried to pull Kite's hand away from the alarm, but he didn't have the strength.

"So that you can feed me to Macbeth?" Lennox snorted. "The way you fed Angus to us?"

"I was in the same predicament as you, Lennox. I had no choice. He threatened my family."

Lennox gave up and slumped back. "And what do you want now? Have you got a knife with you? Poison?"

"Yes. This." Kite waved the microphone.

"Are you going to kill me with *that*?"

"Not you, but Macbeth."

"Oh?"

Walt Kite put down the microphone, unbuttoned his jacket and wiped the fug from his glasses.

"When Tourtell rang I knew they had enough to get him. Tourtell persuaded the doctor to give me five minutes, so we have to hurry. Give me the story, and I'll go straight to the radio station and broadcast it, raw and unedited."

"In the middle of the night?"

"I can do it before midnight. And it's enough for some people to hear it. Hear that it's irrefutably your voice. Listen, I'm breaking all the principles of good journalism—the right to respond, the duty to check statements—to save—"

"Your own skin," Lennox said. "To swap sides again. To be sure you're on the winning team."

He saw Kite open his mouth and close it again. Swallow. And blink behind his still fugged-up glasses.

"Admit it, Kite. It's fine. You're not alone. We're not heroes. We're completely normal people who perhaps dream about being heroes, but confronted with the choice between life and the principles we sound off about, we're pretty normal."

Kite flashed a brief smile. "You're right. I've been an arrogant, big-mouthed, cowardly moralist."

Lennox drew breath, no longer sure whether it was him or the morphine talking. "But if you had the chance do you think you could do things any differently?"

"What do you mean?"

"Could you be a different person? Could you make yourself sacrifice something for a higher entity than your own esteem?"

"Such as what?"

"Such as doing something which is really heroic because it will reduce the respected journalist Kite's reputation to rubble?"

Macbeth closed his eyes. He hoped that when he opened them again he would wake up from the bad dream and the much-too-long night. All while the voice coming from the radio on the shelf behind his desk droned away. Every rolled "r" sounded like a machine-gun volley.

"So, Inspector Lennox, to sum up. You maintain that Chief Commissioner Macbeth is behind the murders of Chief Commissioner Duncan and Inspector Banquo, the massacre at the Norse Riders' club house, the murder of Inspector Duff's family, plus the execution of Police Officer Angus carried out at Macbeth's orders by you and Inspector Seyton. And that earlier this afternoon Chief Commissioner Macbeth with the head of SWAT, Inspector Seyton, and Police Officer Olafson were behind the failed attempt on Mayor Tourtell's life."

"That is correct."

"With that we say thank you to Inspector Lennox, who was speaking from his bed in St. Jordi's Hospital. This recording has been made with witnesses present so that it can be used in a court of law, even if Lennox is also murdered. And so, dear listeners, finally I will add that I, Walt Kite, was an accessory to the murder of Police Officer Angus in that I placed the integrity you have honored me with at the disposal of the chief commissioner and murderer, Macbeth. In the law court where I will be judged and in the conversations I will be having with my nearest and dearest, one mitigating circumstance might be that I and my family were threatened. However, professionally, this will not count. I have shown that I can be threatened, used and manipulated to lie to you. I have let myself down and I have let you down, and that means this is the last time you will hear from me, Walt Kite, radio reporter. I will miss you more than you will miss me. Show that you are better citizens than me. Take to the streets and depose Macbeth. Good night and God bless our town."

The signature tune.

Macbeth opened his eyes. But he was still in his office, Seyton was still on the sofa, Olafson still on the chair and the radio was on.

Macbeth got up and turned it off.

"Well?" said Seyton.

"Shh," Macbeth said.

"What?"

"Shut up for a second!" He held the bridge of his nose between his thumb and first finger. He was tired, so tired it was difficult to think as clearly as he needed to. Because he did need to. The next decisions he made were going to be momentous, the next few hours would decide the struggle for the town.

"My name," Olafson said.

"What?"

"They said my name on the radio." He smiled sheepishly. "I don't think anyone in my family has ever had their name mentioned on the radio."

Macbeth listened to the silence. The traffic, where was the regular booming drone of the traffic? It was as though the town was holding its breath. He got up. "Come on."

They took the lift down to the basement.

Passed the SWAT flag with the red dragon.

Seyton unlocked the ammo room and switched on the light.

The boy was sitting between the machine-gun stands, gagged and tied to the safe. The brown irises of his eyes were just a thin ring around the pupils, which were large and black with fear.

"We're taking him to the Inverness," Macbeth said.

"The Inverness?"

"We're not safe here any longer, none of us. But from the Inverness we can bring Tourtell to his knees."

"Who's *we*?"

"The last of the faithful. Those who will be rewarded when the victory is won."

"You, me and Olafson? Are we going to bring the town to its knees?"

"Trust me." Macbeth stroked Kasi's head as if he were a loyal dog. "Hecate needs us and is protecting us."

"Against the whole of the town?" Olafson said.

"Hecate's helpers constitute an army, Olafson. They're as invisible as he is, but they're there—they've already saved me twice. And we have the Gatling sisters and the Kenneth Laws on our side. When Tourtell gives in and declares a state of emergency the town is mine. Well? Loyalty, fraternity?"

Olafson closed his eyes. "Baptized in fire," he whispered. The "z" lisped around the concrete walls.

Seyton scowled at them. But then, slowly, a smile spread across his narrow lips. "United in blood."

40

DUFF WAS SITTING ON THE sofa in Tourtell's living room. The four of them looked nervously at the mayor as he stood with the telephone to his ear. It was two minutes to midnight. Pressure had built up and up and thunder had started to rumble. The town would soon be punished for the hot day. The mayor alternated between "Yes" and "No" on the phone. Then he cradled the receiver. Smacked his lips as though what he had heard had to be chewed and swallowed.

"Well?" said Malcolm impatiently.

"Good and bad news. The good news is that Supreme Court Judge Archibald says that, based on what we have, he's fairly sure they should be able to issue a federal warrant for Macbeth's arrest, and that accordingly they can send federal police here."

"And the bad news?" Malcolm asked.

"It's a politically delicate matter and will take time," Tourtell said. "No one wants to arrest a chief commissioner if it turns out the case won't hold water. In concrete terms all we have is a radio interview with Lennox, who himself has confessed to being an accessory to murder. Archibald says quite a bit more persuasion is needed for him to succeed, but the best-case scenario is that they'll get a ruling tomorrow afternoon."

"But it'll be decided then," Caithness said. "So we just have to hold out tonight and a few hours tomorrow."

"Looks like it," Malcolm said. "Shame the circumstances don't allow for a celebration."

"On the contrary," Tourtell said, turning to the maid, who had just come into the room. "During the war, the more the victories cost us, the harder we celebrated. Champagne, Agnes!"

"Yes, sir, but there's someone on the other line."

Tourtell brightened up. "Kasi?"

"I'm afraid it's Mr. Macbeth."

They looked at each other.

"Put the call through here," Tourtell said.

Macbeth leaned back in the chair with the phone to his ear. Staring up at the ceiling, at the inverted gold spire on the chandelier hanging over him and the empty gaming room. He was alone. He could hear Seyton and Olafson still in the process of assembling the Gatlings on the mezzanine, but he was alone just the same. Lady wasn't here. They had got to work as soon as they arrived back from HQ. It had taken them half an hour to get all the gamblers and diners out. They had tried to do it in a relaxed way. But games had to be finished, chips had to be cashed and some customers insisted on drinking up even though they weren't asked to pay. The last customers had protested that it was a Saturday night and literally had to be pushed out. Lady would of course have managed it in a more elegant way. But Jack, whom Macbeth had sent up to the suite to get her, had returned unaccompanied. That was fine, she needed her sleep, and this was going to be a long fight. They had removed the bars from the windows and sited the machine guns at each end of the mezzanine.

"Tourtell here." The voice struggled to sound neutral.

"Good evening, Mayor. All well?"

"I'm alive."

"Good, good. I'm glad we saved you from the assassination attempt. I suspect Hecate was behind it. Sorry your driver had to pay for it with his life. And that Lennox has lost his senses from the injury he brought on himself."

Tourtell gave a dry laugh. "You're finished, Macbeth. Do you realize?"

"These are indeed wild times, don't you think, Tourtell? Explosions on rooftops, shootings in the streets, assassination attempts on the chief commissioner and mayor. I rang because I think you should declare a state of emergency at once."

"That won't happen, Macbeth. What will happen is that a federal arrest warrant is being issued in your name."

"You've called in the cavalry from Capitol? I thought you would. But the warrant won't be issued before I have control of this town, and then it's too late. I will have immunity. Chief Commissioner Kenneth had more foresight than many give him credit for."

"You're going to rule the town like the dictators before you?"

"In this storm it's probably best to have a stronger hand on the till than yours, Tourtell."

"You're mad, Macbeth. Why on earth would I declare a state of emergency and hand power to you?"

"Because I have your illegitimate son and will cut his head off if you don't do what I say."

Macbeth heard a sharp intake of breath.

"So don't go to sleep, Tourtell. I'll give you a few hours to write and sign the declaration of a state of emergency. And it will come into effect before the sun rises tomorrow. If I haven't heard it broadcast on radio before the first ray of sun hits my eyes, Kasi will die."

Pause. Macbeth had a feeling Tourtell wasn't alone. According to Seyton, Duff, Malcolm and Caithness were three of the four who had prevented them from completing the job at St. Jordi's Hospital.

"And how do you think you will get away with killing my son, Macbeth?"

The tone was tough but couldn't quite conceal his helplessness. And Macbeth noticed he hadn't been prepared for such utter despair. But he shook it off. The mayor's shaking voice confirmed what he had hoped for: Tourtell was willing to do anything at all for the boy.

"Immunity. State of emergency. That'll do the trick, Mayor."

"I don't mean escaping a court of law. I was thinking of your conscience. You've become a monster, Macbeth."

"We never become what we aren't already, Tourtell. You too, you'll always be willing to sell your favors and soul to the highest bidder."

"Can't you hear the thunder outside your house, Macbeth? How can you, in this situation, in this town, still believe there will be sunshine at daybreak?"

"Because I've given orders that there will be. But if you're not a believer, let the sunrise times in this year's almanac be your guide. Until then . . ."

Macbeth rang off. Light played on the crystal above him. Which had to mean it was moving. Perhaps it was rising heat, perhaps it was the strange tremors in the ground or perhaps it was the light outside changing. But there was of course a fourth possibility. That it was he himself who was moving. Who saw things from a different angle. He took the silver dagger from inside his jacket. It was perhaps not the most effective weapon against tanks and thick skin, but Lady was right: silver worked against ghosts. He hadn't seen Banquo, Meredith, Duncan or the young Norse Rider on his knees for a couple of days. He held the dagger up to the light.

"Jack!"

No answer. Louder: "Jack!"

Still no answer.

"Jack! Jack!" He yelled in such a wild, uncontrolled way that he imagined he could feel the inside of his throat tearing.

A door opened at the end of the room. "You called, sir?" Jack's voice echoed.

"Still no sign of life from Lady?"

"No, sir. Perhaps you should wake her?"

Macbeth ran a finger across the tip of the dagger. How long had he been clean now? And how much had he longed for sleep, the deep, dark, dreamless kind? He could go up there, lie down beside her and say that now we're going, you and I, we're going to a place where this, the Inverness and the town, doesn't exist, where nothing else but you and I exist. She wanted to, wanted to as much as he did. They had lost their way, but there had to be a way back, back to where they had come from. Yes, of course there was; he just couldn't see it right now. He had to talk to her, get her to show him where it was, as she always did. So what was stopping him? What strange premonition was stopping him from going up there, holding him back, making him prefer to sit in this cold empty room rather than lie in the warm arms of his beloved?

He turned and looked at the boy. Seyton had chained Tourtell's son to the shiny pole in the middle of the room, with a leg manacle around the boy's long, slim neck. Like a dog. And like a dog he lay motionless on the floor looking at Macbeth with his imploring brown eyes. The way they had stared unflinchingly at him ever since they arrived.

Macbeth stirred from the chair with an exclamation of annoyance.

"Let's go and see her, then," he said.

His own and Jack's soundless footsteps on the thick carpets gave

Macbeth the sense they were floating like ghosts up the stairs and along the corridor. It took Macbeth ages to find the right key on Jack's ring. He examined every single one of them as though they held a code, the answer to a question he didn't yet know.

Then he opened the door and went in. The lamp in the room was switched off, but moonlight shone through gaps in the curtains. He stood listening. The thunder had stopped. It was so still, as though everything was holding its breath.

Her skin was so pale, so bloodless. Her hair spread across the pillow like a red fan and her eyelids seemed to be transparent.

He went over to her and placed his hand on her brow. There was still some warmth in her. Next to her, on the quilt, lay a piece of paper. He picked it up. She had written only a few lines.

Tomorrow, tomorrow and tomorrow. The days crawl in the mud, and in the end all they have accomplished is to kill the sun again and bring all men closer to death.

Macbeth turned to Jack, who had remained in the doorway.

"She's gone."

"Wh . . . what, sir?"

Macbeth pulled a chair to the bed and sat down. Not to be close to her; she wasn't there anymore. He just wanted to sit.

He heard Jack's cry of shock behind him and knew he had seen it, the syringe still hanging from her forearm.

"Is she . . . ?"

"Yes, she's d-d-dead."

"How long . . . ?"

"A l-l-long time."

"But I was talking to—"

"She started d-d-dying the night she found the baby in the shoebox, Jack. She simulated life for a while, but it was only the convulsions of death. She saw her child, saw that she would have to travel into death to see her again. That was when we lost Lady, when she fell for that consoling notion that we meet our loved ones on the other side."

Jack took a step closer. "But you don't believe it?"

"Not when the sun is shining from a clear sky. But we live in a town without sun, where we take all the consolation we can get. So, by and large, I believe."

Macbeth examined himself, amazed that he felt neither sorrow nor despair. Perhaps because he had long known that this is how it would end. He had known it and closed his eyes. And all he felt was emptiness. He was sitting in a waiting room in the middle of the night, he was the only passenger, and his train had been announced but it hadn't arrived. Announced but it hadn't arrived. And what does the passenger do then? He waits. He doesn't go anywhere, he reconciles himself to what is happening and waits for what is to come.

Macbeth picked up the piece of paper again.

The days crawl in the mud, and in the end all they have accomplished is to kill the sun again and bring all men closer to death.

41

THE LIFT TOOK DUFF, MALCOLM and the caretaker down to the basement at police HQ.

"I know it's a weekend, but are you sure there isn't anyone else here?" Duff said to the caretaker, whom Malcolm had spoken to at length on the phone from Tourtell's house.

"On the contrary," the caretaker answered. "They're waiting for you."

Duff was unable to react before the lift arrived and the doors opened in front of him. Three people were there, all armed and dressed in the black SWAT uniform. Duff held his breath.

"Thank you," Malcolm said. "For coming at such short notice."

"For the town," said one of them.

"For Angus," said the second.

"For the chief commissioner," said the third, an erect, dark-skinned man. "In our book his name is now Malcolm."

"Thank you, Ricardo," Malcolm said, exiting the lift.

The stiff-backed officer led the way. "Have you spoken to anyone else, sir?"

"I've been on the phone all evening. It shouldn't be easy to persuade people to risk their lives and jobs to fight against a conspiracy they only have my word for. Especially when I add that we cannot expect any immediate help from Capitol. However, I have around thirty officers from the police, ten to fifteen from Civil Defense and maybe ten from the Fire Service."

"The case may not sound very convincing, but *you* are, Malcolm."

"Thank you, Ricardo, but I think Macbeth's actions speak for themselves."

"I wasn't thinking about your words, sir. Your courage speaks louder."

"I had everything taken from me and didn't have much to lose, Ricardo. Nevertheless I had to come back and fetch my daughter, who has been taken to safety now. It's you who show courage. You're not controlled by a father's heart, you're acting freely, governed by your own sense of justice. Which proves that in this town there are people who want what is good."

They passed the dragon flag.

"And where's the mayor?" Ricardo asked.

"He's got other things on his mind at the moment."

Ricardo stopped in front of a massive iron door, like the entrance to an air-raid shelter. It was open. "Here."

The shelves inside were laden with iron boxes and firearms. In the middle of the floor there was a safe. Malcolm took one of the machine guns from a shelf.

"Someone's taken the Gatling guns and their ammo," Ricardo said. "So this is all we have. Plus an armored car. I can have it brought down to the central station straightaway. There aren't enough guns for everyone, but the firemen don't have any weapon training anyway. My men and I can strike tonight, though."

"We'd far prefer Macbeth to surrender voluntarily," Malcolm said. "The numbers tell us he probably has two men with him: Seyton and Olafson. When he sees how many we've mobilized outside I hope he will release Kasi and capitulate."

"Negotiations." Ricardo nodded. "Modern tactics in hostage situations."

"Precisely."

"Modern and useless, as far as Macbeth is concerned. I've had him as a boss, sir. He has the two best marksmen in the country and two Gatling guns on his side. While we have very little time."

"What can you do against two Gatling guns?" Malcolm asked, taking down a bazooka.

Duff stiffened. He had seen what was behind the bazooka.

"It's not very accurate over a long distance," Ricardo said. "But I'd be happy to draw up a plan of how we can take the Inverness if Macbeth won't surrender."

"Good," Malcolm said, looking at what Duff had found. "Jesus, where's that from?"

"The ruins after the raid on the Norse Riders," Ricardo said. "It's a weapon, even if it's only a saber."

"It's not just any saber," Duff said, gripping the handle tightly. He swung it and felt the weight of the steel. "It's Sweno's saber."

"You're not thinking of taking it, are you? It can't do any harm."

"Wrong." Duff ran his forefinger over the blade. "It can slice open women's stomachs and children's faces."

Malcolm turned to Ricardo. "Can you have the weapons transported to the central station an hour before sunrise?"

"Consider it done."

"Thank you. Let's see if the rest of us can catch a couple of hours' shut-eye."

"Sir?"

Macbeth lifted his head from Lady's cold chest and looked up. It was Jack. He had returned and was standing in the doorway.

"There's someone down in reception who'd like to talk to you."

"Have you let s-s-someone in?"

"He's alone and he kept knocking. I had to let him in. And now he doesn't want to go away."

"Who is it?"

"A young man by the name of Sivart."

"Sivart?"

"He says you saved his life down by the quay during the raid on the Norse Riders."

"Oh, the hostage. Wh-wh-what does he want?"

"To volunteer. He says he's been contacted by Malcolm, and Malcolm is getting people together to launch an attack on the Inverness."

"Then," Macbeth said, resting his head back on Lady's chest and closing his eyes, "t-t-tell him to go."

"He won't, sir."

Macbeth sighed heavily, got to his feet and held out a hand. "Lend me the gun I gave you, Jack."

They went down to reception, where the young man was nervously waiting. From the stairs Macbeth pointed the gun at him. "Out!"

"Chief Commissioner . . ." the man stammered.

"Out! You've been sent by Malcolm to kill me. Now out!"

"No, no, I . . ."

"Now! I'll count to three! One . . ."

The man stumbled backward, grabbed the door handle, but it was locked.

"Two!"

Jack rushed forward with the key and helped the man to open the door.

"Three!"

The door slammed behind the man and they heard running footsteps fade in the distance.

"Do you really think he—"

"No," Macbeth said, handing back the gun to Jack. "But a young man like him here would have just got in the way."

"There aren't many of you, and he's the same age as Olafson, sir."

"Have you done what I asked you to do, Jack?"

"I'm still doing it, sir."

"Tell me when you've finished. I'm in the gaming room."

Macbeth opened the double doors to the casino. The night grew old and gray behind the tall windows to the east.

42

THE SUN WAS HIDDEN BEHIND the mountain, but it had sent a red harbinger of its arrival. Inspector Lennox thought he had never seen a finer daybreak in the town. Or perhaps he had, but had never noticed it. Or perhaps it was the morphine more than the sun that colored everything. The streets were adorned with smashed beer bottles, stinking piles of spew and cigarette ends after a lively Saturday night, but no one was about, only a little man in a black maritime uniform and white hat, who hurried past them. Everyone else, as the town's fate was decided, lay at home in bed with the blankets pulled over their heads. And despite this he had never seen his town looking more beautiful.

Lennox gazed down at the tartan blanket Priscilla had spread over his knees. They were approaching the modest eastern entrance to the central station. He noticed the wheelchair was moving more slowly. She was hesitant; he guessed she had hardly ever been to the station before.

"There's nothing to be afraid of, Priscilla. They only want to sell dope. Or buy it." He saw from her shadow as they passed under a streetlight that she had straightened up. Their speed increased.

As arranged, she had picked him up while it was still dark outside, before the corridors were full of nurses and doctors who would have stopped them. And she had brought various things from the office which he had requested. He didn't even need to persuade her or explain anything to her; she had immediately done what he had said, even if officially he was no longer her boss.

"That's fine," she had said. "You'll always be my boss. And Macbeth won't continue as chief commissioner, will he?"

"Why not?"

"He's off his trolley, isn't he."

They passed cigarette-smoking pushers and junkies dozing on blankets who woke up and automatically reached out a begging hand.

But Priscilla didn't stop until they were in front of the stairs by the toilets.

It was here they used to collect him. All he had to do was stand there and they came. Lennox had never worked out where they took him because they not only put goggles on him but also gave him earplugs so that he couldn't speculate from the background noises.

It was a part of the agreement. When he needed a real trip, one that couldn't happen at home or at the office in the evening without the risk of being caught, they took him into the kitchen, the place where they made brew. And there he was given the purest drug that could be produced, injected by specialists. He was placed in a reclining chair, a bit like they did in the old days in opium dens, and after sleeping off his high in safe surroundings he could go into town and move around for a while like a new and better man.

In a way which he would never be able to do again.

He had felt how helpless he was when Priscilla freed him from all the wires and tubes and maneuvered him across into the wheelchair. How useless he had become. How little he could be expected to do.

"Go," he said now.

"What? Are we going?"

"*You* are."

"And just leave you here, you mean?"

"It'll be fine. I'll ring you. Go now."

She didn't move.

"It's an order, Priscilla—" he smiled "—from the man who will always be your boss."

She sighed. Gently placed a hand on his shoulder. Then she left.

Less than ten minutes passed before Strega was standing in front of him with her arms crossed. "Wow!" was all she said.

"I know," Lennox said. "It's an ungodly hour."

She laughed briefly. "You're in good humor despite the wheelchair. What can I do for you?"

"Something to stop the pain and an hour in the recliner."

She passed him the earplugs and the goggles.

"My legs are not what they were, so you might have to help me get there."

"A feather like you?" she said.

"I need the wheelchair with me."

"We'll have to skip the car trip today."

She pushed him. The pains had come and gone all morning, but when she lifted him out of the wheelchair a few minutes later and lowered him onto what felt like crushed stone it hurt so much he cried. He felt Strega's muscular arms around him, the almost overwhelming scent of her. After she managed to get him back in the wheelchair she began to push it. Every meter the wheelchair hit something in the gravel. A sleeper. There was a smell of tar and burned metal. He was being pushed along a railway track.

Fancy not realizing. The other times they had ridden in a car, not a long way, but clearly in a circle, back to their starting point at the central station. He had known before that they were under cover as he hadn't felt the rain, but not that the brewing took place in one of the disused tunnels right under their noses! He groaned with impotence as Strega lifted him and laid him cheek down on something cold and damp. Concrete. Then she put him back in the wheelchair. Pushed it. The air was getting warmer, drier. They were approaching the kitchen now, the easily recognizable smells activating something in his brain which made his heart beat faster and gave him a foretaste of the trip. Someone removed the goggles and earplugs and he caught the tail end of Strega's sentence.

". . . wash the trail of blood after him."

"All right," said one of the sisters stirring the tank.

Strega was about to lift him into the reclining chair, but Lennox waved her away and rolled up his left shirtsleeve. Brew straight from the pot. It didn't get any better than that. A junkie's heaven. This was where he wanted to go. Or not. He would see. Or not.

"Isn't that Inspector Lennox from the Anti-Corruption Unit?" Jack said. He was standing by the one-way glass looking in at the kitchen and the man in the wheelchair.

"Yes," Hecate said. He was wearing a white linen suit and hat. "It's not enough to have eyes and ears in the Inverness."

"Did you hear that Lennox has accused Macbeth of murder? Doesn't he know Macbeth is your instrument?"

"No one's allowed to know more than they have to, not even you, Bonus. But back to the matters in hand. Lady has taken her own life, but Macbeth seems paralyzed rather than upset, would you say?"

"That's my interpretation."

"Hm. And if Tourtell declares a state of emergency, do you think Macbeth in his present state of mind will manage to take power, to do what has to be done to establish himself as the town's leader?"

"I don't know. He seems . . . not to care. As though nothing is very important anymore. Either that or he believes himself to be invulnerable. You will save him, whatever happens."

"Hm." Hecate tapped his stick on the floor twice. "Without Lady the value of Macbeth as chief commissioner has sunk."

"He'll still obey."

"He might succeed in taking power now, but without her he won't be able to keep it. She was the one who understood the game, could see the wood for the trees, knew what maneuvers were required. Macbeth can throw daggers, but someone has to tell him why and at whom."

"I could become his new adviser," Jack said. "I'm winning his confidence."

Hecate laughed. "I can't quite make up my mind whether you're a mud-eating flounder or actually a sly predatory fish, Bonus."

"I am a fish though, I gather."

"Even if you could bolster his impaired ability to rule, I doubt you could do much about his will. He lacks Lady's lust for power. He seems to desire things you and I have not been dependent on, dear Bonus."

"Brew?"

"Lady. Women. Friends maybe. You know, this love between humans. And now that Lady's dead he's no longer driven by the desire to satisfy her hunger for power."

"Lady also needed love," Jack said quietly.

"The desire to be loved and the ability to love, which give humans such strength, are also their Achilles' heel. Give them the prospect of love and they move mountains; take it from them and a puff of wind will blow them over."

"Maybe, maybe."

"If the wind blows Macbeth over, what do you think about him there as chief commissioner?" Hecate nodded toward the glass. One of the sisters was drying Lennox's left arm with an alcohol swab and searching for a vein while holding a syringe ready.

"Lennox?" Jack said. "Are you serious?"

Hecate smacked his lips. "He's the man who brought Macbeth down. The hero who sacrificed his mobility to save the town's mayor. And no one knows that Lennox works for me."

"But Malcolm's back. And everyone knows Lennox runs Macbeth's errands."

"Lennox followed orders like a loyal policeman should. And Malcolms and Duffs can disappear again. Roosevelt won a world war from a wheelchair. Yes, I could get Lennox into the chief commissioner's office. What do you reckon?"

Jack looked at Lennox. Without answering.

Hecate laughed and laid a big soft hand on Jack's narrow shoulder. "I know what you're thinking, flounder. What about you? Who will employ you if Macbeth has gone? So let's hope Macbeth rides the storm, eh? Come on, let me show you out."

Jack cast a final glance at Lennox, then he turned and walked back with Hecate to the toilet door and the station.

"Wait," Lennox said as the sister placed the needle against his skin. He put his free right hand into the big side pocket of the wheelchair. Pulled the cord from the end of the handle.

"Now," he said.

She pushed the needle in and pressed the plunger as he took his hand from the pocket, swung his arm low alongside the chair and let go. What Priscilla had brought from the office rumbled along the concrete floor and disappeared under the table bearing the flasks, tubes and pipes beside the tank.

"Hey, what was that?" Strega asked.

"According to my grandfather, it was a grenade he had thrown at his head," Lennox said, feeling the high, which would never be like the first time but still made him shiver with pleasure. Which was, after all these years of searching, still the closest he had come to the meaning of life. Unless it was this. The full stop.

"It might be a Model 24 *Stielhandgranate*. Or an ashtr—"

That was as far as he got.

Jack was halfway up the stairs when the explosion sent him flying. He picked himself up and turned back to the toilet. The door had been blown off and smoke was drifting out. He waited. When there were no more explosions he walked slowly down the stairs and into the toilet. The cubicle and door to the kitchen had gone. There was a fierce fire inside, and in the light of the flames he could see everything had been destroyed. The kitchen and those inside didn't exist anymore. And five seconds earlier he had been—

"Bonus . . ."

The voice came from directly in front of him. And there, from under the steel door on the floor, it crawled out. A smashed cockroach in a white linen suit. The soft face was covered with shit and his eyes were black with shock.

"Help me . . ."

Bonus grabbed hold of the old man's hands and pulled him across the floor to the toilet door. There he turned Hecate onto his back. He was a wreck. His stomach was slashed open and blood was pouring out. The immortal Hecate. The Invisible Hand, he couldn't have many minutes or seconds left to live. All the blood . . . Jack turned away.

"Hurry, Jack. Find something you can—"

"I have to get a doctor," Jack said.

"No! Find something to close the wound with before I run out of blood."

"You need medical help. I'll hurry."

"Don't leave me, Jack! Don't . . ." The body in front of Jack arced and let out a howl.

"What?"

"Stomach acid! Something's leaking. Christ, I'm burning up. Help, Jack! Hel—" The shout morphed into another hoarse howl. Jack watched him, unable to move. He did look like a cockroach lying on its back, its arms and legs thrashing helplessly.

"I'll be back soon," Jack said.

"No, no!" Hecate screamed and made a grab for his legs.

But Jack stepped away, turned and left.

At the top of the stairs he stopped, looked left, west toward the Inverness. Toward Macbeth. Toward St. Jordi's. There was a phone box in the waiting area that way. He turned to the east. To the mountain. To the other side. To new waters. Dangerous, open waters. But these were decisions a man—and a suckerfish—had to make sometimes to survive.

Jack breathed in. Not because he was hesitant, but because he needed air. Then he headed east.

The crystal murmured and sang above Macbeth's head. He looked up. The chandelier swung back and forth, tugging at the ropes from which it hung.

"What was that?" yelled Seyton from the mezzanine, from the Gatling gun in the southeastern corner of the Inverness.

"The end of the world," Macbeth said. And added, in a low voice and to himself, "I hope."

"It came from the station," Olafson shouted from the machine gun in the southwest corner. "Was that an explosion?"

"Yessir!" Seyton sang. "They're bringing up the artillery."

"Are they?" Olafson said, shocked.

Seyton's laughter echoed between the walls. When they had discussed how the Inverness should be defended it had been easy to conclude that any attack would have to come from Workers' Square, as the bricked-up, windowless side facing Thrift Street was nothing less than a fortress wall.

"I can smell your fear from over here, Olafson. Can you smell it down there, boss?"

Macbeth yawned. "I can barely remember the smell of fear, Seyton." He rubbed his face hard. He had dropped off and dreamed he was lying on the bed next to Lady when the door to the suite slid silently open. The figure in the doorway was wearing a cloak, with a hat pulled so low that it was only when the figure stepped in and the light fell on him that he could see it was Banquo. One eye was gone and white; worms were wriggling out of his cheek and forehead. Macbeth had reached inside his jacket, drawn a dagger from his double shoulder holster and thrown. It bored into Banquo's brow with a soft thud as if the bone behind had already been eaten up. But it didn't stop the ghost advancing toward the bed. Macbeth screamed and shook Lady.

"She's dead," the ghost said. "And you have to throw a silver dagger, not steel." It wasn't Banquo's voice. It was . . .

Banquo's head toppled from under the hat, fell on the floor and rolled under the bed, and from the hat Seyton's face laughed at him.

"What do you want?" Macbeth whispered.

"What you want, sir. To give you both a child. Look, she's waiting for me."

"You're crazy."

"Trust me. I don't want much in return."

"She's dead. Go away."

"We're all dead. Do it now, sow your seeds. If you don't I'll sow mine."

"Get away!"

"Move over, Macbeth. I'll take her like Duff took Meredi—"

The second dagger hit Seyton in his open mouth. He clenched his teeth, grasped the handle, broke it off and passed it back to Macbeth. Showed him his bloody, sliced tongue and laughed.

"Anything on the radio?"

Macbeth gave a start. It was Seyton, shouting.

"Nothing," Macbeth said, rubbing his face hard and turning up the volume on the radio. "Still twenty minutes to sunup." He looked at the white line of finely chopped powder on the mirror he had placed on the felt in front of him. Saw his face reflected. The line of power ran like a scar across the shiny surface.

"And then will we really kill the boy?" Olafson shouted.

"Yes, Olafson!" Seyton shouted back. "We're men, not sissies!"

"But . . . what then? We'll have nothing to negotiate with."

"Does that sound familiar, Olafson?" More laughter from the southeast.

"We have nothing to fear," Macbeth said.

"What's that, sir?"

"No man born can harm me. Hecate promised me I'll be chief commissioner until Bertha comes to get me. You can say a lot about Hecate, but he keeps his word. Relax. Tourtell will give in." Macbeth looked at Kasi, who sat quietly with his back to the pole, staring into the distance. "What can you see, Seyton?"

"People have gathered up by Bertha. They look like police officers and civilians. A few automatic weapons, some rifles and handguns. Shouldn't be much of a problem if they attack with those."

"Can you see any gray coats?"

"Gray coats? No."

"And your sector, Olafson?"

"None here either, sir."

But Macbeth knew that they were there. Watching over him.

"Have you heard of Tithonos, Seyton?"

"Nope. Who's he?"

"A Greek. Lady told me about him. I looked him up. Eos was this goddess of the dawn and she stole a young lover, a pretty ordinary guy called Tithonos. Made sure the boss himself, Zeus, gave the guy eternal life, like her. The guy didn't ask for it, he just had it forced on him. But the goddess had forgotten to ask for eternal youth for the guy. Do you understand?"

"Maybe, but I don't understand where you're going with this, sir."

"Everything disappears, everyone else dies, but there's Tithonos rotting away in his old age and loneliness. He hasn't been given anything, the opposite in fact—he's in prison, his eternal life is a bloody curse."

Macbeth got up so quickly he felt giddy. This was just gloom and a hangover from the dope talking. He had a town lying at his feet, and soon it would be irrevocably his, only his, and he could have his every slightest wish fulfilled. Then all he would need to think about were desires and pleasures. Desires and pleasures.

Duff ran a finger over the crack in the base in front of Bertha's nose. Heard Malcolm's voice: "Sorry, let me through!"

He looked up and saw Malcolm forcing his way through the crowd up to the top of the steps.

"Did you hear that too?" he asked, out of breath.

"Yes," Caithness said. "I thought the roof was going to come down. Felt like an underground test explosion."

"Or an earthquake," Duff said, pointing to the crack.

"Looks like a bigger turnout than I'd planned," Malcolm said, scanning the people who had gathered at the foot of the steps behind the barricade of police cars and a big red fire engine. "Are all these people firemen and police officers?"

"No," said a man coming up the steps. Malcolm examined his black uniform.

"Naval captain?"

"Pilot," said the little man. "Fred Ziegler."

"What's a pilot doing here?"

"I heard Kite on the radio last night, rang around and heard rumors about what was going to happen here. Tell me what I can do."

"Have you got a weapon?"

"No."

"Can you shoot?"

"I was in the marines for ten years."

"Good. Go to the man in the police uniform down there and he'll give you a rifle."

"Thank you." The pilot put three fingers to his white cap and left.

"What does Tourtell say?" Duff asked.

"Capitol has been informed about the hostage," Malcolm said. "But they can't help us until an arrest warrant has been issued this afternoon."

"Jesus, there are people's lives at risk here."

"One life. That doesn't qualify for federal intervention unless our chief commissioner requests it."

"Bloody politics! And where's Tourtell now?" Duff stared to the east. At the edge of the mountain the pale blue sky was getting redder and redder.

"He went to the radio studio," Caithness said.

"He's going to declare a state of emergency," Malcolm said. "We have to attack Macbeth now while we can still act under the mayor's orders. As soon as a state of emergency's declared we'll be lawless revolutionaries and none of these people will be with us." He nodded toward the crowd.

"Macbeth has barricaded himself in," Caithness said. "People's lives will be lost."

"Yes." Malcolm put the megaphone to his mouth. "My good men and women! Take up your positions!"

The crowd ran to the barricade at the foot of the steps. Rested their weapons on car roofs, took cover behind the SWAT armored car and the fire engine and aimed at the Inverness.

Malcolm pointed the megaphone in the same direction. "Macbeth! This is Deputy Chief Commissioner Malcolm speaking. You know, and we know, you're in a hopeless situation. All you can achieve is to defer the inevitable. So release the hostage and give yourself up. I'll give you one, I repeat, *one* minute."

"What did he say?" Seyton shouted.

"He's giving me a minute," Macbeth said. "Can you see him?"

"Yes, he's standing at the top of the steps."

"Olafson, take your rifle and shut Malcolm up."

"Do you mean—"

"Yes, I mean exactly that."

"All hail Macbeth!" Seyton laughed.

"Listen," Macbeth said.

Duff alternated between looking at the mountain, his watch and the men around him. His elbows and shoulders twitched with nerves. They were shifting position because of his knees and calves, which had started to shake. Apart from the six SWAT volunteers and some of the other policemen, the crowd was made up of people with ordinary jobs in accounting offices and fire stations, who had never fired a shot in anger. Or been shot at. And yet they had come here. They were willing, despite their inadequacy, to sacrifice everything. He counted down the final three seconds.

Nothing happened.

Duff exchanged glances with Malcolm and shrugged.

Malcolm sighed and lifted the megaphone to his mouth.

Duff hardly heard the bang.

Malcolm staggered back, and the megaphone fell to the ground with a clang.

Duff and Fleance reacted at once, throwing themselves over Malcolm and covering him as he fell to the ground. Duff felt for blood and a pulse.

"I'm fine," Malcolm groaned. "I'm fine. Up you get. He hit the megaphone. That was all."

"When you said shut him up, I thought you meant permanently," Seyton shouted. "Now they'll think we're weak, sir."

"Wrong," Macbeth said. "Now they know we mean business, but we're sane. If we'd killed Malcolm we'd have given them an excuse to attack us with the fury of righteousness. Now they'll still hesitate."

"I think they're going to attack anyway," Olafson said. "Look, there's our armored car. It's coming toward us."

"Well, that's different. A chief commissioner is allowed to defend himself. Seyton?"

"Yes?"

"Let the Gatling girls speak."

Duff peeped from behind Bertha and followed the lumpen armored car—known as a *Sonderwagen*—as it made its way across the square toward the Inverness. Thick, heavy diesel smoke drifted up from the vehicle's exhaust. German engineering, steel plates and bulletproof glass. Ricardo's plan followed usual tactics. The six SWAT volunteers would drive up to the entrance in the *Sonderwagen*, dismount to fire tear-gas canisters through the windows, then break down the doors and storm the building wearing gas masks. The critical point was when they emerged from the armored car to fire the tear gas. This would take only seconds, but in those seconds they needed covering fire from the others.

Malcolm's walkie-talkie crackled, and they heard Ricardo's voice.

"Covering fire in three . . . two . . . one . . ."

"Fire!" Malcolm roared.

It sounded like a drum roll as the weapons fired from the barricade. From an all-too-small drum, Duff thought. And the sound was drowned by a rising howl from the other side.

"Holy Jesus," Caithness whispered.

At first it resembled a shower of rain whipping up dust from the cobbles in front of the *Sonderwagen*. Then with a cackle it hit the vehicle's grille, its armor, the windscreen and the roof. The vehicle seemed to sag at the knees and sink.

"The tires," Fleance said.

The vehicle kept moving, but more slowly, as though it were driving into a hurricane.

"It's fine. It's an armored car," Malcolm said.

The vehicle advanced more and more slowly. And stopped. The side mirrors and bumper fell off.

"It *was* an armored car," Duff said.

"Ricardo?" Malcolm called on the walkie-talkie. "Ricardo? Withdraw!" No answer.

Now the vehicle seemed to be dancing.

Then the barrage stopped. Silence fell over the square, broken only by a seagull's lament as it flew over. Smoke, like red vapor, rose from the armored car.

"Ricardo! Come in, Ricardo!"

Still no answer. Duff stared at the vehicle, at the wreck. There were no signs of life. And now he knew how it had been. That afternoon in Fife.

"Ricardo!"

"They're dead," Duff said. "They're all dead."

Malcolm sent him a sidelong glance.

Duff ran a hand over his face. "What's the next move?"

"I don't know, Duff. That was the move."

"The fire engine," Fleance said.

The others looked at the young man.

He shrank beneath their collective gaze and for a moment seemed to stagger under the weight of it. But he straightened up and said with a slight quiver of his vocal cords, "We have to use the fire engine."

"It's no good," Malcolm objected.

"No, but if we drive it round to the back, to Thrift Street." Fleance paused to swallow before continuing. "You saw they hit the armored car with both machine guns, and that must mean they're not covering their rear."

"Because they know we can't get in there," Duff said. "There are no doors and no windows, there's only brick, which you'd need a pneumatic drill or heavy artillery to go through."

"Not through," Fleance said. His voice was firmer now.

"Round?" Duff queried.

Fleance pointed a finger to the sky.

"Of course!" Caithness said. "The fire engine."

"Spit it out. What's so obvious?" growled Malcolm, snatching a glance at the mountain.

"The ladder," Duff said. "The roof."

"They're moving the fire engine," Seyton shouted.

"Why?" Macbeth yawned. The boy was sitting on the floor with his legs crossed and eyes closed. Calm and silent, he seemed to have reconciled himself to his fate and was just waiting for the end. Like Macbeth.

"I don't know."

"What about you, Olafson?"

"I don't know, sir."

"All right," Macbeth shouted. He had taken out the silver dagger and whittled a match to a point. He poked it between his front teeth. Left the dagger on the felt. Picked up two chips and began to flip them between the fingers of each hand. He had learned how to do this at the circus. It was an exercise to balance the difference between the motor functions of his left and right hands. He sucked the matchstick, flipped the chips and examined what he was feeling. Nothing. He tried to work out what he was thinking. He wasn't thinking about Banquo and he wasn't thinking about Lady. He was just thinking that he didn't feel anything. And he thought one more thing: *Why? Why . . . ?*

He thought about that for a while . . .

Then he closed his eyes and began to count down from ten.

"This is not like a ladder against a house. It's going to sway more the higher we go," said the man in the harbor pilot's uniform to Fleance and the two other volunteers. "But make only one movement at a time, one hand, then one foot. Nothing to be afraid of."

The pilot yawned loudly and smiled quickly before grasping the ladder and starting to climb.

Fleance watched the little man, wishing he was equally unafraid. Thrift Street was empty apart from the fire engine with its fifteen-meter ladder pointing up the windowless wall.

Fleance followed the pilot, and strangely enough the fear diminished with every step. The worst was over, after all. He had spoken. And they had listened. Nodded and said they understood. Then they had got into the fire engine and driven east from the station in a great arc through the Sunday-still streets, arriving at the rear of the Inverness unseen.

Fleance looked up and saw the harbor pilot signaling from the roof that the way was clear.

They had gone through the drawings of the Inverness so thoroughly last night that Fleance knew exactly where everything was. The flat roof led to a door, and inside it there was a narrow ladder down to a boiler room with a door leading to the top corridor in the hotel. There they would split up, two men would take the northern staircase, two the southern. Both led down to the mezzanine. In a few minutes they would start shooting from the station and keep the machine-gunners' attention focused on Workers' Square, drowning out any sounds made by Fleance and the three others, who would sneak up from behind and eliminate the machine gunners. The three volunteers had synchronized their watches with Fleance's without a word of protest that they were being led by a police cadet. The cadet seemed to know the odd thing about such actions. What was it his dad had said? *And if you've got better judgment you should lead, it's your damned duty to the community.*

Fleance heard them open fire from the station.

"Follow me."

They approached the roof door, pulled. Locked. As expected. He nodded to one of the policemen, a guy from the Traffic Unit, who rammed a crowbar into the crack between the door and its frame and pushed hard. The lock broke at the first attempt.

It was dark inside, but Fleance felt the heat coming from the boiler room beneath. The other policeman, a white-haired guy from the Fraud Unit, wanted to go first, but Fleance held him back. "Follow me," he whispered and stepped in over the high metal threshold. In vain he tried to distinguish shapes in the darkness and had to lower his machine gun as he groped for the railing of the ladder. The metal ladder sang as he took his first tentative step and then found the next rung. He froze, dazzled by a light. A torch had been switched on below him and shone at his face.

"Bang," said a voice from behind the torch. "You're dead."

Fleance knew he was standing in the line of fire of the three behind him. And he knew he wouldn't have time to fire his machine gun. Because he knew whose the voice was.

"How did you know . . . ?"

"I wondered to myself, *Why oh why would you move a fire engine when there's no fire alarm to be heard?*" The voice in the darkness became a low chuckle. "Still wearing my shoes, I see." Uncle Mac sounded drunk. "Listen, Fleance, you can save lives today. Your own and those of the other three mutineers with you. Back out now and get behind the barricade. You'll have a better chance of getting me from there."

Fleance ran his tongue around his mouth searching for moisture. "You killed Dad."

"Maybe," the voice slurred. "Or perhaps it was the circumstances. Or perhaps it was Banquo's ambitions for his family. But probably—" in the pause came the sound of a deep sigh "—it was me. Go now, Fleance."

Fluttering through Fleance's brain were all those pretend-fights he'd had with Uncle Mac at home on the sitting-room floor, when he had let Fleance get the upper hand, only to whisk him round at the last minute and pin him flat on the floor. This wasn't due to his uncle's strength, but his speed and precision. But how drunk was Uncle Mac now? And how much better coordinated was Fleance? Perhaps he had a chance after all? If he was quick, perhaps he could get a shot in. Save Kasi. Save the town. Avenge—

"Don't do it, Fleance."

But it was too late. Fleance had already grabbed his machine gun, and the sound of a brief volley hammered against the eardrums of all five men in the cramped boiler room.

"Agh!" Fleance yelled.

Then he fell from the ladder.

He didn't feel himself hit the floor, felt nothing until he opened his eyes again. And then he saw nothing, although there was a hand against his cheek and a voice close to his ear.

"I told you not to."

"Wh . . . where are they?"

"They left as instructed. Sleep now, Fleance."

"But . . ." He knew he had been shot. A leak. He coughed, and his mouth filled.

"Sleep. Say hello to your dad when you arrive and tell him I'm right behind you."

Fleance opened his mouth, but all that came out was blood. He felt Macbeth's fingers on his eyelids, gentle, careful. Closing them. Fleance sucked in air as if for a dive. As he had done when he fell from the bridge into the river, into the black water, to his grave.

"No," Duff said when he saw the fire engine driving toward them. "No!"

He and Malcolm ran to meet the vehicle, and when it stopped they tore open the doors on each side. The driver, two police officers and the harbor pilot tumbled out.

"Macbeth was waiting for us," groaned the pilot, still breathless. "He shot Fleance."

"No, no, no!" Duff leaned back and squeezed his eyes shut.

Someone laid a hand on his neck. A familiar hand. Caithness's.

Two men in black SWAT uniforms ran over and halted in front of Malcolm. "Hansen and Edmunton, sir. We heard about this and came as soon as we could. And there are more coming."

"Thank you, guys, but we're finished." Malcolm pointed. They couldn't see the sun yet, but the silhouette of the upside-down cross at the top of the mountain had already caught its first rays. "Now it's up to Tourtell."

"Let's exchange hostages," Duff said. "Let Macbeth have who he wants, Malcolm. Us two. In exchange for Kasi."

"Don't you think I've considered that?" Malcolm said. "Macbeth will never exchange a mayor's son for small change like you and me. If Tourtell declares a state of emergency Kasi will be spared. You and I will be executed whatever. And who will lead the fight against Macbeth then?"

"Caithness," Duff said, "and all those people in this town you say you have such belief in. Are you afraid or . . . ?"

"Malcolm's right," Caithness said. "You're worth more to this town alive."

"Damn!" Duff tore himself away and went toward the fire engine.

"Where are you going?" Caithness shouted.

"The plinth."

"What?"

"We have to smash the plinth. Hey, Chief!"

The man who had driven the fire engine stood up. "Erm, I'm not—"

"Have you got any fire axes or sledgehammers in the vehicle?"

"Of course."

"Look!" Seyton shouted. "The sun's shining on the top of the Obelisk. The boy has to die!"

"We all have to die," Macbeth said softly and put one chip under the heart symbol on the red part of the felt, the other on black. Leaned to the left and took the ball from the roulette wheel.

"What actually happened up on the roof?" Seyton shouted.

"Banquo's boy," Macbeth shouted back and spun the wheel. Hard. "I took care of it."

"Is he dead?"

"I took care of it, I said." The roulette wheel spun in front of Macbeth, the individual numbers blurring as they formed a clear, unbroken circle. Unclear and yet clear. He had counted down to the zone and he was still there. The wheel whirled. This time it would never stop, this time he would never leave the zone—he had closed the door behind him and locked it. The wheel. Round and round toward an unknown fate, yet so familiar. The casino always wins in the end. "What's that banging out there, Seyton?"

"Why don't you come up for a look yourself, sir?"

"I prefer roulette. Well?"

"They've started banging away at Bertha, the poor thing. And now the sun's out, sir. I can see it. Nice and big. The time's up. Shall we—"

"Are they smashing up Bertha?"

"The base she's standing on, anyway. Keep an eye on the square and shoot at everything approaching, Olafson."

"Right!"

Macbeth heard the pad of feet on the stairs and looked up. The reddish tint to Seyton's face was more noticeable than usual, as though he was sunburned. He walked past the roulette table and over to the pole, where Kasi was sitting hunched with his head lowered and his hair hanging in front of his face.

"Who said you could leave your post?" Macbeth said.

"Won't take long," Seyton said, pulling a black revolver from his belt. Put it to Kasi's head.

"Stop!" Macbeth said.

"We said to the second, sir. We can't—"

"Stop, I said!" Macbeth turned up the volume of the radio behind him.

". . . Mayor Tourtell speaking to you. Last night I was given an ultimatum by Chief Commissioner Macbeth, who has recently been responsible for a number of murders, including that of Chief Commissioner Duncan. Last night he kidnapped my son, Kasi, after a failed attempt to kill me. The ultimatum is that unless I declare a state of emergency, thereby giving Macbeth unlimited power and preventing federal intervention, my son will be killed when the sun rises above our town. But *we* don't want, *I* don't want, *you* don't want, *Kasi* doesn't want, *this town* doesn't want another despot in power. For this, good men have sacrificed their lives over the last few days. And their sons. Sacrificed their sons the way we in this and other towns did during world wars when our democracy was threatened. And now the sun is rising and Macbeth is sitting by his radio waiting for me to confirm that this day and this town are his. Here's my message to you, Macbeth. Take him. Kasi is yours. I'm sacrificing him as I know and hope he would have sacrificed me or the son he will never have. And if you can hear me, Kasi, goodbye, apple of my eye." Tourtell's voice thickened. "You are loved not only by me but by a whole town, and we'll burn candles at your grave for as long as democracy exists." He coughed. "Thank you, Kasi. Thank you, citizens of this town. And now the day is ours."

After a short silence there was a crackly recording of a man's sonorous voice singing "A Mighty Fortress Is Our God."

Macbeth switched off the radio.

Seyton laughed and applied pressure to the trigger. The hammer rose. "Surprised, Kasi? A whore's son isn't worth much to a whoremonger, you know. But if you surrender your soul to me now I promise you a painless shot in the head instead of the stomach. Plus revenge over the whoremonger and his gang. What do you say, boy?"

"No."

"No?" Seyton fixed his disbelieving eyes on the source of the answer.

"No," Macbeth repeated. "He mustn't be killed. Put down your revolver, Seyton."

"And let them out there get what they want?"

"You heard me. We don't shoot defenseless children."

"Defenseless?" Seyton snarled. "What about *us*? Aren't we defenseless? Are we going to let Duff and Malcolm piss all over us again, as they always have? Are you planning to abandon your cause now that—"

"Your revolver's pointing at me, Seyton."

"Perhaps it is. Because I'm not going to let you stop the kingdom that is coming, Macbeth. You're not the only one with a calling. I'm going—"

"I know what you're going to do, and if you don't put that revolver away, you're a dead man. A dead something anyway."

Seyton laughed. "There are things you don't know about me, Macbeth. Such as you can't kill me."

Macbeth looked into the muzzle of the revolver. "Do it then, Seyton. Because only you can send me to her. You're not born of woman, you were made. Made of bad dreams, evil and whatever it is that wants to break and destroy."

Seyton shook his head and pointed the revolver at Kasi's head without taking his eyes off Macbeth. At that moment the first ray of sun penetrated the large windows on the mezzanine. Macbeth saw Seyton raise a hand to shade his eyes as the ray hit his face.

Macbeth threw at the sunshine on the tree trunk out there on the other side, at the heart carved into the wood. Knowing it would hit, for lines, veins from his fingertips, went to that heart.

There was a thud. Seyton wobbled and looked down at the handle of the dagger protruding from his chest. Then dropped the revolver and grabbed the dagger as he sank to his knees. Raised his eyes and looked at Macbeth with a fogged gaze.

"Silver," Macbeth said, poking the matchstick between his front teeth again. "It's said to work."

Seyton fell forward and lay with his head by the boy's naked feet.

Macbeth placed the white ivory ball on the wooden frame around the rotating roulette wheel and sent it hard in the opposite direction.

"Keep going!" Duff shouted to the men beating away with sledgehammers and fire axes at the front of the plinth, where they had already dislodged big lumps of concrete.

And then the plinth cracked, and the locomotive's plow-shaped cow-catcher dropped with an almighty bang. Duff almost fell forward in the driver's cab, but grabbed a lever and managed to hold on tight. The loco-motive's nose, in front of him, was pointing downward, but it didn't move.

"Come on!"

Still nothing.

"Come on then, you old woman!"

And Duff felt something through his feet. It had moved. Hadn't it? Or . . . He heard a sound like a low lament. Yes, it *had* moved, for the first time in eighty years Bertha Birnam had moved, and now the wailing of its movable metal parts rose, rose in a crescendo to a scream of protest. Years of rust and the laws of friction and inertia tried to hold on, but gravity was invincible.

"Keep clear!" Duff shrieked, tightening the strap of his machine gun and holding the butt of the reserve weapon he had tucked inside his belt.

The steam engine's wheels turned, wrenched out of their torpor, rolled slowly down the eight-meter length of rail and tipped off the plinth. The front wheels hit the top of the steps and the flagstones broke with a deafening crunch. For a moment it seemed the train would stop there, but then Duff heard the next step crack. And the next. And he knew that nothing could now stop this slowly accelerating massive force.

Duff stared fixedly ahead, but from the corner of his eye he registered that someone had jumped onto the train and was standing beside him.

"Single to the Inverness, please." It was Caithness.

"Sir!" It was Olafson.

"Yes?" Macbeth's gaze followed the ivory's rumbling revolutions.

"I think it . . . it's . . . coming."

"What's coming?"

"The . . . train."

Macbeth raised his head. "The train?"

"Bertha! She's coming . . . here! It's—"

The rest was drowned. Macbeth got up. From where he was standing in the gaming room he couldn't see up to the station building, only the sloping square outside the tall window. But he could hear. It sounded like something was being crunched to pieces by a bellowing monster. And it was coming closer.

And then, crossing the square in front of the Inverness, it came into his field of vision.

He gulped.

Bertha was coming.

"Fire!"

Deputy Chief Commissioner Malcolm stared in disbelief. Because he knew that whatever happened now he was never going to see the like of this again in his lifetime. A steam engine eating stone and making its own track across Workers' Square. A form of transport their forefathers had built with iron, too heavy and solid to be held back, with ball bearings that didn't rust or dry out after a mere eighty years of neglect, a locomotive against which a hail of bullets from a Gatling gun produced sparks but was repelled like water as it held its course straight toward Inverness Casino.

"That is one solid building," someone said next to him.

Malcolm shook his head. "It's just a gambling den," he said.

"Hold on tight!" Duff yelled.

Caithness had sat down on the iron floor with her back to the side of the cab to avoid ricochets from the bullets screaming over their heads. She shouted something, her facial muscles tensed and her eyes closed.

"What?" yelled Duff.

"I love—"

Then they hit the Inverness.

Macbeth enjoyed the sight of Bertha filling the window before she smashed through. He had a feeling the whole building—the floor he was sitting on, the air in the room—everything was pushed back as the train broke through the wall into the room. The noise lay like a coating on his eardrums. The funnel on the steam engine cut through the eastern part of the mezzanine and its cowcatcher dug into the floor. The Inverness had braked her, but Bertha was still eating her way forward, meter by meter. She stopped half a meter in front of him, with the funnel against the railing of the west mezzanine and the cowcatcher touching the roulette table. For a moment there was total silence. Then came a rattle of crystal. And Macbeth knew what that was. Bertha had sliced the ropes holding the chandelier above him. He made no attempt to move, he didn't even look up. All he noticed before everything went black was that he was covered in Bohemian glass.

Duff climbed up onto the train with the machine gun in his hands. The low rays of sun shone through the dust filling the air.

"The Gatling gun in the southeast corner is unmanned!" Caithness shouted behind him. "What about—"

"Unmanned on the southwest too," Duff said. "Seyton's lying by the roulette table with a dagger in him. Looks pretty dead."

"Kasi's here. Looks like he's unharmed."

Duff scanned what once had been a gaming room. Coughed because of the dust. Listened. Apart from the frenetic rolling of a roulette ball in the wheel, there was silence. Sunday morning. In a few hours the church bells would peal. He clambered down. Stepped over Seyton's body to the chandelier. Used the saber to sweep away the bits of glass from Macbeth's face.

Macbeth's eyes were wide open with surprise, like a child's. The point of the chandelier's gilt spire had disappeared into his right shoulder. Not much blood ran from the wound, which contracted rhythmically as if sucking from the light fitting.

"Good morning, Duff."

"Good morning, Macbeth."

"Heh heh. Do you remember we used to say that every morning when we got up in the orphanage, Duff? You were in the top bunk."

"Where are the others? Where's Olafson?"

"Clever lad, that Olafson. He knows when the time's right to scarper. Like you."

"Your SWAT men don't scarper," Duff said.

Macbeth sighed. "No, you're right. Would you believe me if I said he's behind you and will kill you in . . . erm, two seconds?"

Duff eyed Macbeth for a moment. Then he whirled round. Up where the mezzanine was cut in two, he saw two figures against the morning sun shining in through the hole in the east wall. One was a medieval suit of armor. The second, Olafson, kneeling with his rifle resting on the balustrade. Fifteen meters. Olafson could hit a penny from there.

A shot rang out.

Duff knew he was dead.

So why was he still standing?

The echo of the shot resounded through the room.

Macbeth saw Olafson fall against the suit of armor, which toppled back, fell through the gap in the mezzanine and clattered to the gaming-room floor. On the mezzanine Olafson lay with his face pressed to the railing. His cheek was pushed over one eye, the other was closed, as though he had fallen asleep over his Remington 700 rifle.

"Fleance!" Caithness shouted.

Duff turned to the northern end of the mezzanine.

And there, up where the stairs came down from the upper floors, stood Fleance. His shirt was drenched with blood, he was swaying and clinging to a still-smoking gun.

"Caithness, get Kasi and Fleance out," Duff said. "Now."

Duff slumped into the chair beside the roulette table. The ball in the wheel was slowing; the sound had changed.

"What happens now?" Macbeth groaned.

"We wait here until the others come. They'll patch you up at the hospital. Custody. Federal case. They'll be talking about you for years, Macbeth."

"Still think you've got the top bunk, do you, Duff?"

Crystal rattled. Duff looked up. Macbeth had raised his left hand.

"You know I have the speed of a fly. Before you've let go of that saber and reached for your gun you'll have a dagger in your chest. You know that, don't you?"

"Possibly," Duff said. Instead of feeling fear he felt just an immense weariness creeping over him. "And you'll still lose, as always."

Macbeth laughed. "And why's that?"

"It's just one of those self-fulfilling things. You've always known, all your life, you're doomed to lose in the end. That certainty is and always has been you, Macbeth."

"Oh yes? Haven't you heard? No man born of woman can kill me. That's Hecate's promise, and he's shown several times that he keeps his promises. So do you know what? I can just get up from here and go." He tried to lever himself up into a sitting position, but the weight of the chandelier pressed down on him.

"Hecate forgot to take me into account when he made you that promise," Duff said, keeping an eye on Macbeth's left hand. "I can kill you, so just lie still."

"Are you hard of hearing, Duff? I said—"

"But I wasn't born of woman," Duff wheezed.

"You weren't?"

"No. I was cut out of my mother, not born." Duff leaned forward and ran his forefinger down the scar over his face.

Macbeth was blinking with his child-eyes. "You . . . you weren't born when Sweno killed her?"

"She was pregnant with me. I was told she was trying to stop the bleeding at the house of an officer when Sweno swung this—" Duff raised the saber "—and cut open her stomach."

"And your face."

Duff nodded slowly. "You won't get away from me, Macbeth. You've lost."

"Loss after loss. We start off having everything and then we lose everything. I thought it was the only thing that was certain, the amnesty of death. But not even that is guaranteed. Only you can give me death and send me to where I can be reunited with my beloved, Duff. Be my savior."

"No. You're under arrest and will rot alone in a prison."

Macbeth chuckled. "I can't, and you can't stop yourself. You couldn't stop yourself trying to kill me in the alley and you can't now. We are as we are, Duff. Free will is an illusion. So do what you have to do. Do what you *are*. Or shall I help you and say their names? Meredith, Emily and—"

"Ewan," Duff said. "*You're* the one who can't change from the person you've always wanted to be, Macbeth. That's how I knew there was still hope for Kasi even though the sun had risen over the mountain. You've never been able to kill a defenseless man. And even if you're remembered as more brutal than Sweno, more corrupt than Kenneth, it is your good qualities that have brought you down, your lack of brutality."

"I was always the reverse of you, Duff. And hence your mirror image. So kill me now."

"Why the hurry? The place awaiting the likes of you is hell."

"So let me go."

"If you ask for your sins to be forgiven, maybe you'll escape."

"I've sold that chance, Duff. And happily, because I'm looking forward to meeting my beloved again, even if it's to burn together for all eternity."

"Well, you'll get a fair trial and your sentence will be neither too severe nor too mild. It will be the first proof that this town can be civilized. It can become whole again."

"You fatuous idiot!" Macbeth screamed. "You're fooling yourself. You believe you're thinking the thoughts you *want* to think, you believe you're the person you *want* to be, but your brain's desperately searching right now for a pretext to kill me as I lie here defenseless, and that's precisely why something in you resists. But your hatred is like that train: it can't be stopped once it has got going."

"You're mistaken, Macbeth. We *can* change."

"Oh yes? Then taste this dagger, free man." Macbeth's hand reached inside his jacket.

Duff reacted instinctively, folded both hands round the handle of the saber and thrust.

He was surprised by how easily the blade sliced through Macbeth's chest. And when it met the floor beneath, he felt a tremble spread from

Macbeth's body to the saber and himself. A long sigh issued from Macbeth's lips, and a fine spray of pink blood came from his mouth and settled on Duff's hands like warm rain. He looked down into Macbeth's eyes, not knowing what he was after, only that he didn't find it. All he saw was a light extinguishing as the pupils grew and slowly ousted the irises.

Duff let go of the saber and stepped back two paces.

Stood there in silence.

Sunday morning.

Heard voices approaching from Workers' Square.

He didn't want to. But he knew he would have to. So he did. Pulled Macbeth's jacket open.

Macbeth's left hand lay flat on his chest. There was nothing there, no shoulder holster, no dagger, only a white shirt gradually turning red.

A pecking sound. Duff turned. It came from the roulette table. He got to his feet. On the felt a chip lay on red, under the heart, another on black. But the sound came from the wheel, which was still spinning but more and more slowly. The white ball danced between the numbers. Then it came to rest, finally trapped.

In the one green slot, which means the house takes all.

None of the players wins.

43

CHURCH BELLS PEALED IN THE distance. The one-eyed boy stood in the waiting room at the central station looking out into the daylight. It was a strange sight. From the waiting room Bertha had always blocked the view of the Inverness, but now the old steam engine skewered the facade of the casino. Even in the sharp sunlight he could see the rotating blue lights of the police cars and the flashes of the press photographers. People had flocked to Workers' Square, and occasionally there was a glimpse of light behind the windows in the Inverness too. That would be the SOC team taking pictures of the dead.

The boy turned and went down the corridor. As he approached the stairs down to the toilet he heard something. A low continuous howl, as if from a dog. He had heard it before, a penniless junkie who hadn't had his fix. He peered over the railing and saw pale clothes shining in the fetid darkness below. He was about to go on when he heard a cry, like a scream: "Wait! Don't go! I've got money!"

"Sorry, Granddad. I haven't got any dope and you haven't got any money. Have a not very nice day."

"But I've got your eye!" The boy stopped in his tracks. Went back to the railing. Stared down. That voice. Could it really be . . . ? He went over to the stairs, looked around. There was no one else there. Then he descended into the cold damp darkness. The stench got worse with every step.

The man was lying across the threshold of the men's toilet. Wearing what had perhaps once been a white linen suit. Now it was the ragged remains soaked in blood. Just like the man himself. Ragged, blood-soaked remains. A triangular shard of glass protruded from his forehead under a dark fringe. And there was the stick with the gilt handle. *It damn well was him!* The man he had been searching for all these years. Hecate. The boy's eye gradually got used to the darkness and he saw the gaping wound, a tear across stomach and chest. It was pumping out blood, but not so much, as though he was running dry. Between each new surge of blood he could see the slimy pale-pink intestines inside.

"Bring my suffering to an end," the old man rasped. "Then take the money I have in my inside pocket."

The boy eyed the man. The man from all his dreams, his fantasies. Tears of pain ran down the old man's soft cheeks. If the boy wanted, he could take out the short flick knife that he used to chop powder, the one with the narrow blade that had once removed an eye. He could stick it into the old man. It would be poetic justice.

"Has your stomach sprung a leak?" the boy asked, reaching inside the man's jacket. "Is there acid in the wound?" He examined the contents of the wallet.

"Hurry!" the old man sobbed.

"Macbeth's dead," the boy said, quickly counting the notes. "Do you think that makes the world a better place?"

"What?"

"Do you think Macbeth's successors will be any better, fairer or more compassionate? Is there any reason to think they will be?"

"Shut up, boy, and get it over with. Use the stick if you want."

"If death is what's most precious for you, Hecate, I won't take death from you as you took my eye. Do you know why?"

The old man frowned, stared, and the boy saw signs of recognition in his tear-filled eyes.

"Because I think we have the ability to change and become better people," the boy said, putting the wallet in his ragged trousers. "That's why I think Macbeth's successors will be a little better. Small, small steps, but a little better. A little more humane. Isn't it strange, by the way, that we use the word *humane*, human really, to describe what is good and compassionate?" The boy pulled his knife, and the blade sprang out. "Bearing in mind all we've done to one another all the way through history, I mean?"

"Here," groaned the old man, pointing to his throat. "Quickly."

"Do you remember that I had to cut out my eye myself?"

"What?"

The boy pressed the handle of the knife into the man's hand. "Do it yourself."

"But you said . . . more humane . . . I can't do it . . . please!"

"Small steps, small steps," the boy said, getting up and patting his pocket. "We're getting better, but we won't be saints overnight, you know."

The howls followed the boy through the station, all the way until he emerged into the radiant sunshine.

44

THE SHINY RAINDROP FELL FROM the sky, through the darkness, toward the shivering lights of the port below. Northwesterly gusts of wind drove the raindrop east of the slow-flowing river that divided the town in two and south of the busy train line that split the town diagonally. The wind carried the raindrop over District 4 to the Obelisk and a new building, the Spring, two hotels where businesspeople from Capitol stayed. Occasionally a yokel wandered into the Obelisk and asked whether this hadn't been a casino before. Most had forgotten, but they all remembered the other casino, the one that had been in the railway building which now housed the recently opened town library. The raindrop drifted over police HQ, where lights burned in Chief Commissioner Malcolm's office as he held a management meeting about restructuring. At first there had been some frustration among staff that Mayor Tourtell and the town council were demanding downsizing—a consequence of the statistics showing a strong fall in crime rates. Was this how you rewarded the police for doing such a good job over the last three years? But they realized that Malcolm was right: the job of the police was, as far as possible, to make themselves redundant. Of course this predominantly affected the Narcotics Unit and those departments that had an indirect link to the collapse of the drug trade, such as the Homicide Unit. Staff numbers remained the same at Anti-Corruption, while the new Financial Crime Unit was the only one allowed to employ more staff. This was because of increased financial activity as a consequence of the town attracting more business and a recognition that white-collar criminals had had it too easy, contributing to a feeling that the police first and foremost served the rich. Duff had defended the size of the Organized Crime Unit by saying that he needed resources to prevent crime and that if professional criminals were to gain a foothold in the town again, this would be far more expensive to clear up. But he understood that he, like everyone else, had to accept cuts. The head of the Homicide Unit, Caithness—who had argued convincingly that with present officer numbers they could finally offer citizens a satisfactory level of efficiency in murder investigations—had even been forced to resign. So Duff was happy it was finally the weekend, and he and Caithness had planned a picnic in Fife. He was both looking forward to it and dreading it. The house had been demolished and he had let the plot grow wild. But the cabin was still there. He wanted them to lie there in the boiling sun and smell the fragrance of the tar in the planks. And listen to see if the echo of Emily and Ewan's laughter and joyous shouts still hung there. And then he wanted to swim alone out to the smooth rock. They say there are no roads back to the places—and the person—you were. He just had to find out if this was true. Not to forget. But so that he could finally look ahead.

The raindrop continued eastward, over the expensive shopping streets in District 2 West before descending toward a forest-clad hillside next to the ring road, which glittered like a gold necklace around the town's neck this evening. There, at the top of Gallows Hill, the raindrop fell between the trees until with a splash it hit a large green oak leaf. Ran to the tip of the leaf, hung, collecting gravity, ready to fall the last few meters onto two men standing in the darkness under the tree.

"It's changed," a deep voice said.

"You've been gone a long time, sir," a higher-pitched one answered.

"Gone. Exactly. That's what I thought I was. And you haven't told me how you found me, Mr. Bonus."

"Oh, I keep my eyes and ears open. I listen and look, that's kind of my talent. The only one, I'm afraid."

"I don't know if I believe you entirely there. Listen—I'll make no bones about it—I don't like you, Mr. Bonus. You remind me a bit too much of those creatures you find in the water that attach themselves to bigger animals and suck."

"Suckerfish, sir?"

"I was thinking of leeches. Horrible little things. Though harmless enough. So if you think you can help me to get my town back you can suck a bit by all means. Just watch it, though. If you suck too hard I'll cut you off. Now tell me."

"There are no competitors in the market. Many of the junkies moved to Capitol when the dope dried up here. The town council and the chief commissioner have finally begun to lower their guard. Downsizing. The timing's perfect. The potential for new, young customers is unlimited, and I've also found the sister who survived when Hecate's drug factory exploded. And she still has the recipe. Customers won't have alternatives to what we can offer them, sir."

"And why do you need me?"

"I don't have the capital, the dynamism or your leadership qualities, sir. But I have . . ."

"Eyes and ears. And a suckermouth." The old man threw down a half-smoked Davidoff Long Panatella as the raindrop on the branch above him lengthened. "I'll think about it. Not because of what you've said, Mr. Bonus. All towns are potentially good markets if you've got a good product."

"I see. So why here?"

"Because this town took my brother from me, my clubhouse—everything. So I owe it something."

The raindrop let go. Landed on an animal's horn. Ran down it to the shiny surface of a biker's helmet.

"I owe it hell on earth."

ABOUT THE AUTHOR

Jo Nesbø is a musician, songwriter and economist, as well as a writer. His Harry Hole novels include *The Snowman, The Leopard,* and *Phantom,* and he is the author of several stand-alone novels, including *The Son,* as well as the Doctor Proctor series of children's books. He is the recipient of numerous awards, including the Glass Key for best Nordic crime novel.

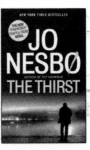